TRUDY KRISHER

On the March

A Novel of the Women's March on Washington

To Kasey, my granddaughter:
may she spread her wings and fly.

The present was an egg laid by the past
that had the future inside its shell.

-Zora Neale Hurston

Trudy Krisher is on Facebook, Twitter, and Instagram.
You can reach her through www.trudykrisher.com or
trudykrisher@trudykrisherauthor.com

Table of Contents

PART I – SOROS, KANSAS

Before she began to pack, Henrietta stood in the middle of Oldham's Antiques and looked around. At the stacks of faded quilts and lace doilies on tabletops. At the sets of dull brass andirons by the fireplace. At the atomizers atop glass vials of perfume, their fragrances long dried out. She lingered over the abandoned brooches in the glass case, feeling a sisterhood with those stones no longer worn: garnet, onyx, marcasite. The shop reminded her of herself: faded, dull, orphaned.

It was time for a change.

There were only two things she *had* to pack: her rosary and her knitting needles. She'd been fingering the rosary since her first communion, kneeling in the sanctuary before Father Cochran, her white-gloved hands trembling, the net of her petticoat scratching her knees, the incense from the censer stinging her lungs. She'd been fingering the knitting needles since Sister Florinda, the cook in Father Cochran's kitchen, had taught her to knit many decades ago. Henrietta would sit on a stool while Sister Florinda, sweat beads gleaming on her black forehead, supervised a stove bubbling with soup, a cloth-covered bowl of rising bread dough, and a young girl struggling with casting on and adjusting the tension of her stitches. As a result, Henrietta's fingers were never far from either her rosary or her needles. They were twin parts of the same impulse: bulwarks against anxiety. Dark-Light. Chaos-Harmony. Doubt-Faith.

Henrietta hoisted her yarn tote onto the red velvet seat of a rosewood chair. She peered inside, double-checking the new knitting project she hoped to work on during the long ride. She checked the hard-boiled eggs rolling around in a plastic newspaper sleeve, her mind floating to that Dr. Seuss story of the patient elephant endlessly sitting on an egg while the lazy Mayzie-bird flew off to Palm Beach. "I'll be Horton no more," she swore under her breath. Then she stuffed in a blanket, a clean pair of underwear, her drugstore supplies, and a couple of pairs of alpaca socks she had knit specifically for this journey. It was January, after all, and alpaca was seven times warmer than wool.

She peered out the shop window. Her taxicab was idling at the curb. For a moment the ache in her heart surfaced. The ache was a longstanding one: she had no child, no companion, no intimate, not even a pet to bid her goodbye. There would be no parting kiss on the cheek, no squeeze of the hand, no arm around a shoulder, not even a wag of a tail. She wondered, "Would the ache ever go away?"

Henrietta turned off the lights, picked up her tote, and checked the lock on the door of the antique shop. She lived by a lifelong muscle memory like the stitches that informed her knitting. Trash on Tuesdays. St. Catherine's on Wednesdays. Mass on Sundays. It was as repetitive as knit, purl. Gripping the handrail, she took one slow step at a time. Reaching the sidewalk, she experienced a little shiver of victory. Nowadays, with her knees, it was a daily miracle to get down her own steps, and she, Henrietta Oldham, was doing *this*.

The cab driver hardly noticed Henrietta; he was checking something on his phone. A gaudy cross was tangled in the chest hair peeking through his open Hawaiian shirt, and he was wearing one of those hats that airline pilots wore. She wondered why men always felt the need to act like a big shot.

The driver didn't get out to open the door or help her with her tote. Henrietta rarely expected to be helped with anything: her life had taught her that. But wasn't she paying for this ride? Couldn't she expect some courtesy?

She backed into the seat fanny first, steadying herself on the door frame and then lowering herself down. Old age, she had learned, was a series of unexpected humiliations: struggles with getting into a car, troubles with standing too long, difficulty seeing the fine print in the Medicare statement.

The driver had tipped his visor back and gawked as she finally sagged into the seat.

"Where you off to, little missy?"

"Trailways," she muttered, determined to stay quiet during the ride. She had no intention of making chit-chat with anyone who called her "little missy," much less a driver who let his cab smell of stale cigarettes while trying to look like some kind of professional pilot.

Quiet came easily to Henrietta. It was another lifelong pattern. She kept quiet at the bedside as she nursed her father, fetching ice water or arranging pills in the weekly pillbox; she kept quiet in her St. Catherine's sewing circle as she bent her head over the walker caddies and adult bibs for the nursing home; she kept quiet about her soundless readings about noisy women: Alice Paul, Susan B. Anthony, Sojourner Truth; she kept quiet as she genuflected before her pew on Sundays, making the sign of the cross over her chest. Isn't that what St. Timothy decreed? Let your women keep silence in the churches? Well, let your women keep silence in the taxicabs, too.

But since November, she had begun to reassess her life, and she had decided she'd been playing the fool. It had infuriated her to see those men swaggering on political stages urging their followers to take up the chant of "Lock Her Up." She knew all about that feeling.

It had scared her to be told she'd need another scan before she had really lived her life. She was angry with herself for having lived each day by certain creeds: Where there is hatred, let me sow love; where there is injury, pardon; let me seek not to be consoled as to console. Well, St. Francis, you can go to hell.

The familiar brownstones of her neighborhood seemed sadder from the passing window of a taxi. They had once been elegant, but their awnings now announced shoe repair shops and thrift stores, bail bond businesses and pawn shops, their owners guarding their businesses with bars on the windows and Shepherds and Rottweilers chained in cramped backyards.

The driver swiped at the neighborhood with a fling of his wrist. "That's what you get when you let certain folks move in."

'Certain folks.' Is that what the cross on your chest teaches you, Mr. Pseudo-Christian Airline Pilot?

'I hear there's a bunch of gals here at the bus station. Planning to go on some kind of march." He smirked.

They were pulling up to the bus station now. "See?" He wagged a finger in the direction of the crowd of women gathering in groups before the bus door. "Bunch of angry gals planning on riding to Washington."

Then he pushed back his pilot's cap and flashed her a toothy grin, the kind men flashed when they patronized. "Seems they're all fired up about the election. They're ready to go, ain't they?" He gave a snort and a shrug.

Henrietta rooted around in her tote bag. She paid the exact fare.

Little missy. Gals. Fired up. Ready to go.

She was going to stop playing the fool.

No to Horton.

No to St. Francis.

No to a tip.

Birdie considered the buttery scrambled eggs Aunt Lou set in front of her.

She had always liked eggs. In a way, she envied them. Eggs were ordinary, but they still had potential: they could be hard-boiled, poached, over easy. Eggs had possibilities. *Unlike me,* she thought, poking at her plate. *Do eggs have a secret life?* she wondered. *Do they dream about what they one day may become – part of a fluffy omelet? Blueberry pancakes? Something for a special occasion, like a wedding or birthday cake?*

"Eat, Birdie," said Aunt Lou.

Birdie was too anxious to eat. Soon she and her aunt would be leaving for the Women's March in Washington, D.C. – the first and only unusual thing she had ever done.

Her mother and aunt were having one of their usual half-hearted arguments.

"I see you're still buying these white eggs," Louise said, waving her hands around. Whenever she got agitated, Aunt Lou talked with her hands.

"Eggs is eggs," Mama said. She was gulping her breakfast. She was late to work. "Brown, white. All the same inside. What I eat for breakfast ain't a political statement, sis."

Aunt Lou shook her head and poured Mama a cup of coffee.

Birdie knew what Lou-Lou thought. To her, everything was a political statement. The hair style you wore. The cracked sidewalks you walked over. The color of Band-Aids at the Walgreens.

Aunt Lou had a desk in her little house she called her Protest Desk. It was not a desk, exactly. More like a utility table. It took up her whole dining room. When the family came for meals, there wasn't room to eat in the dining room, so they ate off of her wobbly aluminum tray tables with pictures of African-American heroes on them.

Lou's protest desk had piles of banker's boxes on it with various labels: Ferguson/Michael Brown, New York/Eric Garner, ADAPT, Voting Rights, Black Lives Matter, and Soros. The Soros box contained her local work and file folders filled with lists: lists of the people who worked for the school levies; lists of local people to contact when there were problems with the schools or police, the city or the county; lists of people who could be counted on during a political season when she wanted to draft poll workers or door-to-door canvassers.

Aunt Lou was always holding up signs or passing petitions or going door-to-door with flyers. One of Birdie's earliest memories was of playing on the floor under Aunt Lou's protest desk, wrapping herself in banners and sashes, t-shirts and sweatshirts with slogans about peace and civil rights and fair wages that she couldn't even read yet.

Lou had even gone all the way to Ferguson to protest the killing of Michael Brown. She said, "What's a few hours out of your own life to stand up for someone who lost his?"

Birdie took her last bite of the eggs they were still wrangling over.

"White eggs usually cheaper anyway, Lou," Mama said. "I gotta watch my pennies." Then she snapped, "Unlike you."

Birdie knew Mama had to watch her pennies. She wondered what she would do with a few extra bucks. Put a down payment on new brakes for the van? Send it in as deposit on Antoine's graduation cap-and-gown? Buy the family a big chuck roast for Sunday dinner?

Birdie also knew Mama was being unfair. Aunt Lou worked in nonprofits, and her job paid even less than Mama's. But Aunt Lou had no kids. Birdie's mama had four.

If you still counted Shanice.

Birdie's aunt had organized this trip. She'd called the families in Soros, connected with other families across the country, bought Metro tickets in advance, taken Shanice's wheelchair to the bus station. They were going to leave the wheelchair in Washington as part of the protest and also as a kind of closure for their family.

Closure. Birdie was sick of that word.

One reason for the trip had to do with Shanice. When Shanice entered fourth grade, Aunt Lou started up a chapter of ADAPT, the first one in Kansas. The organization worked for rights for the disabled. The idea was to get Shanice to meet other kids like her, so she wouldn't feel so lonely. No doubt about it: Aunt Lou was a get-up-and-do kind of woman. Birdie was a sit-around-and-think-about-it kind of girl.

Shanice loved the ADAPT group, and that was the point. Kids like Shanice and Armando Rodriguez and Nicole Snyder did crafts together or met at the coffee shop and just talked. Once Lou-Lou organized a trip to Topeka so they could hold up signs and get lawmakers to pay attention to them. ADAPT helped Shanice feel normal.

Thinking of the ADAPT group reminded Birdie that she wasn't even sure she wanted to go on the march. She would miss Friday night's basketball game and a chance to see Jamil Washington, a friend of her older brother Antoine. Birdie's heart pounded whenever Jamil stopped by her locker now and again to ask her something about Twanny.

Jamil was four heads taller than Birdie, and he had long, curled lashes that gave his eyes a soft, sleepy look. But those sleepy brown eyes didn't match the wide-awake moves he made as a point guard on the varsity team. Aunt Lou always said appearances were deceiving; in Jamil's case, Lou was right.

But Jamil had a girlfriend now. Sabrina Banks stood closer to him than was necessary in the lunch room and tucked her pretty head up against his collarbone. Birdie didn't know her, but she hated her anyway. Sabrina Banks's breasts were shaped like the jumbo eggs Mama bought at Easter.

Jamil Washington was one reason Birdie had started stuffing her bra. Toilet paper was cheap, and when she looked at herself sideways in the cracked mirror in the bathroom, she liked the rounded slope she saw. She hoped appearances *could* be deceiving.

"I vote with my pocketbook," Mama said, ending the egg conversation while Aunt Lou drained the bacon grease. The grease was still spattering and popping as it crackled into a coffee can. It reminded Birdie of her mother's anger.

While Birdie chewed on her bacon, Aunt Lou stood at the stove, sipping her coffee and gazing at the pictures on the shelf above the canisters. The pictures were in cardboard frames from the Dollar Store. Aunt Lou had given the set to the family one Christmas, hoping they might study them from time to time, but they never did. Birdie knew some of the pictures. Martin Luther King, Jr. Nelson Mandela. Kareem Abdul-Jabbar. Thurgood Marshall. Lou-Lou had debated putting the picture of Thurgood Marshall up there because she'd heard he was a womanizer, but since he'd been on that special case in Topeka, he was too important to leave out. Aunt Lou had added a couple of pictures of women. Other than Rosa Parks, Birdie didn't know who they were.

Aunt Lou stirred some extra cream and sugar in her coffee and turned to Mama. "Do you remember what MLK said that time?"

Mama squinted, annoyed. "MLK said lots of things, lots of times. A preacher's never at a loss for words."

Birdie glanced up at the framed picture of Dr. Martin Luther King, Jr. She thought he looked young in the picture. And handsome. His hands were folded quietly, the fingers of his left hand spread outward, his eyes gazing off into space.

Louise ignored her sister. "I'm thinking of the time he said, '*If*

7

you can't fly, then run. If you can't run, then walk. If you can't walk, then crawl. But by all means keep moving.'"

That was Birdie's Aunt Lou. She was always saying things that were just above your head, something like an apple on a tree branch that you had to stand on tiptoes to pick. Mama said things that were straight out in front of you: oil the wheelchair, run up to Mims's for bread and milk, ask Antoine to see if it's the starter or the battery.

Mama stared into Aunt Lou's dreamy face. "I wouldn't call that one of my favorites," she said, scowling at her sister. "Wish he'd said something about sitting down now and again."

Birdie's mama never sat down. She didn't have time. Either it was one of the four kids, especially Shanice. Or Beanie. Or it was the girls at work. Or the toilet that was stopped up. Unlike Lou, Mama didn't have time to take her coffee any way but black.

"Well, even Martin Luther King had to eat," Mama said, rapping the spatula on Aunt Lou's plate. Aunt Lou had cooked everything but hadn't taken a bite herself. Birdie's mama always said Lou preferred dreaming to eating. "Get going, Princess Lou, or you'll be late for the ball."

Birdie took her plate to the sink and headed to the living room, observing its daily chaos: the stray pajama bottoms and headphones; the plastic bowls, cups, and glasses, dried milk or juice lining their lips; the empty cereal boxes spread around the room. Fruit Loops. Lucky Charms.

The ventilator.

The living room had once been neat. Her mama's tours of duty in the Army had taught her about order: shoes were to be slipped off by the door, backpacks were to be hung from the coat tree.

"Yes, Mama." The kids did everything but salute.

Mama had gotten rid of much of Shanice's equipment, but the ventilator still sat in the corner next to the plywood bookcase Antoine made in shop class.

Birdie thought the ventilator looked all lonesome there in the corner without Shanice; she missed the in-and-out rhythm of its sucking sound that made her feel like it was something alive, something breathing. Mama would be donating the ventilator to the Sunny Days Nursing Home while Lou and Birdie were away.

Birdie crossed the room, knowing it would be gone when she returned, wanting to somehow kiss it goodbye. She ran her hand over it instead.

Then she grabbed the framed eighth-grade picture of Shanice that sat next to it on the bookcase. She zipped open her backpack, laying the picture right on top of the purple shawl and the crepe paper and garlands and mementos they were taking to the ADAPT protest in Washington.

Mama and Lou were standing by the front screen door. They had finally finished talking about eggs and Martin Luther King. Even in her work clothes and heels, Mama looked like someone dressed in camo. Mama was pinning something to Aunt Lou's jacket. Birdie heard her say, "Remember what our mama taught us. 'A lady don't leave the house without a pin or a scarf.'"

While they were laughing and cutting up, Birdie met them at the door. Then Mama surprised her. She threw her big wide arms around both of them, mashing them into a great big hug. When Birdie turned to head out the door, she read the words on the round black pin Mama had stuck on Aunt Lou's jacket. "Black Lives Matter," they said.

Emily Messer was eager to leave. She knew her parents were also eager for her to leave. "My parents are sick of me," she muttered. "But I'm sick of them, too."

"Get yourself out of that basement!" her stepfather shouted daily. "A college graduate, and you can't find a job?"

"I *have* a job, Dave."

She did. She worked part time at the coffee shop, making lattes, espressos, chais, and fancy coffees. Dave had assumed her communications degree from a third-tier college would be a ticket to success.

"At least it gives me a chance to get out of your basement," Emily snarled under her breath.

It also gave her a chance to keep in touch with people her age. Most of them were addicted to pleasures like sex and cappuccino.

"Then at least try to find a job at a Starbucks, Emily," he yelled. "They pay health benefits to part-timers."

Emily started to shout back that she still had four more years to stay on her parents' health plan. Instead, she mumbled to herself, "Thank you, Mr. Obama."

She bid goodbye to the basement room. She had tried to brighten it with pictures from college. There were Sonia, Jenny, and Katie, toasting each other with red plastic Solo cups full of beer. She'd snapped a few pictures of the cute mustached bartender at Roosters, the bottles of Gray Goose and Bailey's behind him. And she had dozens of pictures of her dog: Bravo at the beach, Bravo on her lap at Great Clips, Bravo swinging on their back porch swing.

Victoria Stewart peered around the basement door. "Aren't you going to fix your hair?"

Emily was familiar with her mother's complaints.

She wore her hair gathered on top of her head and fastened with a claw. Her mother thought the way her hair fell every-which-way over her crown was ridiculous. "Take some pride in yourself, Em," she said. Not for the first time.

Another complaint was Emily's clothes. She and Jenny and Katie and Sonia had decided to dress alike for the trip. Yoga pants. Stanton College sweatshirts.

"Aren't you going to wear a *coat*? It's *January*, Em!"

Emily shrugged. Her weather app had said the temps would be around fifty.

"Here, Mother, *see?*" She stuck the weather app in her mother's face. "I don't need a coat."

Emily turned away from her mother. She didn't need to face her. She knew too well the way Victoria Stewart rolled her eyes.

Emily had packed only her phone, her charger, and her earbuds: all of it would fit in the pockets of her sweatshirt. Maybe that would be all she would take if her parents split up. They'd been screaming about it for years. She wore her earbuds to bed to drown out the shouting and to escape from what it meant for her future. That's why this trip was so appealing. Sonia, Jenny, Katie, and she were thinking about getting an apartment together in Philadelphia, where Sonia was from. They were going to make plans in Washington. Maybe she could finally escape.

Emily Messer knew one thing: she was stuck. Stuck with debt. Stuck in her parents' house. Stuck with few job prospects. The Internet had shown her all kinds of stimulating possibilities: elephant preserves in Africa, river rafting companies in Brazil, tranquil monasteries in Tibet. And here she was. Stuck, stuck, stuck in a basement in Soros, Kansas.

She couldn't wait to hook up with her college friends. Even though Katie and Jenny lived in towns not far from Soros, somehow they never really connected anymore. And of course Sonia was all the way across the country in Philadelphia. This trip would be their first reunion. Emily was reminded that she hadn't attended a really good party since graduation. The drinking sessions at the Lucky Duck and the predictable people at the karaoke bar in Soros were lame compared to the parties at Stanton College. Still, a guy at the karaoke bar had been texting her some. He had backed her against the wall and thrust himself close to her, breathing in her ear when he'd asked for her number. Emily wasn't sure how she felt about that. Whatever. At least something interesting might still happen to her.

As her mother headed to the garage, Emily followed from a shuffling distance. It was humiliating living at home. But it was scary to imagine anything else. Maybe Sonia, Jenny, and Katie would be the answer.

As always, it was comforting to look down and see Bravo bouncing behind her. The terrier was always on her heels, and she was amazed by his devotion: it was the only thing that came to mind when people mumbled about "unconditional love."

Emily opened the car door to let Bravo jump in ahead of her. As Emily slipped into the car, Victoria Stewart noticed her daughter's feet. "It's January, Emily," she scolded, her voice icier than the weather. "You're wearing sandals?"

"Don't freak, Mom. I *told you* I checked the weather app." The weather app had said it would be unseasonably warm, and that was good enough for her.

On the way to the bus, the only sound in the Lexus was of Bravo panting. Emily kept her eyes fixed on her phone. That way she wouldn't have to talk to her mother.

Whenever she drove through her neighborhood, Emily was reminded that she was sick of that, too. The parents with Lexuses. The kids with Grand Cherokees. The lawns that sported parallel green lines that looked like vacuum cleaner marks and told you they'd just been mowed by a family gardener.

While they drove in silence, Emily scrolled the Facebook posts. There was a new one about a Fattest Cat contest, and she private-messaged Cheryl at the coffee shop about the liqueur-laced coffees that were trending in Australia. Then she uploaded the new photo of her and Bravo at the lake onto Instagram.

When they pulled up to the bus, Emily kissed the dog square on the mouth, slammed the car door, and headed to the bus line. It was better for her mother to think her rude than scared.

Standing in line at the Trailways station, the first thing Birdie noticed was the shoes. Sneakers and high-tops and clogs. Leather loafers and Mary Janes. Beaded Indian moccasins. Doc Martens. Crocs. Old lady shoes that laced all the way up the ankle. Boots. Lots of different boots. Rain boots and hiking boots. Ankle boots and knee boots. Boots that zipped. Boots that laced.

There was one kind of boot that was missing: Army boots. The kind that Mama wore.

Snatches of conversation swirled around her.

"Did you hear they've got a permit in Antarctica?"

"No!"

"It's true. That makes all seven continents now."

"And I read that they have over two thousand bus permits."

Aunt Lou handed Birdie her phone and said, "We can share it on the trip."

Birdie was astonished. Mama wouldn't allow her kids to have phones. Not just because they were expensive, but because of what happened to Shanice. Most of the white girls had phones, of course, but if Black girls had phones, they were the cheap kind like you get at Wal-Mart. Birdie beamed: her Aunt Lou's phone was the expensive kind.

She studied the phone lying across her open palm. It was light as an egg; yet it seemed heavy with possibilities. It wasn't the first time Aunt Lou had done something for her.

Birdie pressed the camera icon and found the round white button. She aimed the camera at the dozens of different shoes on the asphalt and pushed.

"Good idea," Aunt Lou said.

Birdie looked back at the photo. She liked what she saw. For once she was glad to be a shy person, the kind of person who looked down a lot, the kind of person who silenced her questions. *If I had been looking up, I might have missed this picture.*

She passed the camera to Aunt Lou. Lou pointed to all the different shoes in the picture and nodded. "You're not the only one trying to get free, Birdie."

"Lines are stupid," Emily thought. She eyed the bus driver with his ancient clipboard, pencil behind his ear, and wondered if this trip would be stupid, too. You ought to be able to gather any which way and use your phone app to check in. Lines were for kindergarten.

Emily was impatient. Where were Katie and Jenny? She wished they'd hurry up and get here. A lot of the women were her mother's age. You could tell by the Coach bags, the Kate Spade wallets. She felt out of place.

Emily was also anxious. She had texted that guy she'd met at the karaoke bar. "Gd Mrning. How R U?" She went back and added an emoji of a yellow sun before she hit "Send."

He hadn't replied. "Where was he?" she wondered. "What was he doing?"

Emily looked around. If Jen and Kate didn't hurry, she'd be the youngest rider on the bus. Except for a gangly Black girl who looked about junior-high age. The girl's lips were clamped tight as if she was either angry or super-shy.

Emily perked up when she heard another woman introduce herself.

"Jessica Walters." She had long braided pigtails draped over her shoulders. She was probably in her early thirties. "From Wamego."

Emily thought Jessica Walters reminded her of someone. It was something to do with the pigtails.

"Oh! That's where they have the Oz Museum," squealed one of the ladies.

Ahhhhh. Dorothy. The Wizard of Oz.

Wamego was only half an hour northwest of Soros, but Emily had never been there.

"I waitress at Toto's Tacos," the braided young woman said proudly. "And no, we don't serve dog meat." She laughed. The others joined in.

Emily thought the rose tattoo at the nape of Jessica's neck was really cool. She remembered what fun she and her friends had in college getting tats together.

To her relief, she spotted Katie and Jenny, skipping across the parking lot to greet her. They hugged and giggled. Emily realized how much she had missed these friends. "After college, she had often wondered, "if you don't get married, what are you supposed to do?"

Henrietta waited patiently in the long line snaking beside the bus. She thought for a moment about how patiently most people waited in line. "Not people," she corrected herself. "Women." They waited. They took their turn. Then some man butted in front of her. Like that scraggly bearded fellow who stepped ahead of her at Elmer's Drugs: He was only buying one item, and she had three. She wondered how his pouch of chewing tobacco trumped her denture paste, her pocket pack of tissues, and her bag of peppermints.

Henrietta took in the conversations of the women chatting together.

"Thank the Lord this January weather is warmer than usual," said a woman wrapped in a red-white-and-blue crocheted sweater-shawl. "January usually means ice dams on the roof."

The woman next to her nodded. "And all the kids with the flu."

Knowing smiles flashed from face to face. Henrietta knew about sickness too. Just not with kids.

Over in the brown grass, three young women were doing yoga. They were wearing identical blue sweatshirts and black yoga pants. They looked to be in their early twenties, like girls just graduated from college. Henrietta wondered why they were wearing sandals without socks in January.

"Gretchen Tsongas. Topeka," another woman said. "I hate to admit it, but I'm still worried about security. Any of you?"

A few of the women tucked their heads, looking sheepish.

"My husband Tom didn't want me to come," Gretchen went on. "We fought about it for a week. Finally he said, 'Don't call me to fetch you from the jail or the hospital.'"

Henrietta patted the money bag tucked tightly inside her blouse. She had no doubt she needed it to guard against robbers, thieves, or worse in a big, crowded city like D.C.

A woman from Tecumseh said she got a flyer telling her only clear plastic backpacks would be allowed at the march. "To guard against explosives," she explained.

The women eyed each other's bags suspiciously. As if one of them might be hiding dynamite right now. "I tried to buy one," another woman moaned, "but they were all sold out."

Henrietta worried that her yarn tote might prevent her from getting in.

A woman in a camel coat and a Burberry scarf who reeked of money blurted, "Any signs attached to a two-by-four are going to be seized as a dangerous weapon."

Henrietta tried not to worry. Still, her St. Catherine crafters had raised her concerns. They met every Wednesday to sew: walker caddies for nursing home residents; turbans for chemo patients; blankets for newborns at the charity hospital. Henrietta found the stitching dreary, and ever since November, she'd found the crafters themselves even more dull and uninteresting. Over the years, she had tried to involve them in new projects, but they preferred the familiar. Somehow after November, their passivity annoyed her.

Naturally none of these women would have been interested in the march. But they loved to yak about it. If only to scoff and fearmonger.

"What if there's an emergency? Say, someone has a heart attack? Or a bomb goes off?"

Henrietta tried to stifle her own fears. "Martha Hodges," she said to herself, "you may make exquisite embroidered hankies, but you're a master of worst-case scenarios."

She reminded herself that the St. Catherine crafters were afraid of lots of things. Traveling. The devil. Anything new. Sharon Sikorski, for example, always rambled on about the latest horror. While she worked on her drawstring tote bags, Sharon swore that the new e-cigarette shop was going to jack up neighborhood crime. And those new chip readers were just as vulnerable as the old swipe-cards.

Henrietta had kept her head down over her work. Her Wednesday crafters would know nothing about this trip. Like everything else, she would keep things to herself.

Birdie was impatient to board. The smoke billowing out the back of the bus made her think of her brother Beanie. Mama had begged him to quit smoking, but like most boys she knew, not listening to their mother proved they were men. But it wasn't just Beanie who was smoking; Birdie kept a clean t-shirt stashed at Destinee's house so she didn't have that piney skunk grass smell when she snuck home. Birdie knew if Mama found out, she'd be in trouble, but she was too shy to say "No" to the few friends she had.

Mama was always so tired she was easy to fool. But not Aunt Lou.

Birdie knew they both worried about her. But Mama was so distracted that she didn't see Birdie as clearly as her aunt. Birdie overheard them whispering when she was supposed to be doing homework.

"She doesn't smile much, sis," Aunt Lou said. "Girls her age are supposed to smile more."

Birdie was familiar with Aunt Lou's complaint. She was always urging Birdie to smile. Birdie lied and said she was ashamed of the gap between her teeth that needed braces.

"And just look at her eyes, Ronnie," Louise said.

"Yep. Birdie's got those long black lashes. Just like Shanice. When I look into them I remember too much."

"I don't mean that. I don't mean the remembering. I mean do you manage to look into them *at all*, sis? They're always downcast. They're like store awnings shuttered for the night."

"I look into them plenty, girl. I see the way those brown eyes are snapping with questions that I can't answer."

Birdie knew Mama was right about the questions.

"You don't have to answer them, Ronnie. Just listen. You just let her say them out loud. That girl's got her lips stapled shut."

Birdie didn't realize that things about herself showed up in her eyes and mouth. But she did realize there were a lot of things her family kept clamped down about now.

"Well, you better start paying more attention before it's too late," said Lou. "Birdie's starting down the wrong path. Wrong friends. Slipping schoolwork. Too much focus on the boys. And those long legs of hers are starting to fill out. Some boy's sure to notice."

Birdie grimaced. She was pretty sure no boy was going to notice a girl with skinny legs and a flat chest.

"I heard," said another woman in line, "that only poster board signs were being allowed. Any signs attached to a two-by-four are going to be seized as a dangerous weapon." Birdie could tell the woman was rich. She was wearing a plaid wool scarf with a tan coat the color of Lou-Lou's coffee when she put in two creams.

Aunt Lou and Birdie listened to other women reciting their fears. Birdie knew neither Lou nor Mama scared easy. *Me? I'm not so sure.*

"Don't worry, ladies," Louise said, cocky as a rooster. "We've got a Cousin Marvin who's a police officer in Maryland. We've got his number in our phone. Open your phone," Lou ordered Birdie.

Your phone. If only. Birdie opened the phone and swiped to the Contacts page. She held it up. "Sergeant Marvin Banks." She didn't add that you never want anything to do with police. Even if it was a relative.

Birdie was well aware that she and Aunt Lou were two of only a handful of Black people in line. Black people knew things white people didn't. That police were nothing but trouble. Trouble if they called *you*. Trouble if you called *them*.

The white ladies looked relieved. But Birdie hoped they wouldn't need Cousin Marvin.

Aunt Lou introduced herself all around. "Louise Marie Franklin. From right here in Soros. And this is my niece, Alberta Sankofa Jackson."

Birdie winced. She wished her aunt had just said "Birdie." She hated being called "Alberta."

The ladies smiled and nodded.

Birdie looked down at all the shoes again.

Henrietta listened as many of the women introduced themselves. A woman named Darcy Phillips. A woman named Penelope Anders, but they're just supposed to call her "Penny." She hoped she wouldn't be asked to introduce herself. She wondered what she would say. "Hello, I'm Henrietta Oldham, owner of a failing antique store, former nurse to a wretched excuse for a parent, closet consumer of feminist memorabilia, bitter lifetime member of the Sisters-of-Perpetual-Do-Gooders."

Henrietta overheard a woman named Louise Franklin introducing her niece and wondered why most of the marchers were white. The girl looked awkward, anxious. She kept her eyes cast down. She looked to be about fourteen or fifteen. Henrietta had always felt protective of girls that age. So much could go wrong for them.

Some of the women were checking their watches.

"It's about eleven a.m, our time. Noon in the East," one of them called out.

A few of the women were dialing into the inauguration on their phones.

"Listen to what he's saying!" one of them cried, her cheeks reddening.

Louise Franklin, the young Black girl's aunt, piped up. "Do we have to?"

Everybody hooted. The girl's aunt had touched a nerve.

After that, the women shouted out comments.

"It's not really a speech. Just another campaign rally."

"Fake news!"

The women laughed. Laughing helped them feel less like strangers now.

One of the younger women turned up the volume on her phone. "From this moment on," the voice crackled, "it's going to be America First."

"Big bully," someone else said. "Me first. Everybody else second."

Henrietta mumbled under her breath: "The opposite of Abraham Lincoln. Charity for none; malice for all."

"Just ignore it, ladies," called the young woman who waitressed at Toto's Tacos. "This isn't about him. It's about us!" She raised a fist.

The gathered group cheered, raising fists together.

Henrietta's spirits soared. She had problems with her rotator cuff, but she could still raise her right arm chin-high. She looked at all the passionate women beside her, fists pumping. Henrietta had never done anything like this in her life.

She saw Louise Franklin poking her niece in the ribs to raise her fist, too.

But the girl shook her off, keeping her arm plastered to her side.

Henrietta touched her rosary beads and said a quiet prayer.

As they finally boarded, Birdie noticed there were as many different kinds of bags as there were shoes. Bags over the shoulder. Bags across the body. Quilted bags and hobo bags. Satchels and totes.

Fanny packs and back packs. The women were crowded up close to each other, jamming the aisle. They were busy finding seats, loading things into the overhead bin, peeling off coats and hats and scarves, fluffing blankets and arranging neck pillows. Birdie thought about taking a picture, but there wasn't room to move.

Aunt Lou's big duffel bag was a problem. It was full, and it was heavy.

Early that morning, Birdie had watched as Mama pulled her Army duffel bag from the front closet and headed to the garage. Aunt Lou had given Mama a list of what to pack, and Birdie had looked on as Mama dragged the heavy lengths of chain into the thick canvas duffel. The chain would help tie Shanice's wheelchair to the black iron fence around the White House. Mama grabbed the channel lock pliers and the Master Lock padlock and loaded them in, too. Then Mama spied an old Walkie-Talkie on the garage floor. Birdie didn't think it had been on Lou's list, and she couldn't be sure it worked, but it had once been Twanny's, and Mama threw that in as well.

"Birdie," Mama said over her shoulder as she filled the bag, "the U.S. Army sure makes one fine duffel bag." Birdie was glad to hear Mama satisfied with something. Mostly she was angry now, an unfamiliar kind of rage Birdie struggled to understand.

Then Mama dragged the heavy bag through the living room. "Good thing this duffel's got wheels," she said, lumbering to the kitchen.

Aunt Lou asked the women around her to step back as she heaved the camouflage-green duffel into the overhead bin. Birdie helped, wishing Mama was here. Mama was stronger than Aunt Lou and Birdie put together. Or at least she used to be.

It was a big bus. The rows of three seats on each side of the aisle were crowded. The women were elbowing each other for seats. In front of them was a gray-haired white lady clutching a big flowered knitting tote.

The gray-haired lady took a window seat. Aunt Lou motioned for Birdie to sit beside her in the middle. Aunt Lou took the aisle seat. The three college girls doing yoga in the grass before boarding took up the row behind them. Birdie looked up, grateful for the phone charger above her seat.

Once the bus was full, the driver stood up to face his passengers. He had a bushy beard, a bald head, and a Middle-Eastern accent. He was a very small man: he reminded Birdie of a Minion.

The driver switched on a hand-held microphone, and his voice crackled over it.

"Good day, lady," he said. "I am Khalid, you driver. I want you enjoy your journey, no?"

As he said the word "no," Khalid nodded his head "yes." Khalid reminded Birdie of herself: unsure. *Yes or no? Forward or back? Good or bad?*

"Two rule on bus. One, restroom in back. Every few hour we stop, right? Two, enjoy you travel."

Henrietta was glad to hear there was a restroom in back. She had a pretty strong bladder, much stronger than her knees. Still, you never knew.

Henrietta had been secretly planning for this trip since November. She had visited the podiatrist and bought the new orthotics around Thanksgiving; ever since, she had been breaking them in on daily walks around the block before the sun came up and the neighbors were out. She had purchased extra-large Band-Aids, hemorrhoid cream, and other supplies at Elmer's corner drug store. She closed the blinds at night and struggled onto the floor to do her knee exercises. She had ruined her knees running up and down the stairs of the twelve-room, three-story apartment building for the fourteen years before her father died.

But the worst was the Depends. The bus ride was supposed to last seventeen hours. Each way. She'd rather be safe than sorry. She'd been embarrassed to lay them on the checkout counter in front of the clerk at Elmer's Drugs, but the clerk on duty wasn't gossipy Ethel Floyd, so Henrietta was grateful for that. She had hurried out of Elmer's, the package pressed tight against her chest, her heart pounding with the fear that someone would see her on the walk home. She'd felt the same way about buying sanitary napkins for her mother and herself when she was a girl. She hadn't remembered that feeling in a long time.

She'd practiced with the Depends in front of the claw-footed antique mirror in her bedroom, turning down the blinds, turning up the lights. Each diaper was individually wrapped: like snack crackers or American cheese slices. But when she took one out of its wrapping, she couldn't tell front from back. They looked the same to her. She'd never diapered a baby, so she had no mother-memory to rely on. When she stuffed the diaper between her legs, it felt as thick and bulky as a roll of paper towels. When she tried to walk, she waddled like a duck.

Henrietta saw her reflection blinking in the mirror against something she had to face: She had reached the final stage in life. First Pampers, then Kotex, now Depends.

She sighed. It was just like everything else in her life. You're on your own, Miss Oldham.

As Khalid revved the engine, Birdie looked around at all the different heads sticking up above the head rests. In the rows in front of her, there were as many kinds of women's hairdos as there were shoes and bags. Bouffants. Pixies. Afros. Buns. Bobs. Curly hair, straight hair, frizzy hair. Hair accented with head bands, hair forks, elastic bands, barrettes. All the heads sticking up from the headrests in front of Birdie made her think of the wig stands at Darlin' Marlin's Wig Shop where Lou-Lou picked out her wigs for Sunday church.

In the rows behind her were even more hairdos. The three white college girls she'd noticed on the lawn sat directly behind her. They reminded her of the Muses she'd studied in her seventh-grade unit on mythology; Muses always seemed to have distinctive hair. Like most white girls, these girls dressed identically. Only their hairdos were different. One had a clawed topknot spewing like a fountain: Birdie was calling her "Fountain Head." Another had straight blonde hair flowing down her shoulders like waterfalls: Birdie was calling her "Waterfall Head." The third had a dark brown frothy swirl falling onto her forehead: Birdie was calling her "Ocean Wave Head."

Beyond the Muses there was hair that was short and angled, hair that was long and straight. There were Muslim women a few rows back whose heads were covered in peach-colored scarves. There were women with dreadlocks, women with bangs, women with pink or blue streaks in their hair; one woman had pigtails beside each ear, and another had a single ponytail draping one shoulder.

But the hairdos reminded Birdie of Mama and the stubble on the top of her head that was such a frightening sign of her anger.

Late last July Mama had shaved off all her hair in a fit of rage. It was around the one-year anniversary of what happened to Shanice, and the family hadn't really healed yet. The hurt had mostly scabbed over.

Mama had been watching something on TV. Birdie hadn't seen exactly what it was, but it was something about the election coming up in November. It was a rally or something. An orange-faced, yellow-haired man on the stage was flailing his hands and making grunting noises. He was mocking someone. Later, Louise told Birdie he'd been mocking a disabled reporter. Birdie understood about mocking: she'd seen kids mocking Shanice in this same way. The man waved his right hand limply like someone who couldn't control his movements. He was waving it just like Shanice: she had trouble with her right hand too.

Birdie was shocked at Mama's expression. She hadn't known that one face could be ripped by a tornado and a hurricane and a tsunami all at once. Unlike Birdie, who was mostly sad, Mama was mostly angry all the time. But this was something different. Later, Lou-Lou said it was like ripping off a scab that had started to heal.

Mama stomped to the bathroom and took Birdie's long-gone daddy's barber kit out of the bathroom closet. Albert Jackson had planned on becoming a barber and opening his own shop. But he just never got around to it.

Birdie watched as Mama flipped the switch and the clippers buzzed. Mama ran the clippers up the back of her head, then up the sides, then straight back from her forehead and down across the crown. *What is she trying to do? Go back to the buzz-cut she wore in the Army?*

As her kinky locks flew to the floor, Birdie blinked hard against something she could not name. She had longed so many times to have those locks brush her cheek to comfort her, and now they never would. The curls looked like something burnt: charred wood, ashes in a grill. Birdie suddenly thought of her brother Beanie and that skull he carved with the wood burning tool in his shop class. *Why couldn't you burn a nice dragon or a fancy sword like the other boys? Why did it have to be a skull, Beanie?* There were questions Birdie wanted to ask Mama now, too. Like *What can I do with my sadness, Mama?* But Veronica Mae Jackson's daughter knew this was a time to hold her tongue.

It seemed to Birdie, though, that it was always time to hold her tongue. *Does tiptoeing around and holding your tongue make things better? If we never talk, how will our family's pain go away?*

Birdie pointed to the different hairdos and tapped Lou's arm. "Do you think I should take a picture?"

"Doesn't matter what *I* think, Birdie. Matters what *you* think."

Birdie felt scolded. In a good way.

Then she pulled the phone from her jacket pocket and located the camera function. She turned the phone horizontally, widened the frame, pushed the button, and listened for the click. She studied the photo she'd captured: it was a good picture. Then Birdie thought about Mama's shaved head not being there. She couldn't decide whether it would have made the photo better or worse.

Henrietta studied the young girl sitting next to her in the middle seat, her eyes drifting to the scene out the window. She reminded Henrietta of a young giraffe. Willowy neck. Limbs long and awkward like a young calf learning to walk. Skin the bronze color of its spots. Curly black frizz corralled by a Kente-cloth headband.

When the girl raised her eyes, Henrietta thought them stunningly beautiful: a soft cinnamon-brown flecked with olive. Yet the eyes themselves gave off one of two expressions: squinting with worry or probing with questions. Yes. It was the girl's eyes that touched Henrietta's heart.

The girl reminded her of herself at that age. Tense. Guarded. Sister Florinda, who had been Henrietta's salvation, would have said the girl was wound "tight as a tick." As if something had hampered her girlhood. Henrietta thought that hampering someone's girlhood was an indignity that cried out for justice.

She noticed that taking pictures seemed to help the girl unwind.

"Dear," Henrietta said, "would you like to trade seats with me? I can see that you like taking pictures. If you have a window seat, you can see even more interesting things."

Birdie had never been called "dear" before. Certainly never by a white person.

"That's very nice of you," Lou answered for her. Lou eyed Birdie, raising her eyebrows, urging a response.

Birdie nodded. *It would be nice to have a window seat. Then I can take photographs outside and inside the bus.*

Khalid put the bus in gear, and Birdie felt the silver rectangle shake as the engine revved.

Louise and Birdie stood up and moved into the aisle. Birdie saw that the old lady would need help moving over. Birdie extended her hand, and the old woman grabbed it in a vise-grip. Birdie could feel bones fragile as chicken wings close to the surface of her thin fingers. The old woman hunched over, moving slowly, a rosary swinging at her neck. The women rearranged themselves, Birdie by the window, the old woman in the middle, Lou still on the aisle. As she settled herself, the old lady reminded Birdie of a hen wiggling down into her nest. Then the old woman looked over and smiled softly at Birdie.

Birdie stared out the window, the familiar landscape of Soros appearing different from this higher perspective. The cars looked smaller, the potholes less visible, the kids hanging out on street corners less menacing. She wondered what it would be like to fly like a bird, soaring above the treetops, gliding across the sky. Maybe from up high, the world below would seem more peaceful.

Now the gray-headed lady turned and tapped Birdie's arm. Birdie looked away from the window. The woman was offering her feeble hands, one to Louise, one to Birdie, bobbing her head like a chicken pecking grain. Birdie wondered if she might have one of those diseases that made old people tremble.

"I'm Henrietta Oldham," she said.

Louise was easy with the handshake. Not Birdie.

"Louise Marie Franklin." She raised an eyebrow in Birdie's direction.

"Birdie Jackson," she said.

She would never in this world introduce herself as "Alberta."

Emily could almost hear Katie's straight blonde hair swish as her friend leaned over to ask, "Do you think we'll meet anyone interesting on this trip?"

Emily wondered why Katie wanted to meet someone interesting. She had Marc. Emily wondered why a boyfriend wasn't interesting enough.

"Not sure," said Emily. "There's a lady a couple rows up from Wamego, where they have the Oz Museum. Jessica Something."

"Oh," Jenny offered. "My folks took me and my sister there when we were little."

Emily remembered that Jenny's sister Alice had some kind of disease. It made her head jerk, and her tongue made clicking noises.

"I think they wanted to take Alice to visit someplace where her Tourette's wouldn't make her feel so strange," Jenny said. "After all, there's nothing stranger than the characters in Oz."

"Well, that lady up a few rows waitresses at Toto's Tacos. She wears her hair in pigtails like Dorothy." Emily wondered if she had to wear a starched blue pinafore to work. Emily didn't want to admit that she was still scared to watch *The Wizard of Oz*. The worst line for her was when the Wicked Witch said "…and your little dog, too."

"I still have my souvenir from the trip. It's a magnet that says 'Are You a Good Witch or a Bad Witch?'"

Emily and Katie laughed. Emily thought she was probably a Bad Witch. If she'd been a Good Witch that guy from the other night would have texted.

"What I remember most was the Flying Monkey," Jenny said. "It was gross. It was all splayed out, wings and all, sort of like that frog we cut up in Biology class at Stanton. And it had these tiny ugly feet. It was dead as a doornail. It was just like a big, ugly dead bat."

Emily shivered. She didn't like thinking of frogs or bats. "Did they have any Munchkins there?"

"They were wax statues. Gave me the creeps. But I think they had Munchkin hands and feet in cement on the walkway as you came in to the museum. Sort of like in Hollywood. Only not."

"I always felt so sorry for those Munchkins," Katie said. "Wouldn't you hate to be born with something wrong with you like that?"

Birdie had been listening to the girls behind her. They'd been talking about the Oz Museum. She cringed when she heard the one they called Katie say "something wrong with you like that."

Now Henrietta Oldham tapped her arm. Birdie was thankful for the interruption; she had started thinking about Shanice again.

"'Birdie,'" she said, tapping while she talked. "That's a nice name for a young girl."

She looked kind, the way Birdie had pictured a grandmother. Rocking chair. Cookies. Only Black.

Birdie puffed up a little. Most people decided "Birdie" was an odd name, and then she had to go into the whole "Alberta" thing.

"It seems an especially good name for a young woman your age. You're about fourteen or fifteen, an age when a girl starts spreading her wings to fly, right?"

Henrietta thought about the fleeting nature of young dreams. Fragile as hatchlings, young dreams tested the edges of the nest, practiced the first whirl and flap of their wings, and then, their tiny hearts pounding, plunged into the risk of ascent.

Henrietta remembered the conversation between her mother and father so many years ago.

"But she's from right here in Kansas, Frank. She's a native son."

Henrietta didn't offer that Amelia Earhart was a native *daughter.* Young Henrietta had learned early on about Amelia Earhart. There was a picture of her above the blackboard in her classroom at the end of a long line of photographs of famous men: George Washington, Abraham Lincoln, Thomas Edison, Henry Ford.

Sister Mary Margaret, who was loved by her students for her irreverent comments, had slipped Amelia up there right next to the picture of Charles Lindbergh. "She's a female pioneer," Sister said, harrumphing, "and not a Nazi sympathizer."

Henrietta didn't understand about Sister's observation, but she had been transfixed by the sunny freckle-faced woman with wind-blown hair who looked more alive than the bearded, periwigged, stiff-collared concoction of men to her left.

"I don't care if she's from right here in Soros. If God had meant women to fly, He wouldn't have sent her plane down halfway across the world."

Henrietta's mother turned back to the pleats she had been measuring, her lips disappearing into her mouth.

Lesson learned. "God," young Henrietta realized, "hadn't meant for women to fly."

Birdie thought of all the ways her fourteen-year-old self was *not* ready to fly. Instead of two wings for lifting her up, she had two lead-weighted feet holding her down. The weights included the other girls at school, the girls who had excluded Shanice and who now excluded her; they included her brother Beanie, whom she both loved and hated; they included her schoolwork, making her less and less likely to pass eighth grade; they included her mama's buzzed head and her absent daddy and her unanswered questions. Those weights included every little thing in the world, big things and little things, the wide world and the narrow one, things Birdie worried about all the time.

Aunt Lou answered for her. "Her daddy, Albert Jackson, named her when she was born. Alberta Sankofa. The 'Alberta' was after himself. The 'Sankofa' was to honor a bird from Ghana, where Birdie's grandmother still lives."

Henrietta looked closely at Louise. "What a coincidence. Sister Florinda, who was the cook in the rectory where I worked as a girl, was born in Ghana. Florinda was like a mother to me. Florinda's niece Serena is meeting our bus in D.C. to join me on the march."

Aunt Louise wasn't finished. Birdie wondered what it was that made it so easy for her aunt to talk to strangers. "So between 'Alberta' and 'Sankofa,' 'Birdie' was bound to be her nickname right away."

Birdie was glad Lou didn't add the part about how she had been an incubator baby, tiny as a bird. Long, scrawny legs. Big feet. Cheeping noises. How she almost didn't make it. How Daddy left soon after she came home from the hospital. How she had missed him ever since. Birdie longed to whisper her ache into Mama's curls: *Why is it that you can miss someone you never knew?*

When the subject of Birdie's daddy came up, Mama sometimes talked about Afghanistan and losing comrades who walked away from the battlefield. You were angry at them. You called them cowards. But Birdie wondered if Mama hoped Daddy might, like those deserters, still come back. If Mama was the question-asking type, she might have whispered a question similar to Birdie's: *Why is it that you can miss someone who deserts you?*

"Well, that's quite a nice story," Henrietta Oldham said, "behind a special nickname." She pulled a butter-yellow ball of yarn and two knitting needles from her tote. She began to wrap some stitches around one of the needles. Her fingers moved lickety-split.

Knitting. Rocking chair. Cookies. But still Black.

As she cast on a row of stitches, Henrietta thought about baby girls given their father's names. Albert. *Alberta.* Eric. *Erica.* Joseph. *Josephina.* George. *Georgia.* Claude. *Claudia.*

It hadn't been her first find, but Henrietta kept a tattered copy of Elizabeth Cady Stanton's autobiography among her treasured artifacts. That's where Henrietta had learned that Stanton's father wished she had been a boy. Ever after, she had felt a kinship with the feminist pioneer.

Girls made up over half the world. She wondered how many of them were given the names of their fathers.

Roberta. Pauline. Thomasina. Henrietta. She wondered if these baby girls were given those names because their fathers were proud – or disappointed.

Birdie had never heard phrases like "nice story" or "special nickname" applied to her before. Henrietta's compliment loosened something inside her.

"We have lots of nicknames in our family," she began, hesitating at first. "Our aunt Louise here is 'Lou-Lou.' Mama, Veronica Franklin Jackson, is 'Ronnie.' My oldest brother Antoine is 'Twanny.' My youngest brother is Bakari, but we call him 'Beanie.'" Birdie left off one name, feeling a familiar twinge of guilt.

"Beanie?" Henrietta stopped knitting.

"Birdie's brother is hardheaded," Aunt Lou explained. "Bakari's daddy used to say, 'Boy, we got to knock some sense into that bean of yours.' It was just natural for them to call him 'Beanie.'" Aunt Louise winked at Henrietta.

But Birdie noticed that Lou-Lou didn't explain how *Mama* described her brother. "My Beanie's just about the most hardheaded boy you ever knew," Mama would say. "If you told him something, he'd do the opposite. Don't swear at the police. Don't play in the ravine behind the YMCA. And he'd done go and do it anyway. Beanie's always actin' the fool."

"Boys!" Henrietta muttered. "Lots of them need sense knocked into them, don't they?"The braided bun on the top of her head shook.

"What about you?" Birdie asked. "What's *your* nickname?"

Henrietta's milky blue eyes peered at Birdie through her rimless glasses. She seemed surprised by the question. "I don't really have a nickname," she said. "When I was born, my father wanted a baby boy. He was going to name him 'Henry.' But he was disappointed when he got a girl. I guess I've been plain 'Henrietta' ever since."

Birdie felt a connection to Henrietta. Birdie had once been a disappointing baby, too. "Well, I'm going to give you a nickname. How about 'Hennie?' It's a lot shorter than 'Henrietta.'"

Henrietta winked. "I expect I like 'Hennie' well enough," she said. She looked satisfied, maybe even a little pleased. Birdie could tell by the way the lines at the corner of her eyes gathered like gently pulled stitches.

As she picked up her knitting again, Henrietta nodded and smiled at Birdie. "Where do you go to school, Miss Birdie Jackson? You seem like a mighty smart girl."

Mighty smart? Me?

"Frederick Douglass Junior High," Birdie answered. She didn't respond to the "mighty smart" part. The closest she ever got to "mighty smart" was when Mrs. Hightower, her fifth grade teacher, said she was "smart enough for a Black girl."

Emily was thinking about the nice rose tattoo on the nape of Jessica Something's neck. "Remember when we got our tats together?"

They all remembered. It had been first semester of freshman year. They had been suite-mates and were beginning to think of each other as friends. They took the bus together to the mall outside of town.

The parlor was called Eternally Yours. It made Emily think about death. She would die with this tattoo on her body. She wondered if the mortician would have a better idea of who she'd been than she did now.

Jenny was getting a lotus flower tattoo on her ankle. Jenny explained that the lotus stood for overcoming obstacles.

Emily knew that Jenny's parents were divorced, like hers. Jenny's mother had remarried a man with three kids from a previous marriage. So that made five kids, Stan's three and Jenny and Alice. Jenny often talked about how the divorce was hardest on Alice. Stan wasn't exactly up on how to respond to a kid with tics. The kids at school called her Alice-Click-Click, and sometimes Stan called her that too. Jenny had worked her way through college updating websites for professors in different departments, inserting professional articles with titles like "Exploring Mind-Body Modalities," "Physics of the Zero-Photonic Gap," or "Carcinogenicity of Oral Squamous Cell Carcinoma."

Katie had been dating Marc since high school, so she decided to get her tat of the letter "M" on her left butt cheek. She asked the tattooist to disguise it somehow in case they should ever break up. He designed the "M" as the high part of a mountain range, the two peaks sticking out of the range with snow on each of the caps. That way, should things not work out, Katie could claim to be a winter-lover or a skier or a mountain-climber.

Emily had finally decided on an infinity tattoo. The infinity sign had two open spaces in it. She decided to put a heart in one of the spaces and a paw print in the other. She had sprung for the extra money to have the heart inked in red. She hadn't anticipated the look on her mother's face when she came home for Thanksgiving and saw the tat on her left shoulder.

Sonia had come with them to Eternally Yours, but she had declined to get a tattoo. She mumbled something about thinking more about it before she decided on something so permanent. Sonia was the only person Emily knew who was always thinking about things.

The girl that Hennie called "mighty smart" had walked up to school a few days before the march. Extra early. To ask permission from Mrs. Opie. Mama wouldn't let Birdie go on the trip without it.

She'd begged Mama to call her in sick. Or at least talk to Mrs. Opie for her. After all, she'd only be missing one Friday.

"No way, Birdie-girl," Mama replied, turning her back. When Mama turned her back, Birdie knew a conversation was over.

It wasn't fair. Mama'd called Shanice in sick lots of times.

Birdie had taken the same route to school every day since first grade. Now, after Shanice, she was noticing things she'd somehow missed before: the ripped screens on front windows, the open garbage cans on front porches, the rusted cars on front lawns. On Jefferson Street, the dusty window of Mr. Mims's corner store displayed boxes of powdered milk, cans of Spam, and packets of Black and Milds. Mama'd warned her to avoid his back parking lot where the boys-who thought-they-were-men dealt drugs and smoked joints and where her friend Destinee sometimes bought them.

Mama had also warned Birdie to avoid the alley beside the hardware store that would cut her walk to school in half. "Nothin' good ever happens in that alley," Mama said. She was right: last December, a dead body was found there, a dried-out Christmas wreath looped over its neck. But Birdie had found out for herself that what Mama warned was true. She never told anyone what had happened to her there; but she didn't go through the alley any more.

From about fourth grade, it had been Birdie's job to push Shanice to school. It was hard work. It was a second-hand wheelchair, and the wheels often got stuck in the mud or the cracks of the sidewalk. Avoiding the alley meant a longer walk, guaranteeing she'd arrive at school tired and out of breath. When Birdie complained that it was a job for her older, stronger brothers, Mama said girls matured faster than boys so they got the jobs that required the most responsibility. When Birdie complained again, Mama said to think of the pioneers coming across the prairies, their wagon wheels stuck in the mud out in the middle of nowhere. "Life isn't all Kansas sunflowers, Birdie," she snapped.

The kids at school arrived in different ways. The kids out in the county, most of them white farm kids, arrived by a bus that looked like a yellow submarine. The richer kids pulled up in their parents' cars which had silver hood ornaments and leather seats. The kids in town were mostly like Birdie, Black or Latino kids who arrived on foot. None of them pushed a wheelchair.

When she finally got to school to ask Mrs. Opie's permission, there was Mr. Morgan Pine, the janitor. From atop an industrial ladder, Mr. Pine waved at her, his keys jangling from a ring at his waist. Mr. Pine was replacing the outside lights that were not just burned out, but shot out. Mr. Pine was always fixing things: soldering the broken links on the playground swings, lining the rusty edges of the slide with duct tape, replacing the frayed tetherball cord.

As Birdie approached the heavy side door to Frederick Douglass Junior High School, she turned around and looked back at Mr. Pine replacing those shot-out bulbs. She knew that the rest of his day would be spent replacing broken chair legs and scouring graffiti from bathroom doors. As she pulled on the heavy side door and entered the dark hallway, Birdie wondered: *Why are so many things broken at our school? Does that include the kids who go here?*

Birdie had never been called "mighty smart," but she'd been a pretty good student most years. But now her grades were failing: it had been a rough year and a half.

Not just the grades had changed. Birdie was doing things she knew she shouldn't be doing: smoking weed with Destinee and La'Keisha in the woods behind the school; staying out past her curfew, her brother Beanie leaving the back door unlatched so she could slip in without Mama noticing; trying to make her flat chest look like Sabrina Banks's C-cup; not studying. After what happened to Shanice, Birdie felt freer in some ways, not all of them good. She'd overheard Lou-Lou tell Mama she was like a former inmate who leaves the clanging prison gates behind. "Then she lines up for drinks at a bar. And ends up in another kind of prison." Mama didn't say anything to that.

Mrs. Miranda Opie had taught all of the Jackson kids in eighth grade. Antoine, Beanie, Shanice, now Birdie. Her brothers loved to make fun of her behind her back. Sometimes they called her "Opie-Dopey." Sometimes they mocked her with the phrase, "Okey-dokey, Mrs. Opie," laughing hysterically in that way that boys do over things plain silly. Birdie was ashamed of her brothers for that because not only was Mrs. Opie a friend of Aunt Lou, but when Shanice graduated from grade school, Mrs. Opie had knit Shanice a shawl for a graduation present. In purple, Shanice's favorite color. Shanice had worn it draped over her shoulders every single day, even during the hot summer after school let out. Birdie was grateful, too. Dressing a person in a wheelchair wasn't easy.

"Why, Miss Birdie Jackson," Mrs. Opie said, her eyebrows lifting in surprise when she saw her. "It's awfully early. You come in to catch up on your homework?"

Birdie studied her shoes. She had a lot of homework to catch up on. The descriptive paragraph. The career exploration project. The quiz on African-American authors.

She'd hardly done a lick of work this year.

"No'm," Birdie said, her eyes peeking upward to meet Mrs. Opie's. "Here to ask permission."

Mrs. Opie propped her elbows on her desk, laced her fingers together, and rested her chin on them. She waited.

Mostly what Birdie had noticed about Mrs. Opie before was from a distance at the back of the classroom, where a girl who preferred to disappear always chose to sit. Mrs. Opie had a broad wide chest, narrow hips, and toothpick-skinny legs. Sometimes when Birdie watched her write on the chalkboard, she wondered if Mrs. Opie might topple over under the weight of her pillowy bosom. Most of the time, though, Birdie just longed to rest her head there.

Now, up close, Birdie noticed that Mrs. Opie had beautiful fingers, long and shapely like someone who played a harp or a piano. They were neatly manicured and squared off at the end, not claws polished with rainbows and butterflies like Mrs. Perkins, the school secretary. She noticed that Mrs. Opie had beautiful soft black ringlets with threads of gray in them that surrounded her face like a picture frame. *Would Mrs. Opie let me bury my head in her curls, now that Mama's are gone?* In the middle of Mrs. Opie's face were walnut-brown eyes, eyes that weren't blinking but were staring straight at her.

35

"I'm asking for permission," Birdie stammered, studying the cracks in the linoleum floor, "to miss school on Friday, January 20."

Mrs. Opie tipped her head at an angle; she was listening for more.

"My Aunt Lou wants to take me to the Women's March on Washington. After Shanice and all, my Aunt Lou told Mama that it was time she paid attention to her other daughter, too."

Mrs. Opie drew in a breath. She was a friend of Aunt Lou. They sang together in the gospel choir at Missionary Baptist. They'd both been trying to get Mama to join, but Mama never felt much like singing.

"Your aunt's a capable woman. She's told me about organizing all of the ADAPT chapters for the march. I didn't know she'd invited you to come along."

Mrs. Opie knew a great deal about Birdie's family. Mama's service to the country. Antoine, in his senior year now, hoping to get a college scholarship. Beanie and Shanice. Birdie and her grades. Birdie hoped she didn't know about the kind of smoking and hanging out she was doing.

"Your aunt Louise is a wise woman," Mrs. Opie went on. "And I imagine it's been hard on you being the baby of the family. With an older sister that took most of your mama's attention. And all the sadness afterwards."

Sadness for me. Anger for Mama.

Birdie wondered how Mrs. Opie managed to guess such things. Maybe it came from the same place that told her to knit a shawl for Shanice for her graduation.

Mrs. Opie unlaced her fingers and pursed her lips, rooting around in a folder on her desk. "I think it's a marvelous idea," she said.

"You *do?*" Birdie blurted out. *'Okay' would have been good. But 'marvelous'?*

"Of course," she answered calmly. "But you'll need to do a special project about your time away," she added. "And you'll have to share your special project with the class."

Birdie gulped at the thought of extra work, especially work she had to share with the class, but she knew enough to stay quiet. "Thank you, Mrs. Opie," she said.

Then Birdie turned to leave, intending to wait outside until the first morning bell rang. Some of the girls gathered outside the gym entrance to sneak on make-up and talk about the boys. Every once in a while one of the boys sat with her now at lunch. Just not Jamil Washington.

Mrs. Opie pulled a paper out of a folder, waving it at Birdie. "Your African-American authors quiz, Birdie," she said.

Birdie could see that Mrs. Opie intended for her to take it. Now. Mrs. Opie handed her a pencil, and Birdie shuffled to a desk.

Birdie stared at the names on the test, names she hadn't studied: James Baldwin, Zora Neale Hurston, Langston Hughes, Alice Walker. She blinked and looked over at Mrs. Opie, who was marking a pile of papers, ignoring her.

Mrs. Opie never looked up when she said, "Don't forget the colon and semicolon worksheets, Birdie. I've got them here after you finish with that."

"Yes, ma'am." Birdie gulped, staring at her quiz, helpless at matching authors with books: *Does* The Color Purple *go with Alice Walker or Zora Neale Hurston?*

"And just a reminder," Mrs. Opie added, rising from her work, "the descriptive paragraph and the career exploration project still need your attention." She moved toward Birdie, patting her on the shoulder with her beautiful hands. Then she marched out of the classroom, leaning forward slightly, broad chest balanced atop narrow legs.

Birdie looked down at the paper in front of her. All she could think of was that *The Color Purple* went with Shanice.

"Where are we?" Emily asked, straining to look out the window.

"Nowhere, Em."

"We're outside of Soros now," Emily said.

"That's what I mean, Emily. Nowhere," Katie said. All of them laughed, including Emily.

The talk about Munchkins gave Emily an idea. "Let's look up all the places in Kansas with odd claims to fame. Like the Oz Museum."

Katie clapped her hands. "Good idea."

Emily thought any excuse to dive into their phones was a good idea.

It didn't take long for them to come up with some Kansas oddities.

"Did you know there's a city called 'Liberal,' Kansas? I didn't think Kansas was liberal about anything," Katie said. Emily knew Katie had voted for Gary Johnson. None of the other candidates wanted to legalize marijuana.

"It depends on how you phrase things," Jenny said. "My guess is that folks in Kansas are *against* Obamacare but *for* the Affordable Care Act."

"Hmmm." That made a lot of sense to Emily. Next to Sonia, Jenny was probably the smartest of them.

"Well," said Katie. "Liberal, Kansas has a really cool library. It's in the shape of an open book." She held up the picture. Emily and Jenny were impressed. It was a lovely building.

"Sonia would love that," said Jenny. "I'm going to text that picture to her." Jenny busied herself tapping and swiping.

Katie said, "There are about a gazillion 'World's Largest' sites. World's Largest Ball of Twine, Cawker City. World's Largest Spur, Abilene. World's Largest Hairball, Garden City."

Emily started to say something nasty about the hairball, but then she remembered both Jenny and Katie had cats. Emily hated cats. The litter boxes. The indifference. The hairballs.

As the bus rattled and shook, picking up speed as it headed into the cornfields, Birdie eavesdropped on the conversations of the women chatting in the row in front of her. The one who worked at Toto's Tacos had the window seat, too. The ladies were introducing themselves.

"Lucinda Martin. Olathe. Shift coordinator at Hy-Vee."

Birdie knew about Hy-Vee. Mama complained about how Hy-Vee was always changing the displays around so she had to spend more time finding her groceries. Mama was always short on time. She only shopped there on account of the fuel points.

"Melanie Snyder," said the lady next to Lucinda. "Manhattan. *Kansas*, of course. I run a nonprofit. We buy gift cards for public schoolteachers so they can buy pencil and paper for their classrooms."

Birdie knew what nonprofits were – charity organizations. Aunt Lou had worked for a slew of them. Lou-Lou was the kind of person who always put her change in the cardboard cylinders next to cash registers collecting for kids' cancer camps or the ASPCA.

Lucinda Martin said, "What a shame. If women ran the world, the first thing they'd do is improve our schools."

Birdie silently agreed with Lucinda Martin. They could start the improvements with Frederick Douglass Junior High. Right away.

Henrietta listened to the repetitive bus noises: the grinding gears, the whirring acceleration. They made background music to her knitting: knit one, purl two. The sounds brought back memories. She hadn't taken a long bus ride since that time she was a young girl, sent across the prairie to somewhere on the western edge of Kansas. She had felt abandoned and alone. No one in her family had come with her to say good-bye. Sister Florinda had driven her to the bus depot, her cook's apron still spattered with gravy. As she sent her up the steps of the bus, Florinda had given her a bag of needles and yarn and whispered four words she would never forget: *I believe in you.* That was over fifty years ago.

Grinding memories, whirring recollections. Knit one, purl two.

"World's Largest," Emily said. "That's too easy. Let's look for interesting things about people instead."

They started searching.

"Wow," said Katie. "This is something. There's a memorial to a guy named 'D-E-A-F-Y Boular' in Atchison. He was a legless bricklayer."

"Is that pronounced 'Deffy' or 'Deefy'?" Jenny asked.

"It must be 'Deffy,'" Katie said, reading more. "He was deaf from the age of four. And because he was deaf, he lost his legs at the age of twelve. Couldn't hear the train coming down the tracks."

"God, that's awful," Jenny said. "Poor kid."

"That was back in the 1870s. He had special boots made to fit his stumps, and he found out that he was the perfect height for paving the streets of Atchison with bricks. Because he didn't have to bend over. They put up a statue to him."

"Good for Deafy," Jenny said.

"I think it's gross," Katie said. "Can you imagine a statue of yourself and all your defects for people to stare at till the end of time?"

Emily thought about the end of time. All that came to mind was her tattoo and the name of that parlor: Eternally Yours.

Birdie shifted to listening to the girls in the row behind her. She cringed when she heard the story of Deafy Boular. Deafy made Birdie think of Shanice. Everyone laughed at Shanice all the time. She didn't pick up on gestures and facial cues, so it was hard for her to understand the kids around her, and it was hard for the kids around her to understand Shanice. *Had they laughed at Deafy, too?*

Still, like Deafy, Shanice went ahead and lived. Painted her nails. Talked Mama into dreadlocks. Wore her purple shawl year-round. Went to a protest in Topeka.

Birdie was grateful Mama didn't make her come to all of Shanice's ADAPT meetings, but she resented even those few times she'd gone. Mama made her help make change for them when they sold bouquets of sunflowers to pay for the protest trip to Topeka. Some of them couldn't do math, and others couldn't do more than hold bunches of sunflowers in their laps, looking pathetic from their wheelchairs.

Birdie had been embarrassed to be seen with her sister and her friends in front of the Hy-Vee. *Who really wants to be a member of a club like this?* She was proud that they sold nearly a hundred bouquets, but she wanted to be with her friends, to separate herself from Shanice, to have her own life.

Birdie thought about the legless bricklayer. He went on laying bricks, even without his legs. *How would Deafy have felt about that statue of him? If there had been a statue to Shanice, would she have felt proud – or ashamed?*

Birdie stared out the window.

There was only a light dusting of snow across the wheat fields, like the talcum powder Mama sprinkled all over when she didn't have time for a bath. The trees were bare, but the weather report said it was "unseasonably warm." Birdie was glad the trees weren't shivering in the usual January weather. She'd be worried about them without their coats of leaves. *Why is it that I worry about everything so much? Every. Single. Thing. Mama's anger, my sadness, Beanie's troublemaking, my own future, even trees.*

As the bus picked up speed, Birdie discovered that staring out the window of a bus had an eerie, dreamlike quality, soft and fuzzy: like a first awakening from sleep. It felt like drifting between two worlds, the outside and the inside. She'd experienced that kind of drifting for the last year and a half, unsure which reality she was in. She flashed back to what she'd learned in Mrs. Madden's social studies class about dates. First there was B.C., and then there was A.D. It was all about Jesus. What happened *before* Jesus and what happened *after*. Birdie wondered: *Are there events in regular people's lives that are so important that they feel time as something 'before' and something 'after'?*

PART II – SOROS TO KANSAS CITY

12:05 p.m. CST, January 20, 2017

Emily watched as a skinny white lady in the front row stood up. She had mostly boy-short black hair except for a very long piece that angled like an arrow across her left eye and down her cheek. Gold bracelets jangled at her wrists. She was wearing a dress that looked like an art smock; the fabric had a pattern of jagged lines and forms that looked like mobiles and reminded Emily of that painter from Art Appreciation 101 at Stanton. Mirro? Muro? She thought of Bernadette Boucher, her mother's friend on the opera board in Topeka who ran a so-called "gallery" there. Mother thought she was a sophisticated artist. Dave thought she was full of herself; he reminded Mother that "Boucher" was French for "butcher."

The lady reached for Khalid's microphone. "Greetings, marchers. I'm Alexandra Hall, the organizer of this trip."

The ladies cheered.

Alexandra Hall spoke up over the cheering. "All right, ladies. A lot of you don't know each other, so we're going to start making friends right now."

At Frederick Douglass, only a few of the Black girls hung around Birdie. Ai'esha. Destinee. La'Keisha. She wasn't hanging with JaNeela any more, of course, after what she did to Shanice. Sometimes Birdie blamed her small group of friends on her shyness. Sometimes she blamed her brother Beanie. Sometimes, she was ashamed to admit it, she blamed Shanice. *Can you just decide to start making friends and expect it to happen 'right now?'*

"O.K., marchers," Alexandra Hall said, "I'm going to ask you to raise your hands, and when I point to you, I want you to give your name, where you're from, and why you're here."

Hands flew into the air.

"Teresa Anders, Topeka. I'm here for my daughters."

Clapping.

"Monica Chiandra. Wichita, Kansas. I'm here for our mothers."

More clapping.

Birdie thought about Mama. She didn't want her to be angry any more. Mama had always had a quick temper, but now she was angry all the time. *Am I here for her somehow?*

"Angela Banner, Sioux City, Iowa. I'm here for my granddaughters."

Clapping and hooting.

Birdie's Grandmother Franklin was gone. Daddy's Mama was still in Ghana, so she'd never met her. Aunt Louise was the closest thing Birdie had to a grandmother. Birdie wondered what a grandmother would be like. *Would she come to my school pageants? Would she let me lick the cake batter off the beaters? Would she have a family cookie recipe to pass on to me?*

44

Henrietta wondered what it would be like to have a granddaughter. It was something Henrietta had wondered about for a long time. She had collections of Little Golden Books in baskets scattered throughout her store, and she could hardly get enough of them. Grandmothers were steady buyers of *The Pokey Little Puppy* or *The Saggy Baggy Elephant*, even copies with torn pages. When Henrietta looked at the gnawed corners of *Scuffy the Tugboat*, she pictured teething grandchildren with Chiclets teeth and felt a tug at her heart.

Henrietta tapped Birdie on the arm and whispered, "Maybe I'm here for the granddaughters I've never had."

When Miss Hennie whispered about granddaughters, Birdie remembered she had never met her Grandma and Grandpa Franklin. She was reminded of them through their casserole dish and carving set. The Jacksons used them every Thanksgiving. Grandma and Grandpa had bought the dish and carving set as souvenirs on a weekend trip to Kansas City. They had gone to see the new American Jazz Museum. After that, they planned to jam at a club all night.

At Thanksgiving, Lou-Lou served her famous corn pudding in Grandma Franklin's casserole dish. When you got to the bottom, you could see the picture of Charlie Parker. Grandpa Franklin's carving set, with pictures of Bennie Moten on the fake-ivory handles, was what Mama always used to carve the turkey.

But Birdie didn't like remembering that Grandma and Grandpa Franklin themselves never got to use them. They were killed in a crash outside of Lawrence on the way home. Their bodies were tangled in a crush of metal, but their souvenirs survived without a scratch. *Do objects like that stir comfort or grief?* Birdie thought of Shanice's ventilator in the corner of the living room.

Mama always wondered out loud whether it was a blessing or

a curse that Grandma and Grandpa Franklin never got to meet Shanice. She never mentioned Birdie.

Emily said, "This feels a little like college, doesn't it? Remember 'Fundamentals of Philosophy?'"

"Yep," Katie said. "We spent a whole semester thinking about questions like 'Why are you here?'"

Jenny laughed. "What is *you?*"

"What is *here?*"

"What is *why?*"

Emily said, "But we spent most of college wondering 'Where's the stash?'"

The girls got quiet, remembering.

"So why are we here *now?*" Emily asked. "For real?"

"To pool our resources," Katie answered. "So we can move to Philadelphia with Sonia."

Emily knew her own resources were slim. She also knew it was the same with the others. Except for Sonia, who was taking a yoga certification course and wanted to open a studio, none of them had jobs with much of a future. Jenny updated lists of donor contacts, funding agencies, and former clients for a private adoption agency, making others' dreams for children come true. Katie worked at a craft store, wondering what kind of life she was building out of plastic flowers, crochet hooks, and scrapbooking supplies.

"*What* resources?" Emily asked.

The girls got quiet again.

Alexandra Hall recognized the raised hand of another woman. Instead of shouting from her seat like the others, the lady moved to the front of the bus. She was tall, her chin raised slightly. She looked like an African queen.

She took Alexandra Hall's microphone from her without asking. She spoke into the microphone with confidence. "Rosalie Helen Randolph. Topeka." Birdie noticed how she said her whole name as if she was proud of it. *No Roz. No Rosie.* "I am here," she said, "because I have some questions. Questions that don't have easy answers."

Birdie held her breath. She had questions, too. But she couldn't see herself standing up in front of a whole bus full of strangers to ask them after taking a microphone from a white woman.

"Why is it," Rosalie Helen Randolph asked, "that when I stand up for myself, I'm accused of being an angry Black woman? Or when I seek justice – like equal pay for equal work - I'm accused of playing the race card?"

Birdie remembered Mama talking about equal pay for equal work and how her bosses threatened to fire any girl who brought it up. And the race card. *What was so wrong about Black people playing the race card? Didn't white people thrive every single day of the year playing their race card?*

The bus was silent. Like it was holding its breath.

The women had been giving easy answers about why they came before Rosalie Helen Randolph stood up. Birdie liked Rosalie Helen Randolph because she understood what was hard about easy answers: "Because you're a girl." "Because she's your sister." "Because I said so." "Just because." The one Birdie hated the most was "because girls mature faster than boys." *Doesn't that mean Mama makes excuses for the boys that she doesn't make for me?*

"Thank you, Ms. Randolph," Alexandra Hall said, taking back the microphone.

Then, as if exhaling on cue, the women clapped. One at a time. Then all together. Wild applause echoed through the bus. Some of the women even stomped their feet.

Another woman stood, moving into the aisle. She had wide cheekbones in a square face. She had straight black hair and olive skin. Her coat was dirty and torn. She was much tinier than the African-American queen, but she was attempting to stand to her full height.

Alexandra Hall moved to her with the microphone. The woman motioned it away. Birdie felt a kinship with the woman: she was too shy to use a microphone.

When she finally spoke, her voice shook.

"I'm undocumented," she said. Her dark eyes squinted as if she was scanning a horizon for danger. "I don't dare to say my name. My family crossed over the border from Mexico. Husband. Two children."

Each sentence came out haltingly.

"We were escaping the violence in my homeland. We paid a moving company to hide in the back of a moving van. Under beds and desks and tables. We were covered with hot moving blankets for five days. We had no food, no water. My children were not allowed to cry. We peed into the blankets like dogs and then choked on the smell."

The woman struggled to get her words out. As if she was still choking on the memory.

"And then I came... to America...and heard us..."

The woman began to cry.

"...heard us called murderers and drug dealers."

A trail of tears slipped down her brown cheek.

Henrietta understood about tears. They were the liquid form of anger.

Birdie thought back to what Mama said. "Big girls don't cry." She wondered if that was why Mama never talked about Shanice.

Birdie watched the undocumented woman struggling to speak through her tears. "People went to rallies…" she stuttered "…and shouted horrible things about us. Called us terrible names."

Birdie knew about terrible names. Savages. Wetbacks. Niggers. Retards.

The woman was now crying hard, bubbles of spit forming in the corners of her mouth as she choked out her words. "The church in El Paso …gave us shelter," she burbled. "They gave me money for this trip."

The bus was silent.

"I am here because what they think…" she paused, finding it impossible to speak now.

A stranger beside her handed her a tissue, and the woman began to dab at her eyes. "What they think about us…" - she struggled to breathe – "… is not true."

Birdie's mind raced with all the other things people said about *her* people that weren't true. Lazy. Stupid. Criminal. She thought about her brother Antoine. He worked hard. He was smart. Yet when he went for an interview at Wichita Community College, they gave him an appointment with the athletic director, not the academic director. Twanny hadn't played sports a day in his life. And there were plenty of names for kids like Shanice. Retard. Crip. Spaz.

The tiny woman blew her nose loudly on the tissue, then drew in her breath. "I came to say that every person has a right to seek freedom. Gracias."

Against the silence, one woman called out "gracias." Soon the word "gracias" was echoing through the cabin. The Mexican woman sat down, her shoulders still shaking.

Nobody was hooting or stomping their feet.

The bus was silent.

Birdie thought about silence. *Does silence give you space to pay attention to things?*

"Because she was Latina, he called her 'Miss Housekeeping.'"

"Who?" Emily asked.

"Cheeto. He shamed the Miss America contestant for gaining a few pounds."

"Fat-shaming. It's disgusting," Katie said.

"Why aren't men ever the subject of fat-shaming?"

Emily thought about Dave, the stepfather whose stomach hung out over his belt. She thought about her mother, who was always stepping on the scale.

"Good question, Jenny," Emily said.

Henrietta heard the bracelets jingling on Alexandra Hall's delicate wrists as she swept her angled hair back from her eyes. Henrietta had never done things that other women did regularly: color their hair, manicure their nails, adorn themselves with jewelry. She wondered how you got to be a woman who jingled.

"See, marchers? You've made new friends already. We have a lot of reasons to be on this trip. Please continue your conversations."

The buzz of talking women swarmed around her.

Henrietta turned to her left and asked, "So why are *you* here, Louise?"

Louise answered quickly. "Lots of reasons. We're part of a group called ADAPT. We're advocating for the disabled. We've got a big protest planned for Washington. But mostly I'm here for our family. For my sister Ronnie. For her kids. For Birdie here."

Henrietta envied Louise Franklin: she was here for her family. Henrietta felt she never really had a family. She had a father, a mother, a brother. But they hadn't been a real family, a family like Louise had, a family you might say you were *here for*. Not only did Henrietta envy Louise Franklin; she admired her. Louise seemed to be the kind of woman who knew what she was doing and why. She didn't seem like the kind of woman who would ever act the fool, sitting on an egg through every season, hoping it might hatch.

Birdie, on Henrietta's right, said, "Aunt Louise has always been there for our family. Fixing supper for us when Mama had to work late. Signing permission slips we'd forgotten. Bringing homework we'd left on the coffee table up to school. Taking my sister to her doctor appointments."

Henrietta was glad to see this young girl talking more. It was a shame to see a young woman with her lips sealed shut.

Henrietta wondered what made Birdie's aunt such a cheerful giver, the kind of giver in Corinthians, the kind of giver the Lord loveth. Maybe that was one reason why she'd come. She liked being a giver. She'd been one all her life. But somehow, after November, she'd begun to rethink her ideas about being a giver. Her life now seemed misdirected, insignificant, small. "Why?" she wondered. "Was all that giving a part of it?"

Birdie noticed that the landscape outside the window was just like her: flat as a pancake. Except for miles and miles of tallgrass, there was nothing to see. Mrs. Holmes, her seventh grade geography teacher, had explained that tallgrass was why there were so many buffalo on these plains. And after barbed wire was invented, farmers could become ranchers. Mrs. Holmes sounded like that was something to be proud of. Birdie wanted to raise her hand and ask why every living thing had to be corralled: by barbed wire, by fencing, by race, by memory.

Birdie didn't tell Hennie about how she ended up on this trip. It came up last November. At Thanksgiving. It had been only the second Thanksgiving since Shanice, and her family still struggled with what to be thankful for.

Mama sat at the head of the table, the carving knife and fork in each fist, her stubbly field of hair starting to grow out. Birdie thought it made her look funny and scary at the same time. At the table was Birdie, Mama, Beanie, Twanny, Aunt Lou, and Tyrone McMaster. Tyrone was Aunt Lou's sort-of boyfriend. Lou always said that as long as she was able to support herself, she'd never get married. She even said that out loud in front of Tyrone.

Right after they said grace, but before they started passing the food, Mama said, "No talking about Freddie Gray, Black Lives Matter, or the Charleston church shooting today, Lou. Thanksgiving's a time to get away from our troubles."

Tyrone nodded his head and Birdie's brothers winked at him over the table.

Still, Aunt Louise managed to speak her mind.

Mama had been passing the corn pudding when she did it.

"I'm going on that march, sis."

"*What* march?"

"The march on Washington. To protest. To stand up against things that aren't right."

Tyrone McMaster studied his green beans. Hard. Beanie and Twanny flashed glances at each other and then studied their plates, too.

Birdie knew Lou-Lou was powerful mad about the election the country had just had. Mama didn't have time to care one way or another about politics. But Aunt Lou did. She was always writing a check to one cause or another, even if the checks were small. She had worked for lots of nonprofits and volunteered at several others: homeless shelters, job centers, free tutoring programs.

"I'm going to see if I can get some of those families who brought their kids to the YMCA dance to come, too. They've got plenty to protest about."

Birdie remembered those families. The Rodriguezes. The Snyders. The McPhersons. They were families with kids like Shanice.

It was dead quiet. Aunt Lou had mentioned the YMCA dance, the dance Birdie's family never, ever talked about. You could almost hear the ice melting in the glasses of tea.

"One more thing." Lou paused. "I'm taking Birdie with me."

Mama looked straight at Birdie.

As if she was seeing her for the first time.

The words of the Black lady and the immigrant lady reminded Emily of that class she took for her Psychology elective at Stanton College. The students sat in a circle. They were supposed to "share." After a while, they actually did. Even though they were forced, Emily had liked those kinds of interactions.

Now that she was out of college, those kinds of interactions never happened.

Emily remembered her father taking her to one of his AA meetings after her parents got divorced. He was trying to get her to sign up for Al-Anon. She never did.

"I'm Eddie Messer," her father said, sitting in the circle, "and I'm an alcoholic." Her father's statement had scared her. He told Emily it had freed him.

It had been a long time since Emily had thought about circles or stories or sharing. She remembered the words her dad had taped to the dashboard of that battered old Chevy he drove. She couldn't remember all the words, but she remembered these: "The courage to change the things I can."

Aunt Lou asked, "So why are *you* here, Miss Hennie?"

Birdie studied Henrietta: the silver-gray braids winding on top of her head like a fancy pie crust; the blue-gray eyes like the sky right before it rains; the white blouse faded to an almost-gray like it had been washed and worn too many times; the watch pin on her blouse that told the time upside down; the old lady lace-up shoes. Birdie wondered why an old woman would come on this trip. *Wouldn't she miss her Metamucil? Her rocking chair? Days of Our Lives?*

"Bucket list," Hennie said.

Then she turned to Birdie and explained that a bucket list was a list of things you wanted to do before you died. "Before you 'kick the bucket,'" she added, grinning.

Lou-Lou nodded. "No trips to Paris, France?"

Henrietta shook her head. The silver-gray braids wiggled like feathers in a breeze.

"Or parachuting out of a helicopter?"

She began to laugh softly, a chuckle that sounded like a cluck. Birdie was glad she could call her "Hennie" now. Somehow, it fit.

Birdie wanted to bust in and say her Mama was in the Army and did all kinds of dangerous things. Parachuting. Demining. Building pontoon bridges. But she kept quiet.

"So for you, this march is a kind of closure, right?"

Birdie had been hearing that word a lot for the last year and a half. "Closure." It meant shutting a door. Closing a chapter. Moving on.

Hennie's eyes were no longer twinkling. She stared straight at Louise. "Yes, closure," she said. "How did you know?"

Aunt Lou spoke for both of them. "We - Birdie and I - need closure, too. I expect a lot of the women on this bus need closure."

Birdie thought about her future bucket list. It seemed far, far away. But she wondered: *When I am Miss Hennie's age, will 'closure' still be on it?*

Closure. Henrietta had never thought of it this way before, but Louise Franklin was right. *Closure* was one reason she was on the march. She wanted closure about the fool of a woman she'd been, about the rule-bound life she'd lived.

Henrietta had never wanted the antique shop. "A casket for dusty old things," her brother Henry had called it, and she wondered if he considered her the casket, the dust, or the old thing. The shop had fallen to her after her father died. It was the pattern of her life: things falling into her lap that she had never asked for. She wondered if other women ever felt this way.

Her brother Henry was always urging her to close the antique shop and work harder at renting out the apartments. That was unfair of him: as a priest, he would always have a home at the rectory.

She had explained to Henry that she was leaving for the weekend to visit their ailing aunt Rita. Aunt Rita, their last living relative on their mother's side, was alone in a nursing home in Wichita. "I'll give her your love, Henry."

Henry shrugged.

"Why," Henrietta wondered, "was she always covering for her brother? Couldn't he give his aunt his love for himself? He was a priest, after all! Why did she always add his name to thank-you notes that he hadn't written? Did all women cover for the men in their lives?"

"You'll watch the shop while I'm gone, won't you?"

Henry snorted. "What's to watch?"

Oldham's Antiques was only open half-days on Saturdays. Still, Henrietta was sure that her brother would open late and close early. If he opened at all.

Henrietta wondered how it had happened that this was her life.

The bus was rounding a curve, so Alexandra Hall held on to a head-rest to steady herself as she took the microphone again.

"You've done a good job on reasons why you've come, marchers!"

Birdie felt like she was back in first grade being rewarded with gold stars.

"I thought I'd go on and ask you to identify yourselves by generations. You know, getting to know you marchers on the bus in another way. By decade."

Henrietta listened as Alexandra Hall said, "I'll be naming a decade, and you just raise your hands based on the decade you were born in. And we'll see how many marchers are from each generation. Ready?"

Henrietta could tell that the ladies were not ready. Everyone was holding their breath. Some of the ladies squirmed in their seats. Alexandra Hall was asking these women to identify their age. Henrietta knew that age brought up not-so-subtle questions for women. Hennie wondered why aging was a woman's problem. Or why a man's gray hair makes him look distinguished but a woman's gray hair makes her look old.

"I was going to start with the 1950s, if that's OK with you."

No one said anything.

"Unless we have somebody here from the 1940s."

Lou-Lou elbowed Henrietta. "Could that be you? The 1940s?"

Birdie had no idea of Henrietta's age. In her mind, she could be anywhere from 60 to 90. *Weren't old people all in one clump? Could they really be sorted out age-wise?*

Timidly Henrietta raised her hand and wiggled a few fingers.

"There, right in the middle of the bus," Alexandra Hall said, calling attention to Hennie that she probably didn't want. "We have someone from the 40s. That's right after World War II, ladies. Congratulations, young lady."

Henrietta's pale white cheeks looked sunburned.

The women in the front half of the bus swivelled their heads to stare at her. As if someone this old had to be seen to be believed.

Henrietta thought back to that arrogant taxi driver with his "young lady" and "little missy."

Henrietta remembered little about the 1940s, but she knew she'd been a "baby boomer," one of those children born right after World War II. It was a time when people were starting families, hoping to take up the American Dream again. Suburbanites were buying washing machines, refrigerators, patio furniture. They were celebrating at cocktail hours and backyard barbeques.

But the American Dream had somehow passed the Oldhams by.

Henrietta's father came home wounded from the war. He had lost a foot in Belgium, in the Ardennes forest, and he dragged his left leg when he walked. The injury had limited his employment possibilities. He spent most of his time cutting insoles on the kitchen table for Antonio's corner shoe shop and making phone calls to find renters for the run-down apartment building he had inherited from his parents.

Henrietta's mother had taken in sewing. She was an excellent seamstress, and she had a couple of regular contracts with two department stores in Topeka. The sewing allowed her to earn money and attend to Henrietta's father at the same time. Henrietta had a stark, single memory of her mother: lips braced in a tight straight line, clamping a xylophone of pins.

When their first child turned out to be a girl, the Oldhams were devastated. They had hoped their shattered dreams could be fulfilled by a son. Still, after a while, Henrietta's father began to discover a daughter's uses: running errands, cleaning apartments after renters left, climbing the stairs for late rent payments. Henrietta hoped that her sturdy feet marching around on his behalf might become her salvation. If she worked hard enough to please him, perhaps she could ease the disappointments of his life. Like having a first-born daughter.

The family's only recreation was the church. Fish fries, fall bazaars, Christmas pageants. Father Cochran came about the time of Henrietta's confirmation. She remembered wearing the white dotted-swiss dress her mother had stitched by hand and the too-tight white gloves because her parents couldn't afford a new pair. She remembered pledging to renounce Satan and believe in God and the Church. She remembered the sign of the cross made on her forehead by holy oil. By the end of the ceremony, she had received her first rosary.

Henry had just started school. After the ceremony, she remembered standing stiffly alone while the other confirmands were being congratulated by their parents. She had watched her father offering congratulations to Father Cochran with a handshake that lasted too long and her mother standing meekly behind. Then he had turned to Henrietta's brother Henry: "We have high hopes for him," her father said, guiding him in front of the priest.

On that day, Henrietta was in possession of a different kind of confirmation: she may have been confirmed in the church, but she knew that her own feet were unimportant. It was Henry, not she, whose footsteps would become her family's salvation.

Alexandra Hall rushed ahead. "Anyone from the 50s?"

A dozen or so hands shot up.

"Remember the start of television?" Alexandra Hall asked.

A woman shouted, "And Elvis?"

The ladies laughed. Then clapped.

"What about the 1960s? Any of you from that decade?"

Several dozen hands shot up. Birdie saw that the majority of the marchers were from the 60s. From what she knew about the 60s, all they *did* was march.

"The Vietnam War," Alexandra Hall reminded them. "Protests." She tilted her head, and the arrowhead bangs tilted, too. "Most people think of protests against the war, but I remember a woman's-only protest that happened back then. It was shocking. Anyone remember?"

Emily was playing with her phone. That guy from the karaoke bar still hadn't responded.

A marcher in a red-white-and-blue crocheted shawl stood up. She announced her name was Beulah Knapke. "Atlantic City!" Beulah Knapke shouted. "I was there. Bra burning!"

Katie nudged Emily with her elbow, then pointed to the front of the bus. "Listen to this, Em!"

Emily looked up from her phone.

"That's right," Alexandra Hall said. "Can you tell us about it?"

Emily and Katie and Jenny were looking from each other to Beulah Knapke and back, listening intently.

"Well, we were protesting the Miss America Pageant. I remember bringing a poster with a woman's body marked up like a side of beef for sale in the grocery store."

The marchers were all ears.

Jenny volunteered, "Yep. That's just about right. Then and now. Men see women like sides of beef. Not much has changed."

Emily wasn't sure what to think about that. Her mother always said a woman had only two jobs in the world: to learn to drink coffee and to get herself a man. Emily had failed miserably at both. She was a barista at a coffee shop who hated coffee. And she was still a virgin.

"We didn't actually burn our bras," Beulah Knapke said. "But we did throw them in Freedom Trash Cans. Along with *Playboy* magazines, high-heels, fake eyelashes, and girdles."

Then she swept her patriotic shawl from her shoulders. Emily had never seen breasts so huge; they hung down like oversized pendant earrings weighing down ear lobes. "I wish we could go without them *now*," Beulah said.

The marchers were cheering and laughing, clapping and whistling.

Inspired by Beulah Knapke, some of the marchers in the back lifted their shirts to expose their brassieres. Emily had never seen so many different types of bras. Push-ups, strapless, Wonderbras. Soft cups, underwires, sports bras. Maximizers, minimizers. Emily took note of the sizes, too. Some looked like boa constrictors that had swallowed chickens. Some looked like boa constrictors that had swallowed mice. Emily wore a 32A. She was in the mice category. Emily wondered: "Is that why that guy hasn't called?"

Emily caught Khalid's eyes. He was watching all the women through his rearview mirror.

Emily felt her pulse racing. "This is cool," she said, poking Katie with her elbow. "It's a lot more interesting than karaoke night at the Lucky Duck."

Birdie couldn't believe what she was seeing. She only wished Mama was here to see this, too. The first thing Mama did after getting home from work was take off her bra. But Birdie thought about bras differently. *Aren't bras a sign of pride? In your own womanhood? Didn't you long for the day when you could wear high heels, fake eyelashes, and fill out a C-cup?*

The Muses in the row behind Birdie were excited. She'd eavesdropped on their conversations now and again when conversation slowed. One of them, the Ocean Wave, had a sister with Tourette's. Birdie wondered if Aunt Lou should invite her to the protest. The Muses had argued fiercely about their yoga pants. "Even though we love the pants we all wear," Ocean Wave asked, "was it right to support the brand since the male CEO was a chauvinist?"

Now The Muses were laughing and cutting up.

Birdie had begun to identify them by now.

Waterfall, the one with the straight blonde hair whose name might be Katie, said, "Why not identify each other by bra size instead of decade?"

Fountain, the one with the hair spraying on top of her head, said, "No fair. You'd win hands down. You're a D cup, and I'm not going to tell you what I am." Birdie thought her name might be Emily.

Ocean Wave, the one whose hair made a swirl across her forehead and whose name might be Jenny, said, "It's sports bras all the way for me, ladies. I don't think they come in sizes. They just stretch to fit."

A trucker had pulled up beside the bus and was honking.

Some of the women were waving at him.

Their bus swerved.

Keep your eyes on the road, Khalid!

Henrietta and Louise were holding their sides, laughing so hard it hurt.

Young Birdie looked embarrassed.

"Marchers! Marchers!" Alexandra Hall shouted. "No, please! Enough of this!"

After the ladies calmed down, Rosalie Helen Randolph stood up. All eyes were on her. She was dead serious. "We were talking about the 60s," she reminded them. "There were more important things back then than bra-burning. You didn't mention the 16th Street Baptist Church bombing. 1963."

Aunt Lou reached across Henrietta to poke at Birdie "Four little girls were killed. In church. In Birmingham. It was terrorism. I want you to remember this. Always."

Henrietta would never forget it. Sister Florinda had heard the news crackling over the kitchen radio, and she had wept about it instantly. "They were just babies," Florinda sobbed, tears making gray spots on her crisp white apron. They had held each other – the older woman, the younger girl - in a sisterhood of sympathy.

Hennie murmured under her breath. "Angry white people. Hate. Terrorism."

Didn't 'terrorism' begin with 9-11?

Birdie had never heard of these little girls. Or maybe she'd heard but didn't *listen*.

Alexandra Hall cleared her throat. "Thank you for that good reminder, Ms. Randolph." Birdie noticed that she addressed most of the women by "Miz." Not "Mrs." Or "Miss."

"Anybody from the 1970s?"

About a dozen hands flew up.

"And what do we remember about the '70s, girls?"

Henrietta answered quickly. "Roe vee Wade," she whispered loudly to Lou.

Lou said, "Amen, sister."

Responses bounced in from all over. The marchers were answering what Hennie had whispered. Birdie had no idea what that was. All she knew was that Mama was born in in the 70s, in 1976, during something called the Bi-Centennial. That was the 200th anniversary of America.

Which Mama said was nothing for Black folks to celebrate.

Henrietta remembered the tradition that started soon after her confirmation. Her parents took whatever stray dollars they could muster and invited Father Cochran to breakfast at their home after Sunday Mass. Mother bought the best quality bacon she could afford, and she served pancakes and eggs and hash browns and Maxwell House coffee. They were building a relationship that one day might benefit Henry. Henrietta still remembered how Father Cochran liked his eggs. Fried over easy with the yolks popped right at the last minute.

So when Father Cochran told them that the rectory needed a girl to clean two days a week, Frank Oldham had volunteered Henrietta. On Tuesdays and Fridays she went straight to the rectory from school in her blue plaid Catholic school uniform. Her parents were ecstatic, especially her father. Here was another connection that might help get Henry into seminary.

Emily recognized some of the phrases the marchers shouted when Alexandra Hall got to the 1980s.

"Michael Jackson."

"Madonna."

"*E.T.*"

"Ronald Reagan." Emily wasn't sure, but she thought he was a president who had also been in show business.

Jenny asked, "How does being on T.V. prepare you for being a president?"

A stocky young woman with pink hair and a ring through her nose got up. "AIDS," she said. "The '80s were all about AIDS."

Emily was shocked into remembering what she'd heard about all the AIDS funerals. She remembered her college friend Carl Withers talking about his uncle. She couldn't even remember the uncle's name. All she remembered was that it was so sad. He had died just before decent AIDS treatments came along. She remembered what Carl had said. About the sores all over, sores that covered the nose, mouth, and throat and made it difficult for him to breathe or eat or swallow. But Carl said the worst thing for his uncle was the shame. Shame was the very worst thing of all.

When Alexandra Hall got to the 1990s, the three girls in the row behind Birdie stood up and started pumping their fists like their decade was a football team they were rooting for. They were so much alike that they remind Birdie of the cool kids at school. Identical shoes. Identical slang. Identical notebooks. They shouted out their memories of the 90s.

"The Internet!"

"Monica Lewinsky."

"Funk! Hip-hop! Rap!"

Birdie could relate to that last one. Mama was OK with Ice Cube and Pharrell, but Mama wouldn't allow Twanny or Beanie to mention Dr. Dre in their house. Dre was nasty to women.

"Settle down, ladies," Alexandra Hall said as the three young women behind Birdie continued to butt-bump and high-five each other, pumping their fists again and again.

Finally they flopped down in a pile of giggles.

Louise stuck her head way out into the aisle and swivelled it around to say something to the three rowdy girls sitting behind her.

"Rodney King," she said, scowling. "You forgot to mention Rodney King."

Henrietta thought about all the things she'd witnessed in her lifetime. Korea. Buddy Holly. The Freedom Rides. Viet Nam. The Moon Landing. The Beatles. The Chicago Convention of 1968. Watergate. Assassinations: John Kennedy, Martin Luther King, Bobby Kennedy. Columbine. The Internet. Princess Diana. Same-sex marriage. Hillary.

Birdie stayed quiet.

Henrietta was pretty sure Birdie didn't know about Rodney King, either.

"I'm guessing we don't have any marchers from the 2000s here," Alexandra Hall said. "Do we?"

Aunt Lou raised her hand, and Birdie slunk down in her seat.

"My niece here was born in 2002," Lou said.

Please don't call me 'Alberta.'

"Birdie Jackson. Right here," Lou said, pointing.

"Well, stand up, Birdie Jackson. I think you're our youngest rider."

Birdie didn't want to stand up. She was nothing like Rosalie Helen Randolph. But Birdie saw Aunt Lou's raised eyebrow.

There was head-swivelling and clapping. The women stared at her just like they had at Hennie. Birdie felt the blood rushing to her cheeks.

She sat down quickly and stared at her lap.

Emily Googled "Rodney King." She passed the Wikipedia article over to Katie who passed it to Jenny. They glanced at the photos of the billy clubs, the mug shots, the police officers just standing by, the riots.

Jenny said, "Listen to this! This is what Sonia always says. 'People, you know, can't we all get along?' I think it's her favorite quote."

Emily asked, "Do you think she knows it's from Rodney King?"

"What do we know about the 2000s, marchers?"

The marchers called things out. Birdie thought it was like Sunday service at Aunt Lou's Missionary Baptist.

Facebook.

9-11.

Barack Obama.

The bus went wild at the mention of Obama. Lou's hands were flapping. She was head of the Obama team that canvassed all over Soros. Twice. Even now, whenever their family got the grumps, Lou reminded us: *Yes, We Can!*

Tattoos.

Global warming.

Birdie thought about the 2000s and what else she knew about her decade.

Daddy gone.

Worries about Shanice.

The opposite of 'Yes, We Can!'

Emily glimpsed the green exit sign for Leavenworth flying by. She shuddered, thinking about the Leavenworth Penitentiary. "Are there any famous prisoners there now?"

"Don't know about now. But I bet there've been plenty," Katie said.

Emily looked up "Leavenworth." She wondered why "The Bird Man of Alcatraz" had been locked up in Kansas. She thought he belonged in California.

She read down the list of other famous inmates and got to "Michael Vick." He'd been a pro football player who had done time for dogfighting and animal cruelty.

Emily looked away from the pictures of the dogs with their teeth hanging from their lips, their caved-in snouts, their eyes bulging from their sockets. She thought about Bravo. Emily loved him more than anything in her life. She thought animal cruelty was worse than human cruelty. After all, animals were powerless to stop it.

From the window Birdie spied the exit sign and the off ramp for Leavenworth. Leavenworth made her think of Mama. Mama was always reminding her kids that Leavenworth had a famous prisoner. "You behave yourself, hear? Else you'll end up in Leavenworth like James Earl Ray." James Earl Ray, they'd been told again and again, was the one who assassinated Martin Luther King, Jr.

Birdie shuddered to think of one of Mama's kids ending up there. But if he didn't change his ways, Beanie was halfway there already. It was more than just that skull he carved. There was a rumor that he and D'Ante Wallace had been dealing, and one morning after Earth Science, D'Ante had slammed Birdie up against her locker, her left cheek smashed against the cold metal, D'Ante's two strong arms pinning her own behind her, her shoulder blades stuck out like chicken wings. "Don't say nothin' about nothin' you hear, right? Or your family's gonna pay."

Birdie hadn't heard much of anything but rumors, and rumors flew at Frederick Douglass as fast as tacos on Tuesday. She tried to push back against D'Ante to escape, but he held on tight, pain flashing up her arms and into her shoulders.

"Promise?" he snarled. Birdie wouldn't let herself promise something out loud like a threat against her family, so she just nodded her head, and he took it for a promise, finally letting go.

Birdie never said a word to anyone.

Not a single soul.

Henrietta had begun to doze. Suddenly she was awakened by the wail of sirens. There'd been an accident up ahead in their lane. The traffic wasn't moving. A screaming ambulance with its flashing lights sped along the berm beside their bus. The marchers strained their necks to look out the windows.

"Oh, dear," Henrietta said, pulling out her rosary. It's what she did every time she heard a siren shriek. Her lips moved as her fingers played up and down the beads.

A tow truck slipped up the berm beside the bus. In the distance, the westbound lane was moving smoothly, while their eastbound lane was stalled. She wondered if some people's lives were always stalled by accidents. And why God let that happen.

The accident ahead made Birdie think of Grandma and Grandpa Franklin on their way to the American Jazz Museum. She was glad they'd made it safely to Kansas City. At least they got to enjoy the museum and the clubs. Their accident happened on the way back.

Birdie watched Henrietta finger her rosary. She suspected this was something she did whenever she was afraid or anxious. Sort of like that stress ball that Mr. Fox, the guidance counselor, gave her at the start of school in September. It didn't work.

Would a rosary work better?

The traffic wasn't moving.

Henrietta fished a road map from her tote. "Where are we?"

The map opened up like an accordion and filled up the space between Birdie and herself.

Birdie found the thick blue line that stood for I-70 East. Henrietta squinted at it.

Birdie showed her that they were almost to Kansas City. "We've passed Stull, Perry, Lawrence, Tonganoxie."

"I love all those Indian names," Henrietta said. "Tonganoxie. Oskaloosa. Topeka."

"We took a field trip to the Pottawatomie Indian Reservation in fourth grade."

Birdie didn't say that the field trip made her sad. She didn't have the money to purchase a souvenir like most of the white kids. On the bus ride home, they shared their beaded wrist bracelets and their miniature hatchets, their babies in papooses and their totem poles. But that wasn't why Birdie was sad. Birdie was sad because the reservation had seemed a kind of prison to her. Sort of like a Leavenworth for Indians. *Weren't the Indians the real native Americans? Weren't they here first, roaming a land that was supposed to be theirs? Hadn't wypipo rounded them up and herded them into reservations like buffalo?*

"Here," Birdie said, "we can look up all those Indian names in my phone."

"We can?"

"Sure. Just fold up the map, and we'll find out what they mean."

Henrietta struggled with the map. It took her several tries to get it folded right. Birdie felt sorry for her. She had everything right there on Lou-Lou's phone. She didn't have to struggle with a map.

Henrietta marvelled at people who understood the new technology. She remembered watching the moon landing on an old black-and-white set given to her by a renter who was moving away. She had been spellbound by the wizardry of NASA and the bravery of Neil Armstrong who dared to leave the planet while Henrietta rarely dared to move beyond the comfort zone of her own neighborhood. She had marvelled at the child-like manifestations of such mature technological sorcery. The astronaut had seemed giddy as a child in his fish-bowl helmet, his body somersaulting like a boy on a trampoline, the small round circle of Earth like a blue cat's-eye marble against a black playing field of sky.

Technology was just one more complication in an already complicated world. She marvelled that other people managed to make it look simple.

Emily was bored. She hated waiting for anything. Even if it was because of an accident. She'd been texting with Sonia while they were waiting.

"Sonia says she's sick of 'mansplaining.'"

"What's that?" Katie asked.

"Sonia says it's when men think you're so stupid that they talk down to you."

"Like how, Em?"

"Well, like about sports. It's something my stepfather does. Dave believes baseball is a sport for geniuses, and he puts himself in that category, so naturally it's his favorite game. I don't know how Mom puts up with watching games with him, but watching baseball together always ends in a fight. Dave talks the whole time, explaining things he thinks she doesn't understand like the balk or the infield fly rule. Mom says the best thing about baseball is when a batter hits it out of the park and the worst thing is when they go into extra innings. One time Mom asked, "What kind of sport doesn't have time limits?" After that, Dave didn't speak to her for a week. Sonia says mansplaining happens when a guy acts like *you're* stupid when actually *he's* being patronizing."

A couple more ambulances shrieked up ahead. Emily was impatient to get going again.

Jenny added, "I once had a guy friend at Stanton ask me to proofread a paper on the French Revolution. He knew I was pretty good at proofreading because of all those academic papers I used to post for my professors. The guy thought he was a genius because he was taking an Honors history seminar, but he got furious when I started laughing as soon as I read the first page. I told him he'd spelled 'peasant' as 'pheasant.' I kept imagining all those pheasants being sent to the guillotine to have their heads cut off. He huffed off and never spoke to me again."

Katie said, "Marc explains that I don't like tequila because it has a worm in the bottle and girls don't like worms. Honestly, can't I just not like it because it tastes like rubbing alcohol?"

Emily said, "There are things girls do that are annoying, too. Like complimenting what other women are wearing. Or fake smiling."

Katie and Jenny nodded, considering her words. Emily didn't add that Sonia had pointed out those things to her. They weren't really her own original thoughts.

"Oskaloosa?" Hennie asked.

Birdie punched some buttons.

"Black Rain."

"Hmmm. Interesting. What about 'Topeka'?"

"A good place to dig potatoes."

Hennie grinned. "Pottawatomie?"

"Those who tend the hearth fire."

"Ahhhh. We could bring the potatoes from Topeka and cook them with the Pottawatomies."

Henrietta was enjoying this game. Birdie was a grand traveling companion. "How about 'Tonganoxie'?"

Birdie punched some buttons again.

"Oh," Birdie said, "This is a good one."

"How?"

"It means 'Shorty.'"

"Oh, I see," Henrietta said, laughing. "We can get Shorty to bring the potatoes from Topeka to cook in Pottawatomie even if there is a Black Rain."

By the time they stopped laughing, the bus was moving again.

The bus was rocking, and Birdie was getting sleepy. A road sign announced the Missouri state line coming up, and she thought of Mama. Mama always said Missouri made white folks think of Tom Sawyer and Huck Finn and Black folks think of Ferguson and Michael Brown. Mama worried like crazy about Birdie's brothers, warning them they already had targets on their backs. She said she'd never trust Beanie to have a civil conversation with the police. So she'd bring up Eric Garner, Tamir Rice. "Tamir Rice was only twelve, boy," she'd scold. Then she threatened: "If I ever hear you've been sassing a po-lice, I'll tie you up in the basement. And let you die there."

The rocking of the bus reminded Birdie of Aunt Lou's yard swing. It had been her grandparents' before they died. The aluminum poles had rusted, and the stuffing was peeking out of the plastic seat cover with the pattern of pink flamingos all over it. But rocking in this swing had been a comfort to Birdie as a child. Aunt Lou used to sit beside her and sing, "Rock-A-Bye, *Birdie*, in the tree tops." It was the closest she ever got to a lullaby of her very own.

She returned to the window and a sign that read, "Kansas City KS, 5 miles. Kansas City MO, 20 miles. Two Cities, One Heart."

Against the voices of the other passengers, Birdie dozed, comforted by the rhythm of Hennie's clicking needles. They sounded to Birdie like beaks tapping.

The last thing she remembered before dozing off were the words, "And down will come *Birdie*, cradle and all."

The rhythm of the rocking bus matched the rhythm of Henrietta's needles. *Whirr, whirr. Click, click.* Playing with the Indian names with Birdie set her to wondering what other games she had missed out on with a granddaughter: pat-a-cake, this little piggy, the it-sy-bitsy spider.

In her Wednesday sewing circle, she had envied the other women who had children and grandchildren. They knitted baby sets with matching cradle caps and booties, crocheted blankets embellished with pink or blue ribbons, fashioned quilts with baby lambs or teddy bears or alphabet blocks. Years ago, Hennie had once started on some baby booties during Wednesday circle, but her teeth had clenched, her throat had tightened, and she had felt her eyes growing wet. She'd swallowed hard and then turned her stitches to a pair of crocheted slippers for the nursing home.

Birdie was fully awake now. Her lidded green-flecked eyes snapped open.

She had been napping when someone suddenly shouted, "Kansas City!"

A chorus of voices began to sing out.

"Barbeque!"

"Jazz!"

"The Chiefs!"

Somebody turned up their phone, and the sounds of "Goin' to Kansas City" filled the cabin. Now a few ladies started singing. "Goin' to Kansas City, Kansas City here I come. They got some crazy little women there, and *I count myself as one.*"

Louise and Hennie grinned at each other. They told Birdie that someone had changed the last line of the lyrics.

"For the better," said Louise.

A row of three women in the back was standing up. "Let's *jam*, ladies," one of them shouted. Everybody periscoped their necks to see them.

Birdie pulled out her camera, standing up to snap a picture of the three ladies in the back, butt-bumping, shaking their booties, waving their hands in the air, their big hips swaying, their hoop earrings bouncing. One of the ladies unwound her scarf, swinging it in the air like a stripper. Everybody cheered. Birdie took another photograph.

Now everyone began to pick up the chorus, flailing their arms, fist-bumping, singing extra loud on the last line: "They got some crazy little women there, and I count myself as one." Many of the women had jumped up into the aisle to boogie with the ladies in the back. Birdie switched over to the video function.

Why couldn't Shanice be here?

Birdie remembered the happy Friday nights they spent before what happened to Shanice. They'd huddle in the living room, the afghan stretched across all of them, eating popcorn and listening to Mama's stories about Afghanistan. She'd describe her soldiers and the nicknames they had: Tank, Champ, Ringo the Dingo. "Ringo was one wild dog," she'd say. Birdie's brothers bent over double with laughter when she ordered them to line up like she'd ordered her recruits: "Nuts to butts, soldiers; nuts to butts." Sometimes Beanie and Twanny scattered the popcorn everywhere, pretending it was grenades exploding.

On those happy Friday nights, they always ended up dancing. Twanny and Beanie and Birdie would put on their socks and slip-slide across the living room floor. Shanice loved to dance. She'd wave both her hands, the good one and the bad one, and she'd wiggle her feet, but it was her head that danced the most. Down. Back. Side-to-Side. Neck circles. Then all over again. Shanice loved Michael Jackson. Somehow she thought because her own last name was "Jackson," too, that she might have been related to him. The last song they'd play on Friday nights before what happened was Shanice's favorite: "Don't Stop 'til You Get Enough."

Birdie looked over at Lou-Lou and Henrietta. They were grooving with the rest of them. "They got some crazy little women there, and I count myself as one."

Cars on either side of the bus were honking and waving. Children in car seats were gawking; dogs were barking. An 18-wheeler whizzed by, flashing its lights. Khalid honked his horn in answer.

Birdie joined in, her spirits lifting as she sang. She had never thought about being a "crazy little woman," but it felt good to shout out that last line with everybody else, young and old, Black and white, Hispanic and Muslim.

Crazy little women.

I count myself as one.

PART III - KANSAS CITY
TO ST.LOUIS

1:50 p.m. CST, January 20, 2017

Alexandra Hall stepped to the microphone again. She announced that the first rest stop would be coming up on the other side of Kansas City. In Columbia, Missouri.

The women clapped.

"Just a couple of hours to 'stretch time.'" The women groaned, and Birdie groaned with them. Her knees were stiff; her shoulders were tight; her back ached. She worried about Miss Hennie; her body parts were much older than hers.

"But while you're waiting, I'm going to pass out this paper to see how well you know your history, ladies. Take your time. There's no hurry to finish. We've got 17 hours on this bus! *One way!*"

The women grumbled and laughed at the same time. The way they do when someone's told a corny joke.

Alexandra Hall and a couple of volunteers were passing out pencils and paper. Birdie thought it was starting to feel like school.

Birdie stared at her paper. It was a crossword puzzle with the boldface title "HOW WELL DO YOU KNOW WOMEN'S HISTORY?" She was pretty sure she wouldn't know any of the answers.

"Let's work together on this," Aunt Lou said. "Three heads are better than one."

Birdie liked that idea.

Aunt Lou and Henrietta figured out 1 ACROSS straight off. One ACROSS was "Anthony."

"That's for Susan B. Anthony," Aunt Louise said.

Birdie kept quiet. She didn't want to admit she didn't know who "Susan B. Anthony" was. She also wanted to open Lou's phone to Google the name. But she was afraid Lou-Lou and Hennie would call that cheating. She knew Mrs. Opie would.

Henrietta filled 10 ACROSS with "Elizabeth." "That's for Elizabeth Cady Stanton. Her father was like my father: he had wanted a boy. But," she added, "she never let being a girl be an obstacle."

Birdie was curious. *How could being a girl not be an obstacle? Especially if you were a Black girl? Fewer sports teams. Fewer leadership roles. Fewer opportunities to speak up. Fewer possibilities that someone might notice you. For the right reasons.*

She scanned the page, relieved to find something she knew. "I've got 6 DOWN," she said, punching at her paper. She knew the answer to "Launched the Montgomery Bus Boycott by refusing to give up her seat on a city bus."

"That's 'Rosa,'" Birdie said. "Four letters. It fits."

Birdie thought back to the framed picture that sat on the Jacksons' kitchen shelf. Rosa Parks was sitting alone, her hands quietly folded on her lap. She wore rimless glasses just like Hennie's. She was staring out a window that looked a lot like the one on this bus.

Aunt Lou and Henrietta were scribbling away. They were writing down words like "Sojourner," "Morrison," "Angelou." Birdie struggled to keep up with the answers.

Hennie put down her pencil and sighed when she came to 7 ACROSS. SEVEN ACROSS was thirteen whole letters that streamed across the entire middle of the page.

"That woman was my salvation," Hennie said.

Henrietta remembered the magazine rack up at Elmer's Drugs. In fact, she still had the very first copy of *Ms.* magazine from back in the early seventies. The first cover showed a woman with eight arms, looking like a Hindu goddess. Henrietta knew that cover by heart. The woman's arms were holding a clock, a skillet, a typewriter, a rake, a mirror, a telephone, a steering wheel, and an iron. She kept the magazine in a secret stash with her other treasures like copies of those *Boston Globe* articles from the early 2000s. *Ms.* magazine and the *Boston Globe* had helped her understand the black hole into which her life had disappeared. The November election confirmed just how long she'd been playing the fool and just how little time she had to turn things around.

"The only magazines I could buy until she came along," Henrietta said to Birdie and Louise, "were things about beautifying your home or satisfying your husband. I didn't have a home to beautify or a husband to satisfy, and I wasn't interested in filling my mind with how to make hollandaise sauce or macramé pot hangers. *Ms.* magazine gave me more important things to think about."

"Like what?"

"Well, Birdie, one thing it was famous for was 'consciousness raising.'"

"What's that?"

Louise answered for her. "Just getting yourself aware of how many things, big and small, work against women. Who's kept down by the welfare system. Who lacks opportunities for promotions. Who's victimized by job discrimination. Who gets to have a credit card. Who picks up the kids' toys at night."

Hennie said, "And look at how she got us to think about even our own language. Before her, women felt left out of words like "*man*kind." They couldn't begin to think about a career in certain jobs because most of the jobs were held by "police*men*" or "mail*men*."

Louise said, "One of my favorite articles to come out of *Ms.* magazine was 'I Want a Wife.'"

Hennie smirked. "You, too?"

Louise gave Hennie a high-five. Hennie had never been high-fived in her life.

"Yes, Birdie," Hennie said, "think about these women on the bus around us. That woman got us to think about the power of sisterhood."

"And how the personal is the political," added Louise.

Birdie thought about what Lou-Lou and Hennie were saying.

She thought about the welfare system and Mama and her brothers and Shanice and that awful Nurse Axelrod.

She thought about Mama and promotions and the Kingswood Plumbing Company.

She thought about Mama and credit cards and picking up toys and how much she needed a wife. *Was I somehow a stand-in for the wife Mama needed?*

Mostly she thought about Aunt Lou and her protest desk and her tray tables with pictures of famous African-Americans and her voter registration drives and her ADAPT efforts and her hatred of Aunt Jemima syrup and Uncle Ben's rice and how she thought everything was political. Birdie was beginning to wonder if maybe Aunt Lou *was* right.

"So who *was* 7 ACROSS?" Birdie asked.

"Gloria Steinem," Hennie answered. Her cheeks puffed up like little white cotton balls when she smiled.

Birdie had never heard of her. She wrote down the letters while Hennie spelled her name.

"By the way," Aunt Lou said, a twinkle in her eye, "The website says she's going to be at the march."

Hennie's eyes snapped to attention. "You wouldn't kid me like that, would you, Louise Franklin?"

"Not on your life, sister," Lou said.

Emily stared at the page, annoyed. For one thing, she took all her tests at college online. A pencil-and-paper test was for the 20th century.

Sonia was the only one of them to take a women's studies class, and she wasn't here. Katie identified the easiest one, "Hillary Clinton," 20 ACROSS. Emily only had two answers: "Rosa" and "Eleanor." Well, three. If you counted overhearing "Gloria Steinem" from the marchers in the row in front of her.

"Hey," Emily whispered loudly to her seatmates, "should we get some help from the ladies in the row ahead?"

The lady who was probably the young girl's aunt lifted her head above her headrest. She whispered back just as loudly. "Of course!"

The girls stood up and leaned over the headrest, introducing themselves: Emily, Katie, Jenny.

Louise, Hennie, and Birdie introduced themselves, too.

Emily copied most of their answers, bracing her paper and pencil against Louise's headrest. Working together, they added a couple more. Louise knew "Shirley Chisholm," 2 DOWN. Birdie knew "Helen Keller," 13 ACROSS.

Jenny said, "I read a biography of Helen Keller to Alice. She's my little sister. She has Tourette's. Alice loved hearing about Helen Keller because not only did she work for the disabled, but she was disabled herself."

Louise swivelled her head around to speak to Jenny. "Those are the activists I admire most. Anyone who fights for legislation or stages protests is admirable, but you're right, Jenny. I tip my hat to the people who work for the disabled when they're disabled themselves. Their work is doubly hard."

The girl named Birdie asked, "Anybody have a clue about 21 DOWN? It has something to do with a Supreme Court case."

Both Louise and Hennie shook their heads. They didn't know the answer, either.

Jenny said, "I'm guessing it's 'Carrie Buck.' It fits. Ten letters."

"Who's 'Carrie Buck'?" Katie asked.

"She was part of a Supreme Court case that said it was okay to forcibly sterilize people with disabilities.'"

Katie and Emily shuddered.

Birdie swivelled around, looking surprised. "They can *do* that?" she asked.

Jenny shook her head. "Not anymore, thank God. I accidentally learned about Carrie Buck when I was studying up on Tourette's to help my sister."

Katie said, "You mean they could have done that to Alice?"

Jenny glared at Katie. "No shit, Sherlock," she said.

Emily was grateful for Louise. She was managing to smooth things over between Katie and Jenny.

"Well, then," Louise said. "It sounds like you three should join our ADAPT group. We're staging an action on behalf of the disabled. Lafayette Square. Noon. We'd love to have you."

"Thanks," Jenny answered for all of them. "I'd like that. I know Alice would enjoy hearing about it."

Katie got out a cellophane package of Twizzlers and passed them around, starting with Jenny. Emily thought it was a peace offering.

Only Hennie declined. "My dentures," she explained.

The rest of them chewed on the twisty red vines.

Emily checked her messages. That guy from the karaoke bar still hadn't texted her back.

Emily Googled the answer to 4 ACROSS. She read that Wilma Mankiller was the first woman Chief of the Cherokee Nation. When Emily thought of Indians, she imagined hatchets, scalping, and war cries.

Emily checked her phone again. No answer to her text.

Mankiller! What a great name!

Birdie could see that Henrietta was a whiz at this, but after a while, even she slowed down. The questions were getting harder. She was stuck now, stumped by how to spell the name of a young girl, 12 DOWN.

"Is it M-E-L-L-A-L-A?" Henrietta asked.

"Can I use my phone to help? We can Google it."

Lou-Lou's face brightened. "Good idea, Birdie! We can Google the clues on our phone!"

Our phone. Birdie liked that.

Henrietta's eyebrows lifted at the word "Google." They looked like double question marks at the end of a sentence.

Lou-Lou read out the clues for 12 DOWN. "Type in the words 'Pakistan,' 'education,' 'Taliban,' and 'Nobel,' Birdie."

While Birdie was typing, she thought of Mama. How strong she had been. She had been a soldier in a faraway part of the world. She had fired mortars, driven tanks, rescued wounded soldiers in the field. *Where had that strong soldier disappeared to?*

The name "Malala" popped up. Birdie had never heard of her, but she spelled it for them. "M-A-L-A-L-A. Six letters." Her last name – "Yousafzai" – nine letters - was too long.

"It fits!" Henrietta filled in the six letters.

Birdie read about Malala.

Henrietta was leaning over her shoulder, squinting to read the words on the phone. "The print's too small for my eyes, dear. But tell us about her, Birdie."

Aunt Lou leaned in to listen, too.

"She is about my age. Or a little bit older. She stood up for a girl's right to learn. The Taliban tried to kill her on account of it. They didn't want girls to have an education. She won the Nobel Prize for her bravery."

Birdie showed them the picture on the phone. Malala had brown skin and dark hair. She had beautiful dark eyes framed by heavy black eyebrows. She was wearing a bright red and yellow head scarf. Her mouth was soft and hard at the same time. It said she was kind but determined. *She isn't anything like me. Malala wouldn't allow herself to bully or be bullied.*

"Don't you have to do some kind of project for Mrs. Opie?" Aunt Lou asked. "You could start by looking into the women on this puzzle," she suggested.

Birdie had forgotten about Mrs. Opie's project. She clicked "save" to keep the picture of Malala Yousafzai and the article that described her.

Birdie typed in the clues for 11 DOWN while Lou and Henrietta were chatting about Malala and education for girls. "Maryland," "rescue," "slaves."

Google answered: "Harriet Tubman."

Birdie stared at her picture. Harriet Tubman had a shiny dark black face like Mr. Pine. She had a clean white bib at her throat. Her eyes were cast down. Birdie wondered if she was maybe shy. But then she caught the deep wrinkles in her forehead that looked like the lines Beanie and his friends made on cars with keys after dark. The lines told Birdie that Harriet Tubman was powerful determined.

Then Birdie read the description: "Harriet Tubman was an escaped slave. With a bounty on her own head, she rescued dozens of slaves, leading them to freedom through a network of safe houses called the Underground Railroad." Birdie pushed "save" again.

Aunt Lou and Henrietta had stopped working on the puzzle to chat. Birdie continued to look up clues. She was learning about all kinds of women who were brave. Malala and Harriet Tubman and Ida B. Wells and Eleanor Roosevelt. Susan B. Anthony and Elizabeth Cady Stanton. When she read their stories, she felt both shame and longing: shame for her own lack of courage and a longing to possess it. As she saved biography after biography onto the phone, she wondered: *Would I ever be able to add 'courage' next to 'closure' on my bucket list?*

Henrietta put the crossword down and picked up her needles. She felt Birdie's eyes on her.

"How do you know so much about so many of these women?" Birdie asked. "Did you study them in school?"

Henrietta wrinkled her lips in a kind of grin. "There wasn't much school for me. I had to skip school to help my family." Then she told Birdie about her father's war wound, the errand-running, the rent collection, and the death of her mother when Henrietta was in her thirties. She saw Birdie counting decades on her fingers. "About forty years ago," Henrietta said, confirming Birdie's finger-count.

"I fixed up one of the rooms in our apartment building as an antique shop. Nothing very fine to buy there, but our tenants were always moving in or out, and they always left things behind. Desks. Kitchen tables. Old-fashioned gadgets like ice chippers or apple corers. When Mr. Schmidt died, he had no relatives, so he left everything he had behind, and when I sold his hutch for a princely sum, I had enough to acquire even more. I got myself an education, finally, by studying antiques."

Birdie asked, "How did antiques give you an education? Don't you have to go to school for that?"

Henrietta considered the earnest expression on the young girl's face: pursed lips, wrinkled brow. "Life sometimes gets in the way of going to school. Sometimes I think life's just one thing after another that gets in the way of what you might want to do. Antiques gave me my own schooling. I learned history through the antiques that turned up. Old druggist's chests with their chloroform tins taught me about the history of medicine. Furniture's an education in itself. Furniture taught me about the periods of history: Louis the sixteenth, Empire, Art Nouveau."

"But how did you learn about the women stuff?"

"I'd find diaries or postcards from different eras, mostly written by women. My first find was a newspaper article from around 1850. It was written by a man mocking a women's rights convention. So I began to learn about why he was mocking, and all these wonderful women began to appear: Elizabeth Cady Stanton, Dorothea Dix, Sarah and Angelina Grimke. I began to study women and their contributions through the things I began to acquire: books, jewelry, suffrage collectibles. When we needed money, I sold something. I hated to part with my Ballots for Both button, a contest slogan-winner back in 1915, but it brought in four hundred dollars, and that sustained us for a while."

Henrietta realized that she'd been talking more than she usually did. Usually she was a listener. Still, Birdie's green-flecked eyes were wide with astonishment. "My life taught me that going to school's not the only way to learn, dear. Think about Abraham Lincoln. Think about your school's Frederick Douglass. He taught himself from old newspapers he picked up in the street. Learning's free for the taking all around you. Most people don't notice that."

Now Khalid made a wide turn, pulling up to a huge rest stop. It was as large as the entire main street of Soros. The long line of buses at the gas tanks looked like giant silver grasshoppers, their nozzle-like limbs feeding on the streams of tanks. *Isn't there something called 'symbiosis' that Mr. Archer, my Earth Science teacher, once talked about?* Birdie decided the tanks feeding the buses would make a good picture. Maybe if it turned out, she might give it a title: "Symbiosis." She'd never given a title to a picture before. She pushed the white button on Lou's phone.

The bus came to a halt with a groan and a belch of gas, and Khalid engaged the grinding gears of the parking brake. The marchers stood to loosen their knees and press their shoulder blades back against their spines. They shuffled backpacks and pillows and blankets and purses, making room to step out into the aisle.

Henrietta was struggling to unlock her knees. Aunt Lou extended a hand and helped her up, bracing her as she stumbled first into the aisle, then to the exit. Lou climbed down the steps ahead of her, then turned back around, watching Henrietta grip the railing to make her shaky way to the asphalt. Lou's outstretched hand steadied her down the last few steps.

When Birdie reached the ground, she took Henrietta's left hand the way she used to take Shanice's, her whole arm under Hennie's, Hennie's over hers like a brace, their hands linked. Henrietta had slipped her knitting bag over her right arm, wearing it like a purse. Slowly they made their way to the service plaza, part of a trail of women exiting all the parked buses, hurrying through the doors like ants to sugar cubes.

"Seems a service plaza's got two purposes for you: to eat and to pee," said a lady in scuffed Keds and a poncho that looked like a woven rug with the head cut out.

"I suggest we do the restroom first," Aunt Lou said to Hennie and me. "I've got food on the bus."

Birdie took in the fast food signs for Popeye's, Arby's, Hardee's, and McDonald's. She knew Lou-Lou wouldn't set foot into a McDonald's. Out of loyalty to Mama.

Mama had been working at McDonald's when Birdie was born and when Shanice was just a toddler. Daddy had been managing the Soros Car Wash back then. Mama always said she'd never have survived without Aunt Lou's help.

What Mama said when Birdie asked if maybe she could get a part-time job at McDonalds one day was seared into her brain.

Mama had flashed her black eyes and said, "None of my flesh and blood is ever going to work there. Especially the flesh and blood that's a daughter. The teenage boys pull up to the drive-in window and say they'll have 'three feels,' 'two hand jobs' and 'one blow' before they order, Birdie. Then they fall all over themselves laughing. All kinds of crazies hang out inside there, all day long if they can. And then the boss orders you to close up and you're by yourself out in the dark by your car, one of the crazies waiting for you with his hands in his pants. No, thank you, McDonald's. Not for any daughter of mine."

Birdie understood what Mama was saying, but she still liked the French fries.

Emily, Katie, and Jenny rushed to line up at Starbucks. It was the longest line in the rest stop. Emily had heard they were promoting kale smoothies now, and she was dying to try one.

While she waited in line, Emily thrilled to the multitude of fleece jackets, woolen shawls, Ugg boots, college gear. She ogled heads topped with multicolored scarves, hijabs, plaid lumberjack caps, corn rows. A group of women doctors had stethoscopes around their necks. Many of the women were carrying signs into the rest stop: "Walls Turned Sideways are Bridges." "Tweet Women as Equals."

What Emily liked best were the hats some of the women were wearing: pink knitted hats with two small cat-like ears sticking out the top.

"What's with the hats?" Emily asked.

"Oh, those are pussy hats," Katie answered. "Don't you remember when the Orange One bragged about grabbing women by the pussy any time he wanted?"

Emily didn't remember.

"Oh, come on, Emily," Jenny said. "It was from that *Access Hollywood* interview. He was saying that when you're a star, women let you do anything. Even grab their pussies."

Emily still wasn't remembering.

Apparently lots of other women were.

From the long line that snaked through the entire plaza, Birdie overheard snatches of conversation from the women around her. They were from all over Kansas and Missouri: Olathe, Leavenworth, Kearney, Independence. One woman was from Reno, Nevada. Another had come all the way from Coeur d'Alene, Idaho. Some were sisters, others aunts and cousins. Most were friends or members of groups. The National Organization for Women. Amnesty International. NAACP. The League of Women Voters. Birdie saw Alexandra Hall chatting up a group of artists.

Aunt Lou was in heaven. "This is my kind of folks," she said, throwing an arm around Birdie's free shoulder. Lou-Lou reminisced about the protests she'd been involved in over the years: against guns; for the environment; against LGBTQ discrimination; for a woman's right to choose. "This is better than any march I've ever been on, even that march in Ferguson."

An elderly Black woman leaning on a walker noticed Henrietta gripping Birdie's arm. She pushed a lever on her walker, and a seat flipped down. "Here," she said to Hennie, "rest yourself."

"Bless you." Hennie sank onto the seat, releasing Birdie's hand.

Birdie pulled out the camera and took a picture of two old ladies, one Black, one white. One steadied herself on the back of the walker, the other rested on its seat in the front. Birdie made sure to get the sign in the background. It said, "A Woman's Place is in the Resistance." Birdie looked at the picture and showed it to them. Both of them laughed out loud.

The lady with the walker reached for the phone to study the picture more carefully. Looking it over, she said, "Spunky gal."

Does she mean Hennie – or me?

Henrietta held out her hand to study the picture again.

She thought the picture was just right. The slogan. Two women of two races sharing one walker. The scene churning with women of all ages.

"It's marvelous, Birdie," she said, passing back the phone.

"A Woman's Place is in the Resistance," she mumbled to herself. She had never resisted anything in her life, and here she was, resisting.

She even had the picture to prove it.

Louise asked for the phone. She had to make a few calls to people heading to Washington from all over. Something about flyers for the Information Booth. Something about the lunch table. Something about updating the thank-you list for the opening ceremony.

After her calls were finished, Lou-Lou passed her phone back to Birdie and struck up a conversation with a woman named Pauline Frazier. Soon they were chatting like old friends. Pauline ran a mini-museum out of a van in Archway, Missouri. The van held miniature displays of just about everything in the world. All the dog breeds and cat breeds. Hundreds of miniature wildflower specimens. The Mini Seven Wonders of the World. She drove the van to schools and festivals so people could go inside and see miniatures of dinosaurs, gems and minerals, a timeline of car models.

"I wanted to go to college and study museum management. But my mother got sick, and my brother had just married and moved to Oregon. So it was college or Mama. I guess you can say I got a degree from the College of Hard Knocks." She chuckled with pride.

Birdie wondered about her own mama. Unlike Lou, who had a two-year degree, Mama never got a college degree. After the Army, she could have taken advantage of the GI Bill, but then there was Daddy gone and Shanice sick and one thing after the other. *What did that mean for her life? What about me? Would I ever go to a real college? Or just a 'College of Hard Knocks?'*

Birdie thought about Hennie. *Hadn't she gone to the College of Hard Knocks, too? Is that related in any way to what Malala was protesting about?*

Pauline Frazier wanted to come back after the march to see the Kansas City National Museum of Toys and Miniatures. "The animal minis are my favorite. There's a miniature cat lounging on a bed. And a miniature birdcage, solid gold, with a parrot on a perch."

Pauline Frazier took out her phone and showed them the pictures of the cat and the parrot from the museum's website.

Hennie's eyes widened with interest. "I believe that cat's sleeping on a genuine replica Louis XVI canopy bed!"

Birdie looked at Pauline's phone. She had no idea who Louis XVI was, but she knew that was one fancy bed and one lucky cat.

Henrietta asked, "What kinds of toys are on display there? I've got an antique store, and I have a few antique toys I enjoy."

Henrietta told Pauline about the metal railroad train circa 1913. And the parrot bank. "You place the coin in his cage and he picks it up with his beak and drops it in the slot. It's from the 40s when people were saving for war bonds."

Pauline clapped her hands in delight. "Oh, I've always wanted to see one of those banks! Maybe we can meet some time in Kansas City and see the museum together after the march is over."

Hennie's face lit up. "Oh," she said, surprised at the invitation. "That would be lovely."

"Would you take our picture?"

Pauline and Lou-Lou and Hennie were like best friends now. Pauline gave a great big smile, even though she was missing a few teeth. Lou was always complaining that Birdie didn't smile enough. Birdie knew it didn't have anything to do with missing teeth.

Birdie checked the picture. She was pleased with it. She managed to capture something happy and free in all of them.

The line still moved slowly.

Birdie's picture of the three women spoke to Henrietta. She admired Pauline, envied her, even. Pauline with the firecracker red hair, the funny line of work, and the degree from the College of Hard Knocks. Pauline who probably had a father with the name of Paul. She wondered where Pauline's sense of freedom came from.

Henrietta felt for the beads around her neck and began to pray that Birdie would develop that sense of freedom one day. The girl was lucky to have an aunt who supported her, an aunt who loaned her a camera for this trip. Henrietta could see that pictures helped Birdie say things without speaking. That was a good thing for a shy young woman. The pictures could talk *for* her. Until she was ready to talk for herself.

Suddenly Emily heard a group of young women in Kansas State Jayhawks sweatshirts begin to sing.

Gimme a strong, nasty woman.
Gimme a strong, nasty woman.
Gimme a strong, nasty woman.
The nasties get things done.

Emily and Katie and Jenny bolted from their place in the Starbucks line to join them.

A group of college students had begun to sing. Birdie recognized the melody: "Gimme that Old Time Religion." She snapped a picture, focusing in on their upper bodies: open mouths, laughing eyes, arms laced around shoulders, big-lettered sweatshirts.

What is a 'Jayhawk,' anyway?

It was close to their turn for the restroom.

Birdie thought about Shanice and all their trips to the bathroom. At school she had special passes from Mr. Roberts, the principal, to come and go as needed to help out with her sister. Mostly that involved leaving the classroom to take her to the bathroom. A buzzer would go off in Birdie's classroom that meant Shanice needed to go. Birdie's teacher would nod at her, and then she would get up from her seat as quietly as possible, leaving the classroom with her head down, hoping to make herself invisible.

Shanice would roll herself to the bathroom door, and Birdie would meet her there. Whenever Shanice saw her sister, her face broke out in a grin. Birdie had to admit: she had the prettiest face of all the Jackson kids. She remembered what Mama said: that Shanice's pretty face was God's way of making up for her twisted body.

Birdie remembered that when you looked at Shanice, your gaze naturally traveled to her eyes. They were dark brown and glistening under thick black lashes, and whenever she looked full on at you, you felt she was seeing down into your heart. Tight twists of glossy black curls circled her head: they reminded Birdie of the ringlets she made swiping ribbon strips with the open blades of scissors for the tops of presents. When Shanice was small, Mama kept her hair cut short because it was easier to care for that way, but before her eighth-grade year, Shanice had stood her ground to grow her hair out so she might have dreadlocks, and Mama had given in. Birdie was proud of Shanice for that.

At school, the first challenge of every bathroom visit was to roll Shanice inside the restroom itself. First you had to prop open the heavy oak door with the brass GIRLS sign on it with your backside. Then you maneuvered the clunky chair through the door. On most trips, the wheels ran over your own feet. One time Mr. Roberts stood by and watched as Birdie struggled with the door. She wondered why Mr. Roberts had never asked Mr. Pine to put on a door stop. Or if it would have made a difference if she'd been one of the white kids, a kid whose mama had time to chaperone field trips or make cupcakes for Valentine's Day.

Inside, there were no special stalls for kids like Shanice, so you had to brake the wheelchair in front of a stall, open the stall door, unbrake the wheelchair, and roll it at a slant to brace the stall door open. Birdie always entered the stall first, scooping her hands under Shanice's armpits as she leaned forward, lifting her tiny body off the chair. Then Birdie reached down and quickly ripped off her diaper, which often stunk to high heaven. There were no containers in the stall, so Birdie just dropped the diaper on the floor.

Then Birdie turned Shanice around so that her backside was to the toilet, and she let her down slowly. While she watched her sister go, Birdie thought of Mrs. Sylvester, who walked her Boston terrier at sunrise: Birdie felt ashamed for Shanice, peeing like a dog in front of the whole world, and, she had to admit, she felt ashamed for feeling ashamed. The worst part was when other girls or teachers came in, either gawking at them or looking intensely away.

When Shanice was finished, it was Birdie's job to wipe: Shanice couldn't reach behind herself without her toilet tongs, which were now kept quietly at home. The sixth-grade boys had once stolen them and humiliated her by swinging them around the playground.

After she was finished, Birdie diapered her again, Shanice holding onto the left side with her good left hand while Birdie pressed the tape on the right. After wheeling her out of the stall, Birdie tossed the soggy diaper in the trash.

Then they washed up. The sink was too high, and Shanice's twisted right hand wouldn't have been able to reach it at any height, so Birdie soaped up brown paper towels and they washed their hands together. Aunt Lou had always taught them to wash for as long as they could sing "Happy Birthday," so if nobody was around, Shanice and Birdie would sing it together. Afterwards, Shanice always put her good left arm around Birdie and gave her a kiss. After she did that, a wetness always surged up behind Birdie's eyes.

When Birdie went back to her classroom, hoping to make herself invisible again, she was usually lost about what was going on, so she'd daydream about being somebody, someday, somehow.

Although she didn't know what or when. Or especially how.

We had finally reached the entry to the restroom. There were about a dozen sinks and about twice that number of stalls. Women were moving between the toilets and sinks to the music of tinkling and flushing.

Henrietta pushed herself up from the walker seat. Her knees shook. Panic flashed through her body like an electric shock. This wouldn't be like the dress rehearsal before her mirror. She would need help.

Birdie could feel Hennie's body trembling as she helped her up.

They thanked the lady with the walker.

Henrietta clawed Birdie's arm with her fingers for support.

They shuffled to the stall with the handicapped sign in front of it. Birdie thought of Shanice, wishing there had been a handicapped stall at Frederick Douglass Junior High.

Lou-Lou sprang ahead of them; she was in and out quickly. "I'll meet you back at the bus, Birdie," she said, waving. "I want to pick up something at the gift shop."

Hennie crooked her finger, asking Birdie to bend down. She whispered, "I hate to ask you this, dear, but would you mind helping me?" She pointed to the stall door. She wanted Birdie inside with her. In that private space.

Birdie gulped. "Sure."

They stepped inside. The stall was roomy. You could probably get *two* wheelchairs in there. Somehow the luxury of the stall reminded Birdie of Mama. She may have hated the way Kingswood Plumbing treated its employees, but she was proud they had provided the fittings for the gold toilets at Mar-A-Lago.

Birdie slid the lock on the door, and Hennie jumped at the metallic click. "Oh!" she exclaimed, "Sorry. I'm a bit afraid of locks. It's an odd fear of being locked in." Henrietta hung her tote over the hook on the door while Birdie slipped a paper cover on the toilet seat. The paper was waxy: like the Cut-Rite Aunt Lou used to roll out pie crust.

Birdie waited. Hennie shuffled to the toilet and stretched the elastic band on her slacks; they fell to her ankles.

Hennie was wearing a paper diaper. Birdie resisted the urge to look away. Hennie's were the small size, just like Shanice's.

Hennie struggled with the tape on one side.

Birdie helped with the tape. She was glad she could drop the diaper into the lined trash can on the side of the stall instead of onto the floor like she did for Shanice.

Hennie gripped Birdie tightly as she lowered herself onto the toilet, her knees shaking.

From the seat, Hennie pointed to her tote bag hanging from the hook. Birdie took out a fresh diaper. As she opened it, she recognized the familiar muffled sound of whispery paper. She knelt at Henny's waist with the open diaper, ready to slip it on.

Hennie said, "My, you seem to know which end is the front, dear. Good for you. It's my first experience with a diaper, I'm proud to say. My bladder's still pretty strong for an old lady. I practiced at home, of course. Before I came. Whenever I unfolded it, it felt as bulky as a roll of paper towels between my legs, and once I put it on, it made me waddle like a duck. I never could figure out which end was the front."

Birdie grinned at her confusion. She never thought knowing the front end of a diaper would be a useful skill. *Can it get me into the College of Hard Knocks?*

Birdie observed Hennie's pale white blotchy skin lined with purple veins and dotted with age spots, so different from Shanice's smooth young brown skin. And yet the private parts, not quite hidden from view, reminded her of the brown eggs and the white eggs Lou and Mama had been wrangling about this morning: different outsides, same insides.

Birdie finished up quickly, helping Hennie with the diaper, the tape, the slacks.

And then she realized she needed the toilet herself. *Will I have to get back in line again?*

Hennie seemed to have heard her silent question.

"Go ahead, dear," she said. "Aren't we all the same somehow, Birdie? We girls?" she asked.

We girls. Does she mean all of us? All shades? Brown? Black? Yellow? All ages? Little girls? Teenagers? Grown women? Old ladies?

Shyly Birdie unbuttoned her jeans, dropped herself onto the toilet, peed, wiped, flushed. She kept her eyes down as she buttoned her jeans again.

Gently Birdie slid the latch on the stall, careful not to alarm Hennie, and they moved to the sink.

Together they washed up, Birdie's unlined brown hands next to

Hennie's wrinkled white ones. Birdie soaped up all the way to the wrists, trying to swallow the memory of lathering Shanice's hands. Silently she sang "Happy Birthday."

When they had finished, Birdie remembered the way Shanice always put her arm around her neck, and a familiar wetness surged up behind her eyes.

As they left the restroom, Birdie noticed the maid on duty. She was as black-skinned as Harriet Tubman. She was offering a linen hand towel or a squirt of perfume. *Why does she make me so sad? Is it the unnecessary towel, the cheap perfume, or the woman herself?*

There was a basket with change and a few bills in it: tips.

Henrietta stopped. She dug around in her tote bag. She pulled out a $20 bill and placed it in the basket, waving off the offer of perfume.

Henrietta could tell that Khalid was annoyed. He had waved his passengers up the steps, checking off names on his clipboard. He had switched on the engine of the bus, and it had roared into life. Now it was idling.

Khalid's usually serene expression had been replaced by a scowl. All of the marchers had retaken their seats. Except for the one empty seat in the row behind her.

Louise, irritated, rose from her seat. "I know who it is," she grumbled. "I'll go get her." Henrietta watched Louise march back into the rest stop.

Louise reappeared with Emily, the young woman with the womperjawed topknot. Lou reminded Henrietta of Sister Marguerite, who had once hauled Harold McFarland to the principal's office, pulling him by the left ear all the way.

Henrietta tried to settle herself, but it was difficult with that young girl behind them slurping a foul-looking green liquid from a plastic cup.

Back on the bus for the second time, Aunt Lou handed Henrietta a bag from the gift shop.

"For you," she said. Inside was a yellow-and-red tube of arthritis cream. "For your knees."

Henrietta's face lit up. "And you got the kind that doesn't smell," she said. "Bless you." She rooted around in her tote for some money, but Aunt Lou waved her off.

It was just like Aunt Lou to bring a gift. Most of the time the gift was her. Sitting with them when Mama had to work late. Bringing homework they'd left on the coffee table up to school. Taking Shanice to her doctor appointments.

Just this morning, Lou-Lou had come over at six in the morning to finish the fried chicken, the potato salad, and the brownies. She had already packed a dozen sleeves of Tom's peanuts.

"I'm using the vinegar-sugar dressing on the potato salad, Ronnie," she called out to Mama, whose heavy footsteps were heading to the kitchen from the garage. "Plus some fresh crumbled bacon."

Mama's big strong frame filled the kitchen doorway. She was grinning at her sister. "You put bacon in every last thing you cook, don't you, Lou-Lou?"

"You complainin', girl?"

"Naw. You know I ain't the cook around here."

"Damn straight. You wouldn't know a collard from a turnip green," huffed Aunt Lou.

"Both green. That's all I need to know."

"And neither of 'ems fit to eat without bacon drippings."

Mama didn't argue with that.

Then Aunt Louise pulled the pan of brownies from the oven. She had spent days debating whether to send the buttermilk chocolate Bundt cake or the frosted walnut brownies. She'd finally decided on the brownies. They'd be easier to pass around, and they had been Shanice's favorite. At the last minute she left out the nuts. Shanice didn't like nuts.

Lou-Lou dived into another bag, pulled out a t-shirt, and held it up. It read, "Dear Aunt Em. Hate You. Hate Kansas. Taking the Dog. Dorothy."

"It's for your Mama," Lou said. "Think she'll like it?"

Birdie knew she would. It was all Mama. Bitter. Resentful. Longing to escape.

Aunt Lou had bought herself a book to read from the gift shop. *The Color Purple*. Birdie sighed. She hadn't guessed right on her test for Mrs. Opie. The author was Alice Walker, not Zora Neale Hurston.

Lou settled herself, opened it up, then began reading.

The bus started up again. Alexandra Hall said our next stop would be St. Louis.

Birdie lay her head against the cool bus window and wondered about what Henrietta had said. *Are we somehow all the same? We girls?*

Henrietta turned to Birdie.

"I'm so lucky to have found you two," she started up, her eyes glittering. She pointed to her feet. "I bought new orthotic insoles last December. I've been breaking them in on daily walks around the block, trying to get in shape for this march."

Birdie opened Lou's phone and scrolled to the very first picture she took while waiting beside the bus.

"See. There they are!"

Henrietta studied the picture of her shoes. They were commonplace black, the high laces designed to support her aging ankles. Still, she was thrilled to place them among the medley of boots and sneakers and moccasins.

"I love seeing my own feet among all these younger women," Henrietta said. "They give me hope for the future."

She studied Birdie's face. It said the girl wasn't hopeful about the future.

"But my knees are a bigger challenge than my feet, dear. I closed my blinds every night and struggled onto the floor to do my knee exercises before I went to bed. I trained for this walk like an athlete."

Henrietta noticed that Birdie had covered her mouth to hide her smile. *Well, it probably was amusing to think of an old lady crawling around on the floor or walking around her neighborhood at dawn to break in her orthotics.* Henrietta was happy to see the young girl smile. She found the gap between the girl's two front teeth endearing; it had made Birdie look younger than her age. She hoped the gap would make room for some happiness to slip through.

"I'm in pretty good shape for my age," Henrietta said. "I've been running up and down the stairs of our apartment building nursing my father for years. Three stories. Twelve rooms. Father was in one of the second-floor apartments. Right next to the bathroom. The upstairs tenants were always needing this or that. Father died four years ago. But the caretaking plain ruined my knees."

Henrietta patted Birdie's arm. "But that's enough about me. What about you?"

"*Me?*"

"Yes, you. It looks like you've had practice as a caregiver, the way you took care of me at the rest stop."

She made caregiving sound like something to be proud of.

"Well, I had practice with my sister Shanice. She was in a wheel-chair. I pushed her to school. Took her to the toilet. Stuff like that. Would you like to see her picture?"

Henrietta nodded. Birdie reached down into her backpack and held up the framed picture. She never tired of looking at it. The shape of her face and the shade of her skin was like an acorn. Wide in the middle, narrow at the tip. But Birdie knew the acorn would never grow into an oak.

"She's very pretty," Henrietta said.

"Mama always said she was the prettiest one of us kids."

Henrietta rested her hands in her lap, thinking. "I hope you don't mind my asking, but you didn't mention her when you were telling me about your family. When we first got on the bus."

Birdie looked into Hennie's cloudy gray-blue eyes. They reminded her of the swimming hole out near Cavern's Creek and her early fear of diving in. She took a breath. "She died," Birdie said.

"Oh, I'm so sorry, dear," Hennie said. Hennie looked down as if she was embarrassed. Then she laid her soft hand on Birdie's arm. Quietly, she whispered, "Do you want to talk about it?"

Birdie turned away and stared out the window. *Yes and no. I do and I don't.*

Henrietta picked up her knitting. She understood about not wanting to talk about things. But she knew that if you kept silent for too long, parts of you began to die. Still, talking required someone on the other end to listen, someone you could trust. Someone like Sister Florinda.

She didn't know what she would have done without Sister Florinda. One thing she did know: there was nothing worse than losing a child.

Miss Hennie's fingers were flying across her needles. She was making good progress with the butter-yellow yarn. Something about knitting caused a softness to fall all around her like a cloud of cotton candy. *Is it the repetition? The quiet? The opportunity to be alone with just your own thoughts?* Birdie wished Mama had a hobby like knitting.

The bus was moving too swiftly for her to take pictures; the world whirled by like the petals on those whirligig sticks she used to spin as a child. From the bus window, the passing world looked lonely. Birdie made photographs in her mind: run-down train stations, only a few lonely travelers waiting on wooden benches; cold sheets flapping on a line, lonely without warm bodies snoring across them; miles of lonely farmland and then the sudden appearance of a white frame house, a flash in the empty ocean of prairie like a lighthouse signal; glimpses of a river, a flat blue-and-silver mirror, lonely without a face to stare into it.

Birdie pressed her cheek to the cool window, and as she breathed, in and out again, her nose left little patches of condensation on the pane. She began to worry. About the trees. About her schoolwork. About what's behind and what's ahead. About the ventilator back at home, sitting all alone, no longer breathing.

Every time she picked up her needles, Henrietta thought of Sister Florinda, who had taught her to knit decades ago. She was the cook in Father Cochran's kitchen, and Henrietta remembered sitting on the stool near her, struggling over her stitches, while Florinda labored over the bean soup on the stove and the cornbread in the oven, sweat beading across her forehead.

She was certain now, as she hadn't been certain then, that Florinda saw what she was at fourteen. "You're wound tight as a tick, girl," Sister said. "Knitting always helps with that. Once you get the hang of it."

"What if I teach you to knit, Birdie?"

The girl looked frightened. But curious.

"Me? Right now? Or some other time?"

"What about right now? We've got time, don't we?" Henrietta's head bobbed up and down with quiet laughter. "Unless you're too busy."

Birdie rolled her cinnamon-olive eyes.

"Here," Henrietta said, stuffing needles and yarn into her hands so she couldn't object.

Henrietta taught her about casting on. Birdie fumbled with the needles in her hand. Henrietta took back the needles and yarn and cast on the first row herself to make it easier for the girl.

"There," she said, passing it over. "It's all yours."

Henrietta showed her how to make an X with the two needles, the right-hand needle under the left-hand needle, encouraging her to take her first stitch. Immediately the stitch looped off the needle. "That's O.K., dear. No harm. Just try again."

Birdie tried again and again. Once she made a solid stitch, she looked at Henrietta for encouragement. "Did I do that right?" she asked doubtfully.

"Of course you did. Learning to knit – or learning anything, for that matter - is mostly a matter of persistence and support. You supply the persistence. I supply the support."

But Henrietta watched the way the girl held the yarn. Stiff. Taut. The tightness made it impossible for her to make satisfactory stitches.

Henrietta had forgotten how hard it had been to get the hang of knitting. You could pull the yarn too tight. You could hold it too loose. The comfort came when you got it just right. When you got it just right, a space opened up inside and let the comfort slip in.

Henrietta saw frustration written all over the young girl's face. It was time to stop.

"That's enough for now, dear," Hennie said. "And next time we'll do some simple finger knitting. Just yarn. No needles."

Birdie put the work down with relief.

"Yes," Henrietta mumbled to herself, "the girl reminds me of myself at her age. Tight as a tick."

Birdie watched Hennie pick up her own knitting again, relieved to stop the knitting lesson. So far, knitting made her feel all fumble-fingered. She was glad Hennie wasn't her real grandmother. She wouldn't want her real grandmother to have discovered she was such a slow learner.

One of the young women in the row behind them leaned over the headrest to talk to Hennie. Birdie thought it might be Emily, the Fountain, the one who kept the bus waiting so she could get her green drink.

"Do you mind me asking what you're knitting?"

"Oh, not at all, dear. But I'm still not sure. Maybe another lap robe for Sunny Days nursing home back in Soros. I've knit hundreds of them in my day. I find it relaxing. The repetition of it, the rhythm. It's sort of like praying the rosary."

Birdie thought about Mama again. She wished she had a rosary to pray on. *Do you have to be Catholic to pray on a rosary?*

"Do you think you could knit me one of those pussy hats?" Fountain said.

Hennie's needles stopped moving. "What?"

The two other seatmates popped up now, leaning over the headrests and listening.

"You know," Fountain said. "Didn't you see them back in the rest stop?"

Fountain's seatmate took up the thread. Birdie knew her name was Katie, but she still thought of her as Waterfall, for the two blonde Niagaras cascading down her shoulders. "Those pink pussy hats with the ears? Didn't you see them?"

Birdie had certainly noticed them. There had been quite a few of them, actually. Knitted hats. Two cat-ears on top. Pink.

"What did you say they were called?" Hennie looked confused.

"Pussy hats," answered the third seatmate. Her hair was cropped short with a swirl like an ocean wave swishing across her forehead. Birdie remembered her name. Jenny. Her sister had Tourette's. "They were a way to fight back against the Predator-in-Chief who bragged about grabbing women by the pussy."

Hennie's needles fell to her lap, and the three young women laughed together.

"Your pussy," Ocean Wave said. "Surely you know what a pussy is, right?"

"Your snatch. Your beaver," said Fountain.

"Your privates," said Waterfall.

Hennie blinked. "Oh, I thought they were one of those new fads young people adopt. You know, like nose rings, tattoos, or purple streaks in their hair."

Now the three muses all laughed at once. "They *are!*" they giggled.

"But why would you wear your ... umm ... *privates,*" stuttered Hennie, "... well ... on the top of your head?"

Jenny spoke right up. "Because you're *proud*. Proud of being a woman. Proud of your pussy. And you're sending a signal that it's not for grabbing."

Birdie was embarrassed, so she stared out the window. But she didn't stop listening.

Jenny passed the topic around like a runner with a baton. "I'm plain sick of being shamed. Shamed about my own body. Having other people speak for it, claim rights to it, make laws for it. Aren't we sick of being shamed, girls? Shamed about our own pussies?"

Jenny's two seat companions were nodding their heads furiously. Hennie's jaw was open, but no answer was coming out.

Jenny took back the baton. "Doesn't our woman's blood give life to every person on God's green earth? And doesn't it flow from our pussies? What's the shame in that?"

Birdie remembered the shame in that. The blood. The secret flowing of it, like an underground river that nobody else could see. She'd started her period early, at age eleven. Ever after, she avoided wearing white. After all, her woman's blood might seep through her clothing. She wondered why shame had been such a part of those worries.

"Our blood and our pussies," Waterfall declared. "Every one of us holds the secret of life in our own bodies. Hundreds of tiny little eggs just waiting to become living, breathing human beings. We've probably got millions of them sitting right here inside this bus."

Birdie had never thought about it that way. Mostly she thought about those uncomfortable feelings of wondering if her pad was too full, if her underpants were stained, if the restroom would have a Kotex machine, if the boys could notice.

"Yes," Fountain agreed. "Nothin' to be ashamed of. Oughtta make us *proud,*" she announced.

Birdie felt a kind of charged energy running from the ocean wave to the waterfall to the fountain to Hennie. And to her. As if the word *proud* was a powerful river flowing from one woman to another. A deep underground river. Old as time.

Birdie thought back to the alley behind the hardware store and Mama's warning that terrible things happened there. Birdie had never told: something terrible had happened to her there.

It was near dusk, and Birdie had stayed with Destinee too long, so she was going to be late for supper. She had decided to take a short cut through the alley, and Bobby Showalter had followed her there into the darkest part of the alley. He had grabbed her, pushed her down, scraping her knees and hands, bruising her arms, his hands down in her jeans, exploring. *As if my body belonged to him.*

Birdie never said a word. *Who would have believed her?* Bobby Showalter was the superintendent's son. Bobby Showalter was white. Yet she wondered: *Would he have dared if I had been the kind of girl brave enough to wear a pink pussy hat?*

Birdie flashed back to the restroom, to Hennie and her in the bathroom stall. *We girls. Does she mean all of us? All shades? All ages? And all of them quietly harboring new life inside of them like eggs in a nest?*

"Well," said Hennie," taking up her needles again. "I think I can do that. The pattern's simple enough." She began pulling the stitches from her needles. They fell like yellow curlicues onto her lap. "Yes, I think I can knit you one of those hats."

Fountain, Waterfall, and Ocean Wave gave each other high fives. "Thank you," they giggled. "After the trip is over," said Ocean Wave, "we'll put a purple streak in your hair for you. Or take you to get a tattoo."

Hennie was smiling.

Birdie wasn't so sure about the tattoo.

But she thought a purple streak would look awesome in Hennie's gray bun-braids.

Henrietta fished around in her tote bag. She pulled out a pink skein of yarn. She felt for the small fat needles linked together in a circle: they worked better for hats.

She was flattered to have had these young women enlist a skill of hers, yet looping the pink yarn around her circular needle for such an immodest request gave her time to think about things she'd rather not remember. Like her own girlhood.

She remembered how the little white flags and silver wrappings from his jar of Hershey's Kisses were scattered all over the floor of Father Cochran's room when she came to clean. They caught easily in the fibers of the carpet. They weren't easy to pick up. She had to get down on her knees to pick them up.

The memory made her sad. She picked up rubbish from a priest: Henry could actually *be* one. Still, mulling over the memory now, Henrietta realized it wasn't the humiliation of picking up that vexed her: it was the kneeling it required. Catholic girls spent a good deal of time on their knees. She wondered why it taken her so many years to recognize the seeds of humiliation in that.

As the yarn flew over her needles, Henrietta said a quiet prayer for young women. Those on the bus, those behind her, and especially that tense young girl sitting to her right.

Birdie had been curious about something ever since her trip to the restroom, so she dared to ask about what was on her mind.

"Why'd you give," she began, "a twenty dollar bill to the maid in the restroom back there? Was it because she's Black?"

Hennie stopped hooking needle under yarn and squinted her cloudy blue eyes. "You're quite the questioner, aren't you, Miss Birdie?" It was a question that sounded like a statement.

Birdie knew Hennie was right about that. Asking questions was something Mama never understood. *'Who has time for questions, girl? Now get on up to Mr. Mims's store. Your sister's 'bout to run out of diapers.'*

"Well," Hennie confessed, "I appreciate questions." She said it with a mix of pride and frustration. "When St. Timothy said for women to keep silence in the churches, why didn't they all get up and leave? Tell me: If women run the church – and they do - why aren't they allowed to be priests?"

Of course Birdie didn't know the answer since she didn't know much about Catholics. But she knew the scandal up at St. Charles High School last year got Aunt Lou riled up. She'd heard Mama and Lou whispering about it. Miss Borden, the English teacher, got fired for getting pregnant. But Mr. Withers, the Physics teacher and the father, got to keep his job. Lou was part of the crowd that stood outside the school and held up signs. Some of the protesters were even Catholic. Birdie had overheard Lou say that between priests and bishops and archbishops and the Pope, no woman ever stood a chance.

Birdie had lots of questions, especially about the Popes. "Was there ever a lady Pope?"

Hennie tightened her lips. "No."

Birdie didn't have the nerve to ask what she'd heard about Popes. That they had a special test to confirm that the Pope was male. That there was a glass toilet hoisted high above the cardinals. The candidate for Pope had to drop his privates into it. That way they could all look up and make sure he was a man.

"Back to your original question," Hennie said. "I didn't give twenty dollars to the woman in the restroom because she's Black. But because she's a woman. A woman with troubles. No woman – Black or white - ever wants a job like that."

Birdie thought about the woman and wondered what she'd do with the twenty dollars: *Put a down payment on new brakes for the van? Send it in as deposit on her son's graduation cap-and-gown? Buy her family a big chuck roast for Sunday dinner?*

"Women like that usually have a story that makes me sad and angry all at the same time," Hennie said, her fingers moving lickety-split. "I've struggled with both my whole life. They seem like two sides of the same thing, don't you think?"

Birdie wondered whether Miss Hennie was really asking her what she thought. Or if she was just making another statement in the form of a question.

What Hennie said made Birdie think of herself and Mama. Sadness like her. Anger like Mama. *Were they really two sides of the same thing?*

As Henrietta stitched, the memory came floating up, unbidden: She had been leaning over to pick up the silver candy wrappers from the floor.

She felt something brush the backs of her knees, and she jumped: startled.

"I thought you might be in need of this," Father Cochran said kindly. "This study can get mighty dusty."

She hadn't heard him come in. She looked down and wondered why he hadn't been wearing shoes. Father Cochran was only wearing socks.

Henrietta kept her head down. She was too afraid to meet his gaze. If she had, she would have noticed that his friendly smile had wrinkled the corners of his eyes. She kept her own eyes fixed on the silver crucifix hanging from a chain around his neck and dangling across his midriff.

She couldn't think of what to say. "Thank you," she mumbled, taking the feather duster. Decades later she had realized it had been a stupid thing to say.

As he turned, she continued to look down, noticing his black socks again, watching the black skirt of his cassock ripple and swish as he left the room.

Had she imagined it? That faint tickle behind her knees? Perhaps it had been her fault? Of course it had! Hadn't she been bending over deeply? Had her skirt hiked up unbecomingly? Yes! He'd only been offering a gentle warning to pull it down.

Later, much later, the sadness and anger came. Sadness at her youth and innocence. Anger that she'd been such a good Catholic girl. But worst of all was the shame. Shame that she'd been such a fool.

Aunt Lou closed her book. Birdie could tell she'd been listening.

"I've worked in non-profits all my life," Lou-Lou said, jumping into the conversation. "Literacy. Food banks."

Right now Lou was heading a charity that provided used furniture to poor folks. Things like a sofa, a kitchen table, a lamp that worked. When the lease was up this spring, the landlord was raising the rent, and Louise would have to find a new location that was cheaper.

"I've met plenty of women like the one in the restroom. They take on the kind of work that's *steeped* in anger and sadness. The only thing to do about it is to seek justice for them."

That's Aunt Lou for you. She spent her life seeking justice. Unlike Mama who only sought a few minutes of quiet.

Birdie piped up at the topic of justice. "Hennie, do you know the story about how Frederick Douglass Junior High got its name?"

Birdie hardly needed to see Hennie shake her head. Lou-Lou and Birdie always had fun telling that story.

Aunt Louise started. "Birdie's school had been Abraham Lincoln Junior High since forever. But in 2004 it was the 50th anniversary of that ruling that happened in Topeka - right next door to Soros. Our folks thought it was high time a building recognized that," she said.

'Our folks' meant Black people.

Birdie had been hearing about the fight since she was little. Aunt Lou and her church friends got together to have the school renamed "Linda Carol Brown Junior High." The ruling said Linda Carol Brown, who was Black like us, didn't have to go to her crummy school any more. No more rusty slides. No more frayed tetherball ropes. No more shot-out building lights. No more third-hand textbooks.

Birdie didn't understand all the details at the time, but she did now. She kept quiet against the questions rising up in her mind: *Doesn't it make sense to name a building filled with kids after a famous kid who lived right next door? Wouldn't that be something? A school named after a kid, a kid who was the same color as us?*

As she listened, Hennie was making good progress on her hat. Something about knitting seemed to make it easier for a person to listen and work at the same time. Birdie hoped maybe she'd get the hang of it some time. But it wouldn't be today.

Lou-Lou said, "White folks never want anything to ever change, so they were stuck on 'Abraham Lincoln.'"

Hennie nodded. Maybe she understood about folks never wanting anything to ever change. After all, she knew there were no lady Popes.

"Somehow they thought that since Lincoln had signed the Emancipation Proclamation," Lou-Lou said, her hands beginning to dance, "Black folks were free. The white folks, of course, didn't understand that freed slaves still aren't free. They said Blacks should be happy to celebrate something that was the best thing that happened to us. Ever."

Lou's hands were flying up like doves rising from a cage.

"If it was the best thing to happen to us ever, it had happened almost 150 years ago, so wasn't it high time for another good thing to happen?" Lou-Lou huffed at injustice the way Mama did when one of her kids back-talked.

Birdie wondered: *Did you have to wait over 150 years for an egg to hatch?*

Then it was Birdie's turn. She explained how Aunt Lou and her friends put on their Sunday clothes and stood outside the school and held up signs. For days on end. "Mama used to joke that Lou went to a protest in her church gloves and hat."

Hennie grinned over her stitches.

Birdie didn't tell the part about how Mama always shrugged and reminded Lou how she had kids and Louise didn't, so Lou had time for protest marches.

Birdie also didn't tell about how Mama was distracted that year. In 2004, she was almost two. While Aunt Lou held up her signs reminding people that things still weren't equal, no matter what Abraham Lincoln did 150 years ago, Mama noticed that something might be wrong with Shanice. Everything was different after that.

"It was awful," Aunt Lou said. "The two groups scratched and hissed like cats. Helped us to know what 'Bleeding Kansas' must have been like. The whites held up signs and taunted us protesters with questions."

Birdie remembered some of the questions on the signs from Lou-Lou's retellings. "What's wrong with Abraham Lincoln?" "Do you hate the president who gave you freedom?" "Why don't you go back to Africa?"

"Black folks," Lou-Lou said, "were tired of having to understand the white folks' world when white folks never had to understand ours."

Birdie knew enough to believe that getting the white folks to understand the Black folks' world would take longer than 150 years.

Aunt Lou wrapped up the story by telling about the final decision: it was for Frederick Douglass. The whites declared that he was Black and a friend of Blacks as well as a friend of Abraham Lincoln, too. After 150 years, Frederick Douglass wouldn't ruffle any feathers.

How come the only feathers that ever get ruffled are the feathers of Black folks?

Lou's fingers were doing somersaults. "It wasn't a compromise at all, since me and my friends had the most votes. But 'Linda Carol Brown' was overruled by the Principal and the Superintendent and the State Board of Education. All white."

Hennie's hands stopped knitting. Birdie wondered if she was thinking about priests and bishops and archbishops and popes. All men.

"That's a good story." She rested her knitting in her lap. "Now how about if I ask *you two* about something?"

Lou-Lou and Birdie stared at each other, then nodded. *Fair is fair.*

"See if you can't settle something for me. I sew every Wednesday with my St. Catherine's circle. We make simple things, things that don't require much skill. Walker caddies for the nursing home. Adult bibs. Baby blankets."

Hennie turned to Aunt Louise and pointed to the pin she was wearing that said, "Black Lives Matter."

"Help me with something," Hennie said. "The ladies in my St. Catherine's sewing circle don't agree with the 'Black Lives Matter' slogan. They think it should be '*All* Lives Matter.' What do you two think?"

Birdie couldn't believe that a white woman was asking such a question. *White people never want to know what Black people think, do they?*

Aunt Lou's eyes widened. "White folks don't need to be told they matter," she insisted. "They've got all the privileges right along."

Hennie turned to Birdie.

Birdie thought about privileges and white folks. Better schools. Better houses. Better health. Better jobs. Better opportunities. Better justice. She thought about Aunt Lou's "right along." She meant *from birth.*

Hennie was waiting for Birdie to say something.

Birdie studied her face. While she struggled for an answer, she wanted to take out her camera and snap a picture of Hennie. Her face was full of expectation: eyelids and eyebrows lifted over wide-open nickel-blue eyes. Birdie wondered if a picture could capture a look like that.

"I guess," Birdie said, hesitating, "I think of all the things I worry about." She took in a breath. "Things that white folks don't have to worry about."

Hennie was listening. She lifted her rosary from around her neck and began fingering the beads. Then she asked, "But *all* folks worry, don't they? White and Black? At least that's what my St. Catherine sisters would say."

Birdie blurted out a question that was like an answer. "But do they have to worry about their *whiteness?*"

Hennie's fingers stopped moving down her beads. She was considering Birdie's question. "Hmmm," she mused, biting her lip. Her slate eyes narrowed as if she was trying to see something that was off in the distance. "You ask good questions, Miss Birdie Jackson," she said. "You remind me of myself at your age."

Birdie was suddenly glad Mama wasn't here. "I can't see that questions get you anywhere," Mama said. More than once. "Questions just slow you down." Mama never had time in her life for questions. She had to keep moving. Deal with the body bags in the Army. Deal with Shanice. Deal with Daddy's leaving. Deal with the girls in her office. Deal with her kids. Deal with her own anger. Deal with Birdie's sadness. Mama had no time to stop for questions. "Questions just add to your worries," she always said.

Now it was Aunt Lou's turn for a question. "So what caused you to be so woke about Black folks, Miss Hennie?"

Hennie picked up her knitting again. "Maybe I'll tell you about Sister Florinda some time," she said.

Birdie wanted her to tell them about Sister Florinda right now, but Hennie had closed her eyes and leaned back against the headrest to nap, her lips moved as if she was counting stitches. Or praying the rosary.

Birdie's mind was swirling: *Can I survive without thinking about my blackness? Can it be possible that we have a white problem, not a Black problem?*

Emily's phone dinged. It was a text from Sonia. She'd been tracking their bus on her GPS.

"Yr near Ferguson?"

Emily remembered Jenny pointing out the sign that had just whizzed past: FERGUSON, MISSOURI.

"Yep," Emily texted back. "Just passed. Almost to St. Louis."

Katie knew there'd been a big riot there. Marc had told her about it. Marc had been training as a police officer. "Marc finally dropped out of the program," Katie said, "after the Michael Brown killing there. He didn't like it that nowadays white officers were being unfairly accused of everything. Including murder."

Emily hadn't known that Marc had been interested in the police program. All she knew was he was managing an Outback Steakhouse.

Emily's phone dinged. "Sonia asks us to send healing thoughts to the people there," she said.

Jenny nodded. Katie didn't.

Emily couldn't think of a good 'healing thought.' All she could think about was that Black man she learned about earlier, the one who said, "Why can't we all get along?"

Henrietta had been listening to the girls behind her while she worked on the hat. She had finally been able to keep their names straight.

Birdie and Louise must have been listening, too, because Birdie said that her aunt and her teacher had taken up a collection at Missionary Baptist to support the Ferguson community and the Michael Brown family.

"Lou-Lou and Mrs. Opie have also taken up collections to support Laquan McDonald and Tamir Rice and a few others I can't remember," Birdie said.

When Louise said that Eric Garner's Mama, Gwen Carr, was going to be at the march, her hands flailed with excitement. "I can't imagine anything worse than having your child killed in a chokehold by police. And she had pork chops and rice and beans waiting for his supper when he got home. I think that's just the saddest thing in the world." Louise opened up her jacket to show Hennie her t-shirt. "I Can't Breathe," it said.

Hennie reached for her rosary. Her fingers moved up and down the beads, each bead a memory about breathing, too.

Henrietta had just asked Birdie a question. "Did you ever resent taking care of her? Your sister?"

Birdie felt as if a big gaping hole had opened up beneath her feet and she was falling into it.

Birdie had no answer. She thought of Mama, living on the bitter edge of resentment.

"It's hard to admit, but I took care of my sick father by myself for fourteen years after he got fell ill, and he was not an easy man. Sitting by his bedside. Taking his temperature. Massaging his back. Fetching this, fetching that. The ladies at church say I'm a saint. I'm not. Saints don't give in to resentment."

Birdie thought about all the things she had given up to help with Shanice over the years. Entertaining her at home instead of spending time with other girls. Not trying out for the volleyball team because she wouldn't have time for practices. Sitting in the lunchroom with Shanice while the other kids avoided her table. All those things plus no daddy and a mama worn out.

"And Father was never one to say 'thank you.'"

Birdie felt the need to stick up for Shanice. "Shanice wasn't like that," she said.

Birdie explained about how happy Shanice was with their weekend routines. On Saturdays she would play beauty parlor with Shanice, painting her toenails, washing and drying her hair, watching her chuckle with delight. Antoine would clean the ventilator, and after that he'd helped Shanice with the range-of-motion and stretching exercises that stimulated her muscles. She loved the attention of her handsome big brother. Beanie cleaned out the van, which was trashed with fast food wrappers, empty soda cans, and cigarette butts at the end of the week. Afterwards, Twanny would use the lift to hoist Shanice into the clean van, and they'd have picnics with her out in the country. Birdie didn't mention how Mama never went along. How she needed the time to catch up on laundry, dusting, vacuuming, and grocery shopping for the following week. How when they came home she was passed out fast asleep on the couch.

Birdie held Shanice's picture up again, pointing to her plump nut-brown cheeks. "We gave her the nick-name 'Chipmunk.' After a while, we just shortened it to 'Chip' or 'Munk,' and Shanice shook with giggles whenever we called her that."

"So does that mean you didn't resent taking care of her?"

Birdie didn't answer. She took a deep breath as if to force her thoughts down into a place where they couldn't be found. Resentments hid there: being embarrassed for both Shanice *and* herself for the teasing, the mocking, the stealing of things like diaper bags, toilet tongs.

"Well, *I* did," Hennie said, her lips tightening. "Mostly I resented my brother. Henry. He wasn't expected to help out with Father. He was the one who was given the education. I always felt my parents looked past me and focused on Henry. As if I was invisible."

Birdie thought back to last November and the Thanksgiving table and the way Mama had looked straight at her when Lou-Lou said she was taking her on the march. As if Mama was seeing her for the first time. As if before that she'd been invisible, too.

"You remind me of myself at your age," Henrietta said. "Thoughtful. Smart. Capable. The whole world in front of you."

Birdie counted. Hennie had mentioned three good things about her. But Hennie didn't know the bad things, especially that she was nothing like Malala, Rosa, Harriet.

"But it's a dangerous age, too, Birdie. Things can go either way for a young girl at your age. Sometimes they can set a pattern for your life."

Birdie turned away from Hennie and stared out the window as if she hadn't heard her. Her thoughts flew to Mama. A pattern had been set for her life. Birdie's heart ached just thinking about it. *Hate you. Hate Kansas.* She didn't want that kind of pattern for herself. *But am I setting a pattern? Smoking? Sneaking out at night? Stuffing my bra? Ignoring my schoolwork? Is Hennie right? Am I really at the age where a pattern's being set?*

"Do you know what a Jayhawk is, dear?"

Birdie turned and blinked at her. She had seen "Jayhawks" on the sweatshirts and pennants at the rest station. She had thought it was a mascot for a college team.

"Jayhawks are lawless birds. They fly around after dark, seeking out the nests of smaller birds. They not only rob the eggs in the nests but often kill the chicks, too."

Birdie shuddered, wondering why Henrietta was telling her this.

Henrietta didn't explain that Sister Florinda had told her about Jayhawks many decades ago. "They were Kansans who would go to Missouri and steal back slaves, Henrietta," Florinda had said. "Jayhawks tried to keep you a slave. And there's all kinds of different ways to be kept in slavery. Watch out for the Jayhawks, Birdie. Don't let anyone rob you of your future."

Her future. *Does this old lady guess that I long to be someone, someday, somehow? Does Jayhawks mean more than just birds?*

Emily watched the road signs. They were almost to St. Louis.

Katie chirped, "Is it Saint Lew-ISS or Saint Lew-EEE?"

Then Jenny asked, "For that matter, is it Mi-sur-EE or Mi-sur-UH?"

"I don't know," Emily piped up. "But given the stiff state of my body, I'd choose *Mi-sur-EE.*"

Outside, the sun dipped lower in the sky, warming the bare corn fields huddled under thin shawls of snow. The landscape was beginning to change from flatland to rolling hills. The bus passed through a small city that reminded Birdie of Soros: dusty shop windows, limp piles of slush, kids her age hanging out at a convenience store and smoking. The fading light allowed her to see Hennie's reflection in the window glass. Birdie thought her reflected face would make a nice picture. She pulled out Aunt Lou's phone. She aimed the camera at the window, opened the lens for a close-up, pushed the white button, and then examined the image.

Birdie liked the picture. It was both soft and clear at the same time. She could see Hennie's wrinkles like slivers of straw. She could see her flat, woven braids sitting like a nest on the crown of her head. She could see that there was something steady about her, something reliable, something patient. She sat like a hen warming her nest, a nest heavy with eggs and their possibilities. Yet she looked alert, aware, purposeful. Like someone who knew to keep an eye out for Jayhawks.

Against the voices of the other passengers, Birdie was comforted by the rhythm of Hennie's clicking needles. They sounded like beaks tapping.

Louise nudged Henrietta. "Wasn't St. Louis where that awful Presidential debate happened?"

Henrietta replied quickly. "Yes. He came up right behind her like a stalker. Loomed over her. Bullied. Did what men often do to women: invade their personal space. As if they own her and everything around her."

Henrietta understood all about that.

The bus was approaching St. Louis, and Birdie thought back to what she knew about stalking because of Bobby Showalter. He'd leer at her in the cafeteria, brush up against her at her locker, block her path as she tried to enter the gym.

Personal space? Are girls entitled to it? How much space can girls claim as theirs?

Hennie sounded excited. "Even the landscape tells you something important is coming up, Birdie. First rolling farmlands. Then valleys.

Now bluffs. And then terraces along the bluffs." She pointed out the window. She was right. The landscape was different.

"Soon the Mississippi and the Missouri Rivers will meet and flow together. Like branches to a limb," Hennie said. "Birdie, imagine what Lewis and Clark thought when they first saw this!"

Birdie kept quiet. History wasn't her best subject.

Birdie had never seen so many road signs promoting a single attraction: "Gateway to the West." "We have no ARCH-rival". There was highway construction everywhere, and every other billboard announced a different riverboat cruise or blues bar. "Queen of the Mississippi." "American Steamboat Cruises." "Tipsy Pony Party Bar." "Pop's Blue Moon."

"It's the Gateway Arch!" someone shouted. Cheers broke out on the bus. Marchers pressed their noses to the glass to get a better look.

Birdie strained her eyes to see it. She thought she glimpsed some of it, but smog was clouding the top. She was sure Mama wouldn't be impressed: it would remind her of McDonald's.

A group at the back of the bus started singing "Proud Mary." They were led by a soloist who began by announcing that she was "gonna start off nice and easy" but was "gonna finish off nice and rough." The ladies hooted and hollered. When she got to the chorus of "Rolling, rolling, rolling on a river," the noise level swelled, gathering steam as it reached all the way to the front of the bus. Soon a few ladies were jumping into the aisles to dance.

Behind her, The Muses were discussing the song. Jenny said that the inspiration for it wasn't a riverboat. It was a poor woman who worked all day in a rich woman's house and then went home to try to hold things together for her own family: Proud Mary.

The women in the back were singing the line about "Workin' for the man every night and day."

Birdie remembered how Mama used to talk about the conflict between her pride and her family. "You swallow one to feed the other," she said. At McDonald's, her boss used to tell her to tie her apron tighter so customers could see the size of her breasts. "If I had wanted folks staring at my boobs," Mama had scolded him, "I'd have applied at Hooters." Mama was surprised she hadn't got fired for saying that.

Mama said the customers were just as bad. "They comment on the size of your backside and look down your cleavage when you bend over to clean up somebody's sloppy kids' milkshake mess." Stories like this made Birdie ache for her Mama. *Proud Mary. Mama.*

Outside the window it looked like there were nearly ten lanes of traffic. Birdie had never seen so many cars in so many lanes merging in and out, getting on and off. Khalid operated the bus like a dancer, sure of every move.

Now Khalid's voice came up over the microphone. "A little bit of American history from a Syrian. For you ladies." "Little" sounded like "leetle" and "history" sounded like "heestirry."

The ladies were holding their breath. Khalid was merging from lane to lane as he spoke.

"Who know biggest year in history of St. Louis?"

No one.

Birdie could see Khalid smiling in his rearview mirror. He was proud to know some history Americans didn't.

"1904," he said.

A tractor trailer pulled right up next to their bus while Khalid was talking. If the window had been open, Birdie could have reached out and touched the red cab.

"Year for many things. American Olympics here. World's Fair here. And invention by the Hamwi family here. My family." As he said "my family," Khalid thumped his chest, taking his hand off the steering wheel as the tractor trailer pulled even closer.

"Great-grandfather Hamwi. *My* great-grandfather. Famous invention at the World's Fair. Right here. Syrian-American invention. Very famous." "Famous" sounded to Birdie like "fay-moose."

Birdie couldn't imagine what famous invention Khalid had in mind.

"Hamwi family famous for their zalibis. Zalibis like a waffle. How you say, 'Dee-lish?' Great-grandfather have booth at World's Fair. Right next to ice cream seller. You like ice cream, ladies?"

Khalid glanced at the nodding ladies in his rearview mirror, taking in their appreciation with his eyes off the road.

"Ice cream so popular at World's Fair, ice cream seller run out of dishes. So great-grandfather passed his waffles over to hold ice cream. Ice cream cone born. Ice cream cone. Famous invention. So when I bring my family over from Syria in '09, Hamwis already famous Americans, no?"

The marchers were clapping.

Khalid Hamwi had enjoyed sharing his story. "Hamwis as American as pie with the apples."

"Good for him," Aunt Lou said. "Syrians as American as apple pie."

PART IV – ST. LOUIS TO WASHINGTON, D.C.

6:30 p.m. CST, January 20, 2017

Birdie's stomach grumbled. She hadn't had anything to eat since breakfast. She needed a snack. Everyone else must have been hungry, too, because all at once the riders began breaking out food. There wasn't any room, but Birdie wanted to arrange a picture to take: triangles of Doritos, rectangles of Twinkies, squares of Little Debbie cakes. It would look like one of those modern paintings she remembered from art class.

Aunt Lou popped the lid of a large Tupperware container she'd kept under her seat. The smell of fried chicken floated under noses throughout the cabin. Birdie took a drumstick and Hennie took a thigh. Then Aunt Lou traveled up and down the aisle offering her famous fried chicken all around. The women chatted excitedly with each other as they passed rounds of homemade cupcakes and cinnamon rolls and chocolate chip cookies down the aisles and over the headrests. It reminded Birdie of the baking contest at the Soros county fair. Minus judges.

Hennie handed Birdie a tissue from a little pocket pack inside her tote. The gesture touched her. The little cellophane packet seemed like a grandmotherly thing to carry. They wiped chicken grease from their lips and fingers while Aunt Lou was off chatting up riders in the aisle.

"Tell me about your phone," Hennie said.

Birdie reached for the phone. "It's really not mine. It's Lou's. But she's letting me borrow it on the trip." Birdie doesn't tell her the reason Mama won't let her kids have a phone. "Want to hold it?"

Hennie held it in her palm. She stared at it as if it were a newborn chick you could squeeze too hard.

"You can't hurt it."

Then Birdie pointed out the parts. The on-off switch, the audio port, the ringer control. "Here. I'll turn it on for you."

The screen opened up, and Birdie passed the phone back to Hennie.

"My," she said, as Birdie explained about all the apps. The calculator. The weather app. And of course that Google app where she found some of the answers to the crossword. Off and on, Birdie had been using the phone to identify Ida B. Wells and Alice Paul and Shirley Chisholm while Hennie knitted and Louise read.

"But the camera app's my favorite. Want to see more of my pictures?"

Henrietta swiped through Birdie's pictures, fixing on the gauzy picture of herself that captured her reflection in the bus window. She looked at Birdie. "I don't recall ever having my picture taken like this. Just me alone. Never felt like anyone noticed me enough to bother. Thank you, dear."

Henrietta remembered how few pictures her family had. That one of her father going off to war, not yet maimed, handsome in his uniform. The other one of her brother Henry as an altar boy, Father Cochran standing behind him, one hand on Henry's shoulder. She recalled no pictures of herself, not even from confirmation day. The thought of her pictureless confirmation day still hurt her heart. Every Catholic family took pictures of their confirmands on confirmation day. Hers didn't. She understood that happy families had scores of pictures in frames, lining stairwells, on countertops, in drawers waiting to be organized. If no one thought to take your picture, it was a sign you were invisible.

Miss Hennie whispered confidentially to Birdie. "Didn't tell a soul I was going on this trip. That included my own brother Henry. Said I was heading to Wichita to visit my Aunt Rita in the nursing home there. She was Mother's last living sibling."

Birdie liked thinking that old ladies – not just teenage girls - lied to their relatives about where they were going.

Suddenly Pauline Frazier appeared at the aisle headrest. She had intentionally staggered from the back of the bus to find them.

"Hello, there." When she smiled, her face cracked into a million wrinkles. Birdie thought she'd probably been a smoker.

"Can you text me that picture of the three of us? I want to post it on my website."

"Sure," Birdie said. She opened the Contacts file and recorded Pauline's name, address, phone number, and web address. Then she texted the picture to her. She was astonished to think that a stranger might like a picture of hers enough to share it with the world.

Pauline handed Birdie three Ziploc bags of fist-size blueberry muffins. "Mighty grateful," she said.

Hennie poked Birdie in the arm. "Website? Of course I've heard of them, but I've never really seen one."

"Oh," Birdie said, typing in Pauline's web address. Up popped a picture of Pauline's rusty van next to two cactus trees. Then there was another showing a group of school children smiling into the camera. An interior shot focused on the miniature displays: butterflies of the world, famous inventions, U.S. Presidents.

Hennie tapped on the picture. "No women," she said, frowning. She meant the presidents.

"*Yet*," Hennie added. "Maybe the first one will be named Birdie Jackson. It's possible, right?"

"Nooooo," Birdie said, thinking of her grades.

"Well, then, Birdie Jackson," Hennie said. "At least admit that it's not *im*-possible."

'Not im-*possible? Was that just a tad under 'possible?'* Birdie liked the way Hennie talked to her, even though the words made her uneasy. Like a shirt tag that itches your neck.

Birdie changed the subject. "Don't you have a website, Hennie? For your store?"

She just blinked. That meant "no."

"Well, would you like one? It might be good for your business."

Hennie sighed. "The shop's got some French cachepots, a sterling silver inkwell, and a few nice Jumeau dolls. But mostly it's just Depression glassware and attic trinkets and finds scoured from estate sales."

Birdie didn't know what any of those things were, but she let Hennie go on.

"Henry's right. He says, 'Nobody wants this junk anymore. Everybody wants Pottery Barn.'"

Birdie knew about Pottery Barn. It was for rich people. People who could afford fancy mixers with bread hooks and kitchen cabinets with built-in trash compactors. It sold way more than pottery. It was nothing like a barn.

"Well, hardly anybody can sell anything without a website nowadays, Hennie. What's the name of your store?"

"Oldham's Antiques."

Birdie bit her lip to stall for time before she asked, "Are you sure you like that name?"

Birdie knew names sold things. Even if the names hurt your feelings. Aunt Jemima. Uncle Ben.

"Well, it's been in the family all these years. I'd never really wanted the shop. It just sort of fell into my lap after Father died. Somehow I feel like that's been the pattern of my life. Things just sort of falling into my lap." Hennie's face was twisted with a sad kind of surprise. Like a frayed tissue suddenly discovered in a coat pocket when you suddenly needed to sneeze and even a used tissue was welcome. "I wonder if other women ever feel like that."

Birdie wondered, too. But she didn't want to talk about patterns.

Patterns reminded her too much of Mama. And maybe herself. Birdie preferred keeping Hennie focused on the phone. "We could jazz it up a bit. Find a new, cool name. Let's look up some names on the phone."

"You can *do* that?"

"Sure." Birdie began to call out some names that sounded better than "Oldham's Antiques."

"'Shabby Shack.' 'Vintage Village.' 'The Afterlife.' 'Junque,' spelled all French-like with a 'Q,' not a 'K.'"

Hennie's lips were pursed. She was thinking.

"Oh, what about 'Utter Clutter'?" Birdie really liked that one.

Hennie grabbed her arm. "That's brilliant! It's catchy, it's funny, and it perfectly describes the store. No false advertising."

"And you could take pictures of your items and post them on your website, just like Pauline Frazier's doing. And people could buy things without coming into the store."

Hennie looked puzzled. "Well, they don't really come into the store right now anyway. Last week we sold only one item. A silver candlestick. Five dollars was a fair price. It was only plated silver."

She reached over and tapped the phone. "There are a lot of good possibilities in that phone, Birdie."

Birdie let Hennie think only good things came from a phone. She didn't tell her about the bad things. About the bullying that was even easier with a phone.

About the Youtube contest and Shanice.

The contest was to see who could mimic Shanice the best.

The limp right hand. The spastic movements. The smiling face that never would have understood their ugly motives.

The contestants were white boys. Drew Nelson. Ryan Leffler. Bobby Showalter. But a couple of white girls joined in, too.

The cruelest part was the way the video from the contest spread through the school. The kids made the video at Ryan Leffler's house, all of the kids competing and laughing their heads off at Birdie's sister.

Of course the video finally reached Shanice. Birdie learned about it when one of her so-called friends, JaNeela Walters, couldn't resist showing Shanice the video at the lunch table. The boys had dared her to do it, and JaNeela would do anything for the boys.

The winner was Bobby Showalter.

Mama went to school to protest. Aunt Lou offered to come with her, but Mama said this was her fight. Of course Mama's words fell on deaf ears. It didn't help that Bobby Showalter's dad had just been promoted to Superintendent.

After Shanice saw the video and after Mama protested, Beanie beat up Bobby Showalter. Beanie had dragged him back behind the school and punched him over and over. Mostly around the ears, which swelled up as big as cauliflowers. He left bruise marks around Bobby's neck where he'd held him down to punch. What Beanie was proudest of was the way he went for Bobby's right wrist. He twisted it, and Bobby's wrist snapped like a chicken wing. Now Bobby had a hanging right wrist. Just like Shanice.

Of course, Beanie got suspended, and nothing happened to Bobby Showalter. After that, Bobby Showalter stalked Birdie all over the school, but Birdie knew a part of her envied Beanie. She hadn't confronted JaNeela. She had just turned away, swivelling Shanice's wheelchair into the restroom and grabbing those rough brown paper towels to dry her tears. Birdie didn't tell JaNeela or the others how she felt. She kept her mouth shut and started avoiding them. She wasn't anything like Malala Yousafzai.

After that, Mama swore that none of her kids would ever have a phone.

Hennie still seemed keen about a website.

Birdie explained that all she needed for a website was a PayPal and a Go Daddy. A glaze fell over Hennie's eyes. It told Birdie that Hennie was overwhelmed. Hennie tapped the watch on her blouse with her index finger.

"We can talk about it some more later," she said. "It's going to be a long trip."

Emily, Katie, and Jenny all got identical texts from Sonia. "I'm making posters to bring. Which spelling do you like - 'Wimmin,' 'Womin,' or 'Womyn'?"

Emily stayed quiet. She'd never heard of anything like that. Weren't all those spellings just synonyms for 'lesbian'?

None of them knew what to reply except for Jenny.

"Sonia's using these terms now," Jenny said. "She doesn't like "woman" or "women" because they have 'man' or 'men' attached to them."

After a while, their phones dinged again. Sonia had looked up some word origins. She texted what she'd learned. "'Woman' comes from something like 'wifmann,' meaning 'wife of a man.'"

"Sonia doesn't like to be thought of as 'wife of a man,'" Jenny said. "Sonia says language is important."

Emily was confused. "Well, of course language is important, Jenny. How else would we speak if we didn't have language?"

Katie huffed, "I'm tired of all this politically correct stuff. It's like you can't even *talk* any more. You can't call a 'cripple' a 'cripple.' And don't get me started on those gender-neutral pronouns! Good grief!"

Emily hadn't been much of a student like Sonia. This whole language issue made her head spin. Still, Emily wondered, what did Sonia plan to do with the word 'fe-*male*'?

Now Alexandra Hall stepped to the microphone again. "Marchers," she said, "we'll make our last stop of the evening in another hour or so. I know your legs are getting stiff and you need a break. So until the next rest stop, I've got an activity for you."

Birdie was annoyed. Alexandra Hall had decided they were doing school again. Another crossword. Or a word search. That was school: an unending round of some kind of worksheet.

127

"The idea is to get to know each other even better." Her penciled eyebrows lifted in excitement, "What's interesting about you? What kind of work do you do? What about your family? Or where you're from?"

She feathered her angled black hair off her brow. "Each person on the end of a row moves up one row, introduces herself to the others in the new row, and you chat for a while."

Birdie sighed. It was going to be musical chairs. Just like kindergarten.

"I'll set my phone for 10 minutes. After 10 minutes, the end person moves up one again and gets to know a *new* row of people." Alexandra Hall clapped her tiny manicured hands, and her bangle bracelets jingled. "What do you think?"

Most of the women clapped. One of them shouted, "It's like speed dating. Only we wouldn't have to put up with any men!"

The bus burst into hoots and hollers. Even Hennie clapped. From behind her, Birdie could hear one of The Muses whistling. The kind of whistle boys do where they put their fingers between their front teeth.

"Great. You might want to get each other's contact information and photo, okay? So you can text me with memories and pictures after the march. I'll be sending them out on my blog."

Birdie whispered to Hennie. "A blog's like an essay on your website. You write what you're thinking about and people can read it. Like your thoughts on antiques. Or the popes."

Birdie loved laughing with Hennie. *Is this what it's like to have a grandmother?*

Lou got up like the other marchers on the ends of the rows. They stashed pocketbooks and blankets, lunch pouches and fanny packs, each moving up one row.

One of the Three Muses – the one Birdie had thought of as 'Fountain' - moved up and took Aunt Lou's seat. She introduced herself formally as "Emily Anne Messer," and Birdie recorded the contact information for her. Then she snapped a picture to add to her file as well.

Emily Messer's hair was fine, anchored by a claw to the top of her head. Loose wisps like spiderwebs fell across her cheeks and neck. Birdie wondered what it would feel like to have hair as thin as Emily's. She wanted to reach out and touch it, but she was pretty sure she shouldn't. Black girls were always having their hair touched by white girls: it was offensive.

Hennie and Birdie learned a lot about Emily Messer. She worked as a barista at a coffee shop called Higher Grounds.

"What's a 'barista,' dear?"

"A barista makes and serves different types of coffee. Lattes. Cappuccinos. Macchiatos." Birdie added coffee to the list of things Hennie didn't understand.

Mama and Lou always snorted at all those fancy coffees.

"They try to make you feel stupid with all those different names. Lattes. Expressos."

"It's *es*-pressos, Ronnie."

"Well, thank you, Miss Community College. You make my point."

Birdie thought Mama was jealous of Lou-Lou's two-year degree. Mama never understood why Lou got a college degree and then went to work at nonprofits. Lou earned less *with* a degree than Mama did *without*.

"Well, then, explain about those sizes, Louise. Tall. Grande. What's 'venti' anyway?

Aunt Lou said, "It's the next size after *grande* but smaller than *trenta*."

Mama frowned. "What's wrong with plain 'ol 'small,' 'medium,' and 'large,' Lou? And why in this world would anyone pay five bucks for a fifty-cent cup of coffee?"

Birdie thought Emily Messer was showing off about her job to impress Hennie. Birdie wasn't impressed. She knew you probably weren't a barista if you could get a better job.

Emily told them she graduated college but still lived in her parents' basement to save money. To pay off her college loans.

"But if I stay there too long," she said, "I'm going to get stuck there."

So it's possible to get stuck even after you've gone to college?

Emily and the other muses were meeting in Washington. They were hoping to get an apartment together in Philadelphia with Sonia, another college friend.

Alexandra Hall's timer went off. "Ten minutes are up. Time to move on, marchers."

The marchers groaned. They hadn't had enough time. Birdie supposed Miss Emily Fountain Head might have asked Hennie and her about themselves if they'd had more than ten minutes, but she doubted Emily would be much interested in Hennie's silver inkpot or Birdie's unfinished worksheets.

"We'll give you fifteen minutes next time. OK, ladies, let's move."

By now, Emily had moved a few rows up. Next to her, filling up the entire middle seat, was Babs Mildenhaus, a huge bear of a woman. Babs had to sit sideways to fit all of her body in the seat. Her hair was clipped so short she could have been mistaken for a man. Babs was wearing a tan vest that zipped up the front. It had lots of zippered pockets in it, too. Emily wondered what they held: Toenail clippers? A mini-flashlight? Beef jerky? Still, a vest like that beat hauling around a backpack. Or a Coach purse.

Babs Mildenhaus worked at the AAA in Independence, Missouri. She made working at a AAA sound fascinating. Babs bragged that Harry Truman had been a AAA salesman from Independence, Missouri, too. Before he became President.

But Babs was on the trip because she was mad. She'd won last year's fishing tournament at a state park in Kansas, catching the largest fish in the competition ever. That explained the vest. Emily guessed that some of her vest pockets would contain fishing flies, hooks, and dead worms.

But Babs hadn't been declared the winner because no woman had ever won before. Instead, the men created two separate trophies, one for men, the other for women. Babs was still fuming. "Gary Hotchkiss took away a trophy as big as mine, and his bass had been 5 ounces smaller. I'm still stinking mad."

Emily was astonished to learn that a fishing contest could rile you up like that. She wondered what you would call a female fisherman. A fish person? A fisher? A womyn who fished?

Babs was meeting a group called Athlete Allies. "One of the members is a woman soccer player. Another is a Muslim football player in Afghanistan." Emily thought that was one of the coolest things she had ever heard.

Alexandra Hall's phone went off. It was time to move again.

Before Emily moved on, Babs fished around in one of her vest pockets and handed her a handful of buttons. "Equality is a Team Sport," they read.

Emily liked Babs. Women's sports never got the attention they deserved. And she wondered why women's sports didn't have male cheerleaders.

Henrietta liked Amanda Raymond right away. She had a head full of loose brown curls that wiggled when she moved. She was full of confidence. She smiled a lot. Her teeth were so straight and white that Henrietta was sure the girl had worn braces. Amanda sported a teeny-tiny diamond on the left side of her nose. Normally Henrietta was frightened of piercings, but this one looked lovely on Amanda Raymond, a really nice young woman with the whole world before her, a young woman who, she hoped, had escaped the Jayhawks.

Birdie took her picture and typed in her information as Amanda announced that she was a "prosthetist."

Henrietta winced and wondered: "Did this lovely young woman just say 'prostitute'?"

Amanda laughed, reading Hennie's face. "That's what everyone thinks at first."

Amanda explained that a prosthetist designed and fitted people with artificial limbs. She had an engineering degree from Notre Dame and loved her work.

Henrietta remembered that someone famous once said that people had only two problems to solve in their life: love and work. She wondered how many women solved either one – or both – or none. She hoped Amanda Raymond was one of the lucky ones.

"Sometimes I fit people with missing limbs from a birth defect," Amanda Raymond said. "Like a little girl I'm working with now who was born with only one leg." Birdie wished Shanice had had a pretty young nurse like Amanda working with her instead of Nurse Axelrod. She mostly just gave Shanice the once-over and then filled out reports.

But most of Amanda's clients were wounded vets at the John J. Pershing Medical Center. It was somewhere here in Missouri.

"I listen to their heartbreaking stories about Iraq or Afghanistan, and I get great satisfaction out of fitting them with an artificial hand or foot." Birdie thought about Mama and how often she said, "I thank the Lord every day that I returned stateside with all four limbs."

"But there's a problem," Amanda said. Her curls had stopped bouncing. "After my listening and fitting, they feel entitled to touch my breasts. Or kiss my neck. Or grab me and hold me so tight I can smell the cigarettes on their breath."

Birdie's Mama had heard complaints like this from her girls at the plumbing company. Mama was the secretarial pool supervisor at Kingswood Plumbing: "You Flush It, We Rush It." Imelda was supposed to pick up coffee for Mr. Kingswood on her way to work every morning; for that privilege, he expected to be allowed to slide his hand down her back to cup her rear in thanks.

"I complain to my supervisor time after time," Amanda said, "but it does no good. He just shrugs and says I can quit if I don't like it. But I can't quit."

Hennie piped up. "Of *course* you can't quit, dear. Women have a lot on their plates. Alcoholic husbands, foreclosure threats, greedy payday lenders." She didn't add about parents who needed money to send their son to seminary.

Hennie reached for her rosary. Birdie wondered what she was praying about.

Birdie felt sorry for Amanda Raymond.

"Another time I complained, my boss said, 'So sue me!' That was the last time I said anything."

Hennie snapped to attention. "Now where were you going to get the time or money for a lawsuit, dear?" Her chin was sticking out and her lips were turned down.

'So sue me!' Did all bosses know a threat like that from a woman was an empty one? Mama jumped for joy when Mr. Obama signed a law that said bosses had to make sure they were paying their employees fairly. Mama knew her pool girls were paid unequally based on how much freedom they gave Mr. Kingswood to touch them. Over lunch. Under his desk. Around the water cooler.

When Mama stomped into his office with news about the law, Mr. Kingswood said the same thing: "So sue me!"

But Mama wasn't done. She couldn't afford to sue, but she had other ways of getting back. She ordered a cake and announced a company party. She invited everyone at the company: her secretarial pool, Mr. Kingswood, his accountants, his delivery guys, and some of the company's top customers. The cake said, "Congratulations, Lilly Ledbetter, on the Fair Pay Act!" Of course, all the guests assumed that Mr. Kingswood was following this law, and he didn't help them change their mind. But Birdie had often heard Mama say there was a number one rule about work: "Make Sure the Boss Knows You Ain't No Fool." Whenever she said this, Mama's chin stuck out and her lips turned down. Just like Hennie's.

"It helps so much," Amanda said, "to hear that someone else understands." She laid a soft hand on Hennie's arm and gave it a little pat. "I've got a son with epilepsy and a husband who left me when he couldn't handle it. I can't just quit."

When was it that Daddy left? Soon after I was born, right? And wasn't that the same time Mama found out there was something wrong with Shanice? Did the world contain other mamas and daddies like mine? Daddies who left, Mamas who stayed?

"I can't just quit."

Amanda Raymond's words triggered Henrietta's memories.

She remembered sitting at the kitchen table, the same table where her father cut out his shoe soles on weekdays and her family served Father Cochran the best breakfast they could afford on Sundays.

She remembered being frightened about what to do. Should she keep quiet? Tell her family? Would they believe her? Could she expect them to support her?

She had prayed over what to do. She had worried over it for days. Finally, after long talks with Sister Florinda, she had decided to tell them. To speak up. Surely an honest confession of fear could do no harm. She had finally convinced herself that silence – this time – would be wrong.

It was hard for her to raise her eyes to meet their gaze as she spoke about the Hershey's Kisses, the socks, the feather duster, the sensation on the backs of her knees. She never once lifted her eyes as she had stammered about how startled she had been, how uncomfortable she had felt, how frightened she now was, and how ready she was to quit.

When she had finished, the air in the kitchen was still, like the air right before a heavy rain.

"You can't just quit," her father thundered. "What about your brother's future?"

Henrietta had bit her lip so hard she tasted blood. She had been as startled and uncomfortable at her father's response as she had been at Father Cochran's behavior. Her father had simply scowled at her mother and barked, "Frances, go get your needle and thread. And lower the hem on the girl's school uniform. Now."

Lots of other marchers took seats after Amanda Raymond. Birdie took their pictures and recorded their names and numbers, their addresses and websites. Many of their stories surprised her. What surprised her even more was Hennie's reaction to them.

Lois Graves, for example, was an elevator inspector. She had mastered her job in just one year and applied for an upgraded certification program that her company sponsored. Birdie was surprised to learn that there were opportunities for advancement in elevators. Or that you could move up to wheelchair lift systems and after that escalators and then moving sidewalks.

But each time Lois applied for the limited number of spaces, men were always chosen. "They were either friends of my boss or company suck-ups or the sons of the CEO," Lois griped.

"Old boys' network," Hennie snapped. As Lois Graves moved on, Hennie whispered to Birdie. "There's no old boys' network tighter than the Catholic priesthood."

Can old boys' networks also mean the leadership at Frederick Douglass Junior High? Or the folks in charge of scholarships at Wichita Community College? Or Mama's boss at Kingswood Plumbing Company? Or me – the little sister - being full-time caretaker for Shanice instead of my bigger, older brothers?

Emily moved up a row. The woman in the far seat, next to the window, introduced herself as Belinda Gaspard, a mother of five from Kenton, Missouri. She taught AP Biology in high school. Emily never took AP Biology; she was just a mediocre student. All she remembered about high school biology was that report she had to do on insects. Emily chose the praying mantis. She had forgotten to label its body parts in the drawing she made, so she only got a "C."

Belinda Gaspard won a Teacher of the Year award. Three years later, she was replaced by a football coach the school wanted to hire. "He didn't even know how to focus a microscope."

The story reminded her of her high school English teacher. He didn't know the difference between "affect" and "effect" or whether you used "it's" or "its." He'd been hired to coach basketball.

"Male privilege," the woman in the middle grunted.

"Ursula Highman," the woman said to Henrietta and Birdie. The woman had the handshake and eye contact of someone who was used to greeting people. Her gray hair was cropped, and she was wearing a long, flowing peasant skirt under a wrinkled tunic. A silver chalice hung around her neck by a simple black cord.

Ursula Highman introduced herself as a Unitarian Universalist minister. Henrietta was perplexed: she had never heard of that denomination; she had never met a female minister.

Ursula had no trouble talking. Or plunging into a sensitive subject. "I won't insult you by asking if you have children," she said to Henrietta. "That's what everyone wants to know when they meet a woman." Henrietta detected a burr of irritation in Ursula's voice. But she was intrigued: what the woman said was true.

"Perhaps I became a minister to counter that assumption. Children aren't the only way to send love into the world, are they? The worst tradition on Earth is Mother's Day, don't you think?"

Henrietta blinked. She hadn't thought of Mother's Day for decades. Her mother had been gone a long time.

"Mother's Day implies that the only way to show love is to give birth."

Henrietta found Ursula's irreverence both shocking and comforting. Children: The only way to show love. Henrietta had a pack of Old Maid cards in the toy section of the shop. Fifi Fluff. Tumbledown Tess. She hated what the cards implied about her. Yes, Mother's Day was a tradition that made her feel left out. The flowers.

The candy. The paeans to motherhood. She hadn't had particularly warm feelings for her own mother. Sister Florinda had been a kind of mother-substitute for which she had been eternally grateful. Surely, like Ursula said, there were lots of ways to "mother." There were aunts, sisters, friends, neighbors, co-workers, knitting clubs, mentors, altar guild ladies.

"I see you're Catholic," Ursula said, pointing to her rosary. "Knowing a person's religion tells you a lot about them. I loved studying world religions at seminary," Ursula said.

Henrietta had never met a woman who had studied at a seminary.

"Religion's the most fascinating subject in the world. Islam. Confucianism. Bahai. Zoroastrianism. Hinduism."

Henrietta hadn't heard of some of these religions.

"I love the Jewish traditions and the way they're centered around family," Ursula continued. "I love the Muslim tradition of praying five times a day. It's a way of centering yourself, don't you think?"

Henrietta didn't know what to think, but she couldn't find anything wrong with "centering."

"And I adore the way Catholics have all those patron saints that you can pray to for different reasons. Like there's that one you can pray to when you've lost something."

"St. Anthony," Henrietta replied. She didn't share the mantra she had learned as a child when she had lost a doll, a sock, or a plastic decoder ring from a cereal box. "Dear St. Anthony, please come around. My doll is lost and it cannot be found." When the something lost was found, it had helped her believe the church was magic.

"But I'm especially intrigued by the Catholic reverence for Mary."

Henrietta felt a swish of pride. This woman was *especially* intrigued by something about her faith. Henrietta wanted to ask about her curious reverence, but she held her tongue. Ursula, she had discovered, had a way of talking without being prompted.

"It's the one world religion that holds deep reverence for a woman at its core. There's kind of a Mary-worship at the heart of Catholicism, right?"

Henrietta nodded, but she felt it might have been a trick question.

"But isn't that confusing?" Ursula asked. "The church worships a woman but then won't let them be priests or make choices about their own childbearing. There are volumes about the search for the historical Jesus, but little about the historical Mary. It's confusing. And unjust."

Henrietta didn't admit that, once she thought about it, she agreed it might be confusing to her, too. And maybe a smidgen unjust as well. It was like her church had put Mary at the center of things with a halo around her head. And then walked off and ignored her.

"I wrote a Christmas Eve sermon about it once. It contained the usual elements. The star in the East. The shepherds. The wise men. The stable. The lowing cattle. But the Christmas story always outraged me. My sermon spoke to that outrage."

Henrietta was shocked. The Christmas story, she felt, was the most beautiful story in the world. There was no better feeling than hearing it recited at Midnight Mass year after year. There wasn't a single thing outrageous about it.

"Think about it," Ursula went on. "Mary, on Christmas night, was doing what women have always done: laboring in the background. Women know sweat shops and dirty diapers. They mend the world's skinned knees and broken hearts. They educate the world's children. They know what it is to nurse a loved one with everything from a runny nose to terminal cancer without pay or Social Security benefits. They run every last charitable effort in the world from the local church to the International Red Cross. They are the wind beneath the wings of most of the men and children of the world. Here's the irony: Women, like Mary, are as ubiquitous as the air yet somehow just as invisible."

Henrietta detected that double-sided coin of anger and sadness welling up.

Alexandra Hall's phone dinged. It was time for Ursula Highman to move on.

"I suppose that's why I'm on this trip," Ursula said, smoothing her skirt. "If women want to be seen, they have to fight." When she said the word "fight," she gave it her fist.

As she rose, she pressed her palms together in a prayer position. She bowed at Henrietta and Birdie. "Namaste," she said.

Henrietta noticed that, on leaving, Ursula had shared both a fist and a prayer.

As she moved on, Ursula's peasant skirt swished, leaving Henrietta a trail of anger and sadness in her wake. She had somehow spent her own life laboring in the background. She'd been ever-present but invisible as air.

"What does 'Na-mas-tay' mean, Hennie?"

"I'm not really sure exactly. I think it's a kind of prayer. Why don't you look it up in your phone?"

Birdie Googled the word. She couldn't find it.

Hennie said, "I think it's spelled with an 'e' on the end, not a 'y.'"

"Oh, I got it." Birdie read the definition. "It's a greeting that means 'I bow to you.' You're supposed to put your palms together level with your heart and bow your head while saying it. It's a deep form of respect."

"Oh, my," Hennie said. "I like that."

Birdie wondered how the world might change if everybody gave everybody else a deep form of respect.

The minister lady also got Birdie thinking about Mother's Day. Shanice had especially loved Mother's Day. She would fold paper into cards and draw hearts on them with her good hand. Beanie and Twanny and Birdie would clean the house for Mama and make lunch for her. Grilled cheese and tomato soup, with the bread nice and brown and shiny with butter and the cheese all gooey. But Mama always insisted that Aunt Lou come for lunch, too. "An aunt can be the best kind of mother," Mama said. Mama seemed to understand something the minister lady understood, too.

As Emily moved from row to row, she was astonished at the thousands of things in the world to be interested in. Folk dancing. Jewelry making. Pilates. Calligraphy. Mental health. Some of the women were even creating businesses around their interests. They were eager to show her their Twitter accounts and their Facebook pages.

She began to think about career possibilities: beautician, project manager, pharmacist, mortician, mechanic, manicurist. She was astonished that so many of these women encouraged her to explore new work. They weren't that impressed by fancy coffees.

"What do you love?" one of them asked.

Emily wasn't sure. That was the problem. She was unsure about so many things.

"Think about it," said another. "There must be something that interests you, that might point a way forward for you."

Emily was afraid to say it. Finally, she swallowed her fear and said, "Bravo. He's my terrier. He's the one thing I really love."

"Brilliant!" affirmed another stranger. "That's a starting point. You love your dog. Is there a career possibility in that? Veterinary medicine? Vet tech? Dog groomer?"

Emily was surprised to feel her heart lift at these possibilities. She knew of a vet tech program at the community college in Topeka. Might it be possible to find work that involved animals?

She pictured Bravo's face: the tilted ears, the adoring eyes, the wagging tail. Yes, that was what she loved. Could that be a place to start?

Birdie was surprised that each woman who took Lou-Lou's seat seemed interested in her. They said things like "Oh, you're so young" or "How nice for a young girl to come on a trip like this" or "What a blessing our young people care so much about our world." Birdie felt a kinship with Mr. Kingswood, letting them think only good things.

Birdie was also surprised at how many ladies seemed interested in hearing about Oldham's Antiques. When Henrietta described her antiques, they became curious. About her great grandmother's brass tea kettle. About the log cabin quilt made by a group of pioneer woman in Winstead, Oklahoma. About the Tiffany lamp, the nesting dolls, the silver servers. They didn't seem to sense that her shop was on its last legs. Nearly every woman had a question about what Depression glassware was worth and seemed to have a set somewhere in their basement. They told Hennie she should be the host of "Antiques Roadshow." Birdie had no idea what that was, but it was something that made Hennie smile quietly. Maybe was akin to how Birdie felt when she heard herself called "mighty smart."

A lady from Cape Girardeau asked Hennie if she handled music boxes. "I have a nice little collection of them passed down by my great aunt. Would you like to see?"

Henrietta scanned the pictures in the lady's phone. She nodded her appreciation. "There's a brisk market for collectors, but I don't specialize in them. I usually refer sellers to a specialty dealer. Would you like a few names?"

The lady copied Hennie's suggestions into her phone. She thanked her when she moved on. Birdie whispered to Hennie that she could load pictures of her antiques onto her website just like the lady from Cape Girardeau with her music boxes. A flame like a suddenly struck match lit Hennie's eyes.

An elderly marcher from Alton asked, "Would you be interested in buying my Little Golden Books? I have *The Poky Little Puppy* and *A Day on the Farm*. My kids are all grown, and my grandkids are in high school."

"Yes. I'd be interested, dear. Definitely. I love getting those, especially if they're in good condition. There's steady interest from grandmothers."

What kind of grandmother would Hennie have been? Would she sit a grandchild on her lap to read Little Golden Books? Would they bake oatmeal cookies after that? Would she help with her weekly spelling list?

Hennie told a lady from Shawnee Mission about her brass spittoons. "I'm glad I didn't live in the 19th century," Hennie chuckled, the chuckles like clucks. "There was spit flying everywhere. Into the fireplaces. On the streetcars. In the halls of Congress. On ladies' hems. Spittoons were as common as plastic bags now."

Birdie wondered if Beanie would have passed 8th grade history if he could have thought about it this way.

"All right, marchers," Alexandra Hall squawked over the microphone. "Just a couple more interviews. We're about ready for a rest stop."

Sheila Roberts plopped down beside Henrietta. She was an oversized woman with a halo of frizzy blonde hair stiffened with hair spray. She commented straight off on the upside-down watch on Hennie's blouse.

"At first I thought it was a jeweled art-deco wedding pin," Sheila Roberts said. "Like something out of *The Great Gatsby*. But I think it's one of those Votes for Women watches. Am I right?"

The gray braid on the top of Hennie's head wiggled. "Yes! How did you know?"

"I'm a dealer in Larned, Kansas. Grandma's Attic. Here's my card."

"Oldham's Antiques. Soros, Kansas."

Henrietta didn't have a card.

Sheila Roberts and Hennie chattered over the watch. They bent their heads together, admiring the stones. The purple ones were amethysts, the white ones were diamonds, the yellow ones were citrines. Birdie learned that purple, gold, and white were the colors of the suffragettes. The watches were made in a limited edition. Only leaders of the movement got them. Somebody named Alice Paul. Somebody named Lucy Burns. Some others whose names she didn't catch.

Hennie explained that the watch was a lucky find. She got it from a friend of her Aunt Rita at an estate sale. Hennie told Sheila that she never goes without it, and it still worked.

"May I take a picture of it?"

Sheila Roberts pulled out a phone like Aunt Lou's and enlarged the frame so that the watch face filled it. After the button clicked, she asked Hennie if she'd like her to send a text of it.

Hennie looked confused.

"You can send it to me," Birdie said, and she gave Sheila Roberts Lou's contact information. In an instant, the picture of Hennie's watch appeared in her messages app. Birdie showed it to Hennie.

"My," Hennie exclaimed, as if a rabbit had been pulled out of a hat.

"Would you mind if I wrote a blog post about the watch? We dealers know that old things have a history that goes beyond the object itself."

Birdie wasn't sure, but she thought Hennie understood a little bit about blog posts and websites now.

"Of course, not," Hennie said. "I'd be honored, Sheila. But the watch is not for sale, of course."

"I completely understand," Sheila said. "I'm so glad we've met. You must come to Larned this February. In just a few weeks we have the annual Antiques and Collectibles Show. People come from all over for it."

Hennie hesitated.

"You could stay with me. I've got a guest bedroom."

Hennie smiled. "Thank you for the invitation. I've got a doctor's visit when I get home, but perhaps I can."

Perhaps I can. Was that something like not im-possible?

Before she left, Birdie asked Sheila Roberts for a second card. She recorded her information into Lou-Lou's phone and slipped the card into her backpack.

After Sheila Roberts moved on, Hennie whispered to Birdie. "Henry goes to an annual convention of priests in cities all over the world, Birdie. Houston, Buenos Aires, Seattle, Dublin. Do you think I should venture to Larned, Kansas?"

"Of course!" Birdie said. "You could reschedule the doctor, and I could even watch the shop for you. Yes, I think you should add a trip to Larned to your bucket list! And after that you might visit the Kansas City Museum of Toys and Miniatures with Miss Pauline."

Hennie looked flustered. Like a hen trying to decide whether to fluff her nest front to back or back to front.

Emily had engaged in the most interesting conversations. Vaginal deodorants. Doulas. Menopause. Pornography. When a conversation in one row turned to period shaming, Nancy-Something, the woman sitting by the window, reminded her of what The Candidate had said about that female journalist. How she'd been "bleeding from her whatever."

The woman in the middle seat, Evelyn-Somebody, said, "Yep. If we get emotional, people blame it on our periods. We even do that to ourselves. It's a way of dismissing whatever we're upset about."

Nancy-Something agreed. "'No, she's not angry,' they say. 'She's just on the rag.'"

Evelyn-Somebody said, "And explain this one to me. Viagra isn't taxed, but tampons are."

Emily punched some buttons on her phone. "It says here that a female uses nearly 10,000 tampons in her lifetime." She held up the phone so that Something and Somebody could see it.

Emily was surprised at the conclusion she herself had drawn. "That means we get taxed for the privilege of bleeding each month."

Something and Somebody nodded in agreement.

Emily felt a tingle of pride.

The last woman who sat next to Henrietta was a member of an animal rights group. Best Buddies Animal Coalition. Cecile Spyer said there were hundreds of these groups being represented at the march. Cecile worked as a veterinary technician in Branson. She noticed Henrietta's knitting. "Do you ever knit with dog fur? I've got piles of it at the vets. Would you be interested in getting some? I can mail it to you weekly."

Hennie looked over at Birdie. They were both stifling laughs, relieved when Alexandra Hall blew into her microphone. "That's it, ladies. We're approaching Terre Haute and our final rest stop for the evening. About twenty minutes or so."

The women got up and moved into the aisle, on the move a final time. Henrietta and Birdie had finally burst out laughing.

"I could knit scarves out of dog fur," Hennie said.

"Yes," Birdie said. "You could call them 'Arf Scarfs.'"

Aunt Lou returned to her seat. "I met some terrific women," she told Birdie and Hennie. "So many of them have family members or friends with disabilities. I gave them our ADAPT cards and asked them to join our protest tomorrow. I think some of them will."

Aunt Lou was amazing. She could get people to sign up for things in the blink of an eye.

"But there were a few unusual women, too," Aunt Lou said, her eyebrows lifting. "One was an artist who makes tampon art. She showed me pictures on her phone. It was actually pretty interesting."

Hennie and Birdie looked at each other and started to giggle.

Then they told Lou-Lou about the lady who wanted to send Hennie dog fur. They started arf-arfing and bow-wowing. Lou-Lou joined in with some yip-yipping, and then they were all howling with laughter.

Emily couldn't stop talking after she returned to her seat. Katie and Jenny were curious about everything she had heard.

"Well, the most interesting conversation was the one about a woman starting a business selling female body enhancements. Fake boobs. Collagen fillers. Butt pads."

Jenny scoffed. "Why would anyone want those? Besides the Kardashians, I mean."

Emily stayed quiet.

Then Katie said, "I doubt Kim uses butt pads," Katie said. "Her natural ones are big enough."

The girls tittered.

After that, Emily, Katie, and Jenny were quiet again.

Emily felt conflicted: she had been just a tiny bit interested in the fake boobs.

It was getting darker. The tiny overhead lights had been switched on. Lou was reading. Hennie was knitting. Birdie was writing a blog post for Hennie about her watch.

She scrolled to the picture of Hennie's watch and studied the jewels. White. Yellow. Purple. Google explained about the colors. White was the color of the suffragettes and stood for purity; the diamonds represented that. The purple amethysts circling the watch face represented loyalty. The yellow citrines stood for Kansas sunflowers. *Why didn't I know about my own state flower? Or that Elizabeth Cady Stanton and Susan B. Anthony adopted it for their suffrage campaign way back in 1867?*

Birdie found a picture of Hennie's watch on an antique jewelry site. Sure enough, the watch was a limited edition, awarded to a few suffragette leaders like Alice Paul and Lucy Burns. Alice was a Quaker. Lucy was her friend.

Birdie read her blogpost-in-progress to Hennie. Hennie listened while her needles clacked. "Alice Paul was jailed for her protest work. In jail, she organized a hunger strike. Eventually she was force-fed by the authorities."

Birdie turned to Hennie. "Jailed? Force-fed? Just because she wanted to vote?"

Hennie nodded and said it was important to know about women's struggles across history. It helped you identify with your own.

"When we get back, I'll show you some of my collection. I've got a photo from 1917 that shows a group of women sewing a suffragette flag. I've got a box of suffrage postcards. I've got a marble cast of Alice Paul in my shop. Wouldn't sell that for anything."

Birdie felt like she'd been invited into her grandmother's attic. "I'd like that," she said.

Birdie continued reading. "Alice authored the Equal Rights Amendment in 1923." "

"It hasn't been adopted yet, Birdie."

"You mean not even *now?*"

Hennie nodded. "Change takes a long time, Birdie."

Birdie thought about change and the long time it took. For women. For Blacks. For people like Shanice.

Aunt Lou put down her book.

Birdie came to the part in her blogpost about the colors in Hennie's watch. She wondered if Lou-Lou knew about the Kansas sunflower. She'd saved pictures of other kinds of Votes for Women accessories onto the camera roll. Jailed for Freedom pins. Votes for Women necklaces, bracelets, brooches. Stamp pins. Suffrage earrings. Sunflower necklaces. Sashes, gold pins, yellow roses.

After Birdie finished reading the blogpost, Lou-Lou leaned over and asked, "Don't you have to write a descriptive paragraph for Mrs. Opie?"

Birdie didn't know her aunt had been listening.

"I guess so." Birdie knew "I guess so" wasn't the same as "yes."

Birdie wondered if Lou and Mrs. Opie had been talking about her behind her back. If Aunt Lou know about the descriptive paragraph, she probably knew about the career exploration project, too. And also that it was not *im*-possible for her to fail eighth grade.

Birdie was angry. She didn't like it that Lou might have been talking about her with her teacher. Even though they were friends.

Lou-Lou said, "Can't you use that? What you wrote there? The blog post? For your descriptive paragraph?"

Birdie hadn't thought of that. Lou had thought of something Birdie hadn't. She hated admitting her aunt had a good idea about her own schoolwork.

"I guess so."

Still, Birdie felt a quiet relief that one of her assignments might be finished.

"But I haven't got a very good ending. Or a title."

"Hmmm," Hennie said. "An ending is kind of a summary. A final point. Closure, right?"

"Yes." *That word again.*

"So what, after all is said and done, were you trying to say? About this old watch of mine?"

Birdie thought back to what Sheila Roberts had said about old things. How they had a history, a history bigger than the thing itself.

Birdie wrote her summary.

"An old watch can have a history bigger than the watch itself," she read. "What do you two think?"

Aunt Lou piped up first. "Doesn't matter what *we* think, Birdie. What do *you* think?"

Hennie stayed quiet.

Birdie liked her summary, but she didn't say so.

Now she just needed a title.

Birdie thought about watches and time. *Watch. Watches. Watch out. Watch your step. Watch me. Time. Marking time. Wasting time. Keeping time. Time out. Time line. What would make the best title?*

Suddenly a title came to her. "A Time Piece."

She liked it. But she didn't share it for approval. She hugged it to herself.

The pussy hats were an easy project; she should be finished by morning. While it was dark, Henrietta pulled out her special project, the one she made sure to bring on the trip, the one with the double-pointed needles and the softest possible yarn. The project made her think of St. Agatha, the patron saint of breast cancer patients. And whether or not it was worth praying to her.

They pulled into a rest stop somewhere outside of Terre Haute, Indiana. It looked like they were out in the middle of nowhere with only corn stalks for company. Birdie wondered if there was anything in Indiana besides corn fields.

Tall steel lamps bent their heads like swans. Their light loomed ghostly in the darkness. The glass windows of the rest stop looked even more dirty in the half-light. Birdie snapped a picture, wondering what kind of image this light would make.

There were only a few other buses this time. Sleepy-eyed marchers were too tired to make stops at the gift shop or pick up snacks. Hennie didn't ask Birdie to follow her into the restroom stall; she just did.

After they were back on the bus, Alexandra Hall made an announcement. "We're not far from Indianapolis, marchers. After that, we'll pass through Columbus, Ohio, and then West Virginia. Khalid wants to make time overnight. Get some rest. You'll be marching your legs off tomorrow. Good night, marchers."

Khalid started up the engine. "In morning. Wake up DC. Ready to march." The marchers were too tired to clap. Most of the overhead lights had been turned off. Only a few of them winked overhead like fireflies. The darkness and the rocking of the bus put most of the marchers to sleep.

Birdie plugged her phone into the overhead charger: there would be lots of pictures to take tomorrow. Soon Birdie was dreaming.

There is a big picnic table. A vase of sunflowers sits in the middle. The table is heaped with food. Lou-Lou's fried chicken and no-nut brownies. Pauline Frazier's blueberry muffins. It's not Thanksgiving, but there's corn pudding in Grandma Franklin's casserole dish on the table, too.

The skies are blue and filled with fluffy white clouds. Lots of women are seated around the table. Lou-Lou and Hennie and Alice Paul and Malala. Imelda from Kingswood Plumbing. The Three Muses.

Mama is missing.

Shanice is in her wheelchair at the end of the table, but she looks older. Her hair has gray at the temples, and a few wrinkles drape her neck like a necklace. A cake like the ones you can get ready-made at Hy-Vee sits in front of her. The white cake has purple and gold lettering. It says, "Happy 59th Birthday, Shanice."

Suddenly a group of men swoop in from the clouds. Mr. Kingswood. Vets from Amanda Raymond's VA. Bobby Showalter. They dive in and start slicing up Shanice's cake, feeding each other pieces the way brides and grooms do at a wedding. There is no cake left over for the women.

The women scatter. Birdie is pushing Shanice away from the men, breathing hard as she struggles to escape, but the wheelchair slows her down.

Suddenly Mama appears out of nowhere. She is wearing her Wizard of Oz t-shirt and her Army camouflage pants. She slashes at the men with Grandpa Franklin's carving set, and now they scatter, too.

Birdie picks up Shanice, who is gripping her neck, and she brings her to Mama.

Mama smothers her with kisses.

Birdie woke up in a cold sweat. It was pitch-black outside and freezing on the bus. She unzipped her backpack and covered her shoulders with Shanice's purple shawl.

Hennie tapped her arm. She had pulled something from her tote bag. She handed Birdie a pair of socks.

"Put these on, dear. I knit a few pairs for the trip. They're alpaca. It's even warmer than wool."

The gesture seemed to Birdie like something a grandmother would do.

She allowed the socks to warm her.

Then she fell back to sleep.

Henrietta's fingers moved through the yarn in her hands. The repetitive stitches soothed her. Soon she was dozing.

In her dreamscape she is casting on rows of stitches, neat and yellow as cornfields. Under her flying fingers, the rows blossom into ripe ears of sweet corn, August-ready for picking. There are three of them walking among the rows, taking long strides. Her father is at the front, her brother Henry next, then her mother. Henrietta, in her blue plaid school uniform, is at the end of the line, running to keep up, but they don't see her. They begin to pick corn, and soon their arms are heavy with ears of ripe corn. Henrietta's arms are empty.

Suddenly a silver bus appears in the middle of the field. Henrietta's family disappears.

A line of women waits to board the bus.

As Henrietta approaches, the women turn to look at her, and suddenly the women have faces: Elizabeth and Susan B., Harriet and Sojourner, Ida B. and Rosa. They seem to recognize her.

At the door to the bus is Sister Florinda, a clipboard in hand. Recognizing Henrietta, she raises her hand, waving Henrietta to the front of the line. When Henrietta draws near, Sister Florinda makes the sign of the cross and blesses her.

'Namaste,' Henrietta says in reply, and then she begins to climb the steps.

It was dark outside. The bus swayed rhythmically, side to side, soothing Emily into sleep.

In Emily's dream, she sees the coffee shop transformed. Instead of the steaming of espresso machines and the whirring of blenders, the shop is filled with the sounds of dogs: barking, woofing, yapping, baying, howling. The storage room and the supply closet and the restrooms are now separate chambers in which dogs are being bathed, dried, and groomed. A karaoke machine is blasting music: Three Dog Night, Snoop Doggy Dog, Sick Puppies. Hanging on a coatrack are leashes made out of braided ropes of brassieres. The EE-cup leashes are for the Dobermans; the C-cup leashes are for the beagles; the AA-cup leashes are for the chihuahuas.

Emily enters the special room set off for pedicures. Bravo is on the table in front of her, Velcro straps across his paws to hold him still. Emily begins painting his toenails in primary colors: blue and yellow and red.

Suddenly, just like on CNN, a banner announcing 'Breaking News' appears. Everything explodes, and everything in the shop goes flying: the bottles of nail polish, the dog cages, the grooming implements. Emily is being hurled across the globe, searching desperately for Bravo in other places that are exploding, too. Places like Atlanta, Paris, Columbine, London, Aurora, Boston, New York.

When she finally finds him, wandering alone in a wintry field somewhere in the Midwest, she snuggles into his curly fur and fingers his velvet ears, weeping with gratitude. But when she looks into Bravo's face, superimposed on it is the face of the guy from the Lucky Duck who has never texted her back.

Emily woke up frightened and shivering.

Birdie tried to stretch her legs, but the metal footrest wouldn't budge. Her long legs ached like they did when she was a child and Mama called them "growing pains." She wiggled her toes, grateful for the warmth of Hennie's socks. Birdie rubbed her feet and looked over at Hennie, who had just put down her needles. Three little bundles that looked like big pink eggs nested in her lap.

"Good morning, little bird," Hennie said, the words sounding like peeps. "How did you sleep?"

"I slept, but my body's stiff as a board. Thank you for the socks. I could have froze to death."

"Good. Nothing worse than cold feet. And your thick purple shawl warmed your shoulders." Birdie didn't mention that she had a pain stretching from behind her ear to her shoulder blades, despite the shawl. Hennie reached over to pat the shawl. "It's nicely made."

"Thank you. It was Shanice's. Her teacher made it for her."

Birdie thought about Shanice. How she wore the shawl all the time. Even when it was hot.

"What about you?"

"Oh, I just dozed off and on. When you get to be my age, cat naps count as sleep. Besides, I got something done."

Hennie held up three pink hats with kitten ears. "Do you think they'll like them?"

Birdie glanced behind at the Three Muses, leaning into each other, sound asleep. Ocean Wave's wave was sliding to the opposite side of her forehead. Fountain's fountain was hanging limply by its claw. Waterfall's waterfall fell at an angle like blowing sheets of rain, and her open mouth was snoring.

"Here, try one on, Birdie Jackson."

The yarn was soft under her fingers. She liked that it was pink. Pink was feminine. It was a color women could claim as their own. She poked her fingers up under the two cat ears, looked over at Hennie, and smiled. Hennie was smiling back. Birdie stretched the base of the hat over her headband and across her forehead and ears, then centered the cat ears at the crown. It was a perfect fit.

"One size fits all, Birdie. You look good in it."

Hennie tapped her watch face. "Think about it, Birdie. One day your hat might wind up in a museum. Or in a store like mine."

Birdie reached for Lou's phone. "Can you take a picture for me, Hennie?"

Birdie showed Hennie how to frame her face and push the white button.

Then they both hovered over the image.

Birdie liked what she saw. She was herself, but she was someone else, too. Someone who was part of something larger. Someone who was not just Birdie Jackson from Soros, Kansas. The hat made her feel like she wasn't exactly a girl any more. That she was someone to be reckoned with. A girl to be noticed. In a good way.

"I'll make a hat just for you, Birdie. On the way back. Better yet, you'll learn to knit one for yourself."

Has she forgotten my fumblefingers? Or is that what grandmas do – keep their faith in you while they watch you struggle?

Emily stirred and fumbled for her phone. Twitter told her that the march had already started in Japan and New Zealand and Australia. She watched a live-stream from Tokyo, little girls holding up signs in Japanese.

Emily gazed out the window at the streaks of sunrise on the horizon. The gauzy pink-and-blue cotton-candy clouds promised a day of carnival. Emily felt her heart racing and a shiver of excitement she hadn't felt for months. Could we finally be here?

Birdie watched the marchers begin to awake. Like her, they had bedheads, dry mouths, aching limbs. One by one they stretched or fluffed a pillow or studied their tired faces in mirrors. A few opened packages of peanut butter crackers or granola bars. Birdie checked her phone. It was 6:10 a.m.

Khalid switched on the overhead light, and the marchers squinted against the sudden brightness. It was like coming out of a dark movie theater into the bright light of day.

While the bus glided over another bridge, Khalid announced, "Lady, lady. We almost here now. Washington, D.C. Nation capital."

Suddenly the quiet bus burst into loud cheers, and the ladies roused themselves in earnest.

Birdie gazed out the window. Even this early in the morning, the streets were jammed with cars, buses, trucks. On bridges and overpasses, tunnels and one-way streets, every vehicle had slowed. They reminded Birdie of clogged arteries struggling towards a heart. All the traffic was headed *into* Washington; only a few vehicles were heading *out*.

The Three Muses had begun to stir. Birdie had listened carefully to their conversations off and on in the darkness while she dozed in and out of sleep, signs for Columbus, Wheeling, Morgantown, flashing across the window like deer tails in headlamps.

The whisperings reminded her of her late-night gossiping with Destinee and Ai'esha and JaNeela behind the YMCA or in the woods behind the school. Before JaNeela did what she did to Shanice.

Their conversation eventually turned to boys.

Katie, the Waterfall, was still with Marc, her old boyfriend from college. She was afraid he was bored with her after so many years, so she had started doing things in bed with him that she didn't really like. Just to keep him interested. Even so, she was pretty sure Marc was cheating on her.

Jenny, the Ocean Wave, hadn't met anyone since college. She'd been on Match and Tinder, even setting a goal for herself, vowing to go on a coffee date every week for an entire year; then she had changed her vow to once a month; now she had given up entirely.

"What about you, Emily?" Katie asked.

When she explained about the guy at the karaoke bar in Soros, they burst out laughing at his name.

Behind her, The Muses were standing up to stretch. They were rubbing each other's shoulders, massaging each other's backs. Birdie wondered what it would be like to have friends like that, friends who massaged each other's backs, friends who made plans with each other to change their nowhere lives.

Hennie raised her arms as high as she could and waved three knit caps around. The Muses screeched like little girl campers whose cabins had been invaded by the boys.

Hennie was too stiff to move, but Birdie stood up and turned around to watch The Muses put them on.

Birdie pulled out the camera and asked them to put their heads together. In the picture, the hats made it impossible to see the waterfall or the ocean wave or the fountain. The Muses didn't look so individual and separate. They looked like women meant to be part of a more serious group. Not buddies or pals or partiers at college any more. Something bigger than themselves. *Comrades?*

Emily was grateful for the distraction of the hats. She'd been embarrassed the night before when they'd been talking about boyfriends. They had asked her who she'd been seeing. She didn't want to confess that her life was empty. She wasn't even sure she *liked* men.

"There's a guy at the karaoke bar in Soros who's interested," Emily said. "We've been texting."

Katie asked, "Could you really find a decent boyfriend at a karaoke bar? In Soros?"

"Did you really think that texting with a guy meant he was serious?" Jenny followed.

"What's his name?"

"Donnie," Emily said.

The girls exploded into laughter, holding their sides.

"Donnie?"

"As in full name 'Donald'?"

"Donnie?"

"How *could* you, Emily? Not *now?*"

Emily flushed red. She hadn't made the connection.

The Muses, wearing Hennie's hats, were squealing over Birdie's picture and begging her to text it to them.

Suddenly they were scampering into the aisle of the bus, striking yoga poses in their pink hats.

Waterfall was on her stomach. She was reaching behind herself and grabbing her feet at the ankles, rocking her body back and forth.

"I bet that feels good on her shoulders," Birdie said.

Fountain had her legs tucked under her, feet pointing backward, knees pointing forward. She had hunched her body over her knees and stretched her arms forward. Her fountain had flipped over her crown and onto the floor.

"I bet that feels good on her back," Hennie said.

Ocean Wave was sitting upright, the soles of her feet together, her knees falling straight to the floor. She was making little bouncing movements with her knees.

"I bet that feels good on her hips," Aunt Louise said. The Muses' squeals had awakened her.

Suddenly the busful of marchers was fully awake, swivelling their heads or standing to watch The Muses. Then they began to point and shriek. "I want one!" "Where'd you get that?" "Did you use a pattern?"

The Muses got up from the floor and waved their hats in Hennie's direction. "That lady there," Fountain said. "She made them."

"While we were sleeping," Ocean Wave added.

Now the marchers were filling the aisle, heading Hennie's way. Each one of them wanted her to take an order for hats. For her sister. For her granddaughters. In memory of her mother. For her book club. For herself.

Hennie was overwhelmed. But delighted. Her cloudy blue eyes were wet and blinking. Birdie was taking orders on Lou-Lou's phone and was having trouble keeping up.

The microphone squawked. Alexandra Hall had stepped up again. "Good morning, marchers. We'll be there soon. That means coffee."

The marchers cheered.

"But Khalid's asked us to clear the aisles. It's a safety precaution. Still, before we do, I'd like to ask the little lady in the back who made those hats to stand up and introduce herself."

Hennie realized that she was "the little lady in the back."

Birdie braced Hennie's arm, and she stood with difficulty. She didn't introduce herself. She just gave a little wave with a few fingers.

Alexandra Hall took over. "It looks like your hats are making quite a stir. Can you tell us how we might contact you for orders?"

Aunt Lou motioned for Birdie to stand up. "Birdie, get up and give them my phone number."

Birdie was reluctant to stand. She wasn't anything like Rosalie Helen Randolph, whose pride let her stand to her full height.

"Birdie! Stand up!" Aunt Lou wasn't kidding.

Birdie stood. She gave them Hennie's name and Lou-Lou's phone number. All around her, marchers were busily taking them down on notepads, phones, napkins, scraps of paper. Birdie noticed that it wasn't as hard to stand up in front of a group when you were representing someone else.

The three young woman from the row behind us began to chant. "Pussy! Pussy! Pussy!"

The marchers hooted and hollered, then took up the cheer.

Louise stood up in her seat and turned around, waving her hands like a choir director, directing the marchers in the back to cheer. *"Pussy! Pussy! Pussy!"*

Birdie switched her camera to the video function. She began panning the ladies slowly, capturing the raised fists, the open mouths, the bouncing bodies shouting, "Pussy! Pussy! Pussy!"

The Muses returned to their row. They saw that the only one on the bus not chanting was Hennie.

"Come on, Miss Hennie," Ocean Wave said, kneeling next to their row. "Say it. Pussy. *Pussy.*"

Hennie was swallowing hard. Like something in her throat was an anchor, weighing down her words.

Lou-Lou sensed her fear. "Start easy. Just with *Puh.*"

Hennie spoke so quietly she couldn't be heard. *"Puh."*

Fountain, who was hanging over the headrest at Hennie's shoulder, applauded. "Good!"

"But I could barely hear you, girl," Lou said. "Again. Put more air behind it."

Hennie took a deep breath. *"Puh."* It came out louder.

"Good," said Waterfall. "You're a champ, Miss Hennie."

Aunt Louise was like a teacher trying to teach a preschooler to read. "Now say '*see,*' Hennie. Easy peasy. It's a word you say all the time, right?"

Hennie nodded.

Lou said, "Repeat after me. *I see. Let's see. See the dog. See to the accounts. See the priest raise the host. Oh, say can you see?*"

Hennie echoed Lou's words. "See. See. See."

Birdie wondered if Hennie felt like a baby, everyone encouraging a simple *da-da* or *goo-goo.*

When Hennie got to the "sees" about the priest and the host, she began to giggle. Then she burst out with it. *"SEE!"*

The Muses were grinning and clapping. Waterfall was jumping up and down.

"Now, Hennie," said Ocean Wave, taking over for Lou-Lou, "you just got to put the two together. *Puh. See.*"

Hennie looked into Ocean Wave's snapping brown eyes. They said, "courage."

Hennie took a deep breath. "Puh. *See.*"

"Louder!" said Waterfall.

Hennie said it a little bit louder. "Puss-*See.* Puss-*See.* Puss-*See.*"

The Muses picked up her chant, and soon the bus was swelling again with the sounds of "Puss-*See.* Puss-*See.* Puss-*See.*" The women were laughing and clapping, waving their arms, pumping their fists.

Birdie stared into Hennie's smiling face, broken into a thousand dancing wrinkles. She couldn't raise her stiff shoulder too high, but she was pumping her fist with the rest of the marchers. Birdie wondered if Hennie was experiencing a kind of turning, the kind of turning she felt when they were approaching Kansas City. *Crazy little women. I count myself as one.*

Henrietta was out of breath from the chanting and fist pumping. Out of breath. In a good way.

Behind her, the girls were chatting about their pink hats. They were showing pictures of them on their phones to someone named Sonia. Henrietta thought of them now as her girls, her chicks, and how much potential there was in the young. The thought was bittersweet. Any child she'd had would be an older person now, graying perhaps, nearing retirement. Henrietta's heart ached: She'd missed out on being a mother. Still, she began to think of the girls behind her as her chicks. If she'd missed out on being a mother, perhaps she could still be a mother hen, corralling her sweet cheeping adopted chicks.

Birdie stared out the window. Traffic into Washington was snarled. One-ways, overpasses, expressways were stock-still. Their bus wasn't moving.

Alexandra Hall had just finished whispering with Khalid. She picked up the microphone and tapped on its metal head. The sound came up. "Marchers, Khalid has just told me we might be a little bit late." Her voice wasn't as perky as it had been yesterday. "Or maybe quite a *bit* late." There was a growl in her voice that said she was irritated.

Hennie looked down at her watch. Birdie checked Lou's phone. It was 7 a.m., and arrival time was supposed to be 7:30.

"If you're meeting connections in Washington, marchers, Khalid says you should call and tell them you may be late." She sounded irritated with Khalid. As if the traffic was his fault.

Lou-Lou reached for the phone. "I'll make some calls, Birdie."

Most of their group was coming from far away: Vancouver, Bangor, Kenosha. They had only a couple connections from Kansas to meet. The Rodriguezes. The Snyders. Maybe the McPhersons would show at the last minute.

Most of their connections were from the ADAPT group Aunt Lou founded when Shanice was starting school. Birdie was always embarrassed whenever Aunt Louise involved her in the ADAPT group. Mostly because the ADAPT group bonded over stories of bullying and shunning. Armando Rodriguez, who had a cleft palate, had been taken out behind the school, and a gang of boys had set his hair on fire. After that, his parents never let him out of their sight. That was a big reason why the Rodriguezes were traveling separately in their own van.

Every time Birdie met kids in the ADAPT group, feelings of anger and sadness got all balled up together with a sense of helplessness that threatened to overwhelm her. She was embarrassed by her feelings, and she was ashamed of her embarrassment. *Why was it that something that could make someone else feel better make you feel worse?*

"What about you, Hennie?" Lou-Lou asked. "Don't you need to call someone?"

Hennie didn't look worried. "I don't have a phone, dear, but Serena will wait. She knows what Washington traffic is like."

Even if Serena knew Washington traffic on an ordinary day, Birdie thought she was unlikely to imagine Washington traffic on a day like this.

Serena, Birdie gathered, was Sister Florinda's niece. Serena lived in Maryland. Ever since Sister Florinda died, Serena still came to Soros to visit Hennie once a year anyway. They'd be meeting at the McDonald's across from the bus depot. Birdie thought that nearly everything in America ended up at a McDonald's.

Alexandra Hall stepped to the microphone again. "Let's take advantage of the delay, ladies," she said. "It'll give us more time to make our signs. I've asked Ms. Frazier to pass out poster board and markers. You can't go to a protest march without a sign, can you?" She seemed to have recovered from her irritation. Her bangle bracelets were bangling again.

"I didn't have time yesterday to share my own story with you marchers," Alexandra said, hauling a leather portfolio case onto her empty seat. She opened it up to display beautiful posters. There was a poster of a raven-haired Latina with a red rose in her hair under the word "Libertad." There was a poster of hands holding an open eye with the word "WOKE" in the banner. There was a poster of a woman with a whistle between her teeth and a stopwatch on her wrist that said, "Team Work." Each time she revealed another poster, the marchers gasped. Her work was beautiful.

"It's called 'Amplifier Art,'" Alexandra Hall said. "It's art for social change. And, 'no,' I'm not naturally talented," she said. "It's taken me years to learn this skill."

Then she told us her story. When her children were young, she signed up for an evening art class at her local community college.

But she eventually quit after she missed half of the sessions: her husband often failed to get home in time to watch the kids. "Then Ted claimed I never finished anything I started," Alexandra said.

"Sabotage," Henrietta snorted under her breath. "Some men make it so their women can't succeed." She knew she could never count on Henry to run the shop so she could take a break, even though they split the earnings. He was either late or failed to show up at all.

"I finally got the courage to divorce him," Alexandra said. "A woman's group at the community college gave me a scholarship, for which I will always be grateful. My experience taught me that social change was important, so I became attracted to Amplifier Art."

Alexandra Hall held up poster after poster. A portrait of a Navajo woman who had been the U. S. Poet Laureate. A portrait of a woman's flowing, streaming hair under the banner "Peace Like a River."

The women gasped and clapped.

Henrietta was struck by two portraits that reminded her of her conversation with Ursula Highman. One was a portrait of multiracial arms with long forearms like the trunks of trees and broad fists like canopies. Another was a portrait of dozens of multicolored praying hands under the word "Namaste."

Hennie thought back to Ursula's words. She wondered if you had to fight if you wanted to be seen. And if that fight might count as a kind of prayer.

Alexandra Hall's posters were powerful. Birdie's favorite was the one of fists raised above forearms like tree trunks. Birdie was beginning to think Alexandra Hall was more than just bangle bracelets and artsy hair. Maybe Alexandra Hall, like art, had a power she hadn't understood.

Alexandra Hall held up a t-shirt. Birdie had seen the image before. It was an image of three women in profile. The silhouettes represented women of different races and generations. Birdie thought of Hennie, Louise, and herself. The words on the t-shirt said, "Hear Our Voice, Women's March on Washington."

Alexandra Hall announced, "We're going to have a contest. We'll vote on the best protest sign, and the winner can have this t-shirt."

Pauline Frazier, the woman with the mini-museum, was moving down the aisle from the front of the bus. She seemed energized, even this early in the morning. She was passing out poster board and markers.

Now the women were working in earnest, passing different colored markers across the aisles and over the headrests, exclaiming over their lively slogans.

When she reached their row, Pauline passed them stiff poster board and a few markers.

There was not much room for drawing in the crowded row.

Once they had their supplies, The Muses jumped into the aisle. They were on their knees, poster board on the floor of the aisle, markers scribbling, pussy hats flopping. A few others had joined them to create posters on the floor of the aisle, too. As the bus was stock still, Khalid didn't seem to mind.

Katie held up a sign. *WE SHALL OVERCOMB.* The marchers whistled and hooted.

"Anybody trade me a blue marker for a yellow?" Katie asked. "I want to fill in the yellow hair."

There was a scramble to pass Katie a yellow marker.

After that, Emily held up her sign. The front said, I AM A SNOWFLAKE AND TOGETHER WE ARE AN AVALANCHE. The back said, FREE MELANIA.

The ladies applauded wildly.

Jenny pulled two bulky items from her backpack. They looked like empty pop bottles, but she had turned them upside down, and they'd been painted silver. She held them high. The tops of the bottles, pointing downward, had bright red crepe paper flames streaking from them. "I brought these special for the trip, ladies." She strapped the bottles to her poster that said *GIRL POWER.* Everyone clapped.

Alexandra Hall motioned for Jenny to move up front. She hoisted Jenny onto her own front-row seat, and Jenny turned and modeled her sign with its homemade rocket blasters. The marchers went wild.

Henrietta was mesmerized by the chorus of slogans shouted from all over the bus. SEX OFFENDERS CAN'T LIVE IN GOVERNMENT HOUSING; ONE FINGER CAN'T DO MUCH, BUT A WHOLE FIST CAN; IF YOU'RE NOT OUTRAGED, YOU'RE NOT PAYING ATTENTION.

Near the front of the bus, she saw a group of women helping the tiny Mexican woman create her sign. When she finished, she held it up. *THE PILGRIMS WERE UNDOCUMENTED*, it read. Everybody cheered, including Henrietta.

After her, Rosalie Helen Randolph stood up. Henrietta was curious about what this serious, dignified woman would write. Surely she would write something profound. Something quotable. Something by Martin Luther King or James Baldwin.

Instead, when Rosalie Helen Randolph held up her sign, the bus exploded with laugher. Her sign read, *I KNOW, I KNOW, I'M STANDING UP FOR MYSELF. I'M SUCH A BITCH.*

Henrietta laughed so hard her ribs ached.

Aunt Louise finished with her phone calls. She asked Hennie to turn sideways, so she could place her poster board against Hennie's back while making her sign.

Hennie turned with difficulty, so Birdie grasped her wrists and helped her move sideways. Her skin was surprisingly warm.

As Aunt Louise placed her poster board against Hennie's back, Birdie told Hennie about the signs Aunt Lou had made over the years. Signs to save Planned Parenthood. Signs to raise funds for a food co-op in Soros and a school librarian at Frederick Douglass. Signs to gain emergency relief in New Orleans after Hurricane Katrina. Signs against the police shootings of Michael Brown and Eric Garner. Signs to build a handicapped restroom and accessible sidewalks for her school.

Lou-Lou finished her slogan quickly. DISABILITY'S NOT INABILITY, her sign read. She'd drawn a wheelchair inside a circle with a slash mark across it. Then she turned the poster board over to write another slogan on the back. I CAN'T BREATHE, it read.

Birdie turned her back towards the window so that Hennie could use her back to write her slogan. She hesitated.

"I've never written a slogan before,' Hennie said, her eyes blinking behind her rimless glasses.

Lou-Lou said, "Just write what you feel. What are you most angry about? Write about that."

"What if I like *your* slogan best?"

"Mine? You mean DISABILITY'S NOT INABILITY?"

"No, dear. The one that says I CAN'T BREATHE."

Aunt Lou looked shocked.

Is Lou wondering what I am? Whether an old white lady can care as much about Eric Garner and Michael Brown as Black folks?

Hennie confessed, "Sometimes I feel like *I* can't breathe, either. Would you mind if I copied your slogan, Louise?"

I CAN'T BREATHE.

Henrietta remembered that she had been putting fresh sheets on Father Cochran's day bed, smoothing them down with a broom handle, mitering the corners tightly as her father had insisted. She had just reached for the quilt folded over a ladderback chair. She remembered it vividly: it was a gray-and-yellow triangle pattern with a few brown soiled spots; she'd made a note to scrub out the spots next time she came.

As she fluffed out the quilt, Father Cochran appeared in the doorway, closing the door with a quiet "click" behind him. Then she saw the lock in his hand, a brass padlock that he was trying to cover with his palm until he had stepped to the door and bolted it with another "click." Henrietta panicked, confused about whether she was being locked in or whether someone else was being locked out.

Suddenly he grabbed her, thrusting her across the day bed, draping her head with the quilt as he tugged at her white cotton panties. "Stop!" she cried. She struggled to stiffen her knees together. "Stop! Stop!" Her cries were muffled by the quilt tightened over her head like a noose. Soon she was choking, the quilt smothering her, and she was flailing and wailing, "I can't breathe! Stop! I can't breathe!"

After a while, she found herself separating from her own body, floating above herself, dissociating, making herself invisible. And when it was over she was sore and bleeding down there. Sore and bleeding and ashamed. And committed to telling no one. Never. Ever. Committed to silence. Silence and invisibility.

Birdie was confused. "Didn't white people have more breathing room in this world than everybody else?

Aunt Louise looked puzzled, but she nodded. "Sure. You can use my slogan."

"Well, thanks for that. But I'll think of something else," Hennie said, reconsidering. "I don't like the idea of copying."

Hennie leaned up against Birdie's back. Birdie could feel the press of the letters on her skin. There was a closeness about it.

Hennie finished and held up her sign. LOCK HIM UP. FREE HER, it read. She had sketched a lock that looked exactly like the brass Master Lock padlock that was in Mama's duffel bag.

Lou clapped. "Good for you, Hennie. I was furious, too, when that man shouted 'LOCK HER UP' on stage and the audience picked up his chant."

Birdie had never heard about this, but she clapped out of loyalty to Hennie.

Hennie turned her sign to the opposite side. She wrote quickly, then held up her slogan.

I WASN'T BORN YESTERDAY, it read. BUT I FEEL LIKE I'M BEING BORN TODAY.

Lou said, "It's perfect!" She reached over to hug Hennie. Birdie reached over and hugged her, too. Birdie remembered Alexandra Hall's t-shirt: three women, three generations. Embracing.

Henrietta's powder blue eyes fixed on Birdie. "What about you, dear?"

Birdie had taken the cap off the marker to write. She had pressed her poster up against the cold plate glass window. The window was large enough for her to write easily by pressing against it.

But Hennie tapped Birdie on her arm, then turned her back around so it faced Birdie. "Turn about's fair play, Miss Bird."

Birdie liked it that Hennie wanted her to use her back instead of the window. Placing the poster against her back, Birdie carefully made each letter, copying Aunt Lou. DISABILITY'S NOT INABILITY. Birdie thought of Shanice while she wrote.

"That message will get twice as much attention now," Hennie said. "What about the other side?"

Birdie was unsure.

"Just write what you feel," Hennie told her, echoing Aunt Louise. "What makes you angry? Or sad?"

"Well, I love Jenny's GIRL POWER sign, but I don't have the rocket blasters."

Birdie was still thinking.

All around her, women were shouting slogans, raising their fists in approval.

GLASS CEILINGS ARE MEANT TO BE BROKEN. Claps and fists.

WITHOUT HERMIONE, HARRY WOULD HAVE DIED IN BOOK ONE. Claps and fists.

Re-SISTER. Claps and fists.

Birdie remembered how all the marchers raised their fists at the bus stop back in Soros. And how she couldn't.

Then she got an idea, not exactly completely and totally original. But still hers anyway. She remembered Alexandra Hall's poster of the raised arms like tree trunks.

Hennie turned her back again, and Birdie formed the letters, made the underline, then added her drawing. She liked it that Lou leaned on Hennie and Hennie leaned on Birdie and then Birdie leaned back on Hennie again. It was like The Muses being there for each other.

When Birdie finished, she held it up. "BLACK GIRL POWER," it read.

Hennie nodded. Her bun-nest wiggled.

Aunt Lou's jaw dropped. "That drawing is brilliant, Birdie," Aunt Lou said. "It's a brilliant touch."

Birdie felt a surge of something as she held up her sign with the raised fist accompanying the words. *What is it? Pride? Power? Courage?*

Hennie bent nearer and whispered, "Looks like Birdie Jackson's getting ready to *fly.*"

Finally the logjam was broken, and the bus began to move. Alexandra Hall looked happier as she stood at the microphone to announce the winner of the t-shirt. Henrietta was sure it would be Jenny with her rocket blasters.

Instead, "And the winner is….." Alexandra Hall paused for dramatic effect, "Charlotte Harrison for 'The Cat in the Hat!'"

"Oh, I met her when we played musical chairs," Lou-Lou said. "She's a kindergarten teacher from Mecklenville, Missouri." Lou joined in the clapping.

Alexandra Hall lifted Charlotte Harrison onto her own empty seat so the women in the back could see her better. Charlotte was wearing a red-and-white striped stovepipe hat atop her head and a bright red necktie around her neck. She had penciled cat whiskers across her cheeks. She held up her sign that included a cartoon figure of Dr. Seuss's famous character.

"I'm going to read the words line-by-line," announced Alexandra Hall. "And you repeat each line after me. OK, marchers?"

Charlotte Harrison was holding her poster high so the march-er-chorus could follow her words.

I DO NOT LIKE YOU UP MY SKIRT.

I do not like you up my skirt.

I DO NOT LIKE YOU DOWN MY SHIRT.

I do not like you down my shirt.

I DO NOT LIKE YOU NEAR MY RUMP.

I do not like you near my rump

I DO NOT LIKE YOU ... MR. ....

Before Charlotte Harrison could get the last line out, the riders had broken up laughing. Hoots. Hollers. Cheers. Fist bumps. Lou, Henrietta, Birdie, The Muses were all laughing together. The bus was filled with a powerful joy, the joy of women who were reclaiming their power.

Charlotte Harrison bowed, accepting her t-shirt.

And then Khalid tooted his horn and pointed.

Floating in the distance was the dome of the Capitol.

From her window perch high above the sidewalks, Birdie watched the streams of people below her, mostly women, walking in pairs or groups, carrying signs. *Can I really have traveled all the way from Soros, Kansas to Washington, D.C.?*

They were in a run-down part of the city. The streets were dirty and narrow. At each turn, Khalid swung the bus wide before he slid the silver machine into the turn. Each time he was successful, the women cheered. *Who knew driving a bus took so much skill? Was it something underrated like creating mini-museums or learning to repair elevators or selling plumbing supplies?*

An image grabbed Birdie's attention, and she switched on the VIDEO function of the phone's camera. It would be hard to capture, but her mind's eye longed to try. A series of buses was turning one by one into the crowded parking lot, swinging widely and then pirouetting gracefully into their appointed spaces. She needed height to capture it well and wished she was outside, on top of the bus. There she'd be able to get a good picture of this urban ballet. She panned the camera and tried to capture the dance being choreographed against the cityscape of the nation's capital. She imagined uploading her video onto Youtube with waltz music playing in the background.

Finally Khalid turned into a parking lot jammed with buses: Ohio Transport, Cardinal Bus Lines, Granite State Travel.

Birdie examined her video. It was disappointing. Things didn't always turn out as you'd imagined. Still, she thought of the video as "Ballet of the Buses."

Khalid swivelled into one of the empty parking spaces. Below, women were exiting scores of buses with signs, coats, backpacks, fanny packs, jackets and coats, their vests stuffed with phones and keys and protein bars.

The diesel engine ground to a halt, spewing one last cough before it docked.

Khalid switched on the mike. "Lady, lady. We here," he announced.

The ladies shouted out thank-yous.

"Take down address," Khalid said. Birdie typed it into her phone. "Pay attention landmarks. Be back 6 p.m." Khalid was shaking a warning finger at them. "Six p.m. Sharp. No wait for you. 6 p.m."

Then he pointed through the bus window. "Mickey Ds. Across corner. There." Khalid wagged his finger at the brick building with the golden arches. A few of the women clapped, chanting "Coffee, coffee, coffee."

The aisle was crowded with marchers eager to get off. "Step back, ladies," Lou-Lou said as she heaved Mama's heavy duffel bag out of the overhead bin. Even though the duffel was on wheels, the plan was to use Shanice's wheelchair to carry the heavy duffel until they reached the protest site.

Birdie helped Hennie down the steps.

"Do you see Serena?" Lou asked.

"Not yet," Hennie said, scanning the area.

Aunt Louise pointed to a low brick wall surrounding the Mc-Donald's. "Why don't you wait there, Hennie." Birdie took Hennie to the wall and helped her sit while Khalid helped Louise pull Shanice's wheelchair from the bus's deep luggage compartment.

Aunt Lou opened the wheelchair and lifted Mama's duffel onto the seat.

"My," said Hennie. "You don't believe in traveling light, do you, Louise?"

"It's my sister's Army duffel bag," said Lou. "Even with the wheels, it's still heavy."

Birdie thought back to yesterday morning and the packing that went into that bag.

Louise raised her hand to her forehead, shading her eyes from the sharp morning sunshine and scanning the area from the bus to the McDonald's. "You don't see Serena yet, do you?"

"No. But she'll be here. I can wait."

Aunt Lou was annoyed. She knew they had to meet the ADAPT group by twelve o'clock, and there was a lot to see before that. "Do you have Serena's phone number, Hennie? We should call her."

Birdie couldn't imagine going on a trip like this without a phone. She wondered what they did in the olden days.

Hennie rooted around in her tote bag and pulled out a scrap of paper. She handed it to Aunt Lou, and Lou tapped in the number on her phone.

A voice came up.

Louise passed the phone to Hennie.

Hennie listened, then looked confused. "She's stuck in traffic. She's going to be late. What shall I tell her?"

Louise said, "We'll give her our number, and she can keep texting us her location. Maybe for now we'll just say she can meet us at the main pavilion around 10."

"Good idea." Hennie's smoky blue eyes were wide, as if she was astonished by such a practical solution. Hennie repeated numbers into the phone. *Has she never sent a text?*

"Tell her you'll be OK," Aunt Lou offered. "That you're among friends who'll look out for you."

Hennie let out a deep breath. "Yes, Serena," she sighed into the phone. "I'm with friends. I'll be OK. See you soon, darling."

"I'll meet the two of you outside after you get your food," Aunt Lou said. "Remember? I don't do McDonald's. I can pee on the bus, and I've got snacks."

Birdie was starving. She heard her stomach growling. She held Hennie's hand and led her to the restaurant.

"Can we use the bathroom, dear? I'm dry, but I might not be much longer."

Birdie was so hungry she could have eaten her own knuckles.

"Sure," Birdie said between clenched teeth, her stomach turning over.

The McDonald's was wall-to-wall marchers, and the line for the restroom snaked into the parking lot.

"Birdie," Hennie asked. "Is it MICK-Donald's? Or MAC-Donald's?"

Birdie didn't know and Birdie didn't care. She ignored Hennie.

After a while, they were through the door, and the smell of food just made Birdie hungrier. *If I don't get something to eat soon, I'm going to scream.*

"What do they serve here, Birdie?"

Birdie was annoyed with Henrietta Oldham. *Has she never been to a McDonald's? How do you explain a Big Mac – the sauce, the lettuce, the sesame seed bun?* It was how Birdie used to feel with Shanice. *Can she really not reach to wipe her own self? Can she really not pick up cues from the people who were teasing her?*

"It's early enough for breakfast," Birdie said, trying to stay patient. "Does scrambled eggs and toast sound good?"

Hennie nodded. "That would be fine, thank you."

Birdie didn't volunteer that she was getting eggs, toast, hash browns, pancakes, a muffin, bacon, juice, and milk.

Finally they reached the restroom door. Hennie was holding Birdie even tighter. Her knees were probably about to give.

Inside, there was only a single toilet stall. There was no toilet paper, no towel for washing up. In fact, pee laced with strips of wet toilet paper covered the floor. The stall was so tiny Birdie couldn't possibly get inside with Hennie. She let her step inside alone, hoping her knees didn't buckle and send her down into a yellow river.

"Hold the door closed, dear," Hennie said, her voice echoing against the dirty tiles. "I'm afraid of being inside here all alone with the lock latched." Birdie thought of Hennie's sign: LOCK HIM UP. FREE HER. *How many times had I held a door for Shanice? Or stood outside waiting for her somewhere? Or stayed calm against her fears?*

After they were both finished, they ran their hands under the water together, disgusted by the empty soap dispenser. The towel machine was empty, so they dried their hands on their clothes.

Their moods had turned sour.

Hennie muttered, "For the first time I'm wondering why I ever came on this trip."

"Me, too."

Birdie carried their order out in a white paper bag, Hennie's hand squeezing hers in a death grip.

Birdie looked back across at the bus and her gaze moved skyward. The Three Muses had climbed on top of the bus. They had assumed yoga poses, ankles crossed over thighs, palms together in prayer, pussy hats atop their heads.

Hennie, following Birdie's gaze, looked up too. Birdie pulled out her phone and took both a wide shot and a close-up.

Then she showed the pictures to Hennie.

"Maybe, dear," she giggled. "*That's* why we came."

Their moods were starting to brighten again.

Lou-Lou was sitting on the brick wall in front of the McDonald's, eating a packet of Tom's peanuts. Birdie sat next to her and gulped her food. The wheelchair was open beside Aunt Lou.

"We'll wait a few more minutes for Serena to give us an update on her progress," Aunt Lou said. "In the meanwhile, maybe we can decorate Shanice's wheelchair."

Birdie reached into her backpack to pull out their offerings.

The idea had been to memorialize Shanice through her wheelchair. Before Birdie and Lou left Soros, their family had offered farewell remembrances to Shanice. Birdie would carry them in her backpack, and she and Lou would attach these things to her wheelchair when they got to the protest in D.C. There was a note from Twanny; he had put it in an envelope and tied it up with a lavender ribbon. Beanie had left a picture of Michael Jackson, the one where he was wearing his signature glove. Lou had planned to tie bottles of Shanice's nail polishes to the wheelchair's armrests. Mama had put a snip from her growing-back hair in a heart-shaped locket. Birdie had weaved some crepe paper left over from the YMCA dance around Shanice's toilet tongs, and she planned to drape Mrs. Opie's shawl over the back of the wheelchair when they left it at the protest site. Like the others who would join them at noon, they would offer up Shanice's wheelchair and its mementos as a kind of memorial to Shanice and the efforts of ADAPT.

Closure.

When they were finished decorating the wheelchair, they still hadn't heard from Serena.

Lou-Lou stood up. "Well, let's get going, marchers," she said.

She reached out and handed Henrietta her protest sign.

"Have a seat, girl," she said to Hennie. "You're gonna *ride.*"

Gratefully Hennie dropped her body into the wheelchair.

Off they went, Lou-Lou pushing a wheelchair dangling nail polish bottles, a letter wrapped in lavender ribbon, a picture of Michael Jackson, a heart-shaped locket, and a purple shawl; Birdie dragging a rolling Army duffle; Hennie trailing a strand of wet toilet paper on the bottom of her orthopedic shoes. Together they plunged into the crowd going who-knew-where for who-knew what, waving a sign hoisted like a flag: I WASN'T BORN YESTERDAY. BUT I FEEL LIKE I'M BEING BORN TODAY.

PART V – WASHINGTON, D.C.

8:35 a.m. EST, January 18, 2017

Emily paced on the Metro platform. Her head was spinning. She had never seen anything like this. It was nothing like the Lucky Duck, even on a packed night. The trains were so crowded that it was nearly impossible to board without a long wait. All the trains were bursting with passengers, and a logjam was created each time the doors opened: people on the inside forcing their way out, people on the outside forcing their way in.

Katie had overheard that the Metro was running extra trains and that they'd opened at five a.m. instead of the usual seven. Emily overheard someone saying that by nine a.m. they'd had almost 250,000 riders, and she saw the lines for the SmarTrip cards snaking through the tunnels. Jenny had heard that some of the marchers had rented motorcycles in Baltimore and ridden them into the city. Emily thought that was a good idea. It had taken them 45 minutes just to get on and off the Metro.

Once aboard, Emily had to hold her poster high over her head so more people could squeeze in. Riders still in their tuxes from the inauguration gave her the stink-eye when they read her FREE MELANIA sign. It was surprisingly silent inside the train: riders were crowded so tightly that they avoided speech, concentrating only on inhaling gulps of oxygen.

Once off, Emily and her friends headed for 3rd and Independence where they were to meet up with Sonia. Along the way they passed t-shirt vendors, information booths, huddles of police officers. At a souvenir stand along the way, a woman from LA was selling pussy hats. She had hand-knit 500 hats for the event. They were stuffed into Ziplock bags and those bags into dozens of green plastic trash bags. They were selling like hotcakes. Emily bought a pussy hat for Sonia.

It took them forever to catch a train. But one kind soul took pity on Shanice's wheelchair, shoving people out of the way so they could board and finally ride.

Now, standing on the platform outside the train, Birdie pushed the camera function on Lou's phone. She'd been eager to capture a picture that had been impossible inside the train. With the camera to her eye, she snapped the picture she'd been waiting for: riders wearing gowns and tuxedos from last night's inaugural ball jostling riders wearing pussy hats and sandwich boards for this morning's march. Birdie scanned the image. *Can this be the best picture I've taken – ever?*

Activity was exploding all around her. Workmen everywhere were tearing down structures from last night and erecting new structures for this morning. They were setting up bike racks and erecting tents. Store owners and apartment residents were bargaining with marchers for parking spaces. Volunteers were setting up first-aid stations and water bottle kiosks. Birdie's heart jumped when she saw a woman wearing a skirt that showed streaming strands of hair under the words "Peace Like a River": it was Alexandra Hall's own Amplifier art. Birdie snapped a picture of the swirling skirt.

Birdie, Aunt Lou, and Hennie were heading for the Main Stage, and they were in a hurry. The speakers and performers were scheduled to begin at 10 a.m., and the ADAPT protest began at noon. After that, the March itself started at 1 p.m. It was going to be a full day.

Henrietta liked the name of where they were heading: someplace called *Freedom* Plaza, somewhere along Pennsylvania Avenue. Hennie marvelled at the organization of the planners and was grateful for Birdie's phone. Directions to every possible site and every possible venue were mapped out, and all Birdie had to do was press a button for information.

"Hang on, Hennie, we're taking off now," Birdie cried, giving the wheelchair a hard turn and swerving it out of the thick crowds of wall-to-wall people and onto the berm like an emergency vehicle.

"She can be dangerous with that thing," Louise shouted as Hennie lurched ahead. "She's had lots of practice with Shanice."

Hennie gripped the fake-leather arms of the chair and held on for dear life. She rattled over grass and stones, around tree trunks and statues. Occasionally they'd run into a few marchers gathered into small groups along the berm, and they'd quickly step aside while Hennie waved her thanks.

"Isn't that nice of people to let us pass, Birdie?" Hennie said.

"Nice?" Birdie smirked. "Have you ever had your foot run over by a wheelchair?"

Henrietta watched the scenery speed by. There were more advocacy groups with signs and stands than she'd ever imagined in her life: The Dreamers, the Fight for $15, Occupy Wall Street, Black Lives Matter, AFL-CIO, Astraea Lesbian Foundation for Justice, Sierra Club, The National Congress of American Indians, NAACP, the Union of Concerned Scientists. She felt like she'd ridden a roller coaster through a magic kingdom of non-profits far beyond Oldham's Antiques.

Henrietta felt as gleeful as a girl. The capital may have been crowded, its revelers struggling to move, but she was careening through the world in a wheelchair weaponized like an Army tank. She chuckled as they plowed across intersections, hurtled through crowds on the sidewalks, rammed their way through the crush of marchers milling about on street corners and in alleyways.

As they plunged toward the stage area, Henrietta inhaled the warm January air. Even the weather, she exulted, was aligned with the march, defying the season. As she watched feet avoiding the heavy wheels of her rolling chair, feet stepping as lightly as tap dancers, her heart lifted: nobody had ever stepped aside for her in her entire life.

They had agreed to meet Sonia at 3rd and Independence, near the National Museum of the American Indian, close to the Main Stage, and it was just like Sonia to have arrived first. Sonia had always been the dependable one. At Stanton College, you could go to her if you forgot the Western Civ assignment; you could count on her to save a place for you in the student union at lunch; you could rely on her to tell you you'd had too many beers.

Emily was the first to spot Sonia standing on the steps of the museum wearing a "Hear Our Voice" t-shirt under a fleece vest. She was wearing sandals like the rest of the girls, and she had a rainbow bandana tied at her neck. When she saw them in the distance, she swept the air with a broad wave and ran to embrace them, all of them jumping up and down as they huddle-hugged.

As they ran across the promenade toward the Main Stage, holding hands like grade schoolers, Emily cried, "Hurry! We don't want to miss Katy Perry!"

From her wheelchair, Henrietta glimpsed Emily and her friends climbing over the barricades to get to the Main Stage. Emily caught her eye, and Emily and her friends waved at her. Henrietta waved back, her heart happy at the sight of such ecstatic young girls, their whole lives ahead of them. She touched her rosary. Please, God. No Jayhawks.

The stage was crowded with celebrities and musical groups that she'd never heard of. A young Black singer wearing a white shirt with the words "No Is Mi Presidente" on it was performing a song.

"That's Taina Asili singing from *War Cry*," Birdie said, leaning down to her. "It's written in five languages so it can be heard across the world."

Henrietta had never heard of Taina Asili, but if a woman wanted to sing a war cry, that was fine with her. No doubt she was entitled to it.

Henrietta's heart swelled with joy, and she joined in the chorus with thousands of other voices: "We will sing our way home." She sang loudly, hoping their gathered voices would be heard across the world.

Birdie couldn't believe what she was seeing, hearing, feeling. On the Main Stage she had seen Alicia Keys, Madonna, Katy Perry, Cher, Amy Schumer, America Ferrera, and Uzo Aduba. The youngest participant on stage looked no older than six. She was surrounded by her undocumented parents waving their hands and shouting, "Justicia." Birdie searched the crowd for the Latina woman from their bus, hoping she might get a glance at this little girl, but it was nearly impossible in a crowd this big.

On stage now was Janelle Monáe. She was about to perform from Birdie's favorite album, *The Electric Lady*. Aunt Lou knew her music, too. They were proud that she was from Kansas City, not far from Soros. Birdie and Lou-Lou looked at each other and couldn't believe their good luck: they were going to hear her perform Lou's favorite Monáe song, "Hell You Talmbout." It was dedicated to naming the Black victims of police violence.

Hell you talmbout?
Hell you talmbout?
Hell you talmbout?

The steel drums beat out a tribal rhythm.

Eric Garner, *Say his name.*
Trayvon Martin, *Say his name.*
Freddie Gray, *Say his name.*
Sandra Bland, *Say her name.*

Birdie and Lou and the entire crowd said those names over and over. It was like call-and-response in church.

John Crawford, *Say his name.*
Michael Brown, *Say his name.*
Say his name,
Say his name,
Say his name,
Say his name!

The air was filled with the pulse of drums and the cry of names winging through the air like wild geese. Birdie looked over at Hennie. Her gray head was nodding, and her hands, speckled with age spots, were clapping in time to the drums. Aunt Lou's body was lifting on the sound of each name. Her eyes were closed the way they often were when she sang in the gospel choir at Missionary Baptist.

Birdie swallowed hard, still trying to stuff down the feelings that had choked her for so long. But as she said these names into the air and heard them fluttering across the sky to merge with thousands of other voices, she felt her resistance dissolving, rising on the wings of spoken names.

Henrietta felt the drums pulsing through her even after the music stopped. She was thrilled to see Birdie's eyes looking up, not down, her singing sounding like answers, not questions.

And then something shocking happened. Next up on the Main

Stage was a handsome woman dressed in black, her right fist raised, a red fringed scarf wrapped around her neck. It was a woman Henrietta recognized but thought she'd never see. Gloria. *Say Her Name!* Steinem. To Henrietta she represented the embodiment of a long line of powerful women. Sappho. Sojourner. Susan B. Ida B. Eleanor Roosevelt. Maya Angelou. *Say Their Names!*

Henrietta tugged on Birdie's sweat shirt. "Your Aunt Lou was right. It's *Gloria!*" she shouted, pointing.

Birdie stared blankly at Henrietta while Gloria Steinem told the crowd to get to know each other more personally and decide what to do when they got back home.

Henrietta could see that the girl had likely forgotten the name on the crossword puzzle from the bus.

That was okay.

Henrietta had not known about "War Cry," either.

It would be a long bus ride back. There'd be plenty of time for teaching and learning.

For both of them.

Lou-Lou was as happy as she'd ever seen her. Her shoulders were lifting with anticipation, her eyes were riveted to the stage. "This is the biggest protest march I will ever be on, Birdie," Lou said, a look of triumph spread across her face.

Birdie had to agree.

Nothing would ever top this.

And then Aunt Lou jumped up and down. She waved. She pointed.

"Ilyasah Shabazz, Malcolm X's daughter! Maryum Ali, Muhammad Ali's daughter!" Lou-Lou cheered at the women arriving on stage.

And then Aunt Lou saw someone else, someone she had grieved for, someone who had also lost someone dear. In the summer before what happened to Shanice.

Lou was jumping like a jackrabbit, yanking on the sleeve of Birdie's sweatshirt. "Look! Look! Gwen Carr!"

Birdie looked where Lou-Lou pointed, and there she was in the flesh: Gwen Carr, Eric Garner's mother, the mother whose son died from a chokehold by a New York City policeman. Birdie had heard Aunt Lou and Mama hold him up when they warned Twanny and Beanie about how a Black boy should talk to the police. A group of marchers began to chant, "I Can't Breathe! I Can't Breathe!"

"Gwen! Gwen!" Aunt Lou shrieked, waving her hands at the stage, begging to be recognized. And then a miracle occurred. At least that's how Lou described it after they got back home. Gwen Carr caught Lou-Lou's eyes, and Aunt Lou flung open her jacket to reveal her "I Can't Breathe" sweatshirt. As Gwen Carr waved back, Lou-Lou shouted, "Get a picture, Birdie! Get a picture!"

It was not a request: it was an order.

Birdie hurried, aimed, clicked. Although her wave was fuzzy, everything else was clear: the checkered fleece-lined sweatshirt, the leopard print belt, the long, dangly earrings; above all, the "I Can't Breathe" sweatshirt identical to the one Aunt Lou was wearing. Gwen Carr was an impressive woman. She looked directly at the camera: like someone who hid nothing, like someone who could be trusted.

When Birdie looked into Aunt Lou's eyes, she saw tears. "She had supper on the table, Birdie. Think about that. Pork chops with rice and beans. Her son never came home for supper."

Birdie's heart flooded with sadness. She thought about someone else who didn't come home one July, too.

The crowd chanted: *I CAN'T BREATHE! I CAN'T BREATHE! I CAN'T BREATHE!* The words throbbed like a drumbeat. Dah-dah-*DUM!* Dah-dah-*DUM!* Dah-dah-*DUM!*

Henrietta remembered it all. The day bed. The quilt. The silent socked feet. The dangling crucifix. The lock and the finality of its click. The quilt suffocating her as she cried, "I can't breathe! Stop! I can't breathe!"

Alone in her bed that night, she sobbed and prayed into her pillow: "Dear St. Anthony, please come around. I think I'm lost and can't be found."

From the distance of decades, she recalled the lifelong effect of it: separating from her own body, floating above herself, dissociating, making herself invisible. She wondered how many other women across the world had been made invisible like this.

Emily had to admit it: she was basking in Sonia's admiration.

They had just finished listening to the Indigo Girls perform. Emily remembered how Sonia had loved them for their counter-melodies. In college, she had written an essay for her English class that Emily didn't completely understand. It was something about how a countermelody harmonizing with a main melody most closely reflected the way lives were lived. Emily thought Sonia was brilliant.

As the Indigo Girls left the stage, Emily handed Sonia the pink pussy hat, and Sonia had slipped it on her head immediately, giving Emily a hug, modeling it for the other girls. They were no longer a trio but a quartet.

Then Emily had an idea. She plowed through the crowd with Sonia and the others until she reached the spot where she had last seen Miss Henrietta and Birdie and Louise.

Emily introduced Sonia to her friends from the bus. Then she gushed over Hennie's knitting skills, and she chattered about the woman from LA who had hand-made 500 hats to sell. Emily got Birdie to show them how many orders Hennie now had, just from other riders on the bus. Emily thought Sonia would be impressed. She was.

Emily pointed out other marchers in the crowd. Amanda Raymond. Michele Poindexter. Sheila Roberts. TaNeesha Watts. Babs

Mildenhaus was parading tiny Charlotte Harrison, *The Cat in the Hat* lady, on her shoulders. Emily and Katie and Jenny chanted the parody for Sonia. "I do not like you *up my skirt, down my shirt.*" Hennie and Louise and Birdie joined in. "I do not like you *near my rump,*" the final line sending all of them into spasms of laughter.

"Wow," said Sonia, "I missed a great bus ride!"

"Here," Birdie said, "let me get your picture."

The four of them grinned for the camera. They gave toothy smiles and peace signs.

"Can you text it to us?" Emily said.

"Sure."

Louise reminded them of the protest at noon, explaining about ADAPT again and what they had planned. The girls seemed interested, especially Jenny.

Sonia was still carefully studying Birdie's picture. "Remember how many pictures we took of us together in college?"

Emily nodded. "Only we were holding beer mugs in most of them back then. Not wearing pussy hats."

Sonia's eyes narrowed, and Emily felt Sonia's eyes studying her face for a long time.

Henrietta watched as a sweet-faced, apple-cheeked young woman took center stage. She was dressed all in white, a brunette braid over one shoulder, a strand of white pearls at her throat. She looked strong, defiant, unafraid, with the confidence of someone used to being on a stage.

Then the young woman began to recite a poem, stretching out every phrase of its opening line to make sure it was heard:

"I am a *Naaasty* Woman."

The crowd took in a single gathered gasp.

Henrietta remembered that phrase. *Nasty Woman.* It had come in the final moments of the final presidential debate. "Such a nasty woman," the Candidate had sneered at his female opponent. At the time, listening hard, Henrietta's fingers had flown to her rosary, and she prayed that she had misheard. Now, amid this crowd of women, she no longer had to mistrust herself. She had not misheard. Millions of other women had not misheard. And they had gathered to say so.

"Who *is* that?" Henrietta asked Louise.

"Ashley Judd."

Henrietta did not recognize the name, but it hardly mattered, for soon this young woman's words began to pierce the hearts of the crowd.

Ashley Judd had just finished crying, "I am nasty like my bloodstains on my bedsheets."

Sonia bent closer and whispered to Emily, "It's so cool that she's wearing white. Because it means she's unafraid of her monthly bleeding, her messy menses."

Emily noticed that Sonia called it "menses." Not what girls usually called it: "the rag," "my period," "time of the month," "lady business."

Then Emily said, "Or maybe she's wearing white because that was the color of the suffragettes."

Sonia blinked, considering.

Emily felt proud to know something Sonia didn't know.

Birdie was stunned. Ashley Judd was asking questions out loud that she had kept to herself forever.

"Why is the work of a Black woman and a Hispanic woman worth only 63 and 54 cents of a white man's privileged daughter?"

Listening, Birdie ached for Mama, wishing she was here. She

thought back to Mama's Lilly Ledbetter cake and her useless attempts to get raises for her co-workers.

Ashley Judd shouted, "Our wages are still cut with blades sharpened by testosterone." Birdie thought about Amanda Raymond and Mama's Mr. Kingswood: "So sue me!" She remembered Lois Graves, the elevator inspector: "Old boys' network." And Alexandra Hall: "male sabotage."

There were other words that shocked her even more, words Ashley Judd shouted from the stage, calling them out before the whole world: "I am not as nasty as racism ... white supremacy ... white privilege."

Had she really heard these words from the lips of a white woman? Called out so loudly that the whole world could hear?

Aunt Lou reached for her hand, and then suddenly they fell into each other's arms, niece and aunt, girl and woman, baby bird and aunt-mother flying into an unfamiliar kind of freedom.

Emily saw Sonia wince when she heard Ashley Judd cry, "I am not as nasty as a swastika painted on a pride flag."

When the actress began to shout about how shaming gays helped turn "rainbows into suicide notes," she thought back to that time in college. Sonia had been dating a serious young man, a Chemistry major who hoped to be a doctor. When they broke up, Sonia stopped attending classes, slept at odd hours, didn't shower, wouldn't speak. The girls were worried about her. Emily talked her into seeing the college mental health counselor, who put her on antidepressants.

Emily spent hours by her bedside until Sonia slowly recovered.

Emily remembered having been happy to have helped her friend. For the first time in her life, she had felt useful, needed.

Now Ashley Judd was shouting another question: "Why are tampons and pads still taxed when Viagra and Rogaine are not?"

The crowd cheered.

Emily whispered to Sonia, "Did you know that a female uses nearly 10,000 tampons in her lifetime?" She put her hands on her hips, indignant: "Is it fair that we get taxed for the privilege of bleeding each month?"

Sonia's eyes widened and she shook her head.

Then Ashley Judd cried, "Is the bloodstain on my jeans more embarrassing than the thinning of your hair?"

The actress turned around and looked over her shoulder, inspecting the back of her jeans in a gesture every woman in the audience recognized.

The crowd went wild.

And then Henrietta heard these words: "I'm not as nasty as using little girls before their bodies have even developed."

It all came flooding back. The words took her back to the young girl she had been over fifty years ago. To the familiar click of the lock on Father Cochran's bedroom door. To the suffocating stained quilt. To the attack – twice a week – on her most private of parts. To the humiliating pancake breakfasts endured with Father Cochran and her family after Sunday mass, her eyes kept down, the sickening sweet smell of syrup assaulting her nose, the effusive praise for her brother and his fitness for the priesthood assaulting her ears.

The words took her back in time to the lonely ride across the prairie, using the skeins of yarn from Sister Florinda to hide her swelling belly; back in time to the bleak institution sitting high and solitary on a windswept hill; back in time to the tiny closet of a bedroom with the single iron bed, the iron posts of the headboard like prison bars, the crucifix hanging on the wall mocking her; back in time to the months of silent knitting, pink and blue baby blankets, a pink and a blue baby cap, wondering which one would be slipped across a tender newborn scalp.

The words took her back in time to the pains that had suddenly come, sharp as knives; back in time to the bright lights of the delivery room illuminating her shame for strangers to see; back in time to the infant, bundled up and swept away, leaving her with only a glimpse of the wet brown hair across a crown as ruddy as a blush; back in time to the never knowing: which cap, what parents, which home; back in time to the complete and suffocating loneliness; back in time to that sense of floating above herself, dissociating from who she was, adopting the pattern of her life: locked up in her invisibility, in her silence.

She'd been caught by a Jayhawk.

When she was far too young.

The crowd was getting larger and larger, filling up all the blocks around Independence Avenue. It rippled like an ocean of pink hats, signs bobbing on pink water like lifeboats.

Ashley Judd wasn't finished. Birdie was glad more and more people were present to hear: "I'm nasty like the battles my grandmothers fought to get me into that voting booth."

Birdie thought about Alice Paul, Susan B., Elizabeth Cady Stanton, names unfamiliar to her just a day ago.

She glanced down at Hennie. She had her hand on her time piece, and Birdie thought about the gold and white and purple stones, what they stood for, and about how objects were more than the thing itself.

Birdie knelt down to Hennie's wheelchair. She was level with her face. She took Hennie's hand. After she squeezed it, Hennie planted a kiss on Birdie's left cheek. Birdie had never been kissed by a white woman. Or a grandmother. She was tempted to stand and pat the gray nest of hair on her crown in response. But something inside told her to keep kneeling. Hennie's face had grown familiar: the watery blue eyes, the cross-hatched wrinkles, the sweet smile. Birdie leaned across the arm of the wheelchair and softly kissed her cheek in answer.

Birdie returned to Ashley Judd on the Main Stage. "I am unafraid to be nasty," she was crying, "because I am nasty like Susan, Elizabeth, Eleanor, Amelia, Rosa, Gloria, Condoleezza, Sonia, Malala, Michelle, Hillary!"

Birdie was now familiar with some of those names: Susan, Elizabeth, Rosa. At the mention of "Malala," she opened Lou's phone and stared at the picture she'd saved. There she was, with her brown skin and dark eyebrows, her red-and-yellow shawl, and her brave, courageous mouth. She was so young, and yet she had done something to change her world.

"So if you're a nasty woman, or you love one who is, let me hear you say, 'Hell yeah.'"

The crowd roared. "Hell yeah!"
Emily added her voice. "Hell yeah!"
Sonia slipped her arm through Emily's.
"Hell yeah!"

When Ashley Judd had finished, Henrietta raised her fist with the thousands of other women who made up the crowd. "Hell yeah!" she shouted.

And then the most astonishing thing happened: The crowd began to roar. The roaring came in a rolling wave, gathering at the far edges of the crowd and then sweeping to the front. It was a tsunami gathering force deep in the ocean of history and then plunging across the world, its beaches, its cities, its farmlands, its mountains, sweeping the entire globe.

Henrietta was awestruck. It felt like church. Like something sacred, transcendent, holy.

Her decades of silence had been given a voice.

They were heading to the designated meeting spot for the ADAPT protest. Along the way, Aunt Lou wheeled Hennie and encouraged Birdie to take dozens of photographs. Washington, D.C., Birdie discovered, offered amazing vantage points: through the leafless branches of trees for close-in pictures; on a park bench used like a stepstool for a mid-range shot; atop the marble steps of a government building for a bird's-eye view.

Birdie used her fingers to tightly frame the image of two elderly women slumped in folding chairs, their orthopedic shoes crossed at the ankles, their signs still held high. The wrinkles on their faces were as thick as the lines made by the black letters on their signs: "We Haven't Come That Far," said one. "And Don't Call Me Baby," said the other. They waved at Hennie, and Hennie waved back. Then they all gave each other the thumbs-up sign.

Birdie zoomed in to snap a policeman they were passing: he was leaning on a lamp post and wearing a pink pussy hat. Hennie, Lou-Lou, and Birdie gave him a group wave. He waved right back.

Birdie climbed atop the porch of a building to shoot at mid-range. Before her spread a jumble of signs as diverse as the world that unveiled itself whenever she opened Lou's browser. Her lens captured the signs from activists representing Women in Islam, National Domestic Workers Alliance, Planned Parenthood, National Resources Defense Council, Amnesty International, and many others.

She searched for a place where she could get height for a bird's-eye view. She scrambled up dozens of marble steps worn down by generations of camera-toting tourists before her. Everywhere she looked, marchers filled the streets, streets as tightly crowded as the trains of the Metro. Just like the Metro riders struggling to breathe, these marchers struggled to move, taking not strides but baby steps. So immense was the crowd that Birdie realized she could only capture its size on video. She began to pan the lens slowly from left to right; even then she felt the limitations of her camera. Only the view from a blimp or an eagle or an airplane could manage to convey the size of this crowd.

Birdie's pulse quickened. Somehow, the view through Lou's camera eye sparked a passion she had not been aware of. She snapped image after image of the pink landscape stretching for miles below her. The photographs revealed heads bobbing like pink balloons at a circus; beds of pink carnations bordering buildings and fountains; meadows of poppies as in *The Wizard of Oz,* pink rather than red.

The views took her breath away. It felt like a miracle: Her pictures had allowed her to speak.

Emily couldn't believe it: a group of dogs. There were Pomeranians, Rottweilers, Pit Bulls, and other breeds held by owners on leashes. Suddenly she was lonely for Bravo. The loneliness was like an ache. She scrolled through the pictures of him on her phone: Bravo in sunglasses, Bravo with a tennis ball in his mouth, Bravo by a pool, napping in a chaise longue.

Emily scanned the group of dogs and reached out to stroke the back of a German shepherd wearing a sign around its neck that said "Even Dogs Know Better."

She looked up. Its owner, a suntanned, gray-haired woman in a PETA sweatshirt, was passing her a brochure. It was from an organization called Faunalytics. Emily had never heard of it. A woman told her that Faunalytics was a research organization that provided data and resources to help animal rights activists be more effective in their advocacy.

"I can see you're a dog lover by the way you treated Eleanor there."

Emily passed her the phone so the woman could flip through the pictures of Bravo. Emily was warmed by the woman's smile: it said she liked him, too.

"Did you know," the woman said, fanning open the brochure, "that countries all over the world from Algeria to Russia allow dogs to be eaten as food? Horses and cats, too. I think it's well over two dozen now."

Emily shuddered as she looked at the map of the world in the brochure. All the countries allowing pets to be eaten as food were highlighted in blood red.

"Thank you," Emily said, trying to get over the shock.

Then she looked up and down the row of tables accompanied by volunteers. They sported banners and flyers announcing ASPCA, PETA, Vegan Outreach, Animal Ethics. Emily discovered that there was a whole world of people interested in the welfare of animals. She moved from table to table, learning about puppy mills, animal testing, zoos, circuses. She saw gruesome pictures of gored bulls, eviscerated cocks, pit bull terriers who had been drowned, hanged, electrocuted, given to other dogs to be mauled after losing a dog fight. "Why," Emily wondered, "was cruelty to animals considered a form of entertainment?"

There were several tables about ethical eating, factory farming, slaughterhouses.

A tall, skinny man wearing a lei made up of vegetables spoke to her. "Would you like to know more about vegetarianism?" he asked.

"I guess so," Emily said doubtfully. The topic confused her. There was so much to know about it. She wondered what the difference was between a vegan and a vegetarian. She wondered what defined a lacto-ovo or a pescatarian. She wondered if you could mix all the different categories up and still be a vegetarian. She wondered if you were allowed to cheat.

The man was energized by her passivity.

"Do you love animals?" he asked.

"Yes!" she said.

"Do you hate hunting or blood sports?" He was warming to his topic: the brussels sprouts on his lei began to dance.

"Of course!" she said.

"Are you opposed to the cruel conditions for animals on factory farms?"

Emily didn't know much about factory farms. She stared at the radishes on his lei, thinking. But the words "cruel conditions" linked to "animals" inspired her to nod "Yes."

"But do you still eat meat, dairy, eggs, honey?"

"Honey?" Emily asked herself silently. "These people didn't even eat honey?"

Emily was growing uncomfortable. "I'll take one of those," she said, pointing to the "Lettuce Eat Plants" t-shirt. "And your brochures," she said.

Then she hurried off to catch up to the others.

Birdie rolled Hennie over to the Registration Table where they signed in. Aunt Lou had prearranged this meeting site. It was only a block off of Lafayette Square, very close to the White House. The crowd was so thick Birdie could barely see the square white building. Catching a glimpse of it too, Lou-Lou grumbled, "Every damn thing in the world with any power is white, Birdie." The volunteer at the Registration Table handed Birdie and Hennie an ADAPT pin to wear. "You stay close, hear?" Lou said. "I don't want you running off because you've got my phone." Then she hurried away to check in with some of her volunteers.

Birdie had never seen Aunt Lou in action on this scale before. Usually she was training poll workers or protesting the anti-gay policy of the donut shop in Soros. Birdie was too busy with Shanice to pay attention. It was Mama who had always been thought of as the take-charge leader in her family. Mama was the one who had served in Afghanistan, putting careful plans in place, organizing her recruits, their missions, and their supplies. Mama had the duffel bag to prove it.

But it was Lou acting like a soldier now. *Why had I not understood that there were all kinds of battles and lots of ways to serve?*

Birdie wheeled Hennie over to some other tables. Aunt Lou's volunteers had set up an Information Table. It was next to a Sharing Table. At the Information Table were flyers and brochures and handouts. Volunteers with twisted hands or shaking limbs were passing out information about the National Down Syndrome Congress or the Autistic Self-Advocacy Network. Most of the organizations had confusing initials like TASH (The Association for Persons with Severe Handicaps) or DREDF (Disability Rights Education and Defense Fund). Birdie wondered how she had missed knowing the world contained so many people struggling just like Shanice. Birdie picked up all of the information that was available and stuffed it into her backpack. She saw that Amanda Raymond, that nice non-prostitute who worked at the VA, was also picking up information. She looked up and waved at Birdie. Birdie waved back, remembering her son with epilepsy.

The Sharing Table was surrounded with people like Shanice. They were getting to know each other, chatting about their struggles with those who could understand. Birdie and Hennie stood behind them and listened.

One of the women had dark, half-closed eyes bruised with shadows; a seeing-eye German shepherd sat at attention beside her. She was sharing the adaptive clothing line she and her sister had created. Birdie remembered how much trouble Shanice had with zippers and arm sleeves and shoes and how grateful she had been for Mrs. Opie's shawl. Birdie was disappointed in herself that she so often resented helping Shanice, that she never had courage like Malala. Or her Aunt Lou.

Many of the people at the Sharing Table were wearing ADAPT pins. Birdie looked closely at the pin she was now wearing. *How had I never noticed that the logo showed a figure in a wheelchair breaking a chain? Or understood that looking wasn't the same thing as seeing?*

Emily joined Hennie and Birdie at the Sharing Table. Her friends came, too.

Emily was uncomfortable. The people at the Sharing Table had strange-sounding diseases and reminded her of circus freaks. Emily had never heard of Ehlers Danlos Syndrome. The teenage girl at the table was explaining how it was a problem with her connective tissue that made her joints loose and her skin stretchy. Emily learned that the young boy at the table with his mother was hungry all the time. He'd been born with something called Prader-Willi Syndrome.

Emily felt squeamish. It was something like how she felt when she was scanning the brochures on animal cruelty. For some reason, she thought back to Deafy Boular.

Then Katie whispered, far too loudly: "What are you supposed to call them? Cripples? Retards? Invalids?"

Jenny whirled to face her. "*People!*" Jenny snapped.

Katie had obviously forgotten about Jenny's sister Alice. The one with Tourette's.

"I'm so sorry, Jenny," Katie said. "I just didn't understand."

"You and the rest of the world," Jenny snarled.

Henrietta was worried about Birdie. The girl was listening intently to the conversations at the Sharing Table, her body tense, a furrow between her brows. She was surely thinking of her sister. Hennie remembered being young like Birdie, a young person whose light heart had been made heavy. She had carried the weight of that heart for decades. Inside her heavy heart she wondered if it had been a boy or a girl; or what it looked like; or what had been her temperament or his aptitudes; or if her child had ever known about her; or whether the adoptive parents had been as loving as she might have been.

And then there had been that series in the *Boston Globe*. It had been a difficult year. Like the multi-armed woman on the cover of the first *Ms.* magazine, she had been juggling multiple challenges: nursing her father, running the shop, managing the tenants, handling doctor visits, and paying bills. Her brother Henry had dropped by to visit their father, and he had left copies of the newspapers behind on the glass case of the store when he left. Henry had never sought to retrieve the papers, and they never spoke of them after that. But Henrietta had thought it curious. She wondered whether Henry's delivery was accidental or intentional. Or if he had been trying to say something to her and about himself as well.

Henrietta devoured the articles about the number of priests who had been moved from parish to parish to disguise their behavior. And she remembered conversations at their own breakfast table, when Father Cochran had awed her family by all the parishes he had served: Boston; Chicago; Indianapolis; Santa Fe; Miami; finally Soros, Kansas. What a fool she'd been! She thought of her mother, scrimping and saving to buy his expensive bacon. She thought of the coffee pot that deserved an extra celebratory scoop of Maxwell House only on Sundays after Mass. How foolish to have honored someone who behaved so dishonorably! Worst of all for Henrietta had been the pain that had stalked her for a lifetime. The loneliness. The shame. The grief. The loss of trust.

Henrietta studied Birdie's troubled face. She was too young for the worry lines that were already forming between her eyebrows. Henrietta wondered if the pain of the young challenged the idea of a good God in a good world.

Still, Henrietta hoped Birdie might be cheered by the grit and resilience on display. A handsome twenty-something young man had been injured in a diving accident: his legs were paralyzed. He was explaining about the best strength and conditioning workouts to do at home. A curly-haired teenager with a lung disease had pulled out different kinds of nebulizers and was pointing out the good and bad points of each. A lovely young woman with spastic muscular dystrophy was sharing her dream of getting a contract with a modeling agency specializing in models with disabilities.

At the far end of the Sharing Table was a woman autographing a stack of children's books. The title was *ALL the WAY to the TOP.* Henrietta listened to the woman chatting about her story with the crowd. Then Henrietta saw the girl who was Emily's friend, the girl named Jenny, reaching into her pocket and pulling out some money to buy a copy. "For my sister Alice," Jenny said, bending over to get an autograph.

Emily watched the woman at the end of the table signing autographs for a children's book. As a child, this woman had done something remarkable. In order to help pass the Americans with Disabilities Act, she had participated in a protest called "The Capitol Crawl." With a group of about sixty other people with disabilities, she had climbed the steps of the Capitol on her knees. The people around her had abandoned their wheelchairs and crutches and climbed, too. Butt-first, elbow-by-elbow, knee-by-knee. The little girl had climbed all the way to the top.

That little girl was now the grown woman at the Sharing Table autographing her book. Emily remembered Louise, the lady on the bus in the row ahead of her. They had been talking about Helen Keller, and Louise had said that the disabled were the best advocates for the disabled.

Emily watched the woman signing Jenny's book and Jenny sharing something about her sister Alice. The woman nodded as her Sharpie moved across the page. Emily heard Jenny telling her about the time Alice and some of her friends were turned away from a restaurant. Emily heard Jenny say, "The manager said he couldn't let them in because 'people don't want to watch you eat.'"

Emily watched Jenny's face flush as she recounted this story. Then Jenny asked, "Do you have any advice for my sister?"

The woman stilled her Sharpie and looked straight at Jenny. "Tell her 'asking does not work.'"

Birdie thought about the woman signing books and the courage it took to crawl up the steps of the Capitol as a young girl. She remembered Malala too.

Birdie couldn't shake the words she'd just heard: "He couldn't let them in because 'people don't want to watch you eat.'"

Birdie thought of Shanice and how often they sat alone at the school cafeteria table. People didn't want to watch her eat, either. Or watch her use the bathroom. Or accommodate her wheelchair.

Birdie thought about that Martin Luther King, Jr., quote and the fight Mama and Lou-Lou had about it. "'If you can't fly, then run. If you can't run, then walk. If you can't walk, then crawl. But by all means keep moving.'"

Birdie thought about Aunt Louise and her protest work across the years. She wondered if she had understood that "Asking Does Not Work."

Now a girl in her late teens captured Birdie's attention. Her name was Tammy Byerly. She had short blonde hair and the face of a pixie; she had tiny gold studs in her earlobes. They reminded Birdie that Shanice had stamped her crooked feet and begged Mama to take her to have her ears pierced. Mama did. *Good for Shanice. Good for Mama.* Tammy Byerly's neck seemed permanently tilted to one shoulder. She was sharing about the Dancing with Disabilities program she went to twice a week in Tampa, Florida.

Tammy Byerly had drawn a crowd. Jenny had joined Birdie while their other friends took off to explore. Jenny moved closer and slipped her arm around Birdie's waist. *It feels good to know someone else who understands.*

Tammy spoke with enthusiasm, even though her bent neck tilted her mouth sideways. Tammy shared about wheelchair dancing, street dancing, dancing for the deaf, a dancing program for the disabled with their siblings, too. Birdie remembered how much Shanice loved dancing, circling in her wheelchair, moving her head every-which-way, tapping her toes, waving her good left hand.

Birdie remembered that night at the dance. And how thrilled she and Beanie were to see Shanice so happy. They had even talked about trying to find Shanice a better wheelchair, one that swivelled more easily.

Something caught at the back of Birdie's throat. She was remembering.

It had happened two summers ago. It must have been July because Mama's stand of orange day lilies needed deadheading. Like all of us, Lou knew how Shanice loved to dance, but she also knew that the yearly summer YMCA dance was not meant for teens like Shanice. Lou-Lou decided to figure out a way for Shanice to join in.

Lou convinced the Y to rename the event THE EVERYBODY DANCE instead of the usual Y-TEENS DANCE. She called the parents of kids in the county who were struggling in some way – learning disabled, physically disabled, mentally disabled. Over the years, Lou, Mama, and I had gotten to know many of them and their parents. Kids and adults had bonded over stories of shunning, bullying, humiliation.

Charlie Kilpatrick, a boy with autism, would sit in front of his house taking his father's old alarm clock apart for hours on end, and if a fly buzzed around him, he would go wild, flailing his arms, even sometimes hurting himself. Charlie was teased unmercifully by the kids on his block.

Sylvia Peterman was deaf; the kids called her "robot" for the hearing aids that stuck out from her ears. They mocked her by imitating the funny motions she made with her mouth when she tried to talk.

Violet Shelby, a stutterer who was about Shanice's age, had been bullied on the Internet like my sister; one of the 'cool' boys had messaged that he was in love with her, warming her heart; then he took it back, saying she was ugly, stupid, un-l-l-l-l-l-lovable. Violet heard him and his friends snorting with laughter in the background as they imitated her stutter.

Tammy went on, her audience at attention like Mama's recruits. "What makes it fun is that our teachers seem to know what we need," Tammy said. Birdie thought of Mrs. Opie and the purple shawl and teachers who knew about needs. "We even get to wear costumes when we dance. For some of us, it's the first time to wear a sparkly headdress or floaty skirts made of chiffon."

Mama was grateful to Lou. In fact, Mama bought Shanice a new dress, a hot fuchsia pink with rhinestones on the bodice and a flouncy skirt with layers of taffeta. It had been almost impossible to find shoes to match that would fit Shanice's twisted feet, but Louise bought pink flip flops, and I had painted Shanice's toenails to match her dress.

Beanie had just gotten his license, and when he asked if he could drive his sister to the dance, Mama saw the way her little girl's eyes lit up: There was no way she could say 'No' to a request to be escorted by her handsome big brother.

Antoine had to work, so he wouldn't be going to the dance, but he washed the van and polished the grill and vacuumed the lint from the floor and seats. Beanie wore his favorite "Public Enemy" T-shirt and even made sure it was clean. I was coming, too, riding with my brother and sister, Shanice sitting in the place of honor next to Beanie.

'Birdie,' Mama cautioned as she slid the van door closed, 'I'm expecting you to look out for Shanice, you know. Your brother's lots of fun, but no boy's ever as mature as his sister.'

'Yes, Mama,' I said, feeling as I so often did that her praise was both compliment-insult. 'Boys mature much slower than girls' was one of Mama's favorite lines. 'So we make allowances.' Another one of my silent questions rose up. *If that was so, Mama, and girls were more mature, why don't we ever get the privileges?*

Mama called last-minute instructions to Beanie through the window. 'Make sure you and your friends dance with your sister.' Beanie was driving not just Shanice and me but his friends T.J, Stefon, and Carmello. 'It's not enough," Mama said, "to just take her. You need to make sure she has fun, too.'

Now I remembered that picture Lou-Lou snapped when we were just ready to get in. It was taken in front of the newly-washed van, Beanie kneeling beside Shanice's wheelchair on her left, me kneeling beside her wheelchair on her right. I remembered how her pink top sparkled with silver rhinestones, how her toes gleamed with fuchsia polish.

But what I remembered most was Shanice's smile. It was only a half-smile, as the right side of her lips drooped lower than the left and both corners of her mouth struggled to turn upward. But Lou's picture caught the glimmer in her eyes that said what her lips could not: I am happy.

"Our instructors give us visual cues," Tammy Byerly went on, "putting painter's tape and rubber spots on the floor to mark our space. They add props to our dances – pom-poms and glow sticks – and make sure our props are easy for us to handle."

Birdie noticed that she had momentarily forgotten the way this girl's mouth turned sideways, her words tumbling out at an angle. Her passion made her forget her disability. It was like what happened on those Friday nights when Shanice danced to Michael Jackson, moving her limbs as if they functioned as well as anyone's. "And our teachers let us pick out our music. We dance to everything from classic to hip-hop."

I was proud of Beanie. He had driven cautiously, pulling up slowly at the door to the Y, operating the chair lift carefully, wheeling Shanice through the automatic double doors as his friends and I followed behind.

Under the glow of the swirling colored lights, I met up with Destinee and LaKeisha at a table. Munching on the pretzels in plastic bowls, I watched with pride as Beanie and his friends led Shanice to the dance floor for the first song. Beanie even gave her a little bow when the music started.

After that, my friends and I joined in, and I kept my eye on Shanice and Beanie, who was dancing with her song after song, just as Mama said. As the D.J. played 'Shut Up and Dance,' Stefon twirled her wheelchair round and round. Even when she got dizzy, Shanice was still reluctant to stop.

When 'Dancing Queen' came up, T.J. pushed her right into the center of the polished gym floor while Carmello got all the kids to circle around her, making her the center of

attention, clapping as Shanice waved her feet to the beat of
the music, her hot-pink toes flailing. I felt the lyrics pulsing
through me, mimicking the moment.

'You can dance, you can jive
Having the time of your life.
Oh, see that girl, watch that scene
Digging the dancing queen.'

When the DJs played 'Uptown Funk,' everyone joined
in to start the Electric Slide. To my surprise, I found myself
standing next to the tallest dancer on the floor, Jamil Wash-
ington. I'd been familiar with his basketball moves, not his
dance moves. When I looked up at him, he winked at me,
a broad smile on his face. He was having fun, too. I felt a
little like a dancing queen myself.

When they flashed the lights, signaling the end of the
dance, no one wanted to stop dancing, especially Shanice.
She was begging to stay, even when the dance floor was
empty and the DJs had started packing up.

"Best of all," Tammy continued, "our teachers incorporate our disabilities into our dances."

The young man sitting beside her asked, "How do they do that?" Birdie wondered that, too.

"Well," she said, "if somebody can only walk on tiptoes, the dance itself has all the dancers walk on tiptoes."

Jenny spoke up. "My sister has Tourette's. She has tics. Sometimes she makes clicking sounds at the back of her throat, her eyes blinking at the same time. Would your dancers make use of her tics?"

"Of course! Clicks and noises can create a kind of rhythm that adds to the dance. Our Tourette's kids are some of our best choreographers."

Birdie imagined her sister alive, happy, a dance program incorporating her floppy right hand into a dance. She felt hot tears burning the backs of her eyelids.

Tammy said, "Making use of our disabilities in a positive way helps us feel good about ourselves."

I felt good about myself, too, that night. It was a new feeling. Jamil Washington and some of his friends wanted to hang out with my friends and me a while longer, energized by the dancing yet soothed by the loveliness of the summer night. Beanie gave permission for Jamil and his friend Darius to drive us all home.

We leaned up against the brick wall at the side of the YMCA building and talked and talked against the chirping of crickets and the flashing of lightning bugs. We talked about school, basketball, music, our families, sharing our lives while the stars winked against the blue-black sky. We talked about things each of us worried about alone: Freddy Gray, Black Lives Matter, the Charleston church shooting. It felt good to share those worries together.

I told about Aunt Lou and her protest desk, and Jamil Washington said he thought that was really cool. He knew that Aunt Lou and Mrs. Opie had taken up funds for Ferguson at Missionary Baptist because his family attended there, too.

I lost all track of time. I felt grateful. Like it might be possible to belong somehow to a world that was larger than me, yet small enough to feel like it was also my very own.

"We end every dance class with a gratitude circle," Tammy said. Some of her listeners looked puzzled. *Were they thinking what I was thinking: What could kids with disabilities possibly be grateful for?*

"We make a circle and call out our gratitude for the body parts we *do* have. Our eyes. Our feet. Our brains." Birdie wondered if Shanice would have been grateful for her good left hand. But of course, it wouldn't matter. After what happened that night, there was nothing left to be grateful for.

Henrietta felt inspired by young Tammy Byerly. There was some-thing spiritual in what she was sharing. She was enabling even the most compromised among them to raise their spirits through dance. She was teaching them gratitude for what they did have, even if it were only the ability to hear or the use of legs, if not hands, like everybody else.

Listening to Tammy made Henrietta feel like her own contribu-tions over the years had been feeble. Bibs and walker caddies hadn't done much to transform the world. And she hadn't tried to make changes to her church or share what she had come to know about strong women or taken action to do what she most cared about – keeping Jayhawks away from young girls. Above all, she doubted whether a church inside a sanctuary was more powerful than a church acting outside in the world.

Louise came by to say the protest would begin soon, and we might want something to eat before they got started.

Then Louise called out to a tall, muscular Native American woman. "Naomi! You sure the pole's secure?"

Naomi saluted. A thick, raven-black braid streamed down be-tween her powerful shoulder blades. "Yes, Sarge." Naomi grinned. "Even braced it good."

Henrietta remembered hearing about Naomi back on the bus.

Louise had praised her as one of her best volunteers. Naomi lived in the state of Washington and was a veteran of protest campaigns all over the West Coast. Naomi had twin sons, both with multiple sclerosis. They had trouble walking, so Naomi was determined to pass laws making it easier for them to ride. She had picketed Greyhound bus stations throughout the state of Washington with her Lifts on Hounds campaign. She even got arrested at some of the protests she launched. Finally, after years of advocacy, the legislature of the state of Washington had required wheelchair lifts on all buses across the state. Henrietta was glad to see Naomi in the flesh.

Birdie wheeled Henrietta in the direction of the long cafete-ria-style food table. As she looked around, Henrietta observed

Louise's assembled troops. They seemed to have come from every area of the country. Saginaw. Omaha. Bar Harbor. Abilene. Louise had even made it possible for those unable to attend in person to connect through the Internet: a young man in a wheelchair sat in front of a computer and operated the technology.

Henrietta marvelled at the food table. In addition to the usual cold cuts and salads, Louise had thought to include soft foods that the ADAPT participants might need if they had swallowing difficulties or finger foods that didn't need cutting if they had difficulties with their hands and fingers. There were also adaptive devices for eating spread across the table: lidded cups to prevent spilling, high-sided plates to enable scooping, thick-handled rubberized utensils for easy gripping. Louise Franklin seemed to have thought of everything. Henrietta mumbled a quiet prayer of gratitude: "If a good God is powerless to keep suffering at bay, at least good people have been created to ease it."

Henrietta was aware that Birdie was distracted. The young woman who had talked about Dancing with Disabilities had shaken her. Henrietta had watched Birdie's face change from excitement to concern to despair as she listened to the young woman speak. Henrietta was sure it had something to do with her sister Shanice.

Birdie wasn't eating. She was staring at her plate of potato salad and sliced ham. She was lost in thought.

Henrietta laid her hand on Birdie's. "I'm here," she said. "If you want to talk about it."

Birdie looked at Henrietta. The girl's eyes were glistening. They looked grateful for the invitation at first, but then Birdie shook her head. "Not now," she said.

Henrietta considered "not now" a breakthrough. "Not now" was different from "no."

Birdie was obsessing over Tammy Byerly's gratitude prayer, the one they did after each dance session.

She began to think of the things Shanice might have been grateful for. Her hearing. Her eyesight. Her good left hand. Her beautiful face. Her curly eyelashes. Music. Dancing on Friday nights. Her own good nature. The family who loved her. Mrs. Opie. Aunt Lou. Michael Jackson. The ADAPT chapter.

Birdie looked down at the ADAPT pin they had given her at the Registration Table. It was pinned to her jacket, reminding her of the pin that Hennie wore, the one that told the time and reflected the colors of the suffragettes, the one that taught her that an object could be more than the thing itself.

And suddenly she had an idea.

It was almost noon.

Hundreds of protesters were now arriving. They were an army rolling along in power chairs, limping on elbow crutches, sucking on nebulizers, accompanied by children, spouses, friends, nurses, seeing-eye dogs. Most of them juggled signs: "Don't Take Away Our ACA." "Fix the System, Not Me." One man, his gray hair a grizzled halo around his face, sat defiantly in a wheelchair. "Mock Me to my Face," his sign said.

"God is good," Henrietta whispered to herself.

Emily watched as Birdie's aunt Louise directed them away from the black iron fence surrounding Lafayette Park. Apparently there had been a change in plans. Their focus would not be on the black iron fence but on a huge wooden pole erected in a patch of green close to it. Emily overheard someone saying a woman named Naomi had lashed the pole to the top of her van and driven it all the way from the state of Washington. It must have been at least twelve feet high. You'd be able to see it from the White House.

Some kind of opening ceremony was about to begin.

An industrial ladder had been set up right next to the pole, and Emily watched Birdie's aunt Louise climb a few steps onto the ladder to address the crowd. Emily knew that Birdie's aunt was somehow involved in this event, but she hadn't realized that she might have been in charge of the entire thing. Louise thanked about a million people, and she gave out certificates to dozens of groups outside of ADAPT who had participated. They had names like Caregiver Action Network, State Administrators of Vocational Rehabilitation, The Family Caregiver Alliance, and a bunch of others. Emily couldn't remember them all.

Then Birdie's aunt stepped down from the ladder, and a woman named Naomi took her place. Naomi had the square brown face of a Native American. Streaks of gray wound through the long black braid snaking down her back. She was explaining what would happen next.

"We're creating a kind of totem pole, friends. I brought this red cedar all the way from the state of Washington, the land of my ancestors. Totems tell stories. They represent kinship ties, family legends, myths. They preserve those stories so that others can learn about them through the generations. Our totem pole will do that for our ADAPT group, which is our own special tribe."

Emily was mesmerized. This was more interesting than anything that had ever happened in Soros.

"We've asked you to travel here with your assistive devices, ones that have worn out, ones that you've found in thrift stores, ones discarded from nursing homes. And Louise and I encouraged you to decorate them. Any way you wanted. With crepe paper or notes or paint or ribbons or messages you'd like people to read. Hold them up now, friends."

Emily was astonished. A multicolored rainbow of streamers and balloons and pom-poms floated overhead. Garlands of plastic flowers and beads and team pennants attached to grab bars and canes and diaper boxes rained down on everyone, and the gathered protesters cheered.

Then Naomi shouted, "You'll pass them up to me, and I'll hang them from the pole. Lighter things first, heavier things last."

Her strong arms reaching, her muscles bulging, Naomi tied device after device to the protest pole. Reachers and bed rails, canes and leg lifters, shoe horns and no-slip hospital socks. Emily looked over at Jenny. She had removed a red rubber bracelet from her wrist. The bracelet said "You Got This" in white letters. "Alice gave it to me on my birthday. She had one exactly like it, and I always loved the message. It spoke to both of us."

Now Jenny handed her bracelet up to Naomi. "This means Alice is here," Jenny said.

"Being here, Jenny," Emily replied, "beats whatever Alice is doing back in Kansas."

Birdie was surprised at how beautiful the pole was. Streamers in primary reds and yellows and blues hanging from CPAP cables. Dented silverware hanging from grab bars, clinking in the cool air like chimes. Bedpans decorated with silver and gold glitter. Pom-poms waving from the teeth of reachers. Someone had stitched hospital socks into garlands that wrapped around the pole; they were in many colors, but she noticed the purple and white and yellow socks the most: they reminded Birdie of the colors of the suffragettes. She now knew what this protest had in common with every other protest in the world: Asking Doesn't Work.

Birdie snapped dozens of pictures of the pole against the cool winter sky.

"It's time, Birdie," Hennie said.

She meant Shanice's wheelchair. Time to let go of it.

Naomi had reached the bottom of the pole where the heavier devices like braces and crutches could be lashed. Already she had tied on a couple of dented walkers. The wheelchair would fit snugly at the base of the pole.

Hennie gripped the arms of the wheelchair. Slowly she pushed herself up to stand. Hennie looked over at Birdie and smiled. "Time for closure, Birdie. Time to pass it on," she said.

Birdie wondered how Hennie would get around now. It was past noon, and they had only just heard from Serena. She had texted that it was impossible for her to get through the traffic. She had even checked for an Uber. It cost $106 from Maryland, but even an Uber driver would be stuck in traffic. "Give her my apologies. And my love," Serena's text said.

"Don't worry about me," Henny said. "Remember, dear, I trained for this event. I'm stronger than you think."

As she returned to the totem pole, pushing Shanice's wheelchair, Birdie looked one last time at the mementos lovingly attached to it. The nail polish bottles, the ribboned letter, the picture of Michael Jackson, the heart-shaped necklace. She reached into her backpack and took out Mrs. Opie's shawl. She draped it across the back of the wheelchair, remembering how often she had draped it across Shanice's own shoulders.

Birdie wheeled the chair over to the pole. She bent down to heave the length of brass chain from Mama's duffel bag. It was long and heavy, but it would serve to tie Shanice's equally heavy chair to the totem pole. It should wrap around the pole at least a dozen times. Birdie was ready: to pass Shanice's wheelchair into Naomi's hands, to let go of Shanice, to tie up the painful chains of memory, to embrace closure.

Birdie looked over at Hennie. She was standing tall, not sitting, and Birdie wondered how long she could stand before her knees gave out. Hennie was sending a sweet and encouraging wave with a few of her fingers. Birdie remembered Hennie's faith in her: "mighty smart," "ready to fly." She thought back to Tammy Byerly's conversation about gratitude, and Birdie realized that Miss Henrietta Oldham was something she was grateful for.

Suddenly Birdie swerved the chair away from the pole.

Naomi looked surprised.

Birdie pushed Shanice's chair back to the lunch table where Hennie was standing.

Hennie's raincloud-blue eyes narrowed with concern.

And then Birdie said, "Maybe our family story isn't over yet. Maybe it's still like a work in progress. Maybe it's not time for a memorial like this. Just yet."

Henrietta fingered her rosary. From Shanice's wheelchair, she watched Birdie approach Louise and Naomi, whispering something. Henrietta observed their heads tilting, their eyebrows lifting. They were considering what Birdie said.

Henrietta admired the pole, flashing with color, tinkling with chimes, sparkling with glitter, rising high above the White House fence. The faces in the group circling it from the ground gleamed with pride.

Louise stood on the ladder steps again. "This totem symbolizes our struggles, our stories," she said.

The crowd cheered wildly.

"And I'm proud of all our efforts," she said.

The crowd began to chant, "Thank you! Thank you! Thank you!"

Louise beamed.

"I know most of you have accused me of thinking of everything, but I confess I have not."

The crowd sighed and groaned. "Not true!" "No way!" Protesters were shaking their heads.

"It's true. I want to introduce my niece here, Birdie Jackson. She reminded me that we had not come up with a closing ceremony. And she's had an idea for creating one."

Slowly Louise climbed down from the steps of the ladder, and slowly Birdie climbed up. Replacing her aunt, she lifted her eyes from her feet, meeting the upturned eyes of the crowd.

"Take a look at your ADAPT pins, friends," she said. "What do you see?" After she had said a few words, Birdie looked more relaxed. Hennie had noticed this earlier on the bus. She realized that the girl found speaking on behalf of someone else much easier than speaking on behalf of herself.

The members of the crowd looked at their pins. Perhaps for the first time they noticed the wheelchair and the person with a broken chain raised overhead. The expressions on their faces said they had not looked at the image very carefully before.

Birdie took one end of her chain, the heavy chain from her

mother's Army duffel. Henrietta had watched this young girl drag that chain all the way from Soros. It had been heaved into the belly of the bus, onto the Metro, through the streets of Washington, D.C. It had finally arrived here.

Birdie handed her end of the chain to Louise, and then Louise passed a few links to Naomi and Naomi passed the chain to another participant in the crowd until the chain circled, link after link, all the way around the group into dozens of hands, hands that were now linked by a heavy brass chain.

Once the links had reached every hand, Birdie said, "Now lift the chain over your heads like the picture on your pin."

They raised their hands, and Henrietta thought of her church and the way the priest raised the host aloft in an act of cleansing liberation.

"Then," said Birdie, "Think of someone you love who has struggled. And say their name."

Henrietta gasped at Birdie's bravery. Then she listened as, one by one, names lifted onto the air

"Terrence."

"Bernard."

"Linda."

"Grandpa George."

"Jamal."

"Alice." Henrietta recognized the name of Jenny's sister.

"Carolyn."

"Mrs. Posner."

"Su-Ling."

"Andrea."

Henrietta listened attentively for one name.

Finally she heard it. It was said reverently yet firmly. "*Shanice.*"

Henrietta bowed her head. She felt something she could not name floating up to the heavens. She hoped Birdie did, too.

Emily studied Jenny's face as she called out her sister's name. She looked around at the crowd, its spirits lifted, bits and pieces of self-love restored. Emily wondered about self-love. Sonia said it was the first obligation. "Love yourself, Emily," Sonia had said during interludes on the Main Stage, "and then you'll be able to love others and let them love you." Emily wondered if perhaps this gathering was as much about loving as it was about protesting.

And then Emily looked over and saw them.

The police.

Birdie had just finished taking a picture. The sunlight was just right for making a silhouette on the sidewalk. She held the phone to her eye and pushed the button. The camera captured shapes on the sidewalk. The shapes were hunched over canes, propped by braces, cradled in wheelchairs. And all the shapes were linked by a chain.

Suddenly half a dozen officers were approaching the crowd, their badges winking in the sunlight.

The protesters were focused on the pole, but they now turned to face the officers. Some of them looked confused, some looked frightened. Most of them were still gripping heavy links of chain.

Birdie was afraid. For these friends of Shanice. For Aunt Lou. For Hennie. For herself.

Suddenly she knew what to do, grateful for Lou-Lou's phone.

Henrietta watched the officers advancing, and her limbs began to tremble. She kept her eyes on the protesters, hoping they would give her the courage she lacked.

Leaning on crutches, seated in wheelchairs, braced on walkers, they were standing their ground. Their aides and family members stood shoulder-to-shoulder with them. No one was scattering; no one was scuttling off. A few photographers had rushed to the site, and they were snapping pictures.

Henrietta heard Louise's calm voice above the crowd. "No need to panic, everyone. Stay calm. Nothing to fear here. Trust me. We've planned for every possibility."

Henrietta knew Louise was a good organizer, an exquisite planner. But she could hardly have planned for a possibility like this. Henrietta now thought that her St. Catherine's stitchers had it right: protesting was a dangerous act. She was frustrated, her frustration igniting an inner fury. Here she was, rebelling for the first time in her life, and her mild-mannered self was facing arrest.

Suddenly something inside Henrietta shifted, turning into tempered steel, urging her not to turn away. She reached inside her yarn tote and pulled out a pair of long, pointed aluminum knitting needles. They were the closest things she had to weapons. "By God," she muttered, "I'll use them, too!" She held them up in front of her face, pointed them forward like swords, ready to stab an eye, a wrist, a bloated belly. She was spurred on by the words of Ursula Highman: "If women want to be seen, they have to fight!"

Emily watched the police approach.

The crowd, still gripping their chains, stubbornly faced them.

"Who's the leader here?" one of the offers asked, billy club dangling at his waist.

Both Birdie's aunt Louise and Naomi stepped up.

"We are," they answered together.

"What's the trouble, officers?" Naomi asked.

"We've had a complaint from the White House. Someone inside saw this pole and this motley crowd and was offended. Said it was an eyesore. That it insulted the dignity of the President's house."

Emily looked across at the pole with its beads hanging from canes, its pom-poms hanging from the jaws of reachers. She eyed the protesters leaning on arm braces, inhaling nebulizers, kneeling by seeing-eye dogs. She could understand why someone inside the White House would have thought it an affront.

But Emily thought it the cleverest thing she had ever seen.

The officer stepped forward.

Birdie wished one of the officers had been the one she took a photo of earlier, the one in the pink pussy hat who waved at them.

No such luck.

"May I see your permit, please?"

Naomi, standing next to Aunt Lou, spoke up. "We have no permit, sir."

Birdie had often heard Aunt Lou say that if you asked for permits you got denied. One of her mottos was, "It's better to seek forgiveness than ask permission." Birdie thought this idea was related to the notion that asking didn't work.

"We'll have to take you in, then."

"*All* of us?"

Naomi looked behind her at the crowd, chains in hand, surging forward as a single wave.

The officer scanned the crowd, his eyes a searchlight. They lighted on the heavy length of chain separating them from him, the mass of disabled humanity aided by walkers, crutches, prosthetic limbs.

Birdie wondered what the officer was thinking.

And then, from behind him, Birdie saw them coming. The

women from the bus were streaming to the protest site, nearly the whole busload of them. The riders were running toward the pole, their fanny packs and Coach handbags flapping against their bodies, their Ugg boots and Nike sneakers streaking across the pavement.

Her texts!

Henrietta picked them out one by one. Pauline Frazier, her red hair flying, was leading the way. Henrietta spied Lois Graves, the elevator inspector from Wichita; Ursula Highman, the minister, followed by women in long flowered skirts who might have been members of her church; Sheila Roberts was running toward them, her brooch bouncing against her blouse. Charlotte Harrison, still wearing her Cat-in-the-Hat hat, was riding in on the shoulders of Babs Mildenhaus. The lady who worked at a veterinarian's office and had offered the dog hair for knitting had brought her animal rights group, their beagles, Pomeranians, and poodles in tow.

The busload of women was running to the rescue, all of them, the 34Bs and the 44DDs, the manicured and the unmanicured, the booted and the sneakered, and they were waving their signs at the police, distracting them: "1933 Called. Don't Answer"; "Leave No Granny Behind"; "Love Trumps Hate."

Distracted by the gathering throng of women, the police looked baffled. There were going to be even more marchers to arrest, women wild with passion, waving purses and backpacks, stomping boot heels and sneaker soles. They took up positions alongside the ADAPT crowd who were still waving CPAP cables like pennants, their seeing-eye dogs baring their teeth and barking alongside them.

The police officers were outnumbered. They huddled together about what to do.

Finally the short, bald officer stepped forward. "We'll have to make an arrest," he said. "This is an unlawful gathering."

"If you have to arrest someone," Naomi said, "I volunteer." She held out her hands for handcuffs.

The officers looked at each other, surprised by her cooperation. "Handcuffs won't be necessary. Come along with us."

As they moved through the crowd, Naomi's black braid lay straight and defiant against her back. Henrietta noticed that Naomi towered over the officers, her strong torso a contrast with their soft bellies.

"Don't worry," Henrietta heard Naomi shout over her shoulder. "We're prepared. Go on ahead to the march. I should be out by the time of the Native American rally at four. Join me there, freedom fighters."

Hennie was astonished by all she had witnessed, acknowledging that she was now part of something more important than embroidered hankies and drawstring tote bags: She was a freedom fighter!

They huddled in a group. Birdie and Hennie and Aunt Lou and Emily and her friends. Louise had taken back her phone. She was leaving to see to Naomi and to call Cousin Marvin.

Things were confusing. The march was to begin at one, and it was well past that now. The streets were so crowded with marchers that no one could move. Emily's Twitter feed said the organizers were changing the march route from Constitution Avenue to Pennsylvania Avenue. They had been expecting 200,000, and at least 800,000 marchers had shown up. The original route seemed impossible.

Birdie was grateful that Emily still had her phone.

Katie was thirsty. So were the others.

Emily's Google map pointed out a nearby café. "Go, Ghana," it was called. Emily and Birdie took everyone's orders. They waited in a line for fifteen minutes just to get inside.

Birdie liked the shop. It made her think of Daddy's mama in Africa. There were African artifacts everywhere: masks, baskets, carvings, sculptures. Birdie liked thinking the grandmother she had never met lived among things like this.

They finally reached the cashier when the owner announced

they had run out of Coke, Diet and regular, out of Sprite, out of Mountain Dew, out of Gatorade.

"Do you have any water?" Emily asked.

The owner nodded his head.

"We'll take six," Emily said. "And three bags of these."

"That'll be twenty-four dollars," he said casually.

Emily and Birdie looked at each other.

Although Birdie was glad Mama wasn't here, the Mama inside her asked out loud, "How much is the water?"

"Three dollars. Each," he said without skipping a beat. That meant a little bag of potato chips was two dollars each.

Emily fished out some bills, and Birdie added some bills of her own. She imagined what Mama might have said: "Since when did a Black brother become a rip-off capitalist?"

He took their money with a wink as if he was reading her mind.

They found a patch of greenspace, and they sat on the grass beside Shanice's wheelchair.

They drank without talking, observing the marchers and their signs, sharing bags of salty potato chips, washing them down with water. Miss Hennie passed around hard-boiled eggs pulled from a plastic sleeve in her tote bag.

Louise lifted her egg into the air. "Here's to eggs," she said, raising a toast, and they all followed her, lifting their eggs into the air.

While they ate and drank, they pointed out marchers in the passing parade who were streaming across the grass.

Katie pointed to the group of ladies wearing League of Women Voters sashes. They carried signs that said, "We Are the Majority and We Want Justice."

Sonia pointed out the group of young women carrying signs blaring "Women Geologists Rock."

A huge caravan of women marched by, chanting, "A People, United, Can Never be Divided." Their group clapped in support of them.

"I think we should use the john before the march begins," Emily said. Birdie agreed. Mama always said it was a good idea to pee before starting on a mission.

The lines in front of the banks of porta-potties were long.

Emily jumped up. "I'd better get us a place," she said. Emily looked down at Henrietta. She offered to wheel Henrietta along with her as she waited in line. "Come along, Miss Hennie. We'll save places for everyone."

"Why, thank you, dear," Henrietta said.

Henrietta felt gleeful as a girl at an overnight slumber party. Here she was, among young friends, sharing bags of potato chips, sticking her hands into cellophane bags alongside the others, licking salt off each of her fingers. The only thing missing was the pajamas.

She'd never been in a group of friends who saved places for each other. It felt marvelous.

Soon the others got in line behind them.

"Guess what?" Emily asked. She had discovered something when she Googled the sites for the porta-potties: the name of their vendor. Now she was even more embarrassed about that guy from the Lucky Duck. Emily shared the web page with the others.

Everybody laughed, and Hennie' shoulders shook. She was tittering like a teenager.

Sonia pointed to the sign on the front of the dark gray plastic rectangle ahead of them. "How do you know, Em? That sign gives the phone number and other advertising stuff. But it doesn't give the company name."

Emily said, "Yeah, I know. See that bright blue tape covering the heading on the sign? It's hiding the name of the company. The inaugural committee went around to every single john and slapped blue tape over the name so as not to embarrass the president."

"Really?"

"I'll prove it, friends. It's almost our turn."

When they reached the front of the line, Emily stood on tiptoe to reach the sign on the porta-potty, ripping off the blue tape covering the face of the sign with a single swipe.

Sure enough, Emily was right.

"Don's Johns," the words read.

Emily heard applause from her friends. And applause coming from all the way in the back of the line.

Henrietta applauded Emily, too. She was a bold and lively girl, the opposite of herself at that age.

Now it was her turn at the john.

Henrietta let Katie and Jenny and Sonia go ahead of her. It gave her time to gather her thoughts: She had never used a porta-potty before.

"Can't you get deadly diseases in there?" Foul smells were already wafting under her nose.

"For sure," Emily said. "There's nasty germs in there. But I've been to lots of concerts and never caught a thing."

Henrietta did not feel reassured.

"But there's blue liquid in the bottom that's supposed to be a disinfectant and a deodorizer."

Henrietta mused that if the disinfectant worked as well as the deodorizer, it was probably useless.

"Do they have toilet paper in there?"

"Not usually. They're supposed to, but in a big crowd, they usually run out."

Henrietta looked around. She couldn't imagine a crowd bigger than this.

"Do you need help?" said Birdie, sounding worried as she offered Hennie a hand.

Emily held the door open. The stall was far too tiny for anyone else to step inside to help. Emily offered Hennie a steadying hand as well.

221

Henrietta waved them off.

Her legs were shaking as she stepped to the ledge. The tiny rectangle in front of her loomed like an open coffin. It reminded her of years ago, when she was unable to breathe, when she was locked up with no escape.

And suddenly she felt faint.

It was the smells. They sent her back to all the smells that had defined her life. The antiseptic smells in every corner of the charity hospital. The stink of her father's urine in the bedside commode. The sticky-sweet smell of the syrup at those Sunday morning breakfasts. The sharp iodine smell of the enemas which she bought at Elmer's drugs to use on Tuesdays and Fridays after her family was asleep.

She felt woozy, lightheaded, her legs buckling, her arms shaking.

Suddenly she lost control and toppled backwards.

With relief, she felt herself caught under her arms by Birdie and Emily, lifted at her knees by Sonia and Katie, directed by Jenny into the seat of the wheelchair.

Jenny wheeled her out of the line into a shady spot under a tree. Then she took a Wet-Wipe from her backpack and began to swab Hennie's face with the towelette.

Katie fanned her with a Planned Parenthood brochure.

Sonia asked if she needed ice.

Hennie waved her away. "No, thank you, dear. Just give me a minute."

Birdie stared into Hennie's frightened face and thought of Mama.

Mama had often described the faces on her troops after a grenade exploded, after an ambush broke out, after a bleeding soldier had to be Medivacked to the hospital tent. If they recovered, they had something Mama called PTSD.

Birdie wondered if people other than soldiers could have PTSD.

Birdie felt gently around Hennie's neck until her fingers found the beads. Then she pressed the cross between Hennie's fingers.

Hennie gazed into Birdie's face, her silver-blue eyes clouded over. "Thank you, dear," she said. "I'll be all right. Every now and then that old Jayhawk comes back and pecks me."

They were ready to march.

Jenny wheeled Hennie back into the crowd of marchers.

Everyone was exasperated. The marchers were jam-packed, body-to-body, impatient for the signal to begin. They were getting restless from waiting so long. It had been well over an hour. They began to chant, "We Want to March! We Want to March!" It reminded Birdie of the summer movie programs in Soros when the kids in the darkened theater called out "We want the show!"

Their bodies were packed together, touching: women, men, old people, teenagers, children riding shoulders, babies peeking out of slings. They were shoulder to shoulder with all races, all genders, all religions, all people, citizens and foreigners. It was as crowded as the Metro. At least the wheelchair gave them a bit of breathing room.

Birdie watched as Emily checked her Twitter feed, then squeezed through the crowd. Suddenly she was shinnying up a tall post. She was shouting out the latest updates. "They're back to the original plan, marchers."

All heads turned up to stare at Emily.

She checked her phone again. "Listen up," she shouted, "It's Pennsylvania Avenue down to the Ellipse now." Birdie worried she'd fall off the post. Emily was giving the signal, swirling her arms like the guy who waved the green flag at the Indy 500. "Start your engines, marchers. It's time to march!"

The crowd below cheered, and they slowly, very slowly, started to move forward. They were like toddlers learning to walk. First small steps, then larger steps; then, in a block or two, the crowd began to thin out, at first moving at a halting pace, finally reaching a confident stride.

Henrietta and the girls broke out into the avenue, passing columned buildings, avenues of trees, bleachers set up for yesterday's inauguration now crowded with spectators waving signs.

Wheeling through the cool air revived her.

Around her, pink hats were marching, dancing, singing, waving signs to crowds on the Treasury Building steps, accepting hoots and whistles from spectators on the inaugural parade bleachers, giving middle fingers to that notorious gaudy, grandiose hotel as they passed.

Most of all there was chanting, call-and-response, and choruses swirled around her. Henrietta and the girls joined in. "Not just the girls," Henrietta thought. "But her girls."

"Tell Me What Democracy Looks Like.
This is What Democracy Looks Like."

"The People, United.
Will Never Be Divided."

"We want a leader.
Not a creepy tweeter."

Around her on every side were signs whirring like helicopters. "Make Sexism Wrong Again"; "I Won't Stop 'til it Rains Glass"; "You Can't Comb over Misogyny." A man in a yellow wig passed by, leading a group of women wearing American flags like shawls. They carried signs blaring, "I Hate Hate"; "Women's Rights are Human Rights."

Now and then marchers stopped and bent to Hennie's chair, saying they loved her sign about feeling like she'd been born today, agreeing that they felt exactly the same way. Everyone she met exclaimed how they'd never experienced anything like this before.

Her girls took turns pushing her. She felt joy as strangers stepped up to push her, too: women from the gun-control group Moms

Demand Action, women from the female-forward Emily's List. A group of French students marched by, holding up identical signs that read, "Je Suis une Femme." Her girls struck up conversations with other marchers like the Palowski family from Pittsburgh. Mom Adeline; Dad Boris; sister-in-law Francine; kids Avery, Bruce, and Sarah; Avery's boyfriend Henry; Sarah's best friend Tess. It made her happy to see her girls following Gloria Steinem's advice about getting to know each other.

Henrietta was especially heartened by the young families: men, women, and children holding signs aloft and marching. A curly-headed toddler was dressed in a t-shirt broadcasting, "Future Feminist." A father with his son on his shoulders was holding a sign that said, "My wife is a Muslim and not a terrorist but I'm scared of her anyway." A mother carried her daughter's doll to march on behalf of the daughter back in Boston. A babe in arms had a sign dangling from his bunting: "I Stay Woke Even Though I Need a Nap."

And then the Statue of Liberty appeared beside them. Hennie took in the young woman's face and body, painted in the same green copper patina that marked Lady Liberty herself. Her costume was pitch-perfect. The torch, the tablet, the crown. As she passed by, Hennie studied her marching feet. She was uplifted by the sight of broken shackles dangling at her ankles.

Henrietta stared at the broken shackles of the costumed Lady Liberty and called out to Birdie. "I want to march, too, Birdie. I didn't train for this event just to participate by sitting down! I intend to march!"

Birdie grinned and helped her up while Emily directed traffic around her wheelchair. Hennie set her feet hip width, jiggled her knees up and down a few times, and then shifted from foot to foot until she got her balance. Then she put one foot in front of the other, Sonia holding one hand and Birdie holding the other. When she reached a comfortable stride, the girls let go, and Hennie marched, giddy as a girl, taking up the chant that blended with the others: "Tell Me What Democracy Looks Like. This Is What Democracy Looks Like."

The march ended at the Ellipse, a great circle in the park behind the White House. Hennie and Birdie and Emily's friends stared across the grand circle. It was filled to overflowing with signs. Signs beside each other. Signs on top of each other. Signs piled in the center. Signs piled at the edges. Signs written in marker, in crayon, in glitter. Signs of every type and size and style. Signs with thousands of individual messages.

"What's your favorite sign?" Emily asked, looking over the pile in full view of the White House.

Jenny wondered, "Maybe 'We're Not Going to Get Over It.'"

The group nodded.

Hennie picked out the one that said, "I've Been Holding Up Signs Since the 1920s, and My Arms are Tired."

The girls laughed.

"It's hard to decide," Katie said, scanning signs with slogans she hadn't yet read. "I guess, when all is said and done, I like 'Build a Bridge, Not a Wall.'"

Sonia said, "Yes. I think that's right. A bridge to the future."

"Let's add our signs to the pile, too," Emily said. "As a kind of memorial."

Each of them stepped up to place their signs on the pile.

They stood back to admire the Ellipse again with its mountains of signs.

"Those signs remind me of those presentation bouquets. You know, mounds of roses wrapped in tissue paper and given out after a brilliant performance of something high-style. Like an opera," Emily said.

"Bravo," Sonia replied, grinning at Emily.

Henrietta placed her sign on top of the one she felt a kinship with: the sign written by a stranger who was not a stranger because she had been holding up signs since the 1920s. Hennie somehow knew this stranger, understood her. Adding her signs to the pile, she felt euphoric. "Is this what it's like to have sisters?" she wondered. Henrietta looked around at her girls: Birdie and Emily and Jenny and Katie and Sonia. Her mind was racing: "Is this what it's like to have daughters?" Most of all, she wondered: "What would have become of my life had supportive sisterhood been part of it?"

Birdie placed her "Black Girl Power" sign on top of Jenny's pop-bottle jet engines. *Can signs, marches, and chants really change things?*

> *Change whether your family and someone like Shanice can get good health care or only fake-caregivers like Nurse Axelrod?*
>
> *Change whether you get to go to a decent school or just a run-down neighborhood school with shot-out lights like Frederick Douglass Junior High?*
>
> *Change whether you have a real grocery store in your neighborhood, not just a mom-and-pop like Mr. Mims's store with its cans of Vienna sausages and Spam?*
>
> *Change whether you can learn about your race in school every day, not just during Black History Month?*
>
> *Change whether you can see pictures of people of your race in the books you read?*
>
> *Change whether you can be considered uniquely yourself, not a representative of a stereotype like lazy, dumb, oversexed?*

Change whether you and your brothers get treated fairly by police?

Change whether you can be accepted to a college because of your ability, not just to play sports?

Change whether you can avoid the insult of being called 'smart enough for a Black girl'?

As they left the Ellipse to head toward the National Museum of the American Indian, Birdie passed a young white girl with long dreds sitting cross-legged on the sidewalk. She was all alone, picking out "You've Got a Friend" on her guitar.

The building took her breath away. Curved lines. Buff-colored sandstone walls. Overhangs like outcroppings of rock.

"Look, girls," Henrietta said, pointing to the museum in front of them. "What does it make you think of?"

"It makes me think of the West, Miss Hennie."

Emily had never been out west, but she'd seen plenty of pictures of it: the arches, the Pueblo villages, the rough stone cliffs. The museum reminded her of those things.

"The building itself looks like rock formations. It reminds me of Professor Snyder, my Geology professor, and his slides with all the layers of rock built up over time." She remembered the name of only one of the rock layers: sedimentary. She couldn't remember the others. She didn't volunteer that she took Geology as a science elective in college because she knew she couldn't pass Astronomy or Chemistry.

Emily also knew about the West from movies. Her Dad liked

"Tombstone" and "Dances with Wolves." He never watched any movie other than a Western. In college, after Charlie and Sonia broke up, Sonia had made her watch "Brokeback Mountain" over and over again. But Emily wouldn't exactly call it a Western.

"Evolution, Miss Hennie," Sonia said. "The building makes a statement about evolution. Rock walls shaped by wind and water over eons. And the way the landscape around it flows into the building says something else. It's saying we are the rocks, the trees, the water. We are of the earth, too."

Emily could always count on Sonia to say something brilliant.

Henrietta wished Sheila Roberts were here. Sheila would understand the way an artifact can suggest culture, history, environment, people.

Then Birdie touched her shoulder. "The object is more than the thing itself, right, Miss Hennie?" she said.

Henrietta's heart felt full.

Birdie watched hundreds of women gathering in front of the National Museum of the American Indian. Many of them were in native dress, their costumes beautiful with decorative beading, embroidery, feathers.

Lou-Lou and Naomi spied their group, rushing forward to greet them. It was a relief to see them.

"What happened?" Emily said, bounding up like a baby goat.

"Was it Cousin Marvin?" Birdie asked. "Did he get you out?"

"No. He was willing to come," Louise said, "but he couldn't get through all the traffic in time."

"So how did you get free?"

Aunt Louise pointed to Naomi. "This one," she said.

Naomi's serious brown face cracked into a grin. "An ancient trick. Used by my forefathers," she said.

Birdie didn't understand.

Now Aunt Lou was smiling. "She told the magistrate that they can't arrest us for not having a permit because the city doesn't own the land."

Birdie still didn't understand.

Naomi stepped closer to them. The beads around her neck swung slightly as she bent forward. "Native people were here first. White people stole our land. *They* need to get permit from *us*."

Naomi's story reminded Birdie of stories she'd heard as a child, stories about tricksters like foxes, cats, Br'er Rabbit.

Naomi was smiling, satisfaction behind her broad smile.

"But surely they didn't release you because of that," Sonia scoffed.

Naomi sharpened her gaze. "They believed it when I said I have a tribal elder who practices law, who was part of the lawyer team at Standing Rock. Told them he could tie them up in litigation for years."

"Ahhhh," Sonia said.

"So it was easier to just let us go," Aunt Lou said, victory written in her lifted eyebrows.

"Besides," Naomi added, "These white men don't know about the power of Iktomi, the spider god." Naomi patted her pants pocket. "Iktomi stays in my pocket until I need to snare a white man in her web."

Birdie admired her cleverness so much she wanted to ask what other godlike powers she had, but Naomi had wrapped Birdie's shoulders in a vise grip. "Come," she said, moving her towards a display of easels. "Your auntie tells me you like pictures, right?"

Aunt Louise nodded and handed her phone back to Birdie.

Naomi explained that the art on display represented various Native American tribes. She guided Birdie before the tribes of the Pacific Northwest, where she was from, and then she left, heading off to make arrangements for the drum circle.

Birdie strolled from icon to icon, understanding a little more about Naomi's tribe and its reverence for whales and salmon, sea lions and fish, wolves and bears. The colors were mostly black and red, the lines severe and clean, the shapes stark and eerie.

And then she was struck by the icon of a bird. Its long, curved beak was pitched upward; its wings were bent back; its sharp, strong claws were gripping a branch. It was not a gentle bird. It was no dove, no finch, no budgie. It was fierce, powerful, dangerous.

Birdie opened the camera lens so wide that the bird's image filled the entire screen. Then she pushed the white button.

Emily counted. There were seven of them in the group. Sonia and Birdie and Katie and Jenny and Birdie's Aunt Louise, who was now pushing Hennie in Shanice's wheelchair.

They passed image after image of famous Native American women.

"Are you allowed to call 'Indians' 'Indians' anymore?" Katie wondered out loud.

"They're not from India, Katie," Sonia snapped. "You say 'First Nations' or 'Native Americans' or use the name of their tribe."

Strolling the displays, Emily said, "I've never heard of any of these women. Except for Sacagawea." She was grateful for the short biographies below the images: Sarah Winnemucca, advocate for Native American land rights; Maria Tallchief, first Native American prima ballerina; Winona LaDuke, Native American environmental activist.

And then Emily found herself face-to-face with Wilma Mankiller. She studied the heavy face with its square jaw, broad nose, and black eyebrows. And then she read that Wilma Mankiller had been the Cherokee Nation's first female chief.

"I wonder how she got that great name," Emily mused out loud.

She was surprised that Birdie answered.

"I Googled her," Birdie said. "'Mankiller' is a kind of family name, inherited from her Cherokee tradition. It's a kind of military rank. Eventually she got tired of explaining where such a name came from, so she finally started explaining that she earned it."

"Good one, Birdie," Jenny said, smirking.

Sonia looked pleased by Birdie's remark. Not just pleased: impressed.

Hennie leaned forward to read the biography more closely. "Listen here, girls," she said. Then she read a quote out loud. "Gloria Steinem once said of her, 'In a just country, she would have been elected president.'"

The girls were silent, considering.

"What time is it, Birdie?" Lou-Lou asked, breaking the silence.

"Almost four," Birdie said.

"Better get going. It's time for the drum circle. Naomi's leading it."

Emily wheeled Henrietta to a place in the circle. Everyone approached the circle quietly, as if they were walking towards it on bare feet. Emily moved to the center of the circle to the pile of drums. She took one for herself and another for Henrietta. Then she took her place in the circle.

The circle felt familiar, silence falling all around. It reminded her of her father's AA meetings or that Quaker meeting she was required to attend for her Religious Studies elective at Stanton.

Emily was surprised that she liked the quiet. No phone. No Internet. No texting. No talking. Just listening.

Birdie watched as Naomi held up her drum.

"Drum heads made of different things," Naomi said. "Elk, moose, cow, horse, buffalo. All different things. Just like us. All different."

Birdie scanned the circle of women.

All different.

"Drum circle has no head, no tail. In a circle, all equal."

All equal.

"Drum makes sound like a heartbeat. Heartbeat of the earth. Heartbeat of its people." Here Naomi pounded on her drum.

Her drum made a sound like Dub-*DUB*.

A heartbeat.

"We begin. We will share a rhythm. But we do so quietly at first."

Birdie heard another quiet Dub-*DUB* from Naomi's drum.

Naomi nodded her head, and they all began. Their Dub-*DUBs* followed Naomi's.

Under the steady rhythm, Birdie felt her body relaxing. Between her shoulders. At her wrists.

"Now someone may share a new rhythm. A variation for everyone to follow."

Aunt Louise took up the offer. She added a soft foursome of *dub-dub-dub-dubs.*

The women followed. Dub-*DUB- dub-dub-dub-dub.*

The rhythm reminded Birdie of that song she sang as a child: "The FAR-mer in the Dell."

"Now pick up the pace. Gradually get louder."

As the drummers picked up the pace, gradually getting louder, Emily felt her body tingling. It reminded her of her childhood before the divorce, when her father would take her to the river on a hot summer day and let the cold river water tingle her toes.

"Now sing praise to Mother Earth," Naomi said. She offered short, clipped songs to accompany the drumming. The Wolf Song, the Raven Song, the Grizzly Bear song. Her singing was both simple and complicated. Sometimes it was throaty or breathy. Sometimes it was twanging or rumbling.

Emily thought it would be cool to do yoga to the sounds of drumming. The animal poses especially. Downward dog. Cat-cow. The pigeon. The cobra. The swan. As the drumbeat flowed through her, she was already imagining bending backward, folding forward, reaching to her toes, sitting lotus with her cupped palms.

Birdie felt the singing and the drumming throbbing through her. Like her own pulse. It released something inside.

Now Naomi said, "I sing the Mother Song. For all of you. Sisters. Daughters. Friends. Aunts. Cousins. All have mothers. Like you, all mothers different. All mothers special."

All mothers different. All mothers special.

Naomi's voice changed as she sang. Sometimes it sounded plucked like guitar strings. Sometimes it sounded steady in its rhythm. Sometimes it sounded jazzy, with short bursts of notes.

Naomi's song reminded Birdie of Mama. Dub-*DUB- dub-dub-dub-dub.* Beneath the drumbeat was an undertow, and she felt Mama caught in it, something pulling her down. Birdie thought of her frustrating job, her abandonment by her husband, the soldier-strength she had lost. And her grief for Shanice.

> *I was supposed to watch out for her that night. Isn't that what Mama said? I remembered Mama's words as she slid the van door closed: 'I'm expecting you to look out for Shanice, you know. Your brother's lots of fun, but no boy's ever as mature as his sister.'*
>
> *As I gazed up at the stars, feeling a closeness with friends I had never felt before, I heard the shrieks. Out behind the Y in the large grassy space, there was Shanice, shrieking with the boys, wild with joy. Beanie and his friends were spinning her wheelchair around, continuing the dance across the grassy yard. When the wheelchair slowed, Shanice shouted, "Again! Again!" When they started up again, Shanice squealed with delight.*
>
> *I held my breath when I heard the shrieks. I raced behind the Y to the big grassy space behind the back of the building, my friends following behind.*
>
> *Beanie and his friends were taking turns racing the wheelchair across the turf, back and forth, across and back.*

Then I saw them spinning dangerously close to the ravine. All three of the boys had squeezed behind the handles of the wheelchair, attempting to push it as fast as they possibly could and then let it spin until it came to a stop and it was time to push again.

"Boys! Beanie! Stop that!"

I watched, my heart seizing up in my throat, as they let go of the wheelchair, letting it career away under its own momentum.

And then it happened.

Spinning forward, the wheel of Shanice's chair tripped on a rock, and I gasped as my sister's fragile body sailed forward on its own, landing on the sharp rocks at the bottom of the ravine.

Afterward, I had tried to push through my grief, the overwhelming sadness, the unstoppable questions.

It was impossible to forgive myself. I had tried. I had not succeeded. After all, I knew what Mama thought: "Boys mature much slower than girls. So we make allowances." Mama had counted on me. And her faith had been misplaced.

They had buried my sister's broken body in her pink dress, and I had held tight to one last image: of Shanice's tender feet, the fuchsia polish still gleaming on her stiffened toes.

Over the terrible months that followed, I watched Mama struggle with her grief, a grief that was even deeper than my own. Late at night, I heard Mama and Aunt Lou whispering and sobbing, attempting to come to terms with it all. Lou had reminded her that Beanie was a teenage boy with testosterone-laced impulses. Lou had reminded Mama that it was Shanice who had begged to extend the dancing. Lou reminded her that a shortened life span for Shanice had been inevitable all along. Last of all, Lou had reminded her that Shanice had died at the height of happiness, a reminder that was Mama's only consolation.

But Mama returned again and again to something else.

The if onlys. If only Birdie had stayed by her sister's side. If only she had stopped the boys in time. If only she had been the girl she was supposed to be: mature, responsible, more dependable than her brother.

Lou had stuck up for me. She told Mama that, just like Shanice and Beanie, I had just been being myself. Lou had said when tragedies strike, people look for a reason to explain it. Lou said it was simply a terrible accident, one of those tragedies that happened in life that you couldn't explain with a reason.

Mama listened, but she couldn't hear.

Naomi's song reminded Birdie of Mama.

All mothers different. All mothers special.

Birdie was haunted by the undertow beneath the music, and somehow she was no longer sad for herself. She was sad for Mama. She saw her drowning in an undertow of grief. She longed to reach out her hands and rescue her.

The song stopped. The drumming halted. But Birdie could still feel the drumbeats throbbing inside her. Dub-*DUB- dub-dub-dub-dub.*

Dub-*DUB- dub-dub-dub-dub.*

Henrietta pounded the drum in her lap.

Dub-*DUB- dub-dub-dub-dub.*

She had never experienced anything like this. This community of women. This sacred circle. It was nothing like the circle of her St. Catherine stitchers, fumbling with needles, yarn, thread. This went deeper, broader, all the way into the heart of things.

Dub-*DUB.*

A heartbeat.

One heartbeat to another.

Henrietta experienced the drumming like an echo across the vast lake of time. She heard her voice thrown out into a void and yet returned to her as a smaller voice: like a child coming home, welcomed back.

A child coming home. A child. Coming home. Welcomed back. Dub-*DUB*.

She felt the grief wash over her. For her child. Who would never come home. Who would never be welcomed back.

Dub-*DUB*.

Yet an echo continued to return to her as from across a great expanding universe, an echo that was the same yet different.

Dub-dub-dub-dub.

A quartet.

Dub-dub-dub-dub.

Four.

Four daughters.

An echo across time. Different yet the same.

Dub-*DUB*- *dub-dub-dub-dub.*

As they left the circle, Naomi singled Birdie out.

She handed Birdie a feather.

Birdie fingered the feather, gray-brown, with a white patch at the base.

"Eagle," Naomi said. "Bravest of all birds. Gift from the sky. Only for women warriors."

Birdie tucked it into her pocket as if it were her heart.

Emily was enchanted by the drum circle. This was something to remember. The others thought so, too. Emily had the idea of burying artifacts in the grass alongside the museum to memorialize the day.

Birdie stood at the edge of the group, watching. Then she kneeled in the dirt with the others and began to help dig a trench in the soft earth.

One by one they stepped forward.

Katie buried an ankle bracelet Marc sent after a recent breakup.

Jenny buried one of the business cards from the *All the Way to the Top* author.

Emily buried a button from her thrift store jacket.

Sonia buried a Susan B. Anthony silver dollar that she kept in her pocket every day.

"One day these might have significance," Sonia said. "Like the pictographs in the caves of France. Or the fossil bones of dinosaurs."

Birdie dug her hand into her pocket, fingering the eagle feather. Then she pulled it out, adding the eagle feather to the hole in the dirt. "Or maybe they will remember us as women warriors who were brave as eagles," Birdie whispered to herself.

PART VI – WASHINGTON, D.C. TO SOROS, KANSAS

6 p.m. EST, Saturday, January 18, 2017

Henrietta watched out the window as Khalid checked his clipboard and the women boarded the bus. It was almost 6 p.m., and, despite their differences, each bore the same expression of elated exhaustion. She recognized them: Charlotte, her Cat-in-the-Hat hat still perched atop her head; Sheila, whom she definitely would meet for the antiques show; Lois, who longed to catch a ride up in the elevator business; Rosalie Helen Randolph, as tall and dignified as ever. She watched them climb the steps, shove things in the overhead bins, find a seat, greet each other. She found something endearing in each one: she'd begun to think of them as sisters.

Khalid checked his roster. They were missing one rider. The marchers were impatient. They were eager to get going.

"You said six p.m. Sharp," one rider cried out.

Henrietta remembered the rest of Khalid's promise: "No wait for you."

Henrietta looked behind her at the empty seat on the aisle beside Katie and Jenny. She smiled wryly. Suddenly she saw two figures in the distance. They were holding hands and running past the McDonald's toward the bus. Emily and Sonia. As Emily turned to say "good-bye" and board the bus, Sonia leaned in to kiss Emily full on the lips. It was a gesture that both shocked Henrietta and warmed her heart.

Now, as Emily entered the cabin, the women one by one began to stand up and cheer her arrival. Emily looked as stunned by the clapping hands as a celebrity facing the popping flashbulbs of paparazzi.

Khalid started up the bus, and the engine roared to life.

They were heading home.

Birdie was scrolling through Lou-Lou's phone for news reports about the march when Alexandra Hall stood up. From the front of the bus, she asked, "Well, marchers," flipping the switch on her microphone, "how was your day?"

Her answer was a chorus of hand-clapping and foot-stomping.

Alexandra Hall held onto a headrest with her free hand as the bus lurched through the narrow Washington streets.

"Listen up, ladies," she said. "I've got some late estimates. They expected 200,000 marchers to show up. The figure now is that Washington, D.C. saw over half a million marchers today!"

While the marchers cheered again, Birdie nudged Aunt Louise. Birdie showed her the figures popping up on her phone: various sister marches across the U.S. totaling almost 4 million; separate marches in nearly seven hundred places; scores of other facts, figures, and stories.

Birdie was most impressed by the smaller numbers, the statistics about those small bands of women who had stood up one by one, unsupported by the power of a large group surrounding them. They reminded her of the lone police officer wearing a pussy hat and the girl in dreds singing "You've Got a Friend" to herself alone.

Lou-Lou raised her hand, getting Alexandra Hall's attention. "My niece here has some stats you might find interesting, too."

Birdie thought of her gift from the sky and the place the feather held in her heart. She was less reluctant to stand now.

Birdie stood. "A number of places," she began, "are reporting marches of just one person. Breen, Colorado; Conover, Wisconsin; Evanston, Wyoming; Show Low, Arizona. And there were five women in a California hospital who marched inside their cancer ward." Birdie thought of these women as brave birds: eagles.

The marchers weren't clapping. They were holding their breath before these facts.

Before she sat down, Birdie said, "Women warriors, every one."

Now she heard applause against Alexandra Hall's enthusiastic question. "So what did you learn on the march, ladies?"

Emily's head buzzed with Alexandra Hall's question. "So what did you learn on the march, ladies?"

Her lips were still warm from Sonia's kiss when her phone dinged. She had a text message.

It was that guy. "Bet your headed home. My friend and I can't wate to see you." Emily wondered if it was just the sloppiness inherent in a text message or if he really didn't know how to spell "you're" or "wait." And who was his friend?

Then she saw the picture. At first she hadn't understood what it was. It looked like the zippered front fly of someone's jeans. Whose? Then she detected something else. There was something bulging behind the zipper. What?

After she answered her own questions, putting "whose?" and "what?" together, it clicked for her. *Ahhhh.*

Emily felt her brain lurch, her pulse race, her palms sweat. She struggled with how she should respond. With something like "gross," or "ewww," or "in your dreams, buddy." But every response seemed lame.

Emily took a deep breath and thought again. Silence would be the best answer.

Like the women around her, Henrietta was tired. Birdie and Louise must have recognized it because they had insisted she sit by the window where she could rest her head and nap more easily.

But she hadn't napped. She had taken out a skein of yarn and her circular needle. She had decided it was finally time for Birdie to learn to knit. The girl needed a pussy hat of her own.

Henrietta noticed Birdie's squinched up nose. It meant Birdie wanted a pussy hat but she didn't necessarily want to knit it herself.

"Every project has a pattern," Henrietta began. "This hat pattern is pretty straightforward. It doesn't even have any seams."

Birdie held the needle and yarn awkwardly, like Henrietta had felt as a girl first learning to string a cat's cradle. She saw that Birdie needed her help to get started, but after a first few practice cast-ons, Birdie managed to cast on forty-two more stitches pretty handily. Henrietta observed that the knit stitch was fairly easy for the girl to master, especially since she was no longer tightening each stitch in a death grip. Henrietta could see that Birdie was more relaxed than she'd been on the first half of the trip. But when Birdie had to switch to the purl stitch, she needed more help.

"That's O.K. Eventually it'll seem as automatic as the knit stitch. Don't worry."

Birdie didn't look worried. She looked frustrated. Henrietta helped her pull out a few mangled stitches to start again.

"Your fingers will develop a muscle memory of the purl stitch after a while, Birdie."

Birdie looked doubtful.

Henrietta thought about muscle memory and its usefulness. It applied to many things in her life: reflexive kneeling in church, reactive following of her father's orders, unreflective operation of the antique shop, repetitive stitching of lap blankets and adult bibs. Maybe that had been her problem. She had lived by a kind of compulsive pattern for decades. She wondered if those patterns could be changed.

Henrietta thought about Alexandra Hall's question: "So what did you learn on the march, ladies?" Maybe she had learned something about patterns. About varying the patterns. Or creating entirely new patterns. Maybe knitting, like everything else, needed to be re-thought. She could knit almost anything. But she wondered if she could knit anything original, something based on her very own pattern.

The next part of the hat was easy. Birdie had to do nine inches of only straight knitting. Meanwhile, as darkness fell outside, Henrietta rested her head against the window to nap.

Birdie was surprised that knitting could be so soothing. It helped you calm down. The rhythm of it was relaxing: like drumming. It felt like falling into a soft pillow. Knitting gave you time to think.

Birdie wondered about Alexandra Hall's question, about what she'd learned on the march. She had learned so much that she was overwhelmed. The knitting helped her reflect: birds can be fierce; women can be warriors; asking doesn't work.

Birdie looked down at the stitches she was forming and noticed that they made tiny 'v's. She thought of words like 'victory,' 'vows,' 'vigilance.' The 'v's were all hooked into each other, linked. She thought of the thousands of women who had gathered during the march, linking hands and arms that also made 'v's. They had stitched something together. *What was it?*

Outside, night had fallen, black as tar. Pitter-patters of rain were tapping the window. The sound of the raindrops was soothing.

While Katie and Jenny slept, Emily had been texting Sonia. They were going to write a blog about the march.

They'd decided to begin with the people they'd met. The Cat-in-the-Hat lady. Babs Mildenhaus. Naomi. Tammy Byerly. They'd divide it up and write little profiles of each of them. It would be sort of like that Sociology project they'd done with Katie and Jenny back in college, where they volunteered at the homeless shelter and wrote up life stories of the people there. About their hard times raising six kids on welfare, about getting evicted after missing two rent payments, about the teeth they lost because they never saw a dentist. Thinking about that project made Emily realize how stupid her life had become. Making coffee. Living in a basement. Spending free time at the Lucky Duck.

The rain had picked up while they were thinking of a title for their blog. Sonia suggested "Marching Onward." Emily thought that might seem too evangelical and remind people of "Onward, Christian Soldiers." Emily countered with "Sojourner's Truths." When Sonia said that was brilliant, Emily had to admit to herself that maybe it was.

It was no longer just raining. It was storming. The rain pelting the windows of the bus sounded like sacks of thrown rice. Every now and then the bus swayed, buffeted by wind. Emily heard thunder in the distance, and even the purple flashes of lightning through the window didn't illuminate more than dark shadows.

Her eyelids were getting heavy. Emily had always loved sleeping through a storm. Just before she fell asleep, Emily made a vow: she wouldn't tell Sonia about that text from Donnie. Now, even a mouthful of Tic-Tacs couldn't make her want to kiss him.

Birdie was awakened by the piercing flash from the lights of an oncoming truck. When the bus swerved, sending it bumping off the interstate, Henrietta awoke. Lou-Lou awoke when the bus came to a standstill and the women begin to shriek.

Birdie knew Aunt Lou, like Mama, couldn't stand whining, so Lou stood up before Khalid did. "Calm down, people. Nobody's hurt.

We're just probably stuck in mud." A few overhead lights flickered across her shiny dark face.

Khalid was in a panic. He was dialing in to somewhere. Maybe his company. Or a towing service. Or the bus driver's equivalent of AAA.

The women were flipping on their overhead lights, consulting their Google maps.

"We're somewhere between West Virginia and Columbus, Ohio."

One woman booted up her GPS. "We are out in the middle of nowhere, folks."

"It's called somewhere between West Virginia and Ohio," someone else reaffirmed.

Khalid put down his phone. He flipped on a giant flashlight and opened the doors of the bus. The tiny man hurried down the steps. Babs Mildenhaus and Aunt Louise hurried right down behind him. Soon a heaping handful of women, including Birdie, were following them, hurrying into the night.

Birdie looked down at the sea of mud and wished Mama was here. She knew the kind of mud they were facing. Thick. Wet. Slimy. It didn't scare her. Grandpa Franklin had worked construction all his life and come home every evening with dried mud on his boots. Mama'd done those two tours in Afghanistan. When she had to postdate a check or fix mac-and-cheese without the cheese, she'd often say, "Sucking mud has been part of my life."

Khalid was looking helplessly under the right front tire. That was the one most deeply mired in mud.

"Gimme that flashlight," Babs Mildenhaus ordered.

Khalid blinked at her, looking up at the tall, broad-shouldered vest-pocketed woman looming above him.

He handed her the flashlight.

"How long for your service guys to come?"

Khalid shrugged. "We nowhere. Middle of nothing. Hard finding."

"*Guess!*"

"One hour? At least?"

"That's too long," Babs thundered.

Aunt Louise whispered something to Babs, and Babs nodded. "I think we can get you out," Babs said.

"No way. This big bus, little lady."

"Don't call me that!"

Then Lou and Babs got to work. They re-boarded the bus and ordered everybody out. "We gotta take the load off of that tire," Babs barked at the sleepy women.

Against their complaints, she snapped: "Stop your whinin'." Babs reminded Birdie of Mama and what she always said about whining: "You whined when you never had nothin' real to deal with in your life. Afghanistan taught you that. You didn't whine when the firing got rough and you saw a comrade wounded, Medivacked, bled out, near dead. You just got to work."

"Giddyup, ladies! Do you wanna be late gettin' home?"

Henrietta was startled awake when the bus swerved off the road. She wasn't sure what was happening. She was still gripping her hand rest in fear as the fish-trophy lady began ordering them off the bus. While the groggy riders hauled out their jackets and umbrellas, staggering to the exit, Henrietta saw Louise and Birdie getting back on the bus. They were moving against traffic like those annoying people who took the wrong side of the stairs. Henrietta wondered what they were doing.

Then she watched Louise hauling her duffel bag down from the overhead bin. It landed in the aisle beside her with a thud.

"Sweet Jesus," she heard Louise say, "how did I forget how heavy it is?" Then, with Birdie's help, she hoisted it over her shoulders and down the steps.

Behind her, Jenny and Katie were shaking Emily awake. "Come on, girl. Get up." Emily slowly roused herself, sleep marks creasing her right cheek.

Henrietta was the last person left on the bus besides Emily. She wasn't sure she was going to be able to get off. She was stiff all over. Especially her knees.

Suddenly Birdie appeared beside her. "Come on, Miss Hennie," she said. "You can hold on to me."

"One minute, dear," she said. Henrietta reached inside her tote and pulled out her plastic accordion-pleated rain hat, tying it neatly under her chin.

Henrietta moved slowly down the steps, one-by-one, Birdie in front of her, taking the steps backwards while gripping Henrietta's hands in front of her.

Henrietta remembered leaving home for the Trailways station just the day before, gripping the railing as she headed out to the taxi chugging by the sidewalk, wondering what awaited her on the trip. It struck her that she and Birdie were moving in tandem, even though one was moving forward, and one was moving back.

Emily was still half asleep as she listened to Babs Mildenhaus bossing them all around. She had staggered down the steps, after Birdie and Miss Hennie. Birdie's aunt Louise handed Emily Khalid's giant flashlight, ordering her to train it on the right front tire. Emily was glad to have something to do that might help her wake up.

"Come on, ladies, line up," Babs growled while Louise and Khalid bent to the tire, grunting and huffing as they pulled a long length of brass chain from a duffel bag at Louise's muddy feet. Then they wrapped the chain around and under the trapped tire. Emily recognized that chain. It was the same chain they had used back at the ADAPT protest.

When they had finished, both Khalid and Louise wiped their sweating brows. In the glare of the flashlight, Emily noticed that even Khalid's sweat beads were tiny.

"Now, listen up, sports fans." Babs was ordering the women again. "Line up behind me. Big to small. Hurry it up. We gonna pull."

The women balked.

"How is this going to work?"

"Let's just wait for the service man."

"I'm cold."

"I'm wet."

"I need a bathroom."

"Ladies! Shut your traps! We got work to do. It's just mud. Mud ain't no mor'n good wet dirt."

"Any more complaints," Birdie's Aunt Louise shouted, backing up Babs, "and I won't let you back on."

The women saw that she meant it.

They looked around, fearing the deserted landscape populated by mud and darkness.

They lined up.

They shut their traps.

Babs held the end of the chain in her giant hands, and the women, biggest to smallest, held on to each other's waists. Suddenly Birdie thought of Mama. She would have loved this. It was not exactly nuts to butts, but she'd get the idea.

Babs, at the front of the line, gripped the chain with fierceness, digging her boots firmly into the mud. Behind her were descending sizes of women like those little Russian nesting dolls that opened up to reveal smaller and smaller dolls inside. Charlotte Harrison, the tiny kindergarten teacher, was on the very end.

Birdie needed this picture. Before she took her place in line, she pulled out the phone, found the camera app, and fiddled with the light function. In her viewfinder was the busload of women against the backdrop of darkness, biggest to smallest, holding onto her family's brass chain, all pulling together.

After she pushed the white button, Birdie got in line. Hennie was behind her, holding tight against her waist. She had a sense of role reversal. *Which one is the grandparent, which one the grandchild?* Her thoughts flew to Mama. *Does a parent ever need parenting?*

Khalid hopped back on the bus.

"Start the engine, Mr. Khalid," Babs shouted, waving her arms to signal him.

Khalid started the engine. Henrietta heard it turn over. Then he engaged the gears to move the bus forward. As the gears began to grind, the right wheel tire splattered mud everywhere. The women shrieked.

"Now pull!" Babs commanded.

The ladies pulled.

"Harder!"

Henrietta hung onto Birdie as she pulled backwards, and the women in front of her and behind her heaved with all their might. Henrietta ignored the pain in her knees and focused on the shiver of excitement running up her spine.

With the women's arms wrapped around each other, she felt part of a long, tightly-knit chain stitch that was knitting something together, even if she didn't know what.

Suddenly Emily felt the tire give a little.

"Come on! The tire's movin'. Pull it, gals! Tug it! Jerk it! Pull!"

Emily pulled, again and again. Slowly, slowly, the tire began to rise up over the chains and out of the mud. As the bus began to roll forward, the line of ladies fell backward, but then they caught one another, breaking each other's falls, pulling each other out of the puddles of mud and rain. Emily used the flashlight to help them pick up the lipstick tubes and car keys spilled from fanny packs and coat pockets, chuckling and hooting with elation as they did so.

Emily remembered Babs's button. "Equality is a Team Sport."

Back on the bus, Henrietta heard Emily ask to see Birdie's picture.

Birdie said she was happy the flash worked so well and then passed it around.

The photo captured the women, arranged largest to smallest, holding each other by the waist. Henrietta looked over the arresting image: women in boots and sneakers, women with fanny packs and backpacks, women with polished nails and nails bitten down to the quick, women who worked for pay and women who worked without it, women from all over the middle of America: pulling together.

Henrietta thought about what it had taken to get them unstuck. "Maybe," she mused, "you have to lean backward to move forward."

Henrietta was exhausted; her whole body collapsed into sleep. She dreamed.

> *In her dream, she was still on the bus, the only rider. As Khalid passed the familiar streets of Soros and pulled up to her apartment complex, she looked out the window. She was shocked at what she saw. Her apartment building was no longer there. It was a pile of bricks and broken glass and twisted railings.*
>
> *The neighbors were gathered around, staring. She overheard nosy Wilma Green tsk-tsk-ing that there'd been an explosion. Max Schneider, who lived on the second floor, was sitting on what used to be the front porch steps, clamping his pipe a bit too tightly between his teeth. The neighbor kids were peddling up on their rusty bikes to gawk.*
>
> *And then, from the direction of Elmer's Drugs, four figures came running. They were not gripping packages of Depends or enemas; they were gripping knitting needles and yarn. Each skein of yarn was a different color: blue and yellow and pink and green.*
>
> *Politely they asked Max Schneider to move off the steps so they could get to work. They began knitting the broken bricks together, one by one, assembly-line fashion. Forty*

fingers were knitting and purling, their fingers flying. When they'd stitched several bricks together, they stacked them next to each other, then on top of each other, even making space for windows.

The bricks began to take shape. They were like multi-colored Lego blocks knit together to construct the basement, the first floor, the second floor, all the way to the top until the building had been rebuilt. Except that the façade of this building was no longer a predictable pattern of dull red bricks. The new pattern was colorful, bold, original.

Emily didn't really want to sleep. She felt energized by the surprising strength of the women marchers dragging the bus out of the mud. Plus she had an idea she wanted to share with Birdie. And yet suddenly her body had sunk into Katie's anyway, her fountain topknot flopped across Katie's snoring chest.

She dreamed she was in a dog park with all kinds of dogs. Pomeranians, Irish setters, Whippets. The dogs were not running or barking or chasing kids: they were grooming each other. Three beagles were yapping in a bathtub while the Great Danes lathered them with soap. The Golden Retrievers stood on tables, their heads in grooming nooses, while the Great Danes blew them dry with hair dryers. Reddish-gold dog hair floated everywhere. A few poodles lounged in chaises while a Saint Bernard brought them cooling drinks.

Emily herself was setting a tray to bring around. She filled the tray with orange carrot sticks, red radish bulbs, green spinach leaves. She offered the tray to the lounging poodles, who nibbled politely one by one. And then an Airedale terrier broke away from the table where he was having

his nails done, gobbling up the vegetables in one fell swoop.
"Bad dog," Emily scolded him, swatting him with her
mother's Coach purse.

When she awakened, a wisp of the scene floated by like a flick of Bravo's tail. It was then that Emily realized she had been dreaming: after all, she'd never strike an animal.

The last thing Birdie remembered before she fell asleep was that chain of women heaving the bus out of the mud. As she drifted off, she dreamed.

> *The women were back on the bus again, their shoes caked from the effort of sucking mud. Only this time, Khalid was checking off new riders on his clipboard: Beanie and Twanny and Mrs. Opie and Mr. Pine and Jamil Washington and Destinee and Jenny's sister Alice and Shanice. Shanice was climbing the steps to the bus all by herself, without her wheelchair. Mama was the last to get on, and she was dressed in her camouflage, Army boots and all.*
>
> *Khalid started up the bus, and the passengers lined up, making a chain down the center aisle. They held on to each other by the waist. Birdie heard music start up. What were they doing? It looked like they were doing a dance. Is it the Crazy Little Women dance? No, it's that dance she remembered from her childhood, the one where you hopped forward and back, backward and forward. The Bunny Hop. Doo-di-doo-di-da-da, dah-dah-dah. Doo-di-doo-di-da-da. HOP, HOP, HOP!*

After that dream about spanking the terrier, Emily couldn't sleep. She looked up and down the rows of sleeping marchers. Hers was the only overhead light twinkling in the darkness. As she gazed past the slumped forms of Katie and Jenny, she saw a thin band of light rising across the horizon in the window glass.

She was dying to talk to Birdie. She and Sonia had been working on their blog ever since the bus left D.C. Emily had written two profiles so far. One was of Tammy Byerly with the short blonde hair. Emily wondered if she might cut her own hair short when she got back to Soros. Maybe even bleach it blonde, too. The other was of Henrietta Oldham, seated in a crepe paper-draped wheelchair; a photo of Michael Jackson was taped to the back, and bottles of nail polish were dangling from the hand rests, tinkling like wind chimes. Emily liked the way she had described Hennie's sweet upturned lips and her eyes opened wide in endless surprise. Sonia had finished one profile, of Naomi seated on the ground, pounding her drum with her large, strong brown hands, her long braid aimed arrow-straight down her back.

But Emily needed to talk to Birdie. The profile pieces on the blog she and Sonia were writing would be so much better with pictures.

Emily looked out the window again. The band of light was thickening. She didn't want to wait. She leaned sideways into the aisle and tapped Birdie's aunt Louise on the shoulder. The woman opened only one eye. Emily had been so close to the girl's aunt that she could observe the eyelashes on her one open eye. They were as thick and stubby as a windshield wiper blade.

Groggily, Louise stumbled into the aisle, moving like a sleep-walker to change seats with her.

Now Emily settled next to Birdie, poking the sleeping girl awake with her finger.

Birdie felt a poke. It startled her awake.

"Good morning," Emily said.

Birdie bit back the questions that were forming in her mind: *What's so good about it? Where is Lou-Lou? What is that white girl doing here?*

Birdie thought about what she knew about this white girl. Like every other white girl, she reeked of privilege. Fancy coffees, kale smoothies, traveling in a yoga-panted herd of crowd-followers, bearing a white-bread name like Katie or Jenny, indifferent to others waiting in a restroom line or needing her to board so their bus could depart.

But Birdie had noticed a few good things about her during the trip. She had been the first to volunteer to push Hennie in the wheelchair, and she had seemed genuinely moved by the drum circle. Afterward, Birdie had been impressed by the little ceremony she created to commemorate the experience. The ceremony had been Emily's idea. *Well, good for her.*

"I need your help, Birdie," Emily said.

Ahhhh. Wypipo. They always want something.

"It's about your pictures," she went on.

And then Emily told Birdie about her blog and how it would look better with pictures. Birdie didn't say that she was surprised that something by Emily might be better with something by her attached to it. But as they scrolled through the pictures of Pauline Frazier and Tammy Byerly and Naomi and Miss Hennie and the nameless police officer in the pussy hat, Birdie could tell Emily was right.

"Just a second," Emily said, looking down at her own phone. "My battery's low."

Without asking, she stretched a charger cord across Birdie and Hennie. The cord looped and circled over the half-finished pink hat in Birdie's lap and the piles of yarn projects in Hennie's, and Birdie watched Emily plug it in to the overhead charger next to the tiny light above Hennie's head. Birdie saw that Emily's charger cord was different than hers. It was one of those extra-long ones that you can buy if you don't have to worry about money.

Henrietta woke to the chatter of young voices. At first she thought it was bird calls because birds cheep especially fiercely in the morning. And then she realized it was Emily and Birdie, chirping together.

Emily's face was trained on Birdie's phone. She was swiping from picture to picture. They'd been talking about people they'd met on the march. Henrietta recognized some of the names. Alexandra Hall. Babs Mildenhaus. But whatever they were working on had changed direction. Now they were cheeping about events as well as people. Waiting at the Trailways station, all the different shoes ready to march. Dancing into Kansas City like crazy little women. Squeezing onto the Metro, unable to breathe. Gazing up at the protest pole in amazement. Facing the police officers determined to ruin everything.

They'd been nice enough to share each picture, passing them under Henrietta's nose, too. But when they came to the picture of herself that she had never seen, Henrietta sat upright, fully awake. It had been taken during the police round-up at the ADAPT protest, and Birdie had captured a picture of Henrietta in the wheelchair, brandishing her knitting needles like weapons. She was tickled pink. "Old lady," she thought proudly, "you are no longer playing the fool."

Looking at the picture, all three of them laughed out loud.

Suddenly Emily reached across two laps to unplug a strong white cord that looked like a fishing line Babs Mildenhaus might use for a big fish. Salmon. Whales, even.

But the long white cord, looped and curlicued, had found its way into Henrietta's knitting tote. And it had hooked onto the needles of a project she had been keeping quietly to herself.

"What's that?" Birdie asked.

Something strange was hooked onto Hennie's needles with Emily's charger cord.

"Nothing."

It looked like a weird animal pulled from the sea, something you'd stare at, something like a goggle-eyed smooth-skinned crab with bamboo appendages, something you'd definitely have to throw back.

"It's not nothing, Hennie," Birdie said. *It's something. What?*

It was certainly different from anything else Hennie had pulled from her tote. It was a rounded mound, made of blush-colored yarn except for a darker beige-colored circle in the middle. Two bamboo needles were sticking out of the top.

Suddenly it dawned on Birdie. It was a falsie, a soft pillowy mound that could turn an A-cup into a BB. It would be a lot more form-flattering than strips of toilet paper ripped from the roll. Birdie wondered if bra-stuffing still appealed to her.

Hennie stared into her lap, embarrassed. Emily, the rude white girl, hadn't bothered to notice.

Emily snatched the knitted circle from Hennie. She held it in her hand, then squeezed it to see how soft it was.

"Miss Hennie," she said flatly, "it looks like a breast."

Henrietta was still gazing into her lap. She cleared her throat. Then she said, "Well, if you must know, it *is* a breast."

Emily was shocked. As if this quiet old gray-bunned lady were an underground dealer in intimate playthings: vibrators, dildos, sex toys.

"They're inserts. For brassieres," Hennie said. "Prosthetics."

Emily had never given much mind to prosthetics. Prosthetics were appendages, something like those blade runners worn by wounded vets when they ran in disability marathons or like those computerized hands that let disabled people grasp things like cups and forks. She had never thought a prosthetic meant something so very close to your body, something so private.

"They're for breast cancer patients who've had mastectomies." Henrietta looked at Birdie and then at Emily. "In case you're wondering, that's surgery to remove a breast."

Emily's hand flew to her own breast. She patted it to reassure herself that it was still there. It might have been only an A-cup, but it was *her* A-cup, and she couldn't imagine losing it.

Birdie could see that Emily was at a loss for words.

Hennie described the breast as something called a "knitted knocker." It came in many colors – white, beige, cocoa, saffron, black. Hennie said she even filled a request for a woman who wanted purple knockers.

"They're a little tricky to make," Hennie said. "You have to use double pointed needles and soft, soft, soft mercerized pima cotton yarn."

Birdie didn't know what any of that was, but she understood about the yarn when Hennie passed over a beige skein, and she felt how light and soft it was under her fingers.

"That's the beauty of them. They're so soft next to the skin. The old silicone prosthetics were just too stiff. They must have felt terribly uncomfortable." Then she smirked. "Probably designed by a man."

While she spoke, Hennie was fingering the watch face on the right side of her bodice.

"Why do you make them?" Emily asked.

Birdie felt a familiar flicker of anger. White people's privileges could make them clueless.

Before Hennie could answer, Aunt Lou hovered over Emily. She wanted her seat back. Emily didn't want to leave yet. She turned to Hennie. "Can I take a picture?"

Henrietta looked surprised. "Of what?"

"Of those knockers. I think our friend Sonia would be interested in hearing about them. We could write about them on our blog."

Henrietta looked doubtful.

Aunt Lou was still hovering. "If she lets you take a picture, will you give me my seat back?" She was giving Emily the squint eye, the same one Mama used.

Henrietta looked doubtful again, but then she relented.

Emily snapped a picture, then stood. She stopped to pull her hair up and re-fasten her claw again before she moved.

Birdie wondered about that doctor visit Hennie had scheduled after she got home.

Louise plopped down in her seat and hooked the tips of her toes across the foot rest. "What's all the fuss about?"

Birdie looked to Hennie for permission, and she nodded her consent.

Birdie explained about the needles, the soft yarn, the prosthetic breast.

"What a wonderful thing!" Louise exclaimed. "What do you do with them?"

"I mail them to the U.K. where the ladies who invented them send them all over the world. It's a nonprofit."

Birdie cheeped, "Aunt Lou knows all about nonprofits."

"But this is an especially interesting one. Women are so bravely creative, aren't they, Hennie?"

Henrietta answered, "They are. And unlike men, they don't think to take much credit." She thought of her stash of books back home, the books about brave and creative women whom most people had never heard of.

"I think the hospital in Topeka would have a need for them,

Hennie," Louise said. "Or our own local doctors in Soros. Would you like me to check that out for you?"

Henrietta thought about it. Her St. Catherine stitchers wouldn't understand a project like this, but it would be nice to be able to share some of her inserts with women closer to home.

"Well, yes, thank you," Henrietta said. "I must confess that this quiet project has meant the world to me."

Henrietta thought about all the quiet suffering there was in the world. And the army of quiet women who spent their lives relieving it. "You know, it's taken me a lifetime, dear," she said to Birdie and Louise, "But I've finally learned that the best way to free yourself is to free someone else."

Emily returned to her seat. She was not just spellbound but speechless. She wondered if all old ladies harbored secret surprises. She had first judged Miss Hennie as an arthritic, run-of-the-mill old lady, and now this old lady had entirely redefined herself with her hip, radical usefulness.

Gleefully Emily explained to Katie and Jenny about Hennie's project. Then she texted the photo to Sonia.

Lou-Lou's phone said it was 6 a.m, and they'd just passed Indianapolis, heading toward St. Louis. Indiana made Birdie think of Shanice. One time, Mama said Indiana didn't have anything but race car crashes and corn and nobody famous ever came from there, but Shanice interrupted.

"Mama," Shanice said, "that's where Michael's from. So that's at least one famous person."

She meant Michael Jackson.

Beanie added, "A lot more than one. There's Jermaine, Jackie, Tito, Marlon, and Randy. So that's at least six, Chip."

Shanice swatted him with her eyes. "Aren't you forgetting Janet? Don't you dare forget about Janet, Beanie!"

Birdie had been proud of Shanice for that comment. Mama, too. Birdie could tell by Mama's full-on grin that showed her big white teeth.

Still, Indiana felt like a kind of nowhere-land wedged between Ohio and Illinois, and Birdie was anxious to get home. She had a few ideas about what to do when she got back.

Emily and her friends giggled at first, then chortled. They'd been giving different brand names to Hennie's knitted knockers.

"Glam mamms."

"Sweater puppies."

"Mammo ammo."

"Knitty-gritties."

"True falsies."

By the time Katie suggested "Biddie's Titties," they were laughing so hard their ribs hurt.

Birdie was irritated by the conversation of the girls in the row behind her. She knew that people made fun of things they didn't understand. Prosthetics. Kinky hair. Old people. Shanice. Still, she didn't like it. She didn't like thinking of women with breast cancer as "biddies." No matter *what* their age.

St. Louis traffic was less chaotic than before. After all, it was

Sunday morning. They were finally back on Central Time. If she was back in her own time zone, she was that much closer to home. St. Louis made Birdie think of "Proud Mary." And "Proud Mary" made her think of Mama: Working for the man every night and day. Birdie thought back to the drum circle and the Mother Song. She didn't want to see Mama drowning in the undertow of grief-heavy anger any longer. *Is there something I can do?*

Lou-Lou was sound asleep, *The Color Purple* draped across her forehead like a sleep mask. Birdie was glad. Lou had worked hard. She deserved a rest.

Birdie began to wonder what would happen when they got home. *Will I ever see The Muses again? Alexandra Hall or Babs Mildenhaus?* Mostly she wondered if she would ever see Hennie again. There was so much Birdie still wanted to know.

Hennie was resting her head against the window, but she was not sleeping. She seemed lost in her own thoughts. Her lips were moving quietly as if she was talking to herself.

"Hennie," Birdie said. "You never did tell me about Sister Florinda."

"My, my, Birdie Jackson. You read my thoughts. I was just thinking of her."

Henrietta couldn't say everything she had been thinking, but one thing she'd been thinking about was struggle. Her own struggles. The struggles of others. Henrietta knew that her struggles would have been even more distressing without Sister Florinda.

"She was the African-American cook in the rectory where I worked as a girl. She was the closest thing I had to a mother. She's the one who taught me to knit. Oh, how patient she was with my fumble-fingers!"

"Where was your own mother?"

Henrietta thought about how to answer. "Well, she was around, but I think she was distracted by her own problems. She didn't have the energy to focus on me."

Henrietta didn't say any more than that. But she now realized that it wasn't just her mother who had been distracted: Henrietta herself had lacked the energy to focus on anything outside her father. It was her father who was always in her rearview mirror. Footsteps clomping on the stairs. Spoons rapping on the bottles of medicines on the bedside table. She was frightened of him, and she had served him faithfully to stave off his anger, and in hope for his approval. She wondered if her mother had felt the same.

Frances Oldham was a blur. She was a shadow bent over her sewing, her fingers raw from pricking needles. She was a ghost disappearing behind the old treadle machine inherited from a cousin. Her stacks of ladies' dresses and jackets and skirts on the chair beside the kitchen table demanded her attention like phantom children.

Henrietta never told her mother the details about what had happened to her at the rectory. Her mother's awareness had dawned on the day she asked if Henrietta needed any more sanitary napkins from Elmer's Drugs. Henrietta had replied, "No, thank you. I won't be needing them for a very long while."

Hennie and her mother never spoke about it again. The arrangements were turned over to Sister Florinda.

Sometimes, when Henrietta caught her mother's eyes, they blinked for a moment in a glimmer of understanding. But Frances Oldham always looked away. There was never a straight-on gaze. Mother and daughter both lived to serve the man of the house and the men of the church, and neither of them ever broke that pact. Henrietta knew one thing: they had both been prisoners.

Henrietta couldn't tell Birdie that she had entrusted the truth to Sister Florinda. Florinda had tried to sidetrack Father Cochran on Tuesdays and Fridays with diversions. She had filched the Master Lock from Father Cochran's desk drawer and slipped it into the pocket of Henrietta's school uniform one Friday afternoon. Florinda had explained about iodine douches and how they might help. She had gone to the bishop on her behalf, decades before those articles in the *Boston Globe*. Florinda had tried to learn about adoption, but the bishop and the adoption laws had been fortresses against her. Sister Florinda had driven Henrietta to the bus depot for the ride alone across the prairie to somewhere on the western edge of Kansas. She had given her a bag of needles and yarn, and she had whispered four words Henrietta would never forget: *I believe in you.*

That was over fifty years ago: Henrietta remembered it like it was yesterday.

Birdie's mind flew with questions: *Hennie had been fumble-fingered? Her mother had been distracted by her own problems? Did they have more in common than being named for fathers?*

"Florinda and I used to talk. And she listened. My mother wasn't much of a listener, so I depended on Sister. Every young person needs someone to listen, don't you think?"

Birdie didn't answer. She gave only a tiny nod. She doubted Hennie had noticed it.

"I know now what I only sensed then. That if you keep silent for too long, parts of you begin to die."

Birdie thought about how silent she had kept. For too long. *Yes, Hennie, when you keep silent for too long, parts of you begin to die.*

"Still," Hennie went on, "talking requires someone on the other end to listen, someone you can trust. For me it was Sister Florinda."

Birdie looked over at the sweet lady sitting beside her.

The braids atop her head suggested both youth and age. The clutch of fluffy knitting projects nestled into her lap like baby chicks. The grandmotherly things about her were endearing: the pocket pack of tissues, the accordion rain hat. But it was more than that. It was what she had affirmed about Birdie herself. *Mighty smart. An especially good name for a young girl your age. Not IM-possible.*

Birdie thought about what Hennie had said. *Someone on the other end to listen. Someone you could trust.*

And she began.

Birdie seemed full of confusion, full of guilt, full of all the things young girls shouldn't be full of. Henrietta remembered being full of those things long ago, too.

Birdie told her about resenting participation in her sister's ADAPT group. She told her about the wretched video those hateful children made to mock her sister. She told her about how she didn't stand up to her friend about it.

"I'm nothing like Malala," Birdie said, hanging her head.

And then she swiped to a picture on her aunt's phone.

It had been taken on the night of a YMCA dance. Birdie's brother Bakari was kneeling beside Shanice's wheelchair on her left; Birdie was kneeling beside the wheelchair on the right. Shanice's smile lit up the picture.

Birdie explained about what happened that night and about how she had abandoned Shanice, how she had disappointed her mama, and how she had blamed herself.

Henrietta thought about what to say. She understood about the dilemma of women, young and old. It was the tension between duty to others and duty to self. It was like the challenge of knitting: you had to balance the tension just right.

"I'm so sorry, Birdie," she said. "You've been caught by that old Jayhawk. You were just an egg in the nest, and that nasty bird stole something from you. Now it's time to shake that old Jayhawk off. Don't let it peck in your nest any longer."

"But how do I do that, Hennie?"

"Well, dear, sometimes the best way to free yourself is to free someone else." She reached over and patted Birdie's half-finished pussy hat.

Then she added four words: "I believe in you."

Emily had been texting Sonia, urging her to come to Kansas for a visit.

"Why would she want to come to Kansas?" Katie asked. "Kansas isn't as exciting as Philadelphia, is it? I mean Pennsylvania has the Liberty Bell and the Declaration of Independence, right?"

"Maybe so, but I'll bet Pennsylvania doesn't have the World's Largest Ball of Twine or the World's Largest Spur. Or a city that's the Cow Chip Capital of America. We've got the graves of the *In Cold Blood* killers. Or the Sexting Statue in Bucyrus."

"The *what?*" Jenny asked.

"It says here that it's a statue of a headless woman taking a selfie with a phone. A Chinese father wanted to warn his kids of the dangers of selfies. He put up the statue in 2013."

"Was it an I-phone?"

"Don't know what kind of phone."

"Well, it doesn't matter. It's already out of date."

"We can always take Sonia to see Deafy Boular, girls."

"No, thank you," Jenny said. "I think a disabled person would like a different kind of memorial instead of one stuck in concrete for people to gawk at until the end of time."

It had been four hours since St. Louis, and Birdie wasn't yet finished with her pussy hat. The knitting had become easier with practice, and the stitches had reminded her of that preschool story about the Three Bears: not too tight, not too loose, but juuust right. Hennie had offered to help her finish off the top when she got there. But Birdie hadn't got there yet.

Birdie had been listening to the conversation of the Three Muses. They were trying to entice Sonia to visit Kansas by pointing out attractions like the World's Largest Ball of Twine or the graves of the *In Cold Blood* killers. Emily had suggested taking Sonia to the Deafy Boular statue.

Birdie agreed with Jenny. She thought a disabled person would like a different kind of memorial.

The green road sign said they were almost at the turn for Leavenworth. Soros wasn't far now.

The sign for Leavenworth reminded Birdie that there were all kinds of prisons in the world: slave ships, ventilators, reservations, white privilege, male privilege. *How long did you have to sit on a nest in order for the egg of possibility to hatch?*

Birdie checked her phone. "It's 11:30 Central, Miss Hennie," she said.

Birdie watched Hennie's fingers as they changed the time on her upside down watch. Birdie was thankful for a phone that updated the time automatically. Birdie had always found the time changes confusing. Central. Eastern. Daylight Savings. It was like the centuries. She had to think hard when teachers brought up centuries at school. Like how the 1800s were the 19th century. Or the 20th century was the 1900s. *Why can't the 1900s just be the 19th century?*

Birdie thought back to the beginning of this trip. About how time seemed divided into distinct parts. BC and AD. Or BS and AS: Before Shanice and After Shanice. Now she was wondering: *Can I divide time up in new ways? Before the March? And After?*

PART VII – SOROS, KANSAS

After the March

A few days after Birdie got back to Soros, the phone rang. It was hard to hear the person on the line because Beanie was playing Kendrick Lamar's "DNA" at full volume. Birdie covered the receiver and shouted to Beanie to turn down the music. When Birdie realized it was Hennie, she felt her heart pick up its pace. The familiar quiet voice asked, "Would you and Beanie mind driving me in your van to see my doctor at the clinic?"

Birdie was thrilled to hear from Hennie. Now that she was back in Soros, she'd spent a lot of time wondering what it would be like to be home after the march. She was different on the inside, but the outside was still school, friends, her grades, Mama. She wondered if she would ever start living on After the March time.

It didn't seem likely.

Birdie knew that Friday nights had been different after Shanice. They didn't play music and dance anymore, but Twanny insisted that they still try to be together as a family. At least on Fridays. He said he didn't want to leave for college in the fall and see us split up, going our separate stubborn ways.

Friday nights would now be movie nights, not dance nights. The ritual had worked pretty well. Birdie's favorite movie was *Dreamgirls*. Even though they liked Beyonce's music, Twanny and Beanie

267

dismissed the movie as a chick flick. Birdie didn't think that was fair. Her brothers had forced her to sit through the gory woodchipper scene in *Fargo* a million times. After they first watched *Two Can Play That Game*, about women getting back at their cheating men, one movie line became part of the brothers' lives. When Mama tried to get them to do something they didn't want to do, Twanny and Beanie chorused, "The CIA ain't got nothin' on a woman with a plan."

But on the first Friday night after the march, Mama refused to sit and watch with us kids. Beanie even tuned in to her favorite movie, *Love and Basketball*, where the female athlete challenges her man and the status quo. Birdie was looking forward to watching it because Beanie always said the male star was a big pussy, and Twanny always told him to shut up. After the march, Birdie was looking forward to telling him to shut up, too.

But Mama stomped out of the room.

Birdie went after her. "What's wrong, Mama? Don't you like *Love and Basketball* any more?"

Mama stuck out her bottom lip. "Nope," she said. Birdie pictured a turtle pulling his head into his shell. End of discussion.

Even after the march, Birdie didn't know what to do about Mama.

So it was a relief to see Hennie giving them a little four-fingered wave from her front steps as they drove up to her apartment building. Hennie's little wave calmed Birdie down. She'd been mad at Mama and she was now fuming at Beanie. He hadn't thought to clean all the loose drink cups and fast-food wrappers from the van, so she'd done it herself. Birdie offered to help Hennie climb into the van, but Hennie insisted on hoisting herself inside on her own. Once she had figured out about the seat belt, Hennie said, "My, but your brother's as handsome as you said, Birdie." Right to his face.

Beanie gave a grin as toothy as Mama's into his rear-view mirror. "That's what all the women say."

At the clinic, the three of them came in together and got a lot of stares from the people in the waiting room. After her appointment was over and they'd driven her home, Hennie thanked them, pressing a peppermint wrapped in cellophane into their hands. Birdie began to think of Hennie as a grandmother again. Tissue pack. Plastic rain hat. Peppermints.

A few days later, Hennie called to say their trip to the clinic had been something she called a "joyride." "It was a ride," Hennie said, "that ended in joy because all I have to do is go back in six months for a follow-up." When she said that the second scan turned out to be negative, Hennie's voice tinkled like Christmas bells.

To celebrate, Hennie was planning that bus trip to Larned in a few days. She would be visiting Sheila Roberts. Together they would attend the big Antique, Vintage, and Collectible Show.

"Would you like Beanie and me to drive you to the Trailways station?"

"Oh, my," Hennie said, her voice hesitant at first, as if she was surprised at the offer, "that would be lovely, dear."

At the antiques show, Henrietta was overwhelmed by the number of displays. Dealers had come from at least four surrounding states as well as California and New York. The tables were crowded with displays, and the aisles were crowded with people.

Sheila Roberts seemed to know all the dealers and most of the visitors. As she introduced her new friend around, Henrietta realized that most of the dealers ran businesses that were more interesting and profitable than Oldham's Antiques.

It dawned on Henrietta that the most successful dealers specialized in things like Civil War artifacts or vintage jewelry. Even plain junk could turn a profit if it was curated and unique enough. Cheap costume jewelry – pronged, not glued – could bring between thirty and two hundred dollars a piece, and matching sets of rings, necklaces, earrings, and pins could bring even more. One dealer, a man sporting a pencil-thin moustache and a velvet smoking jacket with satin lapels, presided over a display of costume jewelry worn by movie stars. There was Elizabeth Taylor's serpent belt from *Cleopatra*; a snake bracelet worn by Rita Hayworth; and Rhett Butler's cigar case, an artifact from the set of *Gone with the Wind*. The man's fake jewels brought thousands. "Even so," Henrietta snickered to herself, "Can you really trust a man in a smoking jacket?"

Henrietta was most intrigued by a dealer introduced by Sheila as her "dear friend." Margaret Sutherton specialized in suffrage artifacts and said that any friend of Sheila's was a friend of hers; in an act of instant intimacy, Margaret said Henrietta should feel free to call her "Peggy."

Sheila and Henrietta and Peggy chatted for over an hour exploring Peggy's offerings and hearing about their provenance. In addition to the bookplates and stamps, Peggy had a rare "New Woman" stickpin she had acquired twenty years ago for ten dollars at an estate sale in New Haven, Connecticut; it was worth nearly three thousand now. She had an antique tintype of Sojourner Truth from the 1800s; even though it was in poor condition, it was currently worth nearly thirty thousand dollars.

Peggy Sutherton's expertise was astonishing. She knew that Elizabeth Cady Stanton had made a run for Congress in 1866. Peggy explained that the state constitution in New York prohibited women from voting but not from running for office. "Oh, that Elizabeth was a sly one, wasn't she?" Peggy said, raising her eyebrows in delight. Peggy and Henrietta agreed that the fact she got only twenty-four votes wasn't the point. Henrietta was proud of her own few suffrage items, yet she didn't have the knowledge of a real collector or a single artifact of much value.

Henrietta splurged and bought an old ballot box, circa 1920, from Peggy. She told herself she was entitled to an indulgence in herself after all these years. When Peggy Sutherton gave Henrietta her card and asked for one in return, Henrietta realized she needed more than a new business card: she needed to rethink her whole business. Even if she gave the shop a sassy new name like "Junque," her offerings were still junk. It would be a gamble, but Sister Florinda always said it was a waste of time to put lipstick on a pig. Florinda was right. She'd never really liked the antique shop anyway.

Birdie never got mail, so she turned the envelope over in her hand suspiciously, making sure it was really meant for her. The envelope, made of heavy off-white paper, was addressed to "Miss Alberta 'Birdie' Jackson" and suggested something formal like the graduation announcements for Twanny that Mama couldn't afford. Birdie opened the letter and pulled out the sturdy square of paper that matched the shade of the envelope. She studied words written in a script so elegant that she knew the writer must have studied penmanship. "You are cordially invited to a tea party reunion for the women who attended The March." Birdie had never attended a tea party before. Or a reunion, for that matter. The tea party reunion would take place on Saturday at 2 p.m. at Hennie's apartment. At the end of the invitation were these words, double-underlined: "Bring your mother."

Emily called Sonia and Katie and Jenny. They had received invitations, too. Emily begged Sonia to come. She knew Philadelphia was far away and that Sonia was in the middle of her last yoga certification class, but she had missed her with all her heart. Sonia could share her bed in her parents' basement, and other than the bus fare, the trip would be free. Sonia could stay as long as she liked. At the end of the conversation, she reminded Sonia to bring her pussy hat.

Mama didn't really want to come, but Aunt Louise had received an invitation, too, and Lou was more insistent than Birdie had ever seen her, so Mama gave in.

As she greeted them at the door, Birdie saw Hennie in a new light. Without her over-washed blouse and orthopedic shoes, Hennie looked different from the companion she had met on the bus. Hennie was wearing a simple black dress and no-nonsense black pumps. Her hair was no longer in a braided nest atop her head, but it had been swept back and coiled at the nape of her neck into something that looked French.

Birdie and Lou had told Mama about Miss Henrietta Oldham, but when Hennie introduced herself, taking Mama's hand in hers and holding it for a good long while, Mama looked surprised. As if she'd expected someone much older, someone with swollen ankles and a hump, someone ready for a nursing home.

Hennie took their coats, and Birdie was relieved that Hennie didn't offer to take Mama's crocheted red beanie; her hair was growing out but it still looked a fright. Mama looked even more surprised when the Muses rushed through the door together, hugging and babbling. Lou and Birdie had explained about pussy hats beforehand, but Mama stared anyway.

Emily caught the scent of fresh-cut lemons as Hennie ushered them into a sparsely furnished apartment across from the antique store. The round table in the middle of the room made Emily think of the drum circle. Although the surface of the circular table was marred by burn marks and scratches, it looked freshly polished and set with special care. In the middle of the table were two teapots. They were wrapped in cozies patterned with blue and white hydrangeas like the ones she remembered from her grandmother's parlor. The teapots were flanked by cut-glass cream pitchers and sugar bowls.

Emily felt transported back in time to the tufted velvet stools and the chintz curtains of her grandmother's house, a quiet time without ring tones and Alexa. Around the table were eight china tea cups, each cup hand painted with a different flower motif: roses, pansies, daisies, cosmos, bluebells, violets, buttercups, forget-me-nots. A few of the cups were spoiled with spidery cracks that suggested they'd been broken but that someone had cared enough about them to glue them back together. That was how Emily felt about Sonia and herself: broken cups, mended together.

The Muses seemed at ease, but Mama looked stiff, and Birdie admitted to herself that she felt uncomfortable too. She'd never drunk tea from a cup in her life, and she'd never sat at a table set with cloth napkins. In her family, it was always paper - napkins or towels. Birdie stared at the sugar bowls. She'd never seen sugar molded into tiny separate cubes; she knew only the granulated sugar that came in sacks from the Hy-Vee. Miniature silver tongs lay beside each sugar bowl, and Birdie guessed you weren't supposed to pick the sugar cubes up with your fingers.

Still, there was something elegant about the setting that made a statement about the women gathered around it and inspired Birdie to sit a bit taller in her chair. Birdie listened as Hennie explained that the tea cups were from her shop but they weren't fine china and they'd been broken a time or two. She pointed out the two tea pots, one for brewed tea, the other for hot water. The brewed tea was something Hennie called Lemon Verbena, and if they preferred tea bags, there was a glass bowl of them they could choose from.

Birdie thought she'd try the Lemon Verbena, but Mama wanted to explore the different tea bags. "My," she said, "I've never heard of so many teas." She rattled them all off as she flipped through the choices: Jade Citrus, Mint Majesty. Mango Mist. "If I pick 'English Breakfast Tea,'" Mama asked, "do I have to be English?"

"No," Hennie grinned. "And it doesn't have to be breakfast time, either."

That broke the ice.

"I think I'll have some of that 'Peach Tranquility,'" Mama decided, reaching for a gold foil square emblazoned with peaches. "Tranquility's hard to come by, don't you think?"

It was quiet. No one said anything.

Hennie broke the silence. "Yes, Mrs. Jackson," she said. "Especially for women. We learned that on the march, didn't we, ladies?"

After everyone had her cup of tea, Jenny asked, "Aren't you supposed to lift your little pinkie when you drink tea?"

"Hell, no," Hennie said. "Women raise fists, not pinkies," she said, winking at Mama.

After the laughter died down and they had finished raising their fists, Hennie announced, "I'm so glad we can be together again. To celebrate, I've brought each of you something special."

Hennie handed everyone a manila envelope. Emily felt like she did on Christmas morning, anticipating a still-to-be-unwrapped Christmas gift.

Birdie dived into her envelope, shocked by what she pulled out. Inside was a stack of photographs tied with pink ribbon. Her photographs. Every single one.

"I must confess," Hennie said, "that I was in cahoots with Birdie's aunt Louise here. But I'm thrilled that she agreed to help because I think this is the best way to remember our time together. Besides, Mrs. Jackson wasn't able to join us on the march, so we thought she might get to experience it this way."

Birdie felt something hot and stinging behind her eyes. She clamped her eyes shut the way you clamped on a lid to keep a bubbling pot from spilling over. Birdie felt herself breathing harder. She held her teacup under her nose, absorbing the lemony scent, willing herself to take her time, to inhale slowly.

Then Emily had an idea.

"Let's arrange the pictures in chronological order so Mrs. Jackson can learn all about the trip."

They set about arranging the pictures from the first one of shoes on the asphalt outside the Trailways station to the last one of the women pulling together to haul their bus out of the mud. Birdie decided Emily wasn't such a stupid white girl after all. She'd suggested the best way to get Mama to understand their trip.

Birdie glanced over at Hennie. She was smiling softly as she listened to the girls sorting and remembering and exclaiming: All the different hairdos. The two old ladies in the rest stop, one Black and one white, in front of the sign that said "A Woman's Place is in the Resistance." The Muses in yoga poses atop the bus outside the McDonald's. Lady Liberty with her copper-green face and unshackled feet. The birds-eye view of streets jammed with thousands of marchers, pink hats bobbing like balloons at a circus.

But the reaction Birdie was intent on was the reaction of Mama.

"My baby girl," Mama asked, "took all of these?" Her face turned skeptical the way it did when she got a past due notice for a bill she swore she'd paid.

Lou-Lou delivered her answer like a swat. "Young woman. Not baby girl."

After they had laid out the pictures in order, Mrs. Jackson asked, "Which ones are your favorites?"

Birdie said she couldn't pick out just one because they were all so special to her.

Sonia picked out the one of the police officer leaning on the lamp post, a pink pussy hat on his head.

Katie picked out the one of the thousands of memorial signs left behind on the Ellipse.

Jenny picked out the one of herself standing at the front of the bus, her GIRL POWER rocket blasters on full display.

Emily picked out the one of the four friends at the main stage, arms around each other.

Louise picked out the one of Naomi being hauled off to jail by the police, the army of descending marchers swinging their purses and stomping their feet.

"What about you, Miss Hennie?" Mrs. Jackson asked.

Hennie didn't hesitate. "This one," she said.

It was the picture of Hennie wielding her pointed aluminum knitting needles like weapons, one in each fist.

Mrs. Jackson was about to take a sip of Peach Tranquility. She stopped just as the cup reached her lips. "Is that *you,* Miss Hennie?"

Hennie looked out over her curated arrangement of tea pots, linen napkins, and sugar bowls. "If women want to be seen, Mrs. Jackson, they have to fight. Don't you agree?"

Mrs. Jackson's eyes widened under the arches of her eyebrows. Her cup met its saucer with a solid clink. Then she looked over at Hennie. "Please. Call me 'Ronnie.'"

Lou-Lou stood up and pulled out a plastic bag she'd been hiding beneath her chair. "It's something I picked up at the gift shop in Columbia, Missouri. I wanted to save it for a special occasion. I think today is special enough."

Aunt Louise pulled out a large stuffed bird.

Birdie thought it an awkward-looking gangly thing that reminded her of herself. Its body was made of kente cloth in the same colors as her headband: greens, yellows, reds, and blacks. Although the bird's feet were facing forward, its body was twisted backward. It was holding an egg in its beak.

"It's called a Sankofa bird," Lou-Lou said. "It's a bird that hails from Ghana, where Birdie's grandmother lives. "And 'Sankofa' is Birdie's middle name."

All eyes around the circle turned to Birdie.

"The word 'Sankofa' means 'go back to the past to bring forward what is useful for the present.'"

Birdie swallowed hard as Louise passed the bird over to her.

"Thank you, Aunt Lou," Birdie said, her eyes scanning the bird's bloated body and toothpick limbs.

Then Birdie passed the bird around the circle so that the others could examine it too. She wondered what each of them was thinking. Birdie herself was thinking about that egg in the bird's beak. And wondering what it might hatch.

When the Sankofa bird reached Miss Hennie, she nestled the bird in her arms and said, "This bird reminds me that it's important to move forward while looking backward, to see where you've been to know where you want to go. It tells me I've needed a change."

Then she told us her plan. Her friend Sheila Roberts was buying out the contents of Oldham's Antiques. After Max Schneider's lease was up, she'd take no more renters. Hennie was going to turn the antique store into a yarn shop and perhaps retail space. As she talked, she gazed at the air right above her head where cartoon bubbles or dreams might go. She planned to call it YARNS, a place for women to knit and spin their stories. She described it as a calming place filled with beautiful yarns and specialty teas, a place for women who needed a warm, friendly place to relax. She even imagined a logo: the letter "Y" in "yarns" fashioned from a skein of wool.

"I can help," Katie volunteered.

Hennie blinked, surprised.

Katie reminded Hennie that she worked in a crafts store. She knew all about the best discount yarn brokers and the most reliable distributors. She had lots of catalogs to share. She could bring them over this evening.

Encouraged, Hennie asked, "Do you think I could turn this room where we're sitting into a space for knitting classes? Sort of a comfy community for knitters?"

"It's perfect!" Emily exclaimed. "You've got great light through that big window, a bathroom, and a kitchen where knitters can make themselves coffee and tea."

Hennie grinned. "I'm even imagining teaching knitting classes myself. I could teach an introductory class for beginners. We could start with hats. Hats are easy for beginners. We could maybe even knit pussy hats." Hennie looked over at Birdie. "I don't think you've ever finished your hat, dear. Have you?"

Birdie wondered what Mama thought about the Sankofa bird. She studied her face as it was passed around, but Mama seemed even harder to read since Birdie had come back from the march. Even so, when Hennie mentioned finishing the pussy hat, Mama said, "Maybe Destinee or La'Keisha might be interested in knitting one with you while you finish yours up. What do you think?"

"Maybe," Birdie mumbled, unsure whether Mama was trying to support Hennie's shop or implying that Birdie was lazy about finishing things.

As they got ready to leave, Hennie invited them into the shop and asked them to take whatever they wanted. By the end of next week, everything would be gone.

Emily took a few pieces of vintage jewelry for her mother; the Opera Board held a charity auction every fall. Jenny took a cloth doll – a grinning Cheshire Cat for her sister Alice's Wonderland collection. Mama picked up a few antique Christmas ornaments, holding them by their hooks over at the window, watching them glimmer in the light. Louise would send a volunteer with a van next week to pick up some silverware and some end tables for her nonprofit. Sonia offered to set up a computer for Hennie. If she bought it right away, before Sonia went back to Philadelphia, Hennie could have a business plan that included a Facebook page and an Instagram account before she left. Sonia might even be able to get class credit for the project in her current business and marketing class.

Katie had Hennie by the hand, pointing out places for the

checkout counter, the yarn displays. Already she had Hennie imagining cubbyholes for her yarn like they had at the crafts store. "We can put them right here," she said, sweeping her free hand across the largest wall. "I can get Marc to come and take measurements right away. And I get a discount at the crafts store on baskets and bins. Come to think of it, you might need a revolving rack for knitting magazines and small knitting kits."

Listening to these plans, Birdie began to think that she might interest La'Keisha and Destinee in knitting lessons. After all, pussy hats were pretty interesting.

As they stepped to the doorway, Hennie pulled Birdie aside and pointed to her Sankofa bird. "It's excellent for keeping Jayhawks away."

Henrietta couldn't believe how much could be done in two weeks. The yarn cubbies were up, and supplies were being ordered. Jenny had made up a schedule for beginning knitting classes to start the following week. In addition to the battered folding chairs left behind by renters, Henrietta had saved a couple of the antique store's overstuffed chairs and moved them into the knitting space across the hall from the shop.

Katie had brought over a pile of yarn catalogs, and as Henrietta dreamed her way through them, she discovered that there were vacation tours for knitters: woolen mills in Yorkshire, England; knitting tours of the Shetland Islands; an annual sheep shearing event in California. She'd put those brochures in the shop's browsing rack, and keep a few on her bedside table.

"Well, thank you, Katie," Hennie said, dreaming over the knitting tours. "If Henry can travel to Dublin now and again as just a humble priest, maybe I can attend the Northwest Ireland Knitting Retreat."

Sonia piped up. "And you can take it as a business expense, too," she said.

Mama still refused to participate in their Friday night family movie. Birdie had hoped seeing her photographs and experiencing Miss Hennie's tea might have loosened her up. But Mama was still stiff as a board, sitting alone in the kitchen while Beanie pressed "play" for another night of *Fargo*.

Twanny got up. "I'm sick of this," he said. "it's not a family movie night if she's not letting us act like a family."

Twanny meant Mama. Birdie hadn't realized that Antoine was sick of her, too.

Twanny stomped to the kitchen and Birdie followed. "Come on, Mama. Don't be like this."

"Be like what?" She was standing at the kitchen sink, staring into her cup of black coffee.

"You know. Not being with us."

Mama crossed her arms across her chest and huffed.

"Do you want to watch something else, Mama? We don't have to watch *Fargo* again. We can watch something you like, something girlie like *Waiting to Exhale* or something funny with Tyler Perry."

Birdie hoped Tyler Perry might do it. *Why Did I Get Married?* always busted Mama up.

Twanny put his arm around Mama's waist like he did whenever she needed softening up. Then he insisted, taking her arm and pulling her back into the living room. He made Beanie move over so Mama could have her favorite spot at the end of the couch.

"Don't want to sit here," Mama said.

None of them understood.

"But it's your favorite seat, Mama," Beanie said.

"I don't mean here on the couch." She stabbed at the air with a pointed finger. "I mean *here. In this room.*"

Birdie's eyes travelled the length of Mama's arm until it reached the pointed tip of her finger. She had pointed right at Shanice's wheelchair. After the march, it took the place of the ventilator, which had been shipped off to Sunny Days Nursing Home.

"That thing was supposed to be gone after Birdie got home."

Birdie was dumfounded. She hadn't realized Shanice's wheelchair would be an affront to Mama.

Now Antoine was angry. "*That thing*," he said, "belonged to *our sister.*" Twanny glared at Mama. "She wasn't just *your daughter.* Shanice was ours, too."

Birdie had never seen her older brother get mad. He was steady; he worked hard; he brought income into the family. Unlike Birdie and Mama, Twanny never showed a trace of sadness or anger. Even when he was young, Antoine acted like a grown-up man, trying to take the place of their father.

Birdie ran from the room, tears flooding her cheeks. She grabbed something from the bureau and ran back to the living room.

Twanny had stopped glaring and started speaking again. "We thought we'd said our good-byes to Shanice with the Michael Jackson picture and the nail polish bottles and your locket and my letter."

While he spoke, Birdie heard the dialogue in *Fargo* still playing in the background. She thought a Minnesota winter couldn't be any colder than their living room.

"But maybe," Twanny continued, "Birdie wasn't ready to say good-bye yet."

Birdie wiped her eyes with the sleeve of her sweat shirt, feeling affirmed by her brother's words.

Then Beanie rose from the couch and reached for the remote. He switched off the TV. "Mama," he said, moving toward her, "I love seeing that purple shawl draped over her chair every morning." Birdie had never heard the word "love" leak from her brother's mouth. She had never seen his head bowed so humbly before. "Maybe I wasn't ready to say good-bye yet, either."

Everyone was quiet, at a loss for words.

Finally Birdie said, "We need to talk. It's time." She thought back to what she'd learned from Hennie: *If you keep silent for too long, parts of you begin to die.*

Birdie looked over and saw Beanie studying her face. His own face had softened, and there was something like hope in his eyes.

"Tiptoeing around and holding our tongues hasn't made things better," Birdie went on. "The only way our family's pain will go away," she said, "is if we talk about it."

And they did.

Birdie rooted around in the manila envelope in her hand and pulled out a photograph. She held it up.

"I couldn't say what my favorite picture was the other day at the tea, Mama. But I've thought about it some more, and this one's my favorite."

They all studied the picture. It was the picture of the protest pole, gleaming in the January sunlight with its colorful streamers dangling from CPAP cables, its bedpans sparkling with glitter, its garlands of non-skid hospital socks. While they peered into the picture, Birdie explained about what she'd learned about the ADAPT pin and how she'd felt about saying Shanice's name into the universe.

Birdie looked over at Mama. Her shaggy field of a head was bent over, and her hands covered her eyes. But all of them knew what Mama's shaking shoulders meant.

Then Birdie ran to the garage, wheeling the duffel bag into the center of the living room. She zipped it open and began to pull out the length of chain while her brother Beanie helped. "This is our family's chain," Birdie said. "It can either drag us down or lift us up." Together they followed Birdie's lead, passing the links from hand to hand, winding the chain around and around each other, embracing the circle of their family. They talked far into the night. Not just listening. But hearing.

When boxes and boxes of beautiful yarns began to arrive from all corners of the world, Henrietta plunged her hands into the skeins, lifting out the precious cargo and nestling them to her chest as if they were newborns of her very own. She explored the colors and weights and origins of each unique skein before placing it for display, thinking of her cubbyholes as incubators.

Each day, as the morning light flooded the shop, she marvelled at the rainbow of colors winking in the light: they reminded her of stained glass.

Emily couldn't believe their good fortune: Hennie had made them an offer. She was turning her apartment building into living and studio space for them.

Sonia and Emily could take one of the second-floor apartments in the front; Katie and Jenny could take one of the second-floor apartments in the back. The girls would pay what they could each month, but they had to promise to pay something.

Sonia arrived to join them mid-March, her yoga certification in hand, and Hennie agreed that a yoga studio in the first-floor apartment behind the space for knitters would work well.

Emily marvelled at the way Sonia took charge of the yoga studio. Sonia had liked Emily's idea of combining the animal spirits and yoga poses, so they decided to call the studio "Zoo Yoga," and they bought posters to put on the walls to model various poses based on animals: downward dog, the swan, cat-cow, butterfly. The free space was a godsend. All they needed to start was an open area and a certified teacher like Sonia. One day they might sell yoga mats, but for now students could bring their own. Sonia planned to use her phone for the background music, soundscapes like rain on tin roofs, morning bird calls, rolling ocean waves.

Inspired by Sonia, Emily wanted to turn the apartment behind the yoga studio into a dog grooming business. "Don't get ahead of yourself, Emily," Sonia cautioned. Emily had to admit that she had already begun to think about buying sets of grooming brushes and shampoos. "A new business needs to pass inspection and get a license. And it wouldn't hurt for you to take a dog grooming class at the community college in Topeka."

Emily muttered, "Why did running a business have to be so complicated? And why was sensible Sonia usually right?"

Henrietta had to admit it: these young girls were clever. She was especially excited about Jenny's idea. It was clear that the knitting space wouldn't be utilized all day every day, so Jenny thought of expanding the concept into a designated community space. Anyone who wanted to meet there could reserve it for a small donation. If they were open day and evening hours, that meant over seventy hours of meeting time, over eighty if they stayed open on Saturdays.

When Jenny suggested using the space for members of the ADAPT group, Henrietta was excited. Louise provided Jenny with all of the contact information from the ADAPT box that sat on her Protest Desk, and Katie volunteered to help with craft projects for the meetings.

Jenny also suggested that women who were dealing with breast cancer - either in treatment or as survivors – might want a meeting space. They did. One of the first meetings in the new community space featured the Pink Ribbon Girls; these were women who had recovered from breast cancer and who now volunteered to drive those in treatment to doctor visits or to provide child care or to fix a meal. At one of their meetings, the Pink Ribbon Girls made up gift baskets that included information about Henrietta's knitted prosthetics. A few of them signed up for knitting classes as a way of relaxing during treatment. Henrietta was thrilled: Knitting was transforming anxiety into tranquility.

Emily didn't want to travel to Topeka, so she enrolled in a class at the local YMCA. She hated admitting that Sonia was right, but she soon realized she needed to learn about breed temperaments, anatomy, and techniques for grooming like thinning, stripping, and carding. Best of all were the hands-on clinics. Emily discovered that it was one thing to hold a pair of scissors and quite another to face an agitated Yorkie with them.

Through the class, Emily discovered something called pet therapy. It involved using animals to cheer people in nursing homes and hospitals, to lift the spirits of chemo patients and veterans with PTSD. She decided to start a pet therapy group in Soros, and Jenny agreed that Hennie's community center would make a perfect meeting place.

When she consulted Jenny about scheduling, Emily discovered that Jenny had been floating the idea of offering the space for AA meetings. Emily was uncomfortable with the idea at first. But then she realized how proud her dad would be of her when he saw her friends launching alcoholics into recovery. And his daughter launching animals into therapy.

Then, in consultation with Birdie's aunt Louise, Henrietta decided to give the back two apartments on the east end a social service slant. They could serve as a kind of neighborhood charity center. Louise Franklin and her home furnishings for the needy could occupy one of the apartments, enlarging the selections with offerings from garage and estate sales and freeing Louise from having to move her nonprofit from place to place as rents were raised. They would set up the apartment in the back for a soup kitchen, where the hungry could avoid the shame of the front door and simply walk in the back for a free take-out meal. The apartment kitchen already had a stove, refrigerator, and storage space. Katie's boyfriend Marc arranged for leftovers from the Outback Steakhouse to be delivered twice a week, and Louise rounded up donations to stock the pantry from her lists of local churches. Beanie and Twanny and Birdie and their friends helped with the cooking in their free time. Louise supervised, teaching them simple things like chili, egg salad, beans and rice. Later, if they got good and she felt like it, she might share the recipe for her famous fried chicken.

Emily was thrilled at how quickly Hennie had come to appreciate Sonia. Hennie now knew what a whiz Sonia was at marketing. With help from Birdie's aunt Lou, she applied for non-profit status for some of their operations, and she wrote up grant applications to various charities and churches.

Although Emily knew Hennie didn't exactly understand all of it, every venture – Zoo Yoga, YARNS, and the community center they named The Nest - had a Facebook page, a Twitter and an Instagram account. And business cards. Henrietta mostly just understood about the business cards, but Henrietta knew one thing: The Nest deserved a Grand Opening, and she'd put Sonia in charge.

In early May, Henrietta stepped into the kitchen off the shop for her morning cup of tea. The Grand Opening was to be held the next day. Sipping the Lemon Verbena which had been her mother's only pleasure, she thought back to Frances Oldham. Her mother had died in early May, too, and Henrietta regarded that as a final lost pleasure for her. Wistfully she wondered why God hadn't let her live through a final season of flowers.

In the side yard, the lilacs were just starting to fade, and the peonies were just starting to bud. As spring turned to summer, the yard would produce another miracle of creeping myrtle, coreopsis, roses, poppies, and daisies. Henrietta longed for her mother to return to her side by the window, her hands empty of piles of clothes to stitch, her eyes gazing on the anticipated beauty soon to come.

If Frances Oldham had been there, Henrietta was certain her mother's heart would have been full with the knowledge that a measure of happiness had come to her daughter, but Henrietta now ached with the knowledge that only a few spoonfuls of happiness had been measured out for her mother herself. Thinking back to the days through which mother and daughter had lived, Henrietta recognized that there had been no images of multi-armed women juggling impossible demands, no confirmation of women's lived experience, no talk of sisterhood, no sense of a shared destiny. Perhaps Henrietta was changing some of that now. It was a belated gift, but she liked to think of it as a gift not just on behalf of herself but on behalf of her mother.

She thought back to Naomi, to the drum circle, to the Mother Song.

All mothers different. All mothers special.

The image of her mother bent over her needle stitching her dotted swiss communion dress came to mind. She'd had to make over a stranger's pinafore to crab enough material together, but out of the corner of her eye, Henrietta had glimpsed her mother's hands at work, stitch over stitch over stitch, neat chains that said "love" without words. Her mother's life had been one of silent pattern, and now her daughter's silent pattern would soon be broken. Henrietta wondered if that was how change happened: you had to witness another's pain before you could heal your own.

Henrietta sipped her tea, taking in the sunlight through the window with its promise of flowers. She began to whisper her own Mother Song. It offered words of sorrow, hope, forgiveness, love.

All mothers different. All mothers special.

Dub-*DUB.*

Birdie was flattered. Hennie wanted to include her photographs in the Grand Opening.

Sonia had reached out to Alexandra Hall, and they explored the concept of a rotating gallery of works from local artists to brighten the community room throughout the year. Together they agreed to start with Birdie's photographs, printing them through a professional photographer who owed Alexandra Hall a favor.

Birdie struggled to understand the connection among "gallery" and "artists" and "Birdie Jackson," but there they were. Her photographs. Displayed all along the walls of The Nest.

Hennie had christened her apartment building "The Hen House." Sonia was writing an article for the *Soros Sentinel* about the opening. She'd sent out invitations to neighbors and members of Hennie's church and had asked for Aunt Lou's Contacts pages so she could get in touch with all the ladies from the march. Sonia had created a huge e-blast and ordered a big banner to hang over the door of the apartment building. It read, "Grand Opening. The Hen House. Saturday, May 6, 2017, 2 – 4 p.m." Katie's boyfriend Marc suggested that "Light Refreshments" would attract more people, so the banner read "Light Refreshments" at the end.

Birdie couldn't believe the number of guests who showed up for the Grand Opening. The families from the ADAPT group. Hennie's St. Catherine stitchers. Alexandra Hall would be coming, bringing a group of artist friends; she had sent a bouquet of flowers and a beautiful handwritten letter of congratulations.

Some of the marchers who lived closer to Soros came. Beulah Knapke. Lucinda Martin. Jessica Walters rearranged her schedule at Toto's Tacos to come. Belinda Gaspard, the Teacher of the Year who was replaced by the football coach, came with Lois Graves, the ambitious elevator professional. Birdie couldn't believe it when Rosalie Helen Randolph stepped over the threshold, having driven over from Topeka. She looked as regal as ever, and Birdie couldn't wait to introduce her to Mama.

Those who couldn't come sent cards and balloon bouquets and flower arrangements. The Hen House was as colorful as the protest pole in Washington, D.C. Destinee, Ai'esha, and La'Keisha came as promised, and Twanny took off work from the Kwik Stop to be there. But Birdie hadn't expected Beanie to bring his friends along, and she about fainted when she saw Jamil Washington come in with them, minus Sabrina Banks. The boys sped right over to the food table and overloaded their teeny-tiny plates with mounds of pecan dainties and peanut butter fudge. Even though their focus was on the food, Birdie was glad she looked extra nice. Aunt Lou had taken her to The Grateful Dreads for a weave. Mama had taken her shopping for the event, and although Birdie loved her new tunic and pair of leggings, best of all was the feeling of being like a normal girl with a normal mother taking her daughter shopping.

Birdie was afraid of losing her voice from talking so much. Everybody wanted her to explain about the pictures and the march. The members of Shanice's ADAPT group bunched around the pictures taken at the protest. Aunt Lou explained to the white folks about Eric Garner's Mama and "Hellyoutalmbout." Emily described the drum circle and the memorial signs on the Ellipse. Hennie came over and whispered to Birdie that her St. Catherine's stitchers had stood for a long time in front of the pictures of her, looking surprised.

When Mrs. Opie arrived and said she'd never seen such a good career exploration project, Birdie hadn't realized her pictures could count as a grade. Then Mrs. Opie hugged Birdie tight, and Birdie nestled her head in the soft black curls that were just as soft and silky as she'd always imagined.

Over her shoulder Birdie saw the one person she'd been waiting to come through the doorway. Mama. She wore a blue silk turban, which Birdie was relieved to see, because Mama's growing hair was still a spiky mess. Birdie was happy that Mama hadn't borrowed one of Aunt Lou's church wigs that looked fake on an ex-soldier like Mama. Birdie liked it that it was plain 'ol Mama herself under that turban. She liked her mother's simple black dress with the bright blue scarf at the waist that matched her turban. Birdie thought Mama looked beautiful. But she couldn't believe who she saw trailing after her: the girls from the office pool at Kingswood Plumbing. Nearly all of them came. Imelda and Helen and Cathy and Patrice and so many others whose names Birdie couldn't remember. They came tumbling in one after one like those nesting Russian dolls. Birdie could see the pride on Mama's face as she introduced Birdie around and listened to her explain about Birdie's pictures. When the photographer from the local paper started snapping pictures, Mama suggested he take a mother-daughter shot. Birdie couldn't believe it when that photo showed up on the front page of the *Soros Sentinel*. It looked like Mama was getting her toothy grin back.

The weekend after the Grand Opening, Emily decided they should all take a field trip together. She called it a "getaway." Everyone was so tired from all their hard work for the Grand Opening that Emily had designated the Saturday afterwards as a lark, a "day to play." She also wanted to show Sonia that Kansas had just as much going for it as Philadelphia.

It would be a two-hour drive, but it was I-70 all the way. West, not east this time. She had borrowed Dave's work van, and they had all agreed to come. As they headed out of Soros on I-70, in the opposite direction they'd taken for the march, Emily enjoyed seeing the stares from other drivers: Emily, Jenny, and Katie were wearing their pink hats. Everyone kept begging Emily to say where they were going, but Emily said they'd know when they got there.

Along the way, they chatted about Emily's plans for the dog grooming studio behind Sonia's Zoo Yoga. Emily got her mom to talk Dave into loaning her money for the equipment: the grooming table, the kennels, the shears, the towels, the brushes, the shampoos. She would save on a bathtub because there was already a bathtub and sink in the apartment. They couldn't afford a washing machine for all those towels they'd use, but Hennie offered to let them borrow hers, and Emily promised to be careful to replace any laundry supplies she used.

All Emily needed now was a name for the shop. She wanted to call it "Bravo Company" after her dog.

Jenny objected. "How would patrons know it was a dog grooming studio? Wouldn't they think it was a hunting supply store selling ammo and camouflage vests?"

Katie suggested "Nails to Tails."

Sonia suggested "Bowtique."

When Hennie suggested they get more ideas from Google, they all fell out laughing.

It seemed like they were heading nowhere. Corn fields. Barns. More corn fields. Signs for bait and tackle shops, transmission overhauls, tractor supplies. Corn fields. Barns. More corn fields.

When Katie complained, Lou-Lou said, "It's like life, ladies. You mostly don't know where you're heading."

Birdie thought Lou was right about that, only after the march she knew she had only a general idea about where she was heading; she knew she needed a more specific direction.

On the ride, they had fun remembering the march, and Aunt Lou told stories about her own various protest marches. When they'd been riding for about an hour, Emily said they were halfway there, and they started singing "Crazy Little Women" at the top of their lungs.

Emily thought it was an easy drive so far. Straight shot down the interstate. She'd read that you could see it from the road, but so far she hadn't caught a glimpse, so she followed the instructions on her GPS, getting off at Exit 206 for Wilson, heading south and going over the tracks. When she headed west again on Old Highway 40, Emily said, "Almost there."

She knew the girls were excited the way they were sitting forward in their seats and pressing their noses to the window glass.

They passed a sign that said, "You are Entering Wilson, Kansas, population 736." Birdie noticed that many of the small businesses in Wilson were decorated with colorful painted eggs on the window glasses and on signs that hung over doorways. They reminded her of those foreign kinds of art, like glossy nesting dolls or hand-painted flowered shawls. The names of the owners on the businesses had exotic-sounding names, too, names like Novák, Svoboda, and Černý, written with unfamiliar accent marks.

And suddenly there it was, looming before them as they pulled over. The structure looked to be about 20-feet high, higher than even the ADAPT pole at the march. It was an egg. A giant egg enclosed by a fence. A painted egg. But still an egg. Right in the middle of Kansas, smack in the middle of the U.S. of A.

At first the girls looked stunned. They couldn't understand what it was or why they were here. Then they began to laugh.

"Good one, Emily," Jenny said, cracking up. "The World's Largest Egg. Just like the World's Largest Spur or the World's Largest Cow Chip. One of Kansas's famous sites."

"Hoo-boy," Sonia quipped. "It's something, that's for sure. But it isn't exactly the Liberty Bell."

Emily said nothing. Then she began to watch Birdie, who was walking all around the egg, studying it from every angle.

Birdie could always count on Aunt Lou to figure things out first.

"Wait a minute," Lou said. "Let's read the signs." Birdie remembered what Mama always told her kids: "When all else fails, read the directions."

Lou-Lou read the information signs to everyone, and they found out that Wilson was the "Czech Capital of Kansas." In the 1870s, a group of Czechoslovakians came to Kansas, finding work on the railroad. Most of the town, in fact, had been settled by Czech immigrants. They had fled Europe looking for freedom. Birdie remembered what Aunt Lou said as they started on the march. "You're not the only one trying to get free, Birdie."

Birdie pondered what Lou was reading. Strangers had come from across the ocean into the middle of Kansas to find a better life. *Had they been on a kind of march? Had they understood that there are all kinds of prisons in the world? Had they held hope in their hearts?* They brought their heritage with them, a heritage represented by this egg. Birdie noticed the painted colors on the egg: red, white, and black. They were the same colors as those on the fierce bird she was drawn to in the art displays in front of the National Museum of the American Indian.

Birdie listened as Lou explained about the traditional Czech design, the intricate strokes. As Lou-Lou read, Birdie learned that each stroke had a meaning: the radiating sun stood for good fortune, the curved lines with dots stood for new beginnings, the egg itself stood for new life. Birdie thought back to her Sankofa bird, guarding an egg in its beak.

Birdie remembered how she had always liked eggs. She admired their possibilities. They could be scrambled, hard-boiled, poached, over-easy. Eggs had the ability to become part of many things: a fluffy omelet, buttery pancakes, a cake for a birthday party. Or the World's Largest Egg created by the community of Wilson, Kansas, its many hands sanding the egg, applying the base coat, painting the design.

Birdie thought of this egg as something like the protest pole. It was the story of a special tribe, a story about where they had come from, where they were going, and what they wanted to remember. It was an icon, an object more than the thing itself.

And then Birdie had an idea.

Henrietta was excited. She'd never been given a beauty treatment, and now she was getting special attention from all her girls. They'd gone to the beauty supply store together, and there were doo-dads sitting around the sink in the middle of all the dog hair of The Barking Lot, Emily's new dog grooming studio. Things like bleach powder, crème developer, a tint brush, bowls, rubber gloves, and aluminum foil. Henrietta wondered if a surgeon needed this much equipment.

Henrietta was the very last one. Sonia and Katie and Jenny and Emily had gone first. When the purple streak in her braids matched the streaks in their hair and they eyed each other in the tiny bathroom mirror, she felt like she was part of a sisterhood stretching across the generations. She hoped Frances Oldham was watching from above.

After the trip to the World's Largest Egg, Birdie no longer had just a general direction: she had a specific one.

It took most of the early summer to plan it, but she had plenty of help from her friends and the girls at the Hen House. They decided to call it the "Everybody Dances Dance," and Sonia helped them make a timeline of what had to happen when.

By July they'd ticked things off their list. Permission from the Y. Check. Dee-Jays. Check. Advertising. Check. Facebook page. Check. Chaperones. Check. Invitations. Check. Refreshments.

Check. Tables set up. Check. Chairs placed. Check. Balloons, crepe paper streamers, and table decorations. Check.

Birdie insisted on only one thing: the theme color had to be purple. That meant *purple* balloons, *purple* crepe paper streamers, and *purple* table decorations.

It was a beautiful July night, almost three years since Shanice had left them. Destinee and Ai'esha and La'Keisha had arrived early to support her.

When the doors opened, Birdie was feeling jittery. In a good way.

And then people begin to show up. Beanie and Mama and Aunt Lou, of course. But then lots of kids from school. T.J, Stefon, and Carmello. Jamil Washington with his friend Darius. Birdie noticed that Jamil had come without Sabrina Banks again. Birdie couldn't believe it when Mrs. Opie and Mr. Pine showed up.

Armando Rodriguez and his parents came through the door. Charlie Kilpatrick and his little sister followed. Sylvia Peterman and Violet Shelby came together. Strangers Birdie had never seen before arrived on their crutches, in their wheelchairs, with their seeing-eye dogs.

The girls from the Hen House brought Hennie and Jenny's sister Alice, who was in a wheelchair. Birdie busted out laughing when she saw they all had purple streaks in their hair, even Alice.

Antoine was late getting off work, but after he arrived, he pressed a small package into Birdie's hand. It was wrapped in silver foil and tied with the same lavender ribbon he had used on his farewell letter to Shanice.

"Open it now, sister," Twanny said. "You'll need it tonight."

Birdie slipped the ribbon off the package and opened the box. It was a phone. Her very own phone.

"You deserve it," Twanny said. "My little baby sister's got a great big talent."

Birdie tiptoed up to kiss her brother's cheek. "And that little sister's got the best big brother in the world," she said.

Everyone who came through the door got a favor. They were just simple little purple squares knitted at YARNS by beginning knitters, but Birdie knew they'd look nice under coffee cups or perfume bottles. She liked thinking that every time someone sipped their coffee or squirted on perfume that Shanice was somehow there.

They'd asked the dee-jay to play some of Shanice's favorite music. "Don't Stop Till You Get Enough." "Shut Up and Dance." The music pulsed like the throbbing drums of Naomi's drum circle. When the dee-jay played "Uptown Funk," Jamil Washington led everyone in the Electric Slide, and his long, loose limbs made Birdie laugh. After that, Beanie cracked everyone up by leading "The Chicken Dance," the whole group flapping their wings and wiggling their behinds.

But the best part was when Beanie moved Shanice's wheelchair out onto the center of the floor. They had coordinated things ahead of time, intent on starting a tradition. Anyone who wanted to could be wheeled out into the middle of the floor. They'd sit in Shanice's wheelchair, and Birdie would place the purple shawl around their shoulders. The other dancers could take turns whirling them around, making them the center of attention.

Alice, Jenny's sister, volunteered first. Birdie draped her in Shanice's purple shawl and Beanie asked the dee-jays to play "Dancing Queen." Birdie watched Shanice's nail polish bottles weaving and circling as Alice was celebrated.

> *You can dance, you can jive*
> *Having the time of your life*
> *Oh, see that girl, watch that scene*
> *Digging the dancing queen.*

And then Jenny stepped forward. Following Jenny's lead, the others began to incorporate Alice's neck thrusts and clicks into the dance. "Thank you, Tammy Byerly," Birdie said quietly to herself, "wherever you are."

One-by-one, each dancer was celebrated in the center – Darius, Charlie Kilpatrick, Destinee, Violet Shelby, La'Keisha, even Mrs. Opie – and Birdie's heart swelled in a gratitude prayer: *Shanice is here; Shanice is with us.*

Jenny turned to Birdie and said, "This is the best kind of memorial, Birdie."

Jenny was right. Birdie remembered Deafy Boular and knew Shanice wouldn't want to be stuck in concrete for people to gawk at until the end of time. "Yes, Jenny," Birdie said, "she'd want to be remembered this way. Dancing."

As Birdie watched Shanice's wheelchair circling the dance floor, she realized it had become something Hennie had taught her about: an object greater than the thing itself. It was telling a story, the story of her family tribe, the story about where you've come from, where you're going, and what you want to remember.

The girls swooped Henrietta up and put her in the line between a lanky boy who looked like a basketball player and Birdie's teacher, Mrs. Opie. They hung on to each other's waists like they did that time the bus was stuck in the mud and everybody had to pull together. They were all there: Birdie and Emily and Katie and Jenny and Sonia and Alice and Charlie Kilpatrick and the ADAPT kids and Birdie's family and friends and many of the women on the march.

Then the dee-jay played a song Henrietta remembered from her childhood. *Doo-di-doo-di-da-da, dah-dah-dah. Doo-di-doo-di-da-da. HOP, HOP, HOP!* Hanging on, the dancers moved forward and backward, backward and forward. Again and again. *HOP, HOP, HOP!*

Throughout the night, Birdie snapped picture after picture with her new phone. Phone in hand, she decided on a special picture, a picture just for herself. She aimed her camera at all the feet dancing across the floor. Keds. Flats. Sneakers. Stilettos. Chuck Taylors. She pushed the white button, knowing that she'd come a long way from the sneakers and boots, the crocs and moccasins on the day of the march. Now she knew that things were not *im*-possible. Because she carried the egg of possibility inside her own self.

AUTHOR'S NOTE

I've always been an observer, seldom a participant. I think it's in the nature of writers to observe, to notice, to perceive: what we've witnessed gives us the stories we write.

As a result, I was an unlikely participant in the Women's March on Washington. But then my minister-friend, the late Reverend Gregory Martin, encouraged me to march. He knew how distraught the women of his congregation had been at the 2016 election of Donald Trump. I'd been an active leader in the local campaign to elect Hillary Clinton, and, at the age of 70, I was heartsick: I would likely die before I'd see a woman elected President of the United States.

So, like thousands of other women who were also heartsick, I decided to go "on the march." Wearing my sturdiest sneakers, I mounted the steps of a bus outside a Wal-Mart in Dayton, Ohio, for the sixteen-hour round-trip ride to Washington, D.C.

Like hundreds of thousands of other women across the world, the march transformed me. After January 21, 2017, other women ran for office, launched non-profits, and raised their voices like never before. I decided to write a novel.

Writing it stirred unforgettable memories: writing slogans on posters, cheering on the bus, snapping pictures, jostling Inauguration-goers in furs, wearing pink pussy hats, listening to Naomi Judd perform the "Nasty Woman" poem, crowding into a McDonalds, chanting across the streets of Washington, D.C. Many of those moments find their way into ON THE MARCH.

It wasn't easy; writing a novel never is. But, well, #shepersisted. The result is ON THE MARCH, my fictional version of the "Hell yeah" heard around the world.

ACKNOWLEDGEMENTS

Much gratitude is owed to the congregation of the Miami Valley Unitarian Universalist Fellowship in Dayton, Ohio, who are always marching. Over the years, their example has enriched my understanding of social justice.

Heartfelt thanks are also due to Carol Gaskin at Editorial Academy for her careful editing and generous spirit; any serious writer knows the importance of a competent and caring editor, and Carol has no equal.

Thank you to Lindsay Nicole Broadway at The Book Whisperer for her contribution as a sensitivity reader, and of course to the talented Jane Dixon-Smith for another creative cover.

I am blessed to have had many wonderful women march through life with me, especially Lella, Gayle, Laura, and Kathy. This gratitude extends to my Sewing Circus quilters, my Aging Well friends, and my Women-Living-the-Questions sisters, who have enlivened my march with their friendship.

Special thanks are due to people everywhere who work to ensure that progress for women across the globe is not *im*-possible.

DISCUSSION QUESTIONS FOR READING GROUPS

1. What factors drive each of the main characters – Henrietta, Birdie, and Emily – to embark on The Women's March?

2. Many disabilities are featured in ON THE MARCH. What are these? In what ways are many of the characters in the book "disabled?"

3. How does each of the main characters – Henrietta, Birdie, and Emily – change as a result of attending The Women's March?

4. In what ways do the major and minor characters influence each other?

5. Which uniquely "women's" issues in the book resonated with you?

6. Eggs are used as a symbol throughout the book. Can you explain the meaning of the various "egg" references in the novel?

7. In what ways are events like the Women's March on Washington catalysts for change?

CREDITS

Abba, "Dancing Queen" from *Arrival.* Written by Benny Andersson, Bjorn Ulvaeus, and Stig Anderson, 1976.

ADAPT, American Disabled for Attendant Programs Today, www.adapt.org.

Donovan, Nina Mariah, "Nasty Woman," performed by Ashley Judd at the Women's March on Washington, January 21, 2017.

Geisel, Theodore Seuss, *Horton Hatches the Egg.* Random House, 1940.

"Hellyoutalmbout," from *The Electric Lady,* Janelle Monáe and the Wonderland artist collective, 2015.

"Kansas City," written by Jerry Leiber and Mike Stoller, 1952. Recorded by Wilbert Harrison for FURY records, 1959.

Keelan-Chaffins, *All the Way to the Top,* Sourcebooks Explore, 2020.

"Proud Mary" – Creedence Clearwater Revival, 1969.

Taina Asili y Banda Rebelde, *War Cry,* 2010.

Together We Rise: The Women's March, Behind the Scenes at the Protest Heard Around the World by the Women's March Organizers and Conde Nast, The Women's March Foundation, Dey St., an imprint of William Morrow, 2018.